TEARS

of the

PHOENIX

TEARS
of the
PHOENIX

A story to heal the hearts of men & boys
and the women who love them.

LONNIE BEERMAN

Clovercroft/Publishing

Tears of the Phoenix

©2019 by Lonnie Beerman

Published by Clovercroft Publishing, Franklin, Tennessee

Copy Edit by Lee Titus Elliott

Cover and Interior Design by Suzanne Lawing

Printed in the United States of America

978-1-948484-63-3

I dedicate this story to the memory of my beloved brother Frank Albert "Bud" Beerman "We all miss you & the way that you grin."

A special thank you to my wife Firoozeh, without whom I could never have done this.

Also, my gratitude to my niece Staycee and my mother-in-law Zari.

THE QUESTION

"Momma?" Frankie said to his mother, staring out the window of the old Rambler, she gingerly navigated through the gauntlet of potholes in the crudely paved country road.

"Yes, baby," she replied distractedly.

"Why did my daddy have to die?" he asked, his sullen mood overshadowing the crisp spring morning.

"What was that, darlin'?" she asked, the question taking her by surprise.

"Why did my daddy have to die?" he repeated.

Her mind had been on a thousand other things, like the bills she had barely enough money to pay, or the new clicking sound from under the hood that joined the erratic symphony of squeaks and rattles.

"Why do ask such a thing, baby boy?" his mother countered, feeling a little ambushed by his question.

"I dunno. I guess I just wanna know how come I don't have a daddy, an' all the other kids do," he replied poignantly.

He never talked much about his father's death. He vaguely knew when and where; he'd been told all that years before, but his young heart was troubled by "why." Why had his father gone off to war and left him and his mother alone? Why had none of the other kids' fathers had done that? It just wasn't fair.

She drew a deep breath, desperate for a good answer, "Well . . . your daddy was a soldier, hun."

"I know, Momma," he replied, "but why did he have to go?"

"Baby, that's what soldiers do."

"I know that, too," he said, slightly irritated, "but all soldiers don't have to go to war, do they? Why did he have to?"

It was a good question; he had every right to ask it. She could sense his frustration, and she began grasping for a way to explain to a ten-year-old something that she had difficulty understanding herself.

What makes a man leave his family and risk death in a foreign land in the service of his country?

"Well . . . some really bad people in a country far away were killing other helpless people who couldn't fight back," his mother said. "So our government sent . . . "

Some really bad people? his mother thought. *Geez, he's not five! This is so lame . . .*

"Momma . . . " he stopped her. "I know all about the war. We talk about it a lot in school."

But it was never any fun for him. When they did talk about the war, he could feel the looks and hear the whispers aimed at him. Kids would ask him questions as if he were some kind of expert on the war, just because his father was killed in it.

But usually the looks and comments felt more like accusations, as if the war were somehow his responsibility . . . just because his father was killed.

"Why did he think that other folks in a 'nuther country needed him more than you an' me did here at home?" the boy started to ask. "I mean, I know helpin' to protect folks that can't protect themselves is a good thing to do an' all, but . . . " His question faded on his lips.

He thought, *Did my daddy really love us? Maybe it was just me? Maybe he didn't really want a kid.*

Outside, the weather-gnarled fence posts, strung with sagging, rusty barbed wire, clicked slowly by. A white-faced brindle cow chewed contentedly on her cud, while her new calf eagerly sought breakfast from her huge udder.

"Darlin', soldiers don't get to choose what they are sent to do. They just do as they are ordered to do. That's what being a soldier is about, and your daddy was a good soldier."

She understood what soldiering was about. She just never understood why Jack had chosen to be one. She had always admired the nobility of his choice, but that noble choice had cost her a husband and a soul mate, and it had denied their son a father. He had left a huge void in their lives, with no good explanation.

"Well, don't that stupid country have their own soldiers?" he spat bitterly. *Stupid Veet-nam people! Why don't they just fight their own war?*

"Yes, baby, they do, but they're just not very good." She struggled to find the right words. She could hear the anger in his voice.

"The bad guys had help from another big country like ours, so the people they attacked couldn't defend themselves very well," she explained.

She tried to keep her explanation as simple as she could. He would never understand the politics behind the war. Not many grown-ups did.

"You see, their government isn't a very good one or a very strong one, either. They were afraid the bad guys might take over and kill a whole lot of people, so they asked our government for help. We sent soldiers like your daddy . . . and other kids' daddies, too . . . to stop them."

"But they didn't stop 'em, did they?" he asked irritably. He'd seen the evening news often enough to know that the war wasn't going well, or so Walter Cronkite said.

"Well, not completely . . . not yet," she answered. She shared his irritation. "That's why the war is still going on."

She wondered if she was ever going to be able to turn on the television and not see the gruesome battlefield reports or hear the daily body count, so faithfully and morbidly presented by the sanctimonious talking heads.

Network ratings required reporting death and destruction in the name of "public interest," while Americans consumed frozen dinners on their TV trays, amid the soft glow of the smiling faces in living color.

"It's like the Nazis and the Japs in the movies, ain't it?" he asked, as he struggled to understand.

"Well, yeah, sort of, but it's a long story, sweetie, a little too long for Momma to go into it right now. But we'll talk about it later, I promise. We can talk at dinner tonight, if you want."

"Okay, Momma," he replied, mumbling dejectedly. "Why couldn't he just stay home and protect me an' you?"

His question tugged urgently at her heart. She pulled the car off to the side of the road and stopped.

Turning to him, she asked, "Darlin' boy, why do you ask that? Do you need protecting from something . . . or someone?"

"No, Momma, I'm okay. I mean. . .some of the kids

tease me a little . . . sometimes, but I don't really care. They're just bein' buttho . . . " he stopped, seeing his mother's eyebrows rise.

Not having a father was tough on a boy in a small farm town. But at least his parents had been married and his father had died "honorably." He knew about other kids who weren't so fortunate. He knew how they suffered mercilessly at the hands of the "normal" kids.

However, being "fatherless" had still made him an outcast among those "normal" kids. Sadly, being "normal" was desperately important in a small farm town.

"I just wish I had a daddy, too. Like all the other kids," he said, looking down at his worn Red Ball Jet sneakers and fidgeting with the handle on his Superman lunchbox.

Her response stuck in her throat. What could she say? All she could do was lean over and draw her son into an embrace and hope he wouldn't notice her eyes starting to water.

"I know, baby." She managed keep her voice from trembling. "So do I. . . . So do I," she said, rocking back and forth, as much to comfort herself as to comfort him.

After a brief moment, she released him and turned back to the steering wheel, discretely wiping the tears she couldn't hold back.

"I'm sorry, Momma," he apologized sadly, seeing her tears. "I didn't mean to make you cry."

"That's all right, sweetie, you didn't make Momma cry," she said, her voice cracking. "I miss him, too. More than you know. But Frankie . . . baby boy . . . don't ever be afraid to talk to me about your daddy, okay? That's how we keep him alive . . . in our hearts. He was a good man, and a brave man, too. He helped save a lot of people who would have died otherwise. You should be very proud of him."

Smiling a watery-eyed smile, she added, "He was a wonderful father. . . just like you're a wonderful son. He was so proud of you."

It hurt her deeply that her son would never know how great a man his father was. But there wasn't much she could do about it. She could only try and be there for him with answers to his questions and stories about what kind of man his father had been.

She steered the sputtering car back onto the road. Mother and son spent the rest of the drive to school in silence.

He imagined what it would have been like to have a father to play football with or to go fishing with . . . or maybe to even build a model with.

A short while later, they pulled up to the elementary school. Frankie opened the creaking door, but before he got out, he reached up to kiss his mother's cheek.

She smiled warmly and said, "Your daddy would have been so proud of his little man. I know I sure am."

He scrambled out of the car and paused as he closed the door. He looked back at her and said, "I think he'd of been proud of you, too, Momma. I know I sure am."

She sat for a few minutes, wiping fresh tears from her cheek and watching him amble slowly into school with the other children.

Then, with effort, she shoved her emotions back into the heart-shaped box she kept them in and drove off into another day without Jack. But try as she may, thoughts of her husband forced their way out of that box and brought more tears.

One by one, they crept relentlessly into her aching

heart. Her thorny reverie was only briefly interrupted as she pulled up to the gates of the factory. The craggy-faced security guard, as old as the factory he guarded, smiled a toothless smile and waved her through. She wove through the gravel parking lot, searching for the closest spot to the factory entrance as possible. The trek across the rutted lot was dusty but, thankfully, short. *Well, at least it wasn't raining.*

All that day, her son's questions haunted her thoughts. Time after time, driven by mere rote repetition, she pushed the big mushroom-shaped button that brought the hydraulic press slamming down to cut large sheets of asbestos tile into small squares.

Normally, the pounding din of the machines around her was mind-numbing enough to keep her from thinking about anything for very long.

But today, the painful memories relentlessly plagued her thoughts. It was as if they stood in line waiting to take their turn sticking their particular pin into her heart. With each stack of freshly cut tiles she placed on the waiting pallet, another memory imposed itself upon her. There was no escape, no respite.

The monotony of repeatedly moving one tile-filled pallet and replacing it with an empty one only made things worse. Nothing different offered itself to rescue her from the overwhelming brambles and snares her thoughts imposed upon her.

Some small salvation came when the lunch whistle screeched over the cacophonous din of the production line. The usual buzzing chatter of the factory cafeteria managed to push her thoughts aside and brought her some temporary sanctuary.

Taking her usual place among her fellow worker ants

at one of the long rows of picnic tables covered with red-checkered, plastic tablecloths, she made a concerted effort to get caught up in chitchat and the latest gossip around town.

For an all-too-brief a time, life felt normal amidst the chatter and the smoke of hundreds of cigarettes being hurriedly chain-smoked before the whistle herded the worker ants back to their respective anthill duties. She shared her neighbor's Marlboro, whether she wanted to or not.

But, back on the line, the lingering specters shang-haied her once again and promptly marched her back into the shadows of her mind.

She was thankful that no clock had been placed where workers could watch it. Watching the clock would have made things infinitely worse. She could not remember anticipating a shift change so much as she did on this endlessly bothersome day.

Her job was tedious and boring, but it paid the bills . . . barely. Though dusty and hot during the muggy Southern summers, it was better than the noxious fumes and freezing cold Northern winters she had endured at the paint factory she had worked at before returning to Haleyville.

Neither did she did miss the obnoxious advances from every horny hound dog, single and married alike. At least here, the men behaved themselves and were even courteous, in a Southern sort of way. She suspected that such behavior happened because the women work-ing on the line knew their wives and their girlfriends, so the married men behaved and even kept the single men in line.

Cynically, though, she was sure they would gather

after work at any one of the taverns near the plant and crudely speculate about what they would like to do to this woman or to that one.

THE MIGHTY AVENGER

Around noon that same day, the recess bell rang at Haleyville Elementary. Rambunctious children swarmed like buzzing bees out of a red-brick hive onto the large playground, noisily aannouncing their relief to be out from under the teacher bee's scrutiny.

Random games of kickball and dodgeball sprung up, the geeks and dorks being chosen last, of course. The monkey bars were quickly populated with drape apes, swinging and hooting like their primate cousins.

Sometimes Frankie joined in; though, usually, he sat apart from the other kids. He could never understand why, but he always felt like an outsider, never a part of any group . . . especially not the "cool guys." After two, long, arduous years of being an outcast, he had accepted what seemed to be his fate among them . . . being a loner. Eventually, he got to the point where he preferred it . . . usually, but not always. Feeling as though he was unacceptable still hurt. It seemed his only friend was Solitude.

He trusted Solitude.

Solitude never made fun of him for not having a father. Solitude didn't look down at him because his mother couldn't afford the new sneakers. Solitude never laughed at him because he preferred building plastic models instead of playing football, nor did it ridicule him for not caring who John, Paul, George, and Ringo were.

Solitude was a good friend.

Solitude could be whatever he wanted it to be . . . a band of savage Indians attacking the wagon train . . . a squad of Nazis storming his foxhole . . . a trusted and loyal sidekick, like Tonto, to help him rescue the banker's daughter from dastardly villains. Solitude was there when he wanted it, and Solitude left him alone when he wanted to be alone.

Solitude helped him endure.

Right now, he and Solitude were mulling over the talk he had had with his mother that morning. *If only I had a daddy . . .*

Just then, a large group of kids nearby, crowding around something and shouting excitedly, caught his attention. Curiosity caused him to tell Solitude to wait a minute. He ran over to the noisy cluster and weaved his way to the center to see what was going on.

Instantly, he regretted his curiosity.

In the middle of the melee, a circle had formed. In that circle, he saw three, big sixth-grade thugs taunting and shoving a much smaller boy back and forth between them, goaded on by piranhas disguised as kids.

The gleeful fervor of the jeering pack made him as uneasy as the attack on the hapless prey. It reminded him of the time he watched a frenzied pack of hyenas tear a baby antelope apart on a National Geographic television program. His stomach knotted up with disgust.

Frankie recognized the kid being publicly devastated.

He was the new guy who had just moved to town from somewhere up north. He was a small boy of slight build, and his normally well-combed blond hair hung on his forehead, flying this way and that with every shove, his eyes wide with terror.

"Hey ya twerp, why dontcha jabber some of that there Yankee talk now!" Derek, the biggest bully teased, a chipped front tooth dominating the sneer on his face.

"What the hell does 'Yooz guys' mean, anyhow, ya lil' shit?" Steven, a piggish-looking boy with bright orange hair milled into a flattop, taunted. The bold use of forbidden four-letter words made him feel tougher.

The undersized boy's chin began to wrinkle, and his eyes watered, as his self-esteem was being hatefully shattered for all to see.

"Aw . . . look!" Arnie, the third tormentor, teased, "He's fixin' ta cry! Aw . . . boo-hoo lil' baby!"

A tittering of laughter rippled from the surrounding pack. Thin and awkwardly proportioned, the new boy's movements might have been comical, had his tormentors not been so vicious.

Frankie knew the brutes all too well. All the kids in school did. At one time or another, nearly everyone had been terrorized or bullied by the three hoodlums. Once you'd been singled out by them, an unspoken quarantine fell upon you. You became a leper. No kids in the school wanted to be seen sympathizing with their victim, lest they suffer the same fate. The isolation could last for days, weeks, or even months. The bullies were universally feared and hated. But none of the kids had the courage to stand up to them.

The same three dull-witted thugs had teased Frankie earlier in the year, though not quite so brutally. Steven had branded him a "bastard" because "he ain't got no daddy." Their label made him an "untouchable" among the other children.

But if not having a father was all it took to make him an outcast with these kids, then he was better off being a loner. He and Solitude were good at that, anyway.

Some of the more cowardly kids joined in on the torment, laughing and adding a snide insult or two of their own, hoping it would be remembered the next time the predators went on the prowl.

Frankie found himself transfixed by the juvenile brutality. He'd been in the new kid's place. He found himself feeling just as grateful as the others that it wasn't him being shoved around like a rag doll.

Deep inside, though, a feeling of shame began to take root.

He thought about what his mother had told him that very morning. He thought about how his father had died protecting others who couldn't protect themselves.

Not long ago, she had told him how, in high school, his father had stuck up for guys very much like the kid being shoved around in front of him against even bigger bullies than these three. His father had been a fearless champion of the underdog.

But right now he felt like a coward . . . a chicken. Surely he would be a disappointment to his father.

His shame began to grow, becoming deeper with each shove the helpless boy received. In his heart, he knew that doing nothing but standing and watching was just as wrong as the tormenting. But the frightened butterflies that flailed wildly in his stomach kept his feet rooted in place.

Try as he may, he couldn't move, even though he knew

he should do something. Anger and self-loathing welled up in him, feeding the accusing flames of his shame.

Though he was angry with the bullies and the barbaric onlookers, he was even angrier with himself. The more the image of his father's heroism loomed over him, the more he hated his fear . . . and himself.

The new kid's eyes searched the crowd for help, but found none. No one dared cross the knuckle-dragging brutes. Some looked away when his eyes met theirs, afraid or embarrassed; still others laughed, belying their own fears.

Frankie deliberately avoided eye contact with the victim. He was sure that the boy's terror would infect him, further cementing his cowardly feet in place. His father's blood, now pounding in his temple, began compelling him to do something . . . anything.

But there were three of them . . . and they were bigger than him . . . and he didn't know how to fight . . . and he might get hurt. The excuses screamed in his head, deepening his shame. His father's voice, a voice he had never really known, rebuked him with scathing accusations of cowardice. He could almost imagine the contempt and embarrassment in his father's eyes, bearing down on him like a heavy shadow.

His shame grew and became too much. His father's imagined derision began to break through his fear.

He had to act!

His father was a hero, a fearless defender of the weak and helpless. Frankie was the son of a warrior. He could do no less than his father would have done, however terrified he was. A bloody nose or a black eye paled in comparison to what his father had suffered in the defense of others.

His fear be damned, he was going to help the boy!

Nervously, he started to shuffle forward, fighting back the giant knot growing ever tighter in his stomach, intent on overcoming his fear. Steeling his resolve, he told himself, *My daddy would've done this!*

But just as he started to move, a commotion among the hovering spectators on the opposite side of the circle caught his attention.

Suddenly, a scowling face, raised above the other kids and ruddy with anger, plowed through the gawking crowd, shouting for them to get out of the way.

He recognized this boy, too. His name was Aubrey, a normally taciturn kid in his class who had been held back a grade. It was another surefire way to earn the enmity of his fellow students. Some of the kids referred to him as a "retard," but only behind his back. He was quiet, but he was also huge.

He had heard that Aubrey's older brother had a reputation for fighting. But Aubrey had always seemed more of a gentle giant, never a bully, even though he could easily have been. Frankie had heard the cruel jokes and comments about how poor his family was, when the spiteful tongues thought he couldn't hear them. Frankie had never seen him threaten or retaliate; he had only seen him absorbing the abuse. He had even seen the occasional tear that Aubrey thought he had concealed from the world. He was an outcast, too.

He was bigger than any of the three bullies, and right now, that's what counted. The crowd parted like the Red Sea before a raging Moses to let the wrathful giant through.

Arnie was the first of the thugs to see him as he broke from the crowd, his face twisted in a grimace of anger.

Instinctively, Arnie knew that trouble had arrived and was charging like a bull into the fray.

He grabbed Derek's arm to warn him, but it was too late. With the speed and agility that seemed out of place for someone so big, the raging fifth grader spun Arnie around and slammed a pile-driving fist into his surprised face, blood instantly erupting from his shattered nose.

Turning on the other two stunned punks, Aubrey methodically hammered hard blows to their now-frightened faces, one punishing blow after another. None of the tormentors had a chance to defend themselves or to get away.

Within seconds, all three thugs were squirming on the ground, bellowing in pain and clutching bloody noses and busted lips, devastated at having gone from predator to prey so quickly.

"It ain't right ta pick on them that's littler than you!" Aubrey roared, towering over them with fists clenched tight, cocked and ready to deliver more punishment to the first groveling worm that dared lift its head. A thin line of spittle hung from corner of his mouth.

The morbidly curious grade school piranha's who had been watching the torment, scattered like cockroaches when the light is turned on, especially those who had joined in the taunting. They wanted no part of Aubrey's devastating assault.

The oversized avenger stood glowering angrily at the sniveling boys, now desperately clawing at the ground, trying to escape. All three clasped a hand over bleeding faces and watched their assailant with panic-stricken eyes. Their perverse entertainment had gone horribly wrong. The tables had been turned on them, and, this time, they were getting much worse than they gave.

"It ain't right!" he roared again. He took a menacing step toward them, forcing them to scramble to their knees and crawl away as quickly as they could. Blood streamed down their faces, dripping onto their shirts and into the playground dirt, leaving a trail to mark their humiliating retreat.

They didn't notice that some of the kids who had not laughed at their brutality were now laughing at them.

A weak smattering of cheers peppered the scattered crowd after they were sure the thugs were out of earshot.

Only Frankie and the brutalized boy remained were they stood, both stunned by what they'd just witnessed.

Frankie had never seen anything like it. But now, it wasn't fear that stayed his feet. Instead, he stood awe-struck by someone who hadn't hesitated . . . as he had.

Aubrey had fought for someone who couldn't do it for himself. Aubrey had done what Frankie's own father surely would have done. Aubrey had done what Frankie had been too afraid to do.

"You okay?" Aubrey asked the trembling new kid in a gentle voice, sharply contrasting the fearful roar of mere seconds ago. The new kid also stood frozen in place, tears of humiliation now flowing freely down his cheeks. Aubrey reached out to put a comforting hand on his shoulder, but the boy flinched and bolted away, eyes wide with fear and face red with embarrassment.

Aubrey turned to face Frankie and growled, "You want some o' this, too?" the fury instantly returning to his eyes and his fists clenched anew, ready for more battle.

That Aubrey could so easily switch from rage to compassion, and then back again, both fascinated and frightened Frankie. A desire to know and maybe even befriend this magnificent warrior sprouted through his own fear.

Shaken from his thoughts by Aubrey's threatening tone, he quickly put his hands up defensively in front of him.

"Naw, man, naw. I don't wanna fight ya!" Frankie said quickly and emphatically. "Them guys are buttholes. I'm glad ya whooped 'em."

Then he added, somewhat sheepishly, "I . . . ah . . . I was about to do somethin', too."

"Yeah . . . sure ya were!" the lumbering hero spat derisively, fists still at the ready and breathing hard. Frankie pictured John Wayne after whipping a saloon full of drunken rustlers . . . all by himself.

He realized just how phony his claim sounded. "Yeah, I guess that does sound kinda . . . " he trailed off. "But, honest, I . . . I really was," he pleaded.

"I was just . . . scared," he admitted, feeling ridiculous making such a plea and regretting the confession. "Not like you."

The two boys stood, sizing each other up for a few seconds.

Slowly, Frankie stuck a trembling hand out to Aubrey. "I . . . uh . . . I think what ya did was great. You weren't chicken . . . like me," he said, briefly casting his eyes down in shame.

With his trembling hand still extended, he offered, hopefully, "My name is Frankie. Um . . . ya think maybe we could be . . . um . . . pals?"

The rage slowly melted from Aubrey's eyes, as he looked deep into Frankie's, searching for sincerity, but ready for deception.

Frankie stood there, not knowing if he would be

rejected because had confessed to being a coward. *Who wants to be pals with a chicken?*

Aubrey thought his confession was brave. His battle mask fell away, as he unclenched his white-knuckled fists. After some slight hesitation, he reached his own big hand out and accepted Frankie's much smaller one.

"My name's Aubrey . . . Aubrey Denton," he said, then glared threateningly and demanded, "Now, you ain't funnin' me, are ya?"

"Naw, man, I promise I ain't funnin' ya," Frankie reassured him. "I hate them turds, too. They had it comin', an' I'm glad that someone finally had the guts to give it to them."

Still embarrassed by his own fear, he lamented, "I just wish I had your guts."

Aubrey gave Frankie a sympathetic look and said, "Aw, heck . . . ta tell ya the truth, I was kinda scared, too. But I bet that lil' yella-haired feller was prob'ly a lot more scared than me, huh?" he grinned. "Do ya know who he was?"

Frankie appreciated that Aubrey was marginalizing his shame. He never thought he could admire another kid. After all, kids are just kids, but he found himself admiring this one. He had stood up against superior numbers and had shown compassion for someone he didn't even know. How could he not admire that?

"Yeah, he's the new kid from up North," Frankie explained. "I don't know his name, but they were teasin' him 'cause he's a Yankee."

"Naw, they was teasin' him 'cause they got meanness in their hearts," Aubrey retorted.

Wow! Frankie thought. *I hadn't thought of it that way. But Aubrey is right. Those thugs were just plain evil!*

"Man, did you see the look on them bozo's faces?" he laughed, lightening the mood and pushing his shame back into a corner, to be dealt with later. "Scamperin' off like scared rats! Man that was really somethin'!"

The two boys shook hands and stood, searching each other's eyes for possibilities: Aubrey, in his faded and patched, but clean, blue jeans and plaid flannel shirt, his curly, brown hair showing no signs of ever having known a comb; Frankie in his much newer short-sleeved shirt and blue jeans, his own wavy black hair still neatly parted and combed. The unlikely pair came from different backgrounds, but they shared something in common . . . a real hatred for bullies. And that was a start.

"Yer in my class ain'tcha?" Aubrey asked, changing the subject.

"Yeah. Ol' Shock-face's class!" he acknowledged "I sit behind you, one row over."

Suddenly a thought came to mind, and he warned, "Hey, man, you better haul ass; Ol' Man Pike'll getcha."

"Naw," Aubrey accepted. "Ain't no good ta run. He knows who dun' it!"

Frankie was amazed at his courage. Aubrey was a real live hero, even if he was just a kid.

There was something about him that touched Frankie deep inside. He knew he had to be friends with him. Perhaps some of Aubrey's courage would rub off on him. "I'm glad we're gonna be friends," he declared.

Solitude would understand . . . and would still be there if he needed it.

"Yeah, me, too," Aubrey replied. He'd never had anyone ask to be his friend before and was genuinely touched by Frankie's offer. He saw something of his own desperate loneliness in the nervous kid standing hopefully before him.

Then, just as Frankie had warned, Principal Pike came storming through the throng of milling children who had put a safe distance between themselves and the scene of the crime.

"You boys stay right where you are!" the portly principal yelled, more for show than out of necessity, his face screwed into a scowl and his bald head glowing pink with anger.

"I should have known it'd be a Denton!" he barked, as he approached the pair, even though he'd never had a minute of trouble from Aubrey before today.

Scowling at Frankie, he demanded, "You part of this, too, boy?"

"Yessi . . . " he started to confess, feeling inspired by Aubrey's bravery.

But Aubrey quickly stepped forward to meet the irate man's glare, fearlessly saying, "No, sir, Principal Pike, he didn't have nuttin' ta do with it. I dun' it all by myself."

He confessed defiantly, "They was pickin' on the new kid, an' it wudn't right."

Principal Pike grabbed the back of Aubrey's collar in a show of authority.

"Well, boy, it ain't your place to decide what's right and wrong 'round here," the failed former football coach rumbled indignantly. "That's my job!"

"You're coming with me," he said, tugging Aubrey along. "I reckon we'd better be callin' your folks. Not that they'll be surprised."

He began towing Aubrey to the office, then cast a glance at Frankie and spat, "You'd do well to stay away from this one. He ain't nuthin' but trouble, son . . . just like his brother."

"He's my friend!" Frankie heard himself calling defiantly to the principal's back, surprised but thrilled by his newfound boldness. Maybe Aubrey was rubbing off on him already.

Mr. Pike stopped and scowled hard at Frankie, growling through gritted teeth, "You, too, huh? Well, I'll be watchin' you, from now on, boy. You just made a bad choice, son."

I ain't your son! Frankie thought, but he wisely chose not to say it out loud. Boldness was one thing; foolishness was quite another.

Ignoring the irritable principal, Frankie smiled at Aubrey and gave him a "thumbs-up." Aubrey grinned back, stumbling as the flustered principal yanked him forward by his collar.

He didn't see Aubrey for the rest of the day. He found himself being avoided by the other kids even more than normal, but that was just fine with him. He just hoped his new friend would be okay.

Nor did he see the little blonde kid from up North somewhere. *Poor guy*, he thought, *I hope he's okay.*

GREAT LAMENTATIONS

At long last, the whistle screeched quitting time, and the pounding machinery fell temporarily silent, as one shift of worker ants gathered their lunch pails and filed out of the hill to make way for the next shift of ants taking their place.

Shelley joined the mumbling throng exiting the hill, her clunky and definitely unfeminine safety boots—"Mickey Mouse boots," she called them—crunching through the gravel.

The drive home seemed interminably long, yet ultimately not long enough. Again, the trickle of thoughts grew into a stream and then into a torrent. The floodgates threatened to break wide open now that she was alone.

Amid the squeaks and groans of the old car, the relative silence held no distractions for her. The radio had long since ceased working, not that she could get anything but farm reports or the sappy twang of Conway Twitty lamenting a failed relationship or lauding the virtues of a drunken stupor. She certainly didn't need that, though a shot of something strong sounded good, right about now.

As bad as her day had been, the thought of facing her son with no good answers felt worse. How could she comfort him when she could not comfort herself?

She should have spoken to him more about his father. Had she selfishly created a burden for him?

What kind of mother am I?

She pulled up outside her home and sat in the car for several long minutes. Finally, she gathered her wits enough to face him. She exited the car and headed down the flagstone walkway toward the porch steps.

"I'm home, darlin'," she called out in a falsely upbeat tone, as she opened the front door.

Frankie was lying on the floor in front of the television, watching his usual after-school sitcoms.

"Hi, sweetie," she said, as she walked into the living room. "How was school?"

"It was okay," he replied, keeping the events of his day to himself. He knew that if he told her what had happened . . . what he'd sort of been involved in . . . she would start asking questions he didn't feel like answering right now.

Not wanting to show her own anxieties, she let it go at that, relieved that there were no further questions. No further opportunities for her emotions to overwhelm her.

Little was said between them, as he set the kitchen table and she prepared dinner. His one-word responses to her half-hearted inquiries convinced her that his silent mood stemmed from their conversation that morning. He even seemed distant while watching *Zorro*, one of his favorite TV shows. No jabbing at the comically chubby Sergeant Gomez with an imaginary sword or cheering on the masked avenger. She felt useless and insufficient.

"It's bedtime, sweetie-pie," she reminded him, as the announcer beckoned them to "stay tuned for the local news on most of these CBS stations."

"Okay, Momma," he agreed far too easily, rising to go to bed. No last-minute cookie requests or pleas to stay up a little longer.

"Honey?" she asked. "You okay? You're mighty quiet tonight. Is everything okay at school?"

What a coward I am! she thought. *He needs me, and all I can do is feel sorry for myself.*

"Yes, ma'am, I'm all right," he fibbed. "Jus' a little tired; that's all."

In fact, he had not been dwelling on thoughts of his father all day, as she had assumed. After all, he was only ten years old. Instead, he was still mulling over the drama on the playground.

The violence of Aubrey's vengeance had been frightening in its ferocity, beautiful in its execution, and exhilarating in its outcome. He'd never met anyone who hated bullies as much as Aubrey did. He'd never seen bullies get what they deserve before, either.

Still, he felt like he should have done more than just watch someone else hammer out justice. *What a coward I am!* he thought. *I shoulda done something to help that kid.*

He wondered why his mother seemed so sad all evening and felt a little guilty for not asking. But she was a girl, and girls are complicated, even scary sometimes. He shuddered to think how much worse it would be with a grown-up woman. He doubted he could be of any help to his mother and certainly did not want to see her cry again. So he minded his own business and hoped she would do the same.

He kissed her good night and clambered upstairs to his room, where his thoughts and feelings would be safe with just him and Solitude. Solitude was great at keeping secrets.

He fell asleep amid visions of bullies groveling and crying like babies before a giant knight with curly, brown hair. He dreamt that he, too, was in battle-worn armor wielding great axes and slaying red-headed dragons with flattop haircuts and chipped teeth.

Back downstairs in the living room, alone amid the flickering light of the droning anchorman's reading of the day's events, the mental sandbags she had placed against the levies of her past began to leak. She felt them stream down her cheeks and fall onto her robed breast.

And then the levies broke wide open. The flood she had so stoically held back rushed forth. Burying her face in the throw pillow she was hugging, she muffled her sobs so Frankie wouldn't hear them.

Oh, Jack! Why? Couldn't you see how much I needed you? How much WE needed you?

A lifetime ago, when she and Jack had left Haleyville, the sight of the tacky little town fading in the rearview mirror had been a welcome one. She had happily left the narrow minds and wagging tongues behind, never expecting to be at their mercy again.

Upon her return, the sight of the town looming through her windshield felt like a forgotten yoke, long thought left behind, being shackled around her neck again.

That Jack was gone was with her every single day. All she had to do was look at their son, and she was reminded how much she . . . how much *they* had lost.

She couldn't help remembering that Jack was gone . . . but truth be known, she didn't really mind that. Jack had been the center of her universe since the day they met. He was the most beautiful man she had ever seen. No other man in real life or on the silver screen could ever come close to him.

From the way his wavy, black hair framed his angular, Romanesque features to his heart-melting, crystal-blue eyes—everything about him projected the beauty of the heart that beat inside his brawny frame. She missed the way his lips were forever in a disarming, boyish grin— lips she had never tired of kissing, lips she ached to kiss, just once more.

She knew she wasn't the only one who had loved him, though.

For a while, it seemed the entire town had loved him. He had been the star receiver on the high school football team during the first winning streak in a very long time. He had carried the team through two great seasons, and he had been credited with taking them nearly to the state championship single-handedly. He was admired by everyone in the small town. Almost everyone, that is.

Even for Jack, there were those who had felt over-shadowed by his popularity and resented him deeply for it. But he never let the pettiness of others bother him. Instead, he looked for the good in people.

For her part, Shelley had been a fairly popular girl with that small-town beauty that sometimes made it to the big screen. Her circle of friends included all the most popular debutantes, as usually happens among the pretty and more socially acceptable . . . especially in a small town.

In truth, she knew that some of them were merely

circling like opportunistic buzzards, just waiting for a chance to turn Jack's head . . . because girls do that kind of thing . . . especially in a small town.

Being Jack's girl was all she had ever wanted or needed. Her friends joked that the teenage love song "Bobby's Girl" was written about her.

But, like Jack, the envy of girls less pretty or less socially relevant festered in the shadows of her popularity.

She and Jack had the perfect storybook romance. They were the couple envied by all the other couples in town. They were voted King and Queen of the Senior Prom. She had been a cheerleader, and he had been the captain of the football team. They were a "must invite" to any sock hop 'or party whose host or hostess hoped would be talked about the following Monday.

Jack's '32 Deuce Coupe, jet black with custom flames down the sides, ruled the Saturday night cruise at the A&W Drive-In, as well as the short strip down Haley Street.

A more cliché Hollywood romance could not be found.

Half the town attended their wedding, her mother seizing the opportunity to show the locals how grand an affair she could throw.

It seemed that half the town attended the going-away bash that her brother threw for them when Jack joined the army and announced that they were leaving Haleyville to start their new life.

Most seemed sorry to see them go; others seemed delighted. At last, the shining stars would no longer be around to outshine their own less brilliant ones.

She recalled, with sad gratitude, that at least as many attended his funeral, when the beloved favorite son was returned to his home soil. But, even then, there were some who just wanted to make sure the golden boy had really fallen from his lofty pedestal.

When she allowed herself to, she could still hear his last words to her, as he waited to file onto the air force transport with all the other husbands, fathers, brothers, and sons.

He had kissed her, long and tenderly, brushed a tear from her cheek, and cradled her face in his strong hands, saying, "Take care of my boy 'til I get back, babe."

He had then stooped down to face little Frankie, ruffled his thin wisp of baby hair, and said, "Little buddy, you take care of Momma while I'm gone, okay?" Little Frankie had nodded enthusiastically, a broad grin revealing his new front tooth.

"I love you both with all my heart," he had said, standing up and tenderly caressing the shoulders of the only girl he had ever truly loved. "I love you so much, Shelley . . . more than you'll ever know. Never forget that . . . never!"

Catching the lump in his throat, before it became a gasp, he had kissed her once more, then leaned down and kissed his son on the forehead. Then, slowly, he had turned to join the other soldiers going through their own similar dramas.

She watched as he marched reluctantly up the ramp and into the gaping belly of the giant plane. To the man, each one had turned at the last second to wave, catching a last glimpse of the ones they loved and would miss through long nights of terror, death, and mayhem.

That was the last image she had of her one and only love. A love she could never replace. It was the image she cherished and kept in her heart. It was the image that both tormented and blessed her dreams.

Then, her world had come crashing down one bleak autumn day, when an olive drab Ford sedan, the official white star emblazoned on its doors, pulled up in front of her off-base apartment.

She recalled the solemn, strained expressions on the faces of the two soldiers in dress uniforms, standing at her door as she opened it. Instinctively, she knew why they were there, and her heart began its miserable tailspin into darkness.

One of them, a young captain, made the U.S Army's and the president of the United States' apologies, as he regretted to inform her that Sergeant Jack Albert had been . . .

He then handed her a telegram with an ugly black stripe across it, callously announcing its contents.

Neighboring army wives peered through closed curtains on the verge of panic, breathing a guilty sigh of relief that the grim reaper had knocked on someone else's door. Retreating back behind those curtains, they shed tears of relief and fear of their own, as well as tears of sympathy for an unfortunate sister.

Her nights blurred into day and back into night, steeped in endless weeping and punctuated by fits of angry wailing. She barely functioned through the zombie-like motions of motherhood, breaking down into sobs of grief whenever she saw her husband's face looking back at her through their toddling son.

A sympathetic neighbor, an elderly army wife whose first name she could not remember . . . only Mrs. Cardinelli . . . comforted her and helped her with her son. It was precious help she felt she had never properly thanked the woman for.

Several of the other younger wives had also tried to be as comforting as they could. But their sympathy was always tempered by the fear radiating from their eyes. Fear that they themselves might someday be in her place. In the years that followed, she often wondered how many of those young wives had become war widows like her. She prayed that Mrs. Cardinelli was not among them. But then, she really didn't want to know. Her own loss was sufficient.

She had never been able to be among the brave wives . . . the unenviable widows who had offered sympathy and given support to the newly widowed in their darkest hours.

The memories she hated most were those of her child crying only because he saw his mother crying, unable to understand why.

Without Jack, life no longer felt worth living. If not for the innocent smiles of a boy too young to realize what had happened, she wasn't sure she would have made it through the blackness. He was her only light. His need for her kept her sane and gave her the only reason in the world to keep hanging on.

Tear-fogged memories of a silver, flag-draped coffin, at the first military funeral Haleyville had seen since the Korean War, crept up to torment her. The soul-splitting crack of a twenty-one-gun salute to a fallen hero echoed in her heart. The somber, mechanical salute and genuinely sympathetic look the young lieutenant gave her, as he presented her the folded flag, still played vividly in her memory.

In yet another ceremony, she had been given several medals by some general with lots of stars on his shoulders, on behalf of a grateful nation that could not possibly understand her grief or appreciate her loss but that expected her to understand its needs, and to accept its appreciation.

She resented the shining symbols of gratitude with their colorful ribbons, meant to symbolize, celebrate, and even glorify the bravery that had led to her loss. But she also treasured them, knowing what they would have meant to Jack, wishing with every fiber of her being that he had lived to receive them himself.

More than the medals, she resented the ugly, green check so crassly mailed to her by the army. Jack's "Death Benefit," they had called it. *Death Benefit? God . . . she hated those words!* How had his death "benefited" anyone? A mere few thousand dollars? Was that the price of a man's life, of a lost husband and father? It was blood money she couldn't bring herself to touch.

She felt that cashing the foul thing would be admitting that he really was gone. That was something she just couldn't bring herself to do. But eventually her brother convinced her to set up a trust fund for Frankie with it, arguing that not doing so would disrespect Jack's sacrifice.

THE HOMECOMING

The high-pitched tone coming from the television brought her back to the present. The unmoving profile of an Indian chief against a weird-looking bull's-eye pattern told her that the local station had signed off the air. How long ago, she didn't know.

The damp pillow she held close to her heart told her what she had been doing, but as emotionally wrung out as she was, sleep was the last thing she wanted. She knew what dreams it would bring.

No, she had to finish the sorrowful sojourn she had been set upon that morning. As she lay her head back, her eyes fell upon a small cobweb in the corner of the ceiling.

Mother would have been mortified, she thought. *Mommy . . . I really need you now.*

As if remembering Jack hadn't been painful enough, more of her past imposed itself on her already battered heart.

Her parents had died a grizzly death on a country back road at the hands of a drunken hillbilly in a pickup truck. The suddenness of the double closed-casket funeral left a black hole where the heart of a family used to be.

Her brother, Frank, inherited the house they had grown up in, but he couldn't stand the thought of living in it. Instead, he moved to Nashville and enrolled in the Firefighter's Academy, fulfilling a childhood dream and escaping his hometown.

Although he hated Haleyville, or rather some of the people in it, he loved his childhood home and the fond memories it held. He just never wanted to live in it again.

His parents were gone, and nothing that ever made him happy remained. The safety of family lay shattered and buried in the ground or living on some army base far away.

He simply locked the doors and shuttered the windows until he could decide what to do with the house.

When Jack was killed less than a year later, he pleaded with Shelley to move to Nashville, where he could help her with little Frankie. Although tempted, she decided that it was best for her to try to make it on her own and not become a burden for him, a decision he protested passionately, but in vain.

The McKinney homestead was a two-story traditional-style house, with clapboard siding on a stone foundation, built before the Second World War. Like all the neighboring homes along their street, it was centered on a large three-acre lot in the part of Haleyville that was neither fully in the country nor fully in the town.

A low, white picket fence separated the front yard from the gravel parking lane between the fence and the road. On the far right side of the yard, a seldom-used double gate opened to a mostly overgrown gravel driveway that lead to a separate garage, which generally served as a workshop, a garden shed, and a storage building.

A spacious and inviting front porch stretched the full width of the house. Four square, wooden columns sat atop tapered stone bases spaced equally along its length. A white balustrade railing stretched between each base on either side of the steps.

On the back side of the house, a screened-in porch spanned from corner to corner. Secured from mosquitoes and gnats, it overlooked a broad, carefully manicured expanse of green lawn separated from thick woods behind the house by an overgrown barrier of blackberry vines.

An apple tree, a peach tree, and a plum tree were scattered around the backyard. Growing up with fruit trees had been at times both delightful and the source of arduous, messy chores for the two siblings.

Picking fruit was only fun when you wanted to claim the biggest, juiciest apple or plum for yourself. It wasn't much fun when you had to pick it for Mother to make jams and jellies in Mason jars by the dozen. One learned to hate preserves.

The house had been skillfully painted sky blue with white trim by Shelley's father and lovingly landscaped by her mother. Flower beds graced the foot of both front and back porches and encircled each tree in the yard.

Large, mounded bushes of cascading red heirloom roses stood guard at the two corners of the front yard, while forsythia bushes, smothered in yellow blossoms, flanked each of the side yards.

A huge and ancient oak tree dominated one side of the front yard, complete with the obligatory old-tire swing dangling from a thick, low-hanging branch. Wooden slats ascended to the remnants of a tree fort, built long ago by an adventurous young Frank, sitting precariously among the upper branches.

Much like Shelley's life, the house, too, was a cliché from a prime-time television show. One almost expected to see Donna Reed come out onto the porch, waving and smiling, as she called her perfect family to the perfect dinner in the perfect dining room.

The house held its share of ghosts, though. Shelley could still see her mother, crooning breathlessly, tears of sheer joy in her eyes, when she first held little Frank Benjamin Albert, named after his uncle and one of Jack's closest friends and mentor. Even her father, the ever-serious tax attorney, was choked up the first time he held his gurgling grandson.

"Grandpa loves you, little Frankie," he had croaked through the lump in his throat. From then on, the baby boy's name was Frankie.

The proud grandparents eagerly showed pictures to all the people they knew, whether they wanted to see them or not.

Being the dutiful army wife, Shelley lived wherever her husband was stationed. But it was never close enough for frequent visits to her parents. Grandma and Grandpa rarely got to see Baby Frankie. Three short years of sporadic visits were all they had been given to enjoy their grandson, before being tragically torn away, leaving only someone else's memories and a few reels of eight-millimeter home movies for Frankie to know them by.

When Frankie was eight years old, she moved back home.

The first day she opened the house had been a shock for her. She had assumed that her brother had emptied it before boarding it up. But, in fact, he had left everything exactly as it had been the day their parents had walked out for the last time.

He had hired a local handyman to keep the outside of the house and the yard in good shape. The handyman had made extra money selling the fruit from the trees and the bushes at the local farmer's market, which had been perfectly okay with Frank. In fact, he had been sure his mother would have wanted it that way. "Food is meant to be eaten, not wasted!" she had said so often.

A thick layer of dust cloaked everything in a fuzzy film, freezing a moment in time and belying the expectations that her parents would be returning safely home that fateful night. It had been a difficult sight for Shelley to bear.

The yarn, the needles, and the half-finished sweater her mother had been in the midst of knitting lay on the sofa, waiting for her return.

The newspaper her father had been reading awaited him in his favorite armchair, Vice President Johnson's perpetually constipated expression squinting from behind the dust.

Her first reaction was to be angry with her brother, but, seeing how the sight of it had affected him as he had entered the house, she understood and forgave him without a word. He had lost his father, too. Just as her son had.

Three days of dusting, vacuuming, and cleaning, and three nights on her knees in tearful prayer had allowed Shelley to make peace with the ghosts of her parents and the pain of losing them so tragically. On the third day, a Sunday, she finally felt at peace with the house. She began to make a home in which to raise her son, to share the memories of her childhood, his father, and his grandparents with him, and to make new ones of their own.

Life for a young widowed mother was difficult, especially in a small town. Some old friendships that still remained in town were politely revisited, but not necessarily rekindled, as life had changed for others, as well as for her.

Most of the girls she had called friends in school had left town, seeking more from life than the backwater town had to offer, just as she had. She could scarcely blame them. The few that had remained had married and fallen into their own mundane routines, with families and homes of their own to care for. Though congenial and sympathetic, they seemed to have little time for socializing. An awkward and bizarre sense of guilt, or pity, kept many from once again becoming close to their former friend . . . the widow of the man they had wanted.

Some of the men in town sought to take advantage of what they were sure was her lonely need for a man's company. Fending off the sniffing dogs became emotionally tiresome. Some of the jilted mutts were certain that she had turned into a "bull dyke," since no "normal" woman in her right mind would ever turn away their advances.

But a few more sincere men who had been smitten by her beauty called on her, hoping to capture her affections. She had even gone to a movie or a dinner when the monotony of being single wore on her, but she could never get Jack out of her heart and mind.

Before long, even those occasional suitors stopped calling on her, giving her an old maid's reputation at an early age.

She didn't miss the unwanted attention, though. She was still, and would always be, Jack's girl. No other man could ever take his place, and she was content with that. Besides, she had Frankie, and that was all she needed. Let the petty tongues wag as they may.

Yet it seemed old envies and jealousies were more easily revived. Sneers were offered as readily by some as sympathy was by most. The first year had been the toughest. Several times she regretted returning instead of taking her brother up on his offer. At least there she had the luxury of big-city anonymity.

But there was something about Haleyville that had drawn her home. It must have been Jack. Yes, that had to be it. His memory was here, as was his grave. She could visit him, or at least visit the marble monument that presumed to hold his memory.

She took Frankie once, but, seeing how sullen it made him for days afterwards, she decided not to do so again, unless he wanted to, which he never did.

Besides, the tears she always ended up crying upset her son, and she often talked to Jack about things a little boy should not have to concern himself with.

At first, whenever she ventured into town, to the Piggly Wiggly, the Post Office, or to do some other errand, she would inevitably encounter former classmates of hers or Jack's, as well as other townsfolk who had known Jack, or at least had known about him.

Blue-haired, little, old ladies would stop her on the sidewalks of the town square and reminisce about Jack's natural, flirtatious politeness.

Mothers blushingly remembered his dashing good looks and genteel manners. Each of them who had a daughter had wished he would have picked their little darling for his bride. Though now, they must have been grateful that he hadn't.

The men around town remembered the excited football talk at the barber shop about a possible, though unrealized, state championship. At the feed mill, where Jack had worked over summer vacations, former co-workers spoke highly of his work ethic and marveled at his natural strength, as he easily hoisted one-hundred-pound bags of grain onto his shoulder and loaded them onto farmer's trucks.

He was revered by his friends for his unwavering loyalty, his always positive attitude, and the way he frequently stuck up for underdogs, whether he knew them or not. To them, he may as well have had a big red "S" on his chest and a cape flowing in the breeze behind him.

It was one of those underdogs who had stopped Shelley on the square one day and had told her that a job awaited her at the flooring mill anytime she wanted.

With every encounter, with every "I'm so sorry . . . ", and with every "I remember when . . . ", the wound was opened anew, and she was reminded that her life hadn't turned out like a Sandra Dee movie, that she wasn't living happily ever after.

Their sympathetic wishes were sincere, as was her gratitude, but the repeated reminders of her loss were painful, leaving her to wish they would stop.

As late night turned into midnight, the television now silent, she recalled how Jack had told her his life's story one beautiful star-strewn summer night, as they sat on the banks of Lake Owens. She could still hear the crickets chirping their nocturnal serenade to the rhythm of tiny waves gently lapping the muddy shore.

The strange thing was that Jack had no living connection to the town that seemed to hold him in such high regard. Abandoned in some distant city by his mother during World War Two, he had never known who his parents were.

Sister Mary Albert, a nun and a pediatric nurse at the orphanage, randomly chose "Jack" to be the deserted infant's first name, and, after being captivated by his bright blue eyes, she put her own last name on his paperwork. The day he was found on the orphanage steps became his birthday.

War has a way of bringing out certain feelings of fatalistic lust in the young men sent off to fight it and a duty-bound love in the hearts of young girls who watch them go. When the lustful, young fathers did not return, the panic-stricken, young mothers had to make choices, some choices more horrific than others.

An overabundance of wartime orphans taxed the resources of the orphanage, resulting in little Jack reluctantly being dumped into the state foster-care system at the age of five. Sister Mary wept for days, after her favorite little boy was sent away.

For years, he was shuffled from one family to the next. Fortunately for those who knew him and loved him, the repeated dashing of hopes and the constant shuffling of expectations had not broken his spirit or dimmed his enthusiasm for life or his love for people.

The gregarious and energetic twelve-year-old came to Haleyville in a plain white station wagon with out-of-state license plates. Finally, he had been fostered to a good family. They were a caring, but childless, couple who loved him as much as any foster parent could, more than any of the previous families ever had.

After he graduated, married, and joined the army, his foster parents moved to southern California, chasing lucrative employment in the booming defense industry.

It was a move that Jack had encouraged them to make, telling them how much better the weather would be for their health . . . plus there were movie stars in California. He wrote them faithfully about his new family and then about the war.

When he was killed, they dutifully returned to Haleyville for his funeral, mourning and weeping bitterly over his grave. Although their grief was deep and sincere, they were only foster parents, after all.

Like everyone else who had known Jack, they saw him every time they looked at his son. They doted on little Frankie, insisting that Shelley bring him out to San Diego to visit them . . . sometime. Shelley knew the invitation was more polite than sincere, though. After the funeral, she had little contact with them, other than an occasional letter or birthday card for Frankie. Before long, those ceased, as well.

She understood and forgave them.

At some point in the night, she drifted off into sharing a root beer float with Jack, as Marcie Blaine sang " . . . and if I was Bobby's girl . . . what a faithful, thankful girl I'd be . . . " just for them at the A&W.

NEW FRIENDS

The next morning, class had not yet started, as kids milled about the room, chattering as they began taking their seats. Miss Shockley was at her desk, busily correcting papers.

Well known for her strictness, the elderly woman oozed rigid discipline, striking fear in the hearts of all who crossed her. Although later in their lives, most would remember her with admiration and even fondness, Frankie's mother among them.

She was looking down, her reading glasses near the tip of her nose, immersed in her task, when Aubrey walked into the classroom. He had a black eye and a slightly swollen upper lip. A wave of silence swept the room. His classmates whispered behind his back, as he passed down the row to his own seat, but none dared snicker or talk loud enough for him to hear their comments.

He had become instantly infamous after yesterday's carnage on the playground. Rumors rippled through the school of what Aubrey had done to the bullies. One rumor had them in the hospital in critical condition, just barely holding onto life. The truth was that they were embarrassed by their black eyes and that everyone in school knew of how they had crawled away, crying like babies.

Teasing Aubrey now seemed akin to flirting with certain death. Talk in the hallways hinted that he had become the new bully to be feared, further isolating him, however unfairly. Already, he was feeling the eyes of derision casting their disapproval, and masking their fear.

As Aubrey took his seat, Frankie leaned forward and whispered in a voice wrought with concern, "What happened to you?"

He knew for a fact that not one single bully had so much as touched him. He had no idea who could have done such damage to him.

Aubrey hesitated, deciding whether or not he could trust his new-found friend. Taking a chance that he could, he leaned toward Frankie and whispered, "My Paw whooped me fer fightin' in school."

"What?" Frankie's gasped incredulously, louder than he had intended.

The sound of their whispering in a suddenly quiet room got Miss Shockley's attention. She looked up to catch the exchange between them.

"Mr. Denton, Mr. Albert!" she barked, "Is there something you boys would like to share with the rest of the class?"

Aubrey bolted upright to face her; then he quickly turned his eyes down at his desk.

The fresh bruise on his face was impossible to ignore. The teacher got up from her desk to approach him.

Aubrey sat with his hands clasped on the desk in front of him, his head cast down with embarrassment.

"Look at me, Mr. Denton," she ordered, less stern than before.

"What happened to your face?" she inquired. "I heard you were in a fight yesterday. Is that where you got that?" She pointed to his purplish eye, but she knew better. As his teacher, she had been given the details of the altercation by Principal Pike. However biased the man's feelings were toward the Denton family, he had clearly mentioned that Aubrey came through the altercation untouched. She even thought she had detected a tinge of admiration in his voice at that small detail.

"No ma'am!" Aubrey protested politely, but loudly enough for the class to hear. He was not going to let them think that anybody else in school could do this to him. Not even three bullies at the same time.

"Me an' my brother got into it last night," he lied, not wanting anyone to know his shame. He cast a warning glance at Frankie, who simply nodded in silent reassurance.

"So yesterday wasn't enough, eh, Mr. Denton?" she goaded, instantly regretting her remark. "And it's, 'My brother and I,' not, 'Me and my brother'!" she corrected, ever the teacher, as she turned back toward her desk.

That elicited a chuckle from the class, but it only served to provoke Aubrey. Frankie felt offended for his friend, as well.

"They was pickin' on someone littler than them," Aubrey shouted, standing up in defiance, "an' Maw says that ain't right!"

Wheeling in her tracks, the gray-haired teacher shouted, "*Mr. Denton!* That will be quite enough out of you! Now sit down and don't let me hear another word from you unless I address you directly! Do you understand me? Do not make me send for Principal Pike!"

Aubrey stood defiantly for a second, then wisely sat down, his hands clasped again, to hide their shaking.

"I'm sorry, Miss Shockley, truly I am. I shouldn't a dun that," he said in a subdued and contrite voice. "It's jus' that Maw says that only cowards pick on them that's littler then them. There was three of them an' only one o' him. An' they was all bigger 'n him, too."

Her demeanor softened, and she said, "I do admire your chivalry, Mr. Denton; those other boys were wrong to do what they did. But you must realize that violence does not solve things." Seeing the hurt behind the bruises on his face, she added, "I will speak to Principal Pike about them. They should be punished for what they did. But it is not your place to do the punishing."

She almost said that what they had done did not justify fighting, but she knew that he had simply defended someone incapable of defending themselves. If that wasn't justification, then what was? Instead, she said, "Next time you see something like that, you come get me or another teacher. Do not take matters into your own hands. Okay?"

"Yes, ma'am," was all Aubrey said, again with his face cast down.

She knew who the bullies where and was secretly glad they'd been given a dose of their own medicine. She felt a sincere admiration for what Aubrey had done, even though she loathed violence. She also suspected he had lied about his injuries, but she chose not to press it in front of the class. She had seen the same sort thing on his older brother, when he had been a student of hers. Her heart went out to the young man sitting before her. She found it suddenly impossible to be angry with Aubrey. He was suffering for doing what his heart had told him was right. Even the adults knew he was right to defend the helpless, but they were required to take a stance against violence of all kinds, even when it's morally justifiable.

Yeah, sure! Frankie thought. *Run tattling to a teacher and then see what happens to you.* He wouldn't do it, and the thought of Aubrey running to a teacher to squeal about bullies seemed utterly ridiculous to him.

Mercifully, perhaps sympathetically, Miss Shockley barked sternly at the rest of the gawking class, "What are you children looking at? Get your science books out and turn to page 178."

Recess came none too quickly to break the uncomfortable, hovering silence the morning's confrontation had brought to the classroom. Frankie and Aubrey opted not to go out on the playground. They knew that none of the other kids would come anywhere near them, anyway. Nor did they want them to.

Instead, they sat on the steps near the double doors, engaged in the small talk that new friends engage in. "Where do you live?" "Got any brothers or sisters?" "Ever watch *The Lone Ranger*?" "Who's your favorite superhero?"

As it turned out, Aubrey lived on a farm just over a mile down the same road Frankie lived on, past the bridge that crossed Mill Creek. The boys found that they shared common interests in cars, airplanes, movies, and cartoons, though Aubrey had to admit he hadn't seen very many of the latter two and mostly only scattered pictures of the others. His family's decade-old black-and-white TV usually didn't work. Besides, his father felt Saturday mornings were better spent doing chores around the farm, not wasting time in front of a television, watching cartoons and movies.

Frankie felt sorry for his new friend. Most kids lived for Saturday morning cartoons. After enduring long, torturous hours under the glare of tyrannical teachers all week long, Saturday was freedom day.

He couldn't imagine what life would be like without cartoons. He couldn't wait to squat in front of the TV with a bowl of Sugar Smacks, watching *The Little Rascals* to start things off, followed by *Bugs Bunny and the Road Runner, Space Ghost*, and all the rest. Finally to be topped off by an old Tarzan or Three Stooges movie, all the way up to lunch time. Not being able to watch them was simply unthinkable and unacceptable. Frankie didn't think he was going to like Aubrey's father very much.

He shared his Twinkies with Aubrey, who apparently didn't get those very often, either. Aubrey traded some of his mother's homemade brownies. Frankie liked the brownies much more than the Twinkies and told Aubrey so, bringing a smile of pride to the big guy's face. They agreed to make the same trade every day.

Frankie recounted the latest adventures of Superman versus Lex Luthor for his new buddy, using the pictures on his lunchbox and matching thermos as a guide.

He was deep into an animated description of kryptonite when they were interrupted by the new kid Aubrey had rescued the day before.

"Uh. . .Hi," he stuttered nervously, not sure if it was safe to approach his avenger.

"I'm, uh . . . my name is Tony . . . uh, Tony Carillo," he said, slowly sticking a shaky hand out to Aubrey, as if offering it to a ravenous bear. "Um . . . thanks for sticking up for me yesterday. That was a really cool thing to do."

He grinned hopefully, his eyes revealing his apprehension.

I don't know what I wudda done if yooz guys hadn't showed up when ya did." His sharp Northern accent enthralled the two Southern boys.

Aubrey stood up, looming over the small boy, and smiled broadly, taking his tiny hand into his own big paw.

"Aw heck, it ain't nuthin, lil' fella," he said. "Them guys is jus' buttholes. They had it comin' to 'em." He squeezed Tony's hand a little harder than Tony had expected.

"My name's Aubrey Denton," he said. "They didn't hurt ya, did they?"

Tony shook his head no, pulling his hand back and shaking life back into it. He wasn't crazy about being called "lil' fella," but he wasn't going to reprimand his hulking rescuer. His size had made him a target of ridicule many times before. He didn't think many people wanted a runt for a friend.

"Frankie, here was jus' about ta jump in, too, but I reckon I beat 'im to it . . . hogged all the fun!" Aubrey said, nodding toward Frankie, who blushed at being given credit he didn't think he deserved.

"My name's Frankie Albert. Pleased ta meet ya," Frankie said, shaking Tony's hand less vigorously than Aubrey had. Having shaken Aubrey's hand, he understood why Tony had flinched.

"Now, you come git me if they go bother'n ya again, ya hear?" Aubrey said, still grinning. "Tell ya the truth, it kinda felt good whoopin' up on 'em. They been pushin' folks around long enough. It was kinda like stompin' on rats in the feed bin, 'cept ya can forgive the rats, 'cause they're jus' lookin fer food."

Tony had no idea what the big country boy was talking about. Rats? What the heck was a feed bin? Accustomed to the staccato of a Northern accent, he had some difficulty trying to understand Aubrey through his thick country drawl and his mangling of the English language.

"Hey, you wanna be our pal?" Aubrey asked sincerely, nodding toward Frankie.

Frankie added enthusiastically, "Yeah, that'd be real cool."

The diminutive fifth grader's eyes lit up. He was genuinely surprised and pleased at the offer of friendship. The prospect of not one, but two, new friends at school, especially friends big enough to keep the bullies away, was more than he had dared hope for. His heart leapt at the prospect.

"What happened to you?" he asked, pointing at Aubrey's black eye. He, too, knew very well that none of the thugs had touched him. He wondered how big someone had to be to do something like that.

"Oh that!" Aubrey dismissed with false casualness.

"Me an' my brother got into it last night," he lied. "It ain't nuthin', though. We do it all the time."

"Dang!" Tony exclaimed, wide-eyed. "Your brother must be one big palooka!"

"Uh . . . well, I don't know what a 'palooka' is, but, yeah, I s'pose so," he answered, somewhat confused. "He's in middle school. We're both kinda big, like our Paw."

Frankie knew the truth, but Aubrey had trusted him with it, and he would not betray that trust. He knew that, inside, his pal was ashamed and hurting.

"Kinda like a family of Incredible Hulks, huh?" Frankie joked, hoping it would help take his new friend's mind off the beating.

"Incredible whuts?" Aubrey asked, a little puzzled, not sure if his family had just been insulted.

"The Incredible Hulk," Frankie said. "He's another superhero, or sorta like one, anyway. He turns all green an' grows huge when he gets mad. Then he starts smashin' bad guys. You didn't turn green yesterday, but you did turn red, and you sure looked huge to me, compared to them weenies!" Frankie mused, grinning impishly. Then he said, "I got some of his comic books, too. I'll bring one tomorrow for ya to look at, if ya want."

"Yeah, he's far-out," Tony added, happy to be joining the conversation. "He can crush army tanks with his bare hands and stuff like that."

Then, he added, "And Frankie's right, man. You were huge!"

"Carillo, huh?" Aubrey repeated the name, a little embarrassed at both the praise and his lack of knowledge about superhero lore.

"Sounds kinda like gorilla, dudn't it?" he mused innocently.

He saw a shadow cross Tony's face and immediately felt bad for his clumsy, though modest, attempt to divert praise away from himself.

"Hey, man, I'm sorry," he instantly apologized. "That wudn't very thoughtful o' me, was it? I wudn't makin' fun o' ya. Honest!"

"It's okay," Tony said, dismissing Aubrey's gorilla comparison dejectedly. "I'm used to it. Everybody does it."

"I hate my name," he said. "I wish I was big, like you, so's I could do something about it whenever anybody cracked wise with me."

"Naw, it ain't okay," Aubrey protested. "I truly didn't

mean nuthin' by it. I think it's a cool name."

"At least, it don't sound like a dent on some ol' car, like mine does," he added, hoping it would smooth over his awkward remark and maybe even get a laugh out of Tony.

"I shuda kept my big mouth shut," he admonished himself. "Maw says I'm always puttin' my big ol' foot in my big ol' mouth."

In fact, Tony did chuckle at Aubrey's self-deprecating comment, sensing a humbleness and sincerity he couldn't remember ever seeing in other kids his age.

The three boys fell into an awkward silence.

"Hey, you like Superman?" Frankie asked Tony, tactfully filling the gap.

"Heck, yeah, man; who doesn't!" Tony said excitedly. "He's far-out, too."

"I got all his comic books, even the new ones," he said rapidly, in his Northern staccato.

"Hey, yooz guys wanna come over to my place and check 'em out?" he asked, hopefully.

"Sure!" Frankie answered quickly.

Yooz guys?

He asked, "Ya got any with Krypto in 'em? I love dogs, and a Superdog is so cool!"

Then, he added, "I wonder if he gets fleas and ticks?"

Tony laughed out loud at the comment, and said, "I don't think so; they'd probably break their jaws on him."

Aubrey chuckled, too, but then looked down and shuffled his feet in the schoolyard dirt, saying disappointedly, "I don't think Paw will let me come over. I got chores ta do."

The invitation touched him, nonetheless. He'd never been invited to a friend's house before, because he'd never had a real friend before.

"Well," Tony said, searching for an alternative plan, "I, uh . . . I guess I could bring some over to your house, if it's okay."

Again Aubrey was touched, but regretfully said, "That's doggone nice o' you, Tony. Really it is. Ain't nobody ever invited me ta their house before, or wanted ta come ta mine. I 'preciate it a whole bunch—truly I do—but Paw don't much like havin' folks come over, neither. He ain't real sociable. He says I spend enough time foolin' around in school, as it is."

His big heart was breaking. He'd always wondered what it would be like to have friends and go to each other's houses and do all the things he saw friends on TV doing, when he got to watch TV. But now that the dream seemed possible, the reality of his life threatened to derail all of that, because his father hated the world.

Then an idea came to him, and he said, "Hey! Y'all go ta church, dontcha?"

"Yeah, 'course I do," Frankie answered, wondering what Aubrey was thinking. My mom makes me. Haleyville Methodist. Why?"

"Not me, at least not since we moved here," Tony replied. "I'm Catholic, and there's not one of those kind of churches around here." *Thank goodness!* he thought

"What's a Catholic?" Aubrey asked.

"It's just another kind of church, I guess," Tony replied glibly. "It's what my folks say we are. Everybody back home is one, too. We gotta do a lot of kneeling, and the priest speaks Latin, a lot. It's really boring. Mom wanted me to be an altar boy, but I knocked over the holy water, so . . . "

"Well," Aubrey said, "I ain't too sure 'bout what you just said, but if ya'll want to an' it's okay with yer mothers, ya'll can come on down ta my church, Creekwood Baptist, this Sunday, an' be our guests. We'd sure be proud ta have ya." He offered his invitation hopefully.

"After services Maw 'n Paw always hang around fer a little while, so they can talk with the deacons an' other folks," Aubrey said. "We can slip off to the creek an' check out some comic books then."

"Who knows?" he added. "Maybe after Paw meets ya'll, he might be more apt to let me come an' visit ya'll sometime."

"Uh, yeah . . . cool," Tony said hesitantly, not really sure what a "Baptist" or a "deacon" was, either.

Then he asked, incredulously, "You actually *like* going to church?"

"Well . . . yeah," Aubrey answered, a little confused. "Don't you? How else ya gonna learn 'bout right 'n wrong or hear the stories Jesus told?"

Wow! Tony thought.

His first impulse had been to tease Aubrey, the way they used to tease the altar boys back home. But he'd just made friends and didn't want to jeopardize that. Besides, he'd seen what Aubrey's reaction to bullying was. He might not be too fond of teasing someone about something he obviously enjoyed.

But a kid who really . . . actually likes church? That's just bizarre. Tony thought.

"Well, whatcha doin' Saturday?" he asked, instead.

Aubrey kicked the dirt again and sullenly explained to Tony, as he had to Frankie, "I cain't go nowheres on Saturdays. I gotta help Paw and my brother with the garden an' the hogs an' stuff. An' then I gotta help Maw hang out the laundry an' whutever else needs doin.'"

"Paw only lets me play on Sundays, 'cause Maw says

that's what Jesus said we're s'posta do, so she won't let him make us work then." It was one of the very few concessions his irascible father had reluctantly made for his family.

The other two boys stared blankly back at Aubrey. Frankie's heart went out to him. He understood about the chores. He had some of his own around the house, and he didn't mind helping his mother. But he knew his chores paled next to Aubrey's overwhelming burden. To force a kid to slave away all day, especially on Saturday, was just plain wrong. His dislike for Aubrey's father was growing.

Tony huffed his indignation at parents who would make their own children work so hard. As it was, he chafed at having to empty the trash and clean his room. Weekends were for playing, not working. What kind of parents did this guy have? After all, his own father didn't work on the weekend, so why should he? School was enough of a job.

"Well, then," Frankie conceded, accepting Aubrey's offer, "we'll meet on Sunday. I'll bring some of my comics, too. I got Sergeant Rock an' Batman comics, too.

"I even have some *MAD* magazines," he said proudly.

"Wow, you're lucky," Tony griped. "My mother won't let me have *MAD* magazines. She thinks they're for crazy people. She says they'll turn you into a slobbering idiot."

Clearly his new friends were a lot more hip than he was, Aubrey thought. He felt a little intimidated by it, but that had never stopped him before.

"Whut's a *MAD* magazine?" he asked, innocently.

"Huh?" Tony responded, raising his eyebrows in disbelief. "What? Do you live in a cave or something? Everybody knows what a *MAD* magazine is."

Aubrey looked away dejectedly.

Tony realized that, this time, he'd been the insensitive one and immediately regretted his flippant remark.

"Oh, man!" he berated himself.

"Sorry, Aubrey. I didn't mean it that way . . . honest," he apologized. "Don't pay any attention to me. My cousin Ricky says I got a big man's mouth on a little boy's body. I guess he's right, huh?" Tony was hoping he hadn't ruined things before they got started.

"Aw, fergit it!" Aubrey grinned halfheartedly. It wasn't Tony's fault that his father refused to spend money on anything he considered wasteful, like comic books.

The more time Frankie spent around Aubrey, the more he admired him, and the more he was confused by him. His gentle, forgiving nature was at direct odds with the brute force and violence he had seen the day before. Aubrey was intriguing, to say the least.

He liked Tony, too. The wiry little guy standing before them now seemed a sharp contrast to the frightened victim he'd seen yesterday. But who wouldn't have been terrified?

The bell rang, ending recess. Being closest to the door, they were the first ones back into the building. Tony peeled off to his class, while Frankie and Aubrey returned to Miss Shockley's classroom across the hall. Much to their surprise, she greeted them with a warm smile.

The boys wandered to their seats, shrugging their shoulders with eyebrows raised, and giving each other *What the heck?* looks.

After the class had settled down, Miss Shockley quietly asked Aubrey to step out into the hallway with her. She appointed a girl with curly brown hair, in the front row, to be class monitor; then she admonished the class to stay in their seats and begin reading page 140 in their history books, while she was out of the room. Her final, sweeping glare assured that that was exactly what they would do.

A few minutes later, she and Aubrey returned to the room.

Aubrey blushed with embarrassment, as he lumbered between the rows of desks, but he seemed pleased, for some reason. A freckle-faced boy snickered as he walked by.

"Is there something funny you'd like to share with the class, Mr. Evens?" Miss Shockley scolded at the snickering boy, causing him to shrink, red-faced, as far as he could into his seat, in an attempt to escape her piercing glare.

Frankie tugged at his sleeve, as he sat down, but Aubrey just turned to him and shook his head. Frankie thought he saw Aubrey's eyes watering. Confused, he sat back and glanced at Miss Shockley, who returned his glance with a warm smile, compounding his confusion.

"Now class," she said, falling seamlessly back into teacher mode, "who can tell me . . . "

AUBREY'S FARM

When the three o'clock bell finally rang, the hallway erupted with the usual stampede of screaming urchins, racing to escape their daily detainment.

Frankie's mother worked until after five o'clock, so he took the same bus as Aubrey, since he lived on the same road.

Today he thought to ask Aubrey if he wanted to walk home, instead. It wasn't all that far, and the spring weather was beautiful.

Aubrey said he couldn't, explaining that if he did that, he'd be late getting home, and his father would get upset.

Geez, Frankie thought resentfully, *this guy's father is a real jerk!*

So, instead, Frankie decided to ride the bus all the way to Aubrey's farm, even though it meant walking over a mile back to his own house. He didn't mind, though. He was in the mood, and it was a great day to walk; besides, he had no pressing chores like Aubrey, and it got a little lonely waiting for his mother to come home from work.

Aubrey was a little apprehensive at first, but he agreed. Having a buddy to ride with on the bus was new to him, too.

"What did Ol' Shock-face want?" Frankie asked, as soon as they sat down.

"Don't call her that nomore, okay?" Aubrey admonished gently.

"Huh?" Frankie was taken off guard, "Why not?"

"'Cause she's a nice lady; that's why," he answered defensively, "Ya 'member when she called me out ta the hallway?" Frankie nodded.

"Well, she told me that she was sorry fer yellin' at me an' that I had dun a noble thang, stickin' up fer Tony the way I did. She said Maw was right, that bullies are bad and that they need ta be stood up to."

His cheeks turned pink as he continued, "An' then she dun sumthin' really weird."

He hesitated, not sure he should reveal what happened next.

"She hugged me an' told me that if I ever wanted ta talk with a grown-up about stuff at home, that I could talk ta her an' she promised that she'd keep it our secret," he said, stopping himself from touching his bruised face.

Then he looked Frankie in the eye and said, "She also said that she thought you was a good kid and that she was glad I'd found a friend like you."

Frankie was dumbstruck. Miss Shockley, the dreaded she-dragon of Haleyville Elementary, thought he was a good kid? What next? A Martian invasion?

He had been certain that she hated him. On top of that, she had actually hugged Aubrey . . . and called him noble, whatever that meant. This really was weird.

He thought about the episode of *The Twilight Zone,* where the normal people had been replaced with strangely behaving duplicates who where up to something sinister . . . and who had a third eye on their forehead. He gave Aubrey a sidelong look, but decided to keep the thought to himself.

An awkward silence ensued between them, each boy trying to figure out her strange behavior.

"What other comic books you got?" Aubrey finally asked, changing the subject, as the bus lumbered away with its noisy cargo.

The two boys fell into an animated conversation about the things boys talk about. Eventually, the bus came to a stop in front of the entry to a washed-out gravel driveway. Frankie followed Aubrey off the bus into the bright springtime sun. Looking up the hill at Aubrey's house, he understood his reluctance to have visitors.

After the bus lumbered away, Aubrey crossed the road and retrieved a handful of envelopes and a magazine from the mailbox, Frankie climbed up on the sagging gate that blocked entry onto the Denton farm and soaked up the rural panorama before him.

Unlike the pictures that graced the big wall calendar behind Miss Shockley's desk, where pristine farms with bright red barns and crisp, white farmhouses settled neatly into softly rolling hills of velvety green, Aubrey's farmhouse stood atop the rocky hill. From this distance, it looked a little shabby and in need of painting, its metal roof streaked with rust. It was surrounded by a picket fence, also in need of painting and missing a few slats.

From the farmhouse to the gateway where they stood was about the length of a football field. The steep hillside they faced was tightly dappled with large, craggy limestone boulders. A millennium of rainfall had washed away the layers of soil to form miniature canyons and fissures in between the boulders, in which tall, prickly thistles lifted their purple heads. Sienna-tinted combs of leathery-leafed dock weed mixed with bright green milkweed pods grew in the few open spaces between the boulders. It was essentially a patch of wasteland, not good for farming or even grazing.

Climbing up on the gate next to him, Aubrey read his thoughts and described the narrow field of boulders as though it were the best playground anywhere. Sometimes it was a lost world, where he chased, or was chased, by long-extinct man-eating dinosaurs. Other times it was a battlefield full of hidden enemy soldiers he defeated single-handedly or Indians just waiting to ambush the lone warrior. Still other times it was a distant planet, populated by slobbering, hungry alien monsters determined to make him their next meal.

It was where his legion of imaginary playmates patiently awaited his arrival each day, just so that they could exist, if only for a short while. *How would they feel about a real, live addition to their ranks?* Aubrey wondered.

Frankie realized that Solitude was Aubrey's friend, too.

His own thoughts boiled over with possibilities. Aubrey's farm was getting cooler by the minute.

The winding and rutted gravel driveway meandered to the right and then climbed the hill in a wide-sweeping, left-hand curve. The occasional rounded shoulder of rock protruded up into the roadway, scratched and scarred where a half century of cars and trucks had scraped across it.

The driveway wound around the weathered, unpainted barn, its roof a solid expanse of rusty ochre. On the far side of the barn, a dilapidated, fading red International

Farmall tractor and a few other implements sat beneath a corrugated metal overhang that matched the rest of the barn's roof. On the near side, bales of hay bulged from under another broad, fenced-in overhang, supported by stout cedar trunks, hewn and stripped of all branches and bark.

Surrounding the barn was a swamp of black muck from decades of hungry cattle gathering around to be fed, while leaving their previous meals to add to the noxious sea of manure and mud.

At the top of the hill, in front of the house, the driveway ended in a roughly circular parking area in front of the low limestone retaining wall that supported the picket fence atop it.

A beat-up, old, black Ford pickup truck sat in the shade of an overgrown, drooping hackberry tree. Next to the truck, an even older Chevy sedan sat on concrete blocks, all of the wheels missing, the hood lying upside down on the roof of the car.

To the left of the driveway gate, at the base of the hill where they stood, the boulders ended and the ground leveled off into a broad, flat pasture, split down the middle by a thin, trickling stream, which emptied into a small pond in the middle of the pasture.

A sparse herd of white-faced, rust-colored cattle dotted the pasture. The scattered bovine grazed on the rich, green grass or lay in it, lazily basking in the warmth of the sun. Several cows stood in the shade of the scrub trees surrounding the pond, drinking the murky water or idly standing knee deep in it, simply enjoying the shade.

Frankie spotted what he thought were two large, dark brown horses with gray muzzles in a fenced-off lot adjacent to the barn.

"Wow!" he breathed. "You got horses, too! It must be cool to live on a farm." He had seen cows often enough, but he had never seen mules before.

"Them ain't horses!" Aubrey laughed. "They're mules."

"Mules? What're they for?"

Aubrey explained that his father preferred the reliability of a good team of mules over the tractor. He told Frankie how he and his brother had spent many hours behind the mules, plowing and disking the three-acre vegetable garden that was a large part of the family business, as well as an affordable source of food. He didn't explain that they had to use mules because his father couldn't afford to buy a new tractor to replace the broken relic next to the barn.

Frankie guessed that working the mules, as well as all the other farm chores, was the source of much of Aubrey's physical strength.

"Can ya ride 'em?" Frankie asked eagerly.

"Yep," Aubrey answered.

"Matter o' fact, we gotta ride 'em down ta the pond, yonder, every day," he said, pointing to the pond in the middle of the field, "so we can water 'n exercise 'em."

"That is so cool!" Frankie repeated.

"Can I ride 'em sometime? Please?" he pleaded.

"Well, I reckon ya can! I mean, I'll have ta ask Paw first," he replied. "But I don't think he'll mind. Ever rode a horse before?"

"Nope, but I did ride a pony at the carnival once," Frankie replied, immediately embarrassed by his answer.

Aubrey laughed again. "Mules ain't nuthin' like ponies, man!" He chuckled. "They ain't even exactly like horses, neither. They can be danged ornery and outright mean, at times. Heck, they even try ta bite me when I'm puttin' the harness on 'em, sometimes. Ya gotta be careful when yer ridin' 'em, too. It makes 'em nervous if they think yer scared of 'em an' they'll throw ya off."

Looking impishly at Frankie, he challenged, "But I bet you ain't scared of 'em, are ya?"

"Um . . . no! 'Course I'm not." He wasn't sure if he'd just lied or not. If he had been afraid of a sixth grader, why wouldn't he be afraid of a powerful mule? As he looked at the mules, they seemed to grow right before his eyes.

"Man!" Frankie breathed. "Doesn't anything scare you?"

"I don't know. I reckon maybe some thangs do," he answered in an honest tone, devoid of any arrogance or conceit. He didn't say that his father frightened him more than anything in the world.

"I remember once, a long time ago when I was little, I was in the barn feedin' 'em, an' heard a ruckus up in the loft. I thought it was monster, so I ran ta the house yellin' fer Paw. But it turned out ta be just a pissed-off ol' mama 'coon with some pups! Him an' Waylon thought that was perty funny.

"Ya shoulda seen Paw an' Waylon an' me tryin' ta catch them critters," he laughed. "We never did, though. We jus' scared 'em off. But they ain't never come back, neither.

"Anyhow," Aubrey continued, "Paw says there ain't nothin' out there for a strong man ta be scared of, an' Maw says that Jesus has angels that take care of his own, so . . . "

Frankie doubted that Aubrey was ever "little." He was in awe of the stout farm boy. Aubrey had such confidence and a sense of peace about him, as well as size and strength. Frankie had witnessed his courage firsthand, so he knew he had that.

He found himself wishing he was more like Aubrey. His father had taught him to be unafraid. *Maybe he wasn't such a bad father, after all,* he thought. But the black eye told a different tale.

"Ya know . . . you're all right, Aubrey!" Frankie proclaimed, unable to contain his admiration, "I'm glad we're buddies."

"Yeah, I like you, too!" Aubrey replied.

Then, in a voice heavy with loneliness, he lamented, "I ain't never had no real friends before, ya know, that wudn't a cousin or sumpthin'. Yer my first one."

The revelation touched Frankie inside. It was a shame how poverty, or the perception of poverty, kept such a nice guy as Aubrey from having friends. But then, just not having a father around was enough to keep him on the outside. *Kids have funny ways of measuring each other,* he thought.

"My brother Waylon's been my only buddy," Aubrey continued, "but that ain't the same thang. Besides, nowdays he spends all his extra time with his girlfriend, Irene."

"But I cain't blame 'im, she shore is a perty thang!" he added, grinning at Frankie.

"Hey, ya wanna come up an' meet Maw?" he asked, changing his mood in the blink of an eye.

"Yeah, sure," Frankie answered eagerly, remembering the brownies Aubrey had shared with him. Any mom who could bake such delicious brownies had to be a real special lady.

Frankie's enthusiasm made Aubrey feel wanted and

worthy. In the span of a mere two days, they had begun a bond that would last a lifetime.

The boys jumped down from the gate. Aubrey unhooked the chain that held it closed and swung it open for them to slip through.

"I'll race ya!" Aubrey challenged, closing the gate and replacing the chain on its nail. Then, without warning, he dashed off, but he didn't head up the driveway, as Frankie had expected. Instead, he ran straight toward the boulders that cascaded down the hillside. Easily clambering up the nearest weather-worn rock, he began leaping from one boulder to the next, bouncing up the gnarly hill with the agility of a mountain goat. Obviously, it was something he had done often.

Frankie followed as quickly as he could, doing his best to keep up, but his inexperienced legs couldn't match Aubrey's speed and skill. Some gaps were too wide for him to comfortably leap across, so he had jump to the ground and clamber up the next rock.

Within minutes, Aubrey stood at the top of the hill, barely breathing hard, urging Frankie on with wide sweeps of his arm.

"C'mon! Hurry up, Pokey Joe!" he goaded playfully.

Finally, after several interminably long minutes Frankie made it, panting and gasping, to the place where Aubrey stood with an amused look on his face.

"Dang . . . Aubrey . . . that was . . . tough," he wheezed between raspy breaths, bent over with his hands on his knees. He couldn't remember when he'd been so out of breath.

"You . . . do this . . . all the . . . time?" he asked, his legs burning from the climb and his head buzzing with fatigue.

"Every day," Aubrey answered in a confident voice. "Maw sends me down ta fetch the mail, an' I like ta pertend like I'm one o' them bighorn sheep I seen on *Wild Kingdom*." Frankie was mildly annoyed at how even and unlabored Aubrey's breathing was.

Aubrey motioned for Frankie to follow as he turned toward his house.

Frankie realized that the house, which had seemed shabby from a distance, only needed painting. The old homestead looked solid, even comfortable. Though the house itself needed some attention, he could see that someone had spent long, loving hours attending to the landscape around it, painting it with a variety of plantings, sporting every color in the rainbow. The cheerful landscaping lent forgiveness to the neglected appearance of the house.

A row of red and pink geraniums stood in ranks between the stone wall and the picket fence. Beyond the fence, a mix of wild roses and gooseberry vines helped hide the squat, cinder block pump house in the front yard, to the left. Its flat, tar-papered roof barely showed beneath several pots of flowers and herbs lined up along the edge, spilling over like a living waterfall of color.

Chiseled stone steps set in the low limestone wall led from the gravel parking area to a wire gate that seemed out of place with the flanking weathered pickets.

Past the gate, flagstones led to the broad, wooden porch steps. A variety of old cast-iron kettles and pots brimming with vibrantly blooming impatiens colored the ends of each step. Flanking the steps, flower beds displayed an elegant mix of pastel blossoms and the delicate foliage of different herbs.

An old apple tree shaded part of the right side of the

yard, surrounded by a ring of thick-bladed chives and pungent marigolds.

Frankie's interest was drawn to the round planters that dotted the yard in a random pattern. Looking closer, he saw that they had been made from old truck tires that had been sliced like a pie on one side and then turned inside out and painted white. Each one was filled with a different herb. They reminded him of Jughead's hat, from his Archie comic books.

The tire rings and the wide variety of containers used for planting told him that farmers don't waste anything.

Old fashioned rose bushes were widely spaced along the inside of the fence, their fragrant blooms spicing the air with their scent.

Frankie was amazed at the myriad of colors and aromas the yard boasted.

Even the porch was adorned with planters and old pots, overflowing with color, some resting on the porch itself, others hanging from rafters beneath the overhang.

On the ground at each end of the porch, snuggled against the house, sat wooden whiskey barrels, with downspouts from the roof gutters aimed into them to receive and store rainwater.

Far to the left side of the yard, the remains of a diminished pile of coal and a low row of firewood stood, contained by a low, U-shaped stone stall, apparently built just for that purpose. Several scuttle buckets full of coal were lined up on that end of the porch, for easy access on cold days.

To the far right of the yard, a wire fence separated it from the massive vegetable garden, just starting to set its spring blossoms, along with several long rows of knee-high corn stalks.

The front door was centered on the face of the house and flanked by two large double sash windows on either side. A modern aluminum screen door, with a "D" prominently mounted in the middle of it, seemed out of place with the rustic appearance of the rest of the house. To the right of it, a wide porch swing swayed invitingly.

Just as they were about to mount the steps, a long-legged, rust-colored hound came bounding clumsily around the corner of the house, nearly knocking Aubrey off his feet as it jumped up to greet him, its big paws pressing against his chest.

"Hey, Scooter," Aubrey greeted back, amid a barrage of wet, sloppy licks.

"How ya doin', girl?" he said, scratching behind her flopping ears.

"This here's Scooter. She's the best dang dog in the whole world!" he beamed, as he introduced the only other true friend he'd ever had. "She can track down a 'coon better 'n any dog around, an' she likes to swim in the creek with me, too."

"Aw, man . . . that is right on," Frankie exclaimed. "You even have a dog, too! That is so cool!"

Aubrey blushed. He had never been given so much praise from anyone other than his mother or aunt, and never from another kid.

The redbone hound still had her paws on his shoulders, as he said, "Scooter, this here's Frankie. He's my new friend."

As if she understood what her master said, she dropped down and bounded toward Frankie, this time succeeding in knocking her target to the ground, lavishing him with dog kisses just as enthusiastically as she had Aubrey.

Frankie didn't mind one bit, though. He loved dogs and had asked his mother on several occasions if he could have one. She had said yes, but it had to be the right one. That had always puzzled him. How do you tell if it's the right dog, or not?

Instantly, he was convinced that a dog just like Scooter was definitely the right one.

"She's a real cool dog, Aub. I wish I had one just like her," he said.

After several minutes of romping and wrestling with Scooter, the two boys climbed the steps of the porch. Aubrey pulled the door open and motioned Frankie in. His apprehensions at having a friend visit were completely gone.

Inside the spacious foyer, the walls were covered with old, faded floral wallpaper. A single door was centered on each of the interior walls. On either side, family photographs displaying generations of Dentons covered the walls. Most were grainy black-and-white and faded sienna, but occasional, more modern color photos peppered the walls. Several Dentons proudly displaying the uniforms they served their country in, as far back as the Civil War, were nestled among the aged and unsmiling portraits of the previous century.

A large store-bought portrait of Jesus, illuminated in prayer, hung over the door in the far wall, flanked by more Dentons, smiling from within delicately carved picture frames.

Antique bookcases on either side of the room held dusty tomes that had gone largely neglected for years. In the middle of the foyer, a bare lightbulb hung down from the ceiling. A pull chain dangled just low enough to reach the small brass ball at its end.

The doors to the left and straight ahead were closed, but the door on the right was propped wide open by an antique flatiron sitting at its base.

"Hey Maw!" Aubrey called out. "I'm home . . . an' I got someone for you ta meet." Nodding to Frankie to follow, he entered through the open door into the living room.

Frankie felt as if he'd stepped into an antique shop. The walls were covered in a different wallpaper, but every bit as floral and faded as it was in the spacious foyer.

To his right, a Victorian-era couch decorated with richly carved dark wood and dressed in worn burgundy brocade sat beneath the double window, throw pillows neatly arranged along its cushions and a lace shawl draped over its back. A vast oriental rug covered most of the hardwood floor, a worn pathway through the room attesting to its age. An oval-shaped pedestal coffee table sat in front of the couch; a crystal vase filled with fresh blossoms from the yard sat at its center. At each end of the couch, sculpted bronze lamps sat on lace doilies draped across end tables that matched the coffee table.

In the corner, a slightly less-ancient overstuffed and overused leather armchair sat angled between the couch and the large stone fireplace on the far wall. A matching ottoman sat in front of the chair.

An ornate cast-iron shield now covered the fireplace opening, since the cold days of winter had passed. A medium-sized, lavishly carved, glass-faced hutch squatted to the left of the fireplace, filled with porcelain knick-knacks and family heirlooms.

Standing against the adjacent wall between the hutch and the doorway leading to the kitchen, a large, black, metal cube with a television screen and several knobs on its front sat atop a plain, nondescript table. A rabbit ear-style antenna with strips of aluminum foil stretched between the telescoping rods adorned the top of the TV. Both table and television seemed out of place with the rest of the room, lending an air of cheap, modern shabbiness to the otherwise elegantly aged room.

To the left of the doorway to the kitchen, stood a large, ancient radio from a bygone era, its hand-rubbed wooden cabinetry in sharp contrast to the sterile cube that had usurped its place as the source of entertainment and news. The front of the radio sported a huge tuning dial, its small unlit face covered in lines and numbers. Smaller ivory handles served other purposes, and inch-wide slots with narrow strips of wood between them, backed by elaborately woven speaker cloth, ran up and down the front. Frankie was captivated by the beauty of the antique device. He imagined previous generations of Dentons sitting around it, listening to radio shows and news broadcasts, as he'd seen in some of the old black-and-white movies he and his mother sometimes watched on their color television.

In front of the radio sat a cane-bottomed rocking chair that looked to be as old as the house itself. Behind the rocking chair, next to the radio, a wedge-shaped portion of the wall protruded out, angling from floor to ceiling, ending just over the doorway he stood in. At the base of the wedge, a narrow door offered entry to what Frankie guessed was a stairway.

The neatly kept room was a time capsule, but in no way did it project poverty. *Quite the opposite*, Frankie thought. It was rich with generations of stories to tell.

The house, like Aubrey, contained a wealth of beauty hidden within a deceptively simple exterior.

AUBREY'S MOM

"Hi, darlin'," Aubrey's mother said, entering the room from the kitchen.

"Who might this be?" she asked, smiling, but obviously surprised to see Frankie. Aubrey had never brought a friend home before. A feeling of recognition tickled the back of her memory.

"Maw, this here's Frankie Albert," he introduced.

"He's my new friend from school I told ya about, last night," he said proudly, making Frankie feel very special.

"Well, hello, Frankie," she said, offering her hand and a broad smile that immediately put Frankie at ease.

Of course! That was it. How could she miss it? Those eyes, that nose. This was Jack's boy. A wave of nostalgia wafted through her mind.

"I am so pleased to meet you. My name is Sarah," she said, "but you can call me Mrs. Denton." She smiled, the same impish twinkle in her eyes that Aubrey had.

Frankie could see were Aubrey got his serenity and sense of humor, as well as his curly brown hair. Sarah was average in every way. Not tall, not short, and neither skinny nor fat. She was pretty, even attractive, but he wouldn't call her beautiful, like his own mother. Her bright blue dress and white apron reminded him of June Cleaver, or maybe Harriet Nelson.

Her speech was more refined than Aubrey's. She pronounced her words properly, though still with the ubiquitous Southern drawl.

Frankie thought he saw a look of recognition in her eyes. Or was it something else?

"I used to know a boy, way back in high school, named Jack Albert," she said, squeezing his hand gently, "That would be your father, wouldn't it? And I'll bet your mother's name is Shelley, right?"

"Yes, ma'am," Frankie answered, amazed that she knew his parents' names. But her familiarity felt comfortable to him, putting him at ease. Not like the trapped feeling he sometimes got when others recognized who his father was.

"He was such a nice guy, and you're every bit as handsome as he was," she complimented; then she added, with sincerity, "I was so sorry to hear about what happened to him."

Frankie squirmed slightly, casting his eyes away.

"Oh, my," she exclaimed, realizing that she had touched a nerve. "Please excuse me, dear. I'm sure that's a delicate subject for you, isn't it? I tell Aubrey he talks too much, and here I go and do the same thing, myself.

"Please forgive my clumsiness," she implored.

Frankie shrugged his shoulders, not knowing what else to say or do. He could feel the sincere compassion in her voice. It felt warm and comforting. *What a nice lady,* he thought.

"Aubrey told me how much you liked my brownies,"

she said, changing the subject to something all little boys like.

"Oh . . . yes, ma'am," Frankie replied enthusiastically. "They were great! Best I've ever had."

"Why . . . thank you, sweetie," she said, blushing slightly.

"Would you like to try some of my chocolate chip cookies, too?" she asked, winking at Aubrey.

She had baked a batch especially for Aubrey, just as she had done far too many other times after he had been battered by his father. It wasn't much, she knew, but it helped her deal with the guilt she felt at being so helpless to stop the battering, and they always brought a smile to his face, helping to chase away the hurt.

"Heck, yeah!" Aubrey nearly shouted, starting for the doorway.

"Aubrey," she admonished with a raised eyebrow, "you have company. Show some manners, son."

"Sorry, Maw," he apologized, looking like a scolded puppy. Stepping aside, he motioned Frankie through the doorway and waited for his mother to follow before going through himself.

Sarah was adamant about her son's manners. There was more class in the Denton family than the townsfolk realized, at least, as far the mother and her sons were concerned. Sadly, that perception had been grossly over-shadowed by the uncouth nature of their father.

The kitchen was easily the most modern room in the house, though not as modern as the kitchen in Frankie's own home. The stove and refrigerator were electric, but old.

The cabinets, some with panes of glass in their doors to show off the antique china inside, appeared to have several layers of paint on them, blunting the carved detail that adorned them. The walls, like all the other walls in the house, were covered with wallpaper. In this case; however, it was a vertical stripe pattern of mixed pastel colors, only slightly more modern than the rest of the house.

A light smell of boiled eggs hung in the air, causing him to wrinkle his nose slightly.

Sarah noticed.

"Oh, yes . . . that smell. Please try to overlook it. It's the sulfur that's in our water. It doesn't taste all that great, either," she explained, wrinkling her own nose and smiling.

What's sulfur? Frankie thought, but he chose not to ask.

The boys wolfed several of the biggest and best chocolate chip cookies Frankie had ever eaten, washing them down with ice-cold milk fresh from the cow. His own mother made cookies, too, and they were really good. But he was certain that Sarah's cookies and brownies could win a blue ribbon at the State Fair.

She chatted lightly with the boys, as she busied herself around the kitchen, preparing the evening meal. She asked Frankie about his mother, his family, and school, constantly reminding Aubrey not to talk with his mouth full. But after a short while, she glanced up at the grandmother clock hanging next to the aging refrigerator.

"Aubrey, honey," she started, "your father is over at the Waller's helping them ring their hogs. He'll be home before too long. You need to go change."

Looking at Frankie, she said, "I'm sorry, hun, but Aubrey has chores to do. It's been such a pleasure meeting you, though. Please say hello to your mother, for me.

Maybe we can visit sometime."

She handed him a small brown lunch bag half filled with cookies and then headed for the door leading to the screened-in back porch, saying, "Aub, I'm going out to collect the eggs. Your father wants you to water Kitt and Aida, before you start weeding the garden, okay?"

"Sure, Maw," he replied, gulping down the last of his milk.

"Thanks a bunch, Mrs. Denton," Frankie said, pleasantly surprised at his treasure. He wondered if Aubrey ever had any time to just relax, to play, and to be a kid.

"You're very welcome, sweetie. Bye-bye," she waved, as she walked out onto the back porch, closing the door behind her.

"Your mom is awesome," he said to Aubrey, then asked, "Who're Kitt and Aida?"

"They're our mules," Aubrey answered.

"Hey, ya wanna help me?" he asked. "Paw ain't here, but you can ride behind me on Aida, if ya want."

"Shoot, yeah!" Frankie yelped in reply.

Aubrey placed his plate and glass in the sulfur-stained sink. Normally, Frankie's mother took care of such details, but seeing Aubrey do so, Frankie felt embarrassed not to follow suit.

Walking back through the house, Frankie had a sense of hominess and comfort, and of history and tradition. Even though everything in the house was old, it was well cared for and neatly arranged. No doubt that was Aubrey's mother's doing, but previous generations of mothers and grandmothers had left their mark on the family home, as well.

Turning the small strip of wood that held the door behind the ancient rocking chair closed, Aubrey opened it and motioned for Frankie to follow him upstairs. He then twisted the ancient light switch that turned the lights on at the top and the bottom of the stairwell. The stairs were steep and narrow, with very shallow treads to place his foot on. He noticed how Aubrey had to plant his big feet sideways, as he climbed the creaking steps.

At the top, a small foyer separated two narrow doorways centered beneath the peak of the roofline. Aubrey opened the door on the left and stepped into his bedroom, with Frankie close behind.

The doorway to the right led to a room directly above the master bedroom.

"Whose room is that?" Frankie asked.

"Aw, that's just a storage room," Aubrey said.

Apparently, previous Denton parents had realized that embarrassing sounds traveled easily from the master bedroom below through the rough-hewn planks that made up the floor.

Inside Aubrey's room, the walls were covered in thick layers of wallpaper, just like the rest of the house. They rose vertically to just above Frankie's height, then slanted sharply toward each other, meeting in a peak that ran the length of the room. Dusty shafts of bright springtime light shone through two quarter-round windows that flanked the exposed bricks of the chimney at the opposite end of the room.

Between the two windows, in front of a bricked-off hearth, a small cast-iron stove sat on a metal plate. A blackened stovepipe penetrated the wall a foot or two above the rustic mantelpiece. A small scuttle of coal and a bundle of firewood sat nearby.

Like rest of the house, Aubrey's room was furnished with antiques, but everything appeared well kept, if only worn by generations of use.

A bed stood at the right side of the hearth. Frankie saw what he could only describe as a giant pillow, rather than a mattress. Aubrey called it a feather bed.

"Go ahead, take a dive!" he motioned to Frankie. "It's real soft."

Frankie did so, and found himself engulfed in feathery softness.

"This is awesome," he said. "I wish I had one of these."

Aubrey grinned broadly. Frankie thought that even his bed was cool.

"It's real warm in the winter, but sometimes it gets a bit stuffy in the summer," he explained, as he shed his plaid flannel shirt and stripped off his "good" school jeans.

Aubrey was a big kid, but his baggy clothing concealed just how muscular he was for his age. *No wonder he could take on three bullies at a time,* Frankie thought, looking down at his own spindly arms.

Hanging on a piece of bailing twine from the central beam overhead, Frankie saw an airplane. From all the movies he'd watched, he knew it was a World War II twin-engine bomber. But it was all black, without markings of any sort.

"Whoa, that's far out!" he said, pointing to it. "Where'd ya get it?"

"My uncle was a gunner in a bomber, back durin' World War II. Maw says it was a trainin' thang ta help 'em identify the good guys from the bad guys. It used ta have propellers, but Waylon broke 'em off, playin' with it when he was little. That made Maw cry some."

"Why?" Frankie asked.

"He was her big brother an' he got killed when the

Germans shot his plane down. She was a little bitty girl when he gave it to her," Aubrey explained, as he hooked the buttons on his bibb overalls and slipped into his work boots.

"Oh," Frankie said, "that's a bummer!"

"Yeah, it is," he lamented. "I ever knew him, but Maw says he was a really great guy."

Frankie could easily believe that. It had to be a family thing.

"C'mon, I'll race ya to the barn," Aubrey challenged, as he swung the bedroom door open and bounded down the stairwell, two or three steps at a time.

The steepness of the stairs nearly caused Frankie to fall forward into Aubrey, but since Aubrey seemed to want to race everywhere he went, Frankie was going to do his best to keep up.

KITT AND AIDA

The two boys half-skipped, half-ran down the winding driveway to the barn. Aubrey was in heaven, despite the purple badge of shame he wore under his eye.

"Now, be careful an' step where I step, or else you'll end up in really deep cow pooky," he instructed, as he gingerly leapt from one flat stone to another.

He had not exaggerated. Frankie noticed the few cattle that hovered around the barn were knee deep in the muck.

The odor of manure and urine was pungent, but Frankie was surprised at how fast he had become accustomed to it.

Aubrey turned the short slat of wood that held the barn's tack room door closed and stepped up onto the worn, raised floor inside. Frankie followed him and was nearly knocked backward into the foul muck by several panicked chickens, as they flew wildly through the doorway, clucking their indignation at having their nesting area invaded.

"Dang chickens!" Aubrey spat. "If it wudn't fer their eggs and how good they taste when they're all fried up, they wouldn't be worth killin.'"

He reached up and took two bridles off of two different wooden pegs on the wall, just over his head. A makeshift placard with each mule's name crudely painted on it was nailed over each peg.

"Gotta make sure ya put the right bridle on the right mule," he explained. "They get cantankerous if ya mix 'em up. It hurts their teeth."

The air in the cramped room was stale and dusty, heavy with the mixed smell of oiled leather and chickens. A confused mass of leather straps with tarnished brass fittings hung from other pegs on the wall. Apparently, these were not so specific to each animal.

Seeing Frankie's interest, Aubrey said, "That's the harnesses we use ta hook 'em up to the plow an' the disk for the garden. In wintertime, we hook 'em up to the hay wagon out yonder and spread hay for the cattle." He loved the feeling of having knowledge that someone was actually interested in.

A lone, small window provided the daytime source of light for the room. A bare bulb with a pull chain hung in the center of the cramped room. Several steel drums with hand-fashioned wooden lids lined the opposite wall beneath the window. Each drum was stenciled with large white letters on its side: CORN, OATS, and GRAIN. Frankie guessed those were the "feed bins" Aubrey had mentioned at school. He had also mentioned rats, and that caused Frankie's eyes to dart furtively around the floor.

He had to weave his way through other unfamiliar bits and pieces of farm implements hanging from rafters overhead. Aubrey led him through the door at the opposite end of the tack room, and down onto the straw-covered dirt floor of the barn.

"Wait here a second," he told Frankie.

He opened the gate to a large, empty stall, closed it behind him, and then opened yet another wide door that led to the corral outside, where the mules were languishing, letting a flood of sunlight into the darkened barn interior. He then let out a piercing whistle, and stepped aside. Within seconds, the two, huge draft animals sauntered through. Once they were inside, he closed the door.

Closing doors and gates must be very important on a farm, Frankie thought, *so why did his mother say, "Were you raised in a barn, or something?" whenever he left a door open at home?* Like so many other things about parents, it just didn't make sense.

Aubrey walked in front of one of the mammoth beasts, slapping it on the shoulder and saying playfully, "Git back, ya ol' nag!"

Frankie had never been so close to such huge animals before and was surprised that he wasn't intimidated by them. In fact, it was quite the opposite. He was drawn to them, absolutely fascinated by their size. Despite Aubrey's warning about their nasty dispositions, he felt strangely at ease around them.

While Aubrey grabbed one bridle and was busy fixing it onto one mule's head, Frankie climbed up on the stable rails and stuck his hand out toward the other.

Much to his surprise and delight, the mule stepped over and allowed him to rub its great, grey muzzle. It felt like velvet accented by a sparse prickling of stiff whiskers. He gazed into the animal's huge brown eyes. The serenity he saw in them gave him a soothing connection with the beast. It was a feeling he'd never experienced before, and he loved it. He reached up to scratch behind its long, floppy ear. The mule nickered his approval.

"Whut the . . . ," he heard Aubrey mutter.

Turning, he saw Aubrey standing with his mouth agape, a look of utter astonishment on his face.

"What's the matter?" he asked casually, still scratching the mule's ear.

"Kitt ain't never let nobody he didn't know touch him like that before!" he exclaimed incredulously.

"Why?" Frankie asked, as he stroked the mule's face, his eyes meeting Kitts again. "He seems pretty nice to me."

"Nuh-uh!" Aubrey said, still not believing what he was seeing. "He's the mean one. He's tried to bite jus' 'bout every one of us at one time or another. Even tries kickin' at us when he's in a bad mood."

"Naw . . . really?" Frankie felt flattered, even special. The connection he and Kitt had established felt natural. "Well, maybe ya'll weren't being nice enough to him."

"He's a dang mule, fer cryin' out loud," Aubrey proclaimed.

"Well . . . " Frankie started, "don't mules have feelings, too?"

Aubrey's expression changed to a thoughtful one.

"Ya know, I ain't never thought about that," he said. "I spend most of my time lookin' at their backsides, wishin' I was somewhere else. But I reckon yer right, though. They are God's creatures, too, ain't they? I still cain't believe that ol' jackass ain't tryin' ta nip yer fingers off, though. Wait'll Maw hears about that." He finished buckling the last strap on Aida's bridle. Frankie noticed that he didn't say "Paw."

"Well, I gotta bridle him up now, so . . . ," Aubrey said, as he lifted the second bridle toward the Kitt's head.

"Can I do that?" Frankie asked, wanting to further his connection with the animal.

"Uh . . . I dunno if that's such a good idea, but . . . well . . . yeah, if ya want to, ya can," Aubrey answered hesitantly. "Here, let me show ya how."

With that, he stepped up on the stall rail to reach the mule's head. Even as big as he was, the mule's head loomed over him.

"Ya gotta get him ta open his mouth, an' he don't like that. That's usually when he tries ta bite, so ya gotta be real careful," he warned, not sure he should let Frankie do such a hazardous thing.

He showed Frankie how to hold the bridle and the bit. Much to Aubrey's amazement, Kitt opened his mouth for Frankie almost without being prompted to do so, and waited patiently as Aubrey walked his friend through the process of buckling the straps.

The whole time, Frankie cooed into Kitt's ear, "That's a good mule . . . that's a good mule," while frequently stroking his neck.

Aubrey was absolutely incredulous. After both mules had been bridled, he gathered up the reins and led them through the stall gate, stopping at the main door of the barn before leaving the firm dirt floor for the muck outside.

"Grab that crate over there, would ya?" he called to Frankie.

Stepping up on the makeshift platform, he clambered onto Aida's back and reached down to help Frankie up.

"Ya suppose I could ride Kitt?" Frankie asked, still enamored with the beast and feeling braver than he had in a very long time.

"Uh . . . " Aubrey hesitated, taken aback by yet another

dangerous request from Frankie. "I dunno. He might throw ya."

"Aw, come on . . . please!" Frankie pleaded, surprised at his own audacity.

Aubrey took in a deep breath, as he considered it. He was worried that Frankie might get hurt, but, at the same time, he found it hard to turn his newfound friend down.

Letting out a sigh, he said, apprehensively, "Awright, if you want to. But I have ta hold onto the reins. You just grab a handful o' mane an' hang on, okay?"

"Deal!" was all Frankie said as he moved the crate next to Kitt and scrambled onto the mule's back, clumsily mimicking what he saw Aubrey do.

Motioning Aida up to the door latch, he swung the wide door open and led them out into the sea of muck.

That Frankie didn't immediately fall off the animal's bare back impressed Aubrey and made him feel a little easier about his decision.

The ride down to the pond wove through the field of boulders along a well-worn path. The animals descended the steep slope with unerring confidence, born from years of daily routine.

Frankie was ecstatic. He had never had such a thrill before, and he repeatedly leaned forward to pat Kitt on the neck. Aubrey was astounded at the mule's behavior and was truly impressed with Frankie's calm handling of the normally irascible animal. It was as if the two had an understanding between them. He wondered if Aida would behave the same way for his friend.

When they reached the pond, Aubrey jumped gracefully off Aida's back and motioned for Frankie to do the same. Frankie's descent was not quite as graceful, and he landed heavily on his hands and knees. Kitt looked down at him apologetically.

Gathering both sets of reins, Aubrey led the animals to the water's edge. On cue, both mules lowered their heads and began taking long slurps of the cool, murky water.

"So, how'd ya like it?" he asked Frankie.

"It was boss! Totally farout," Frankie proclaimed, giddy from the experience.

"Ya wanna try Aida on the way back?" Aubrey offered.

"Can I?" he answered. "This is great! I know they ain't horses, but . . . I feel like Roy Rogers."

"Well Kitt ain't exactly Trigger, neither, but I know whutcha mean," Aubrey said. "Sometimes I pertend like I'm the Lone Ranger, with Tonto follerin' me on the other one."

He grinned and asked, "Hey . . . ya wanna look fer frogs while they drink? It's about time fer 'em to crawl out of their mud holes."

"Frogs? You bet, man!" Frankie exclaimed. *Can this day get any cooler?*

After the mules had drunk their fill, and the few frogs that had emerged had been found and terrorized into the water, Aubrey led them over to a stump near the pond and handed Aida's reins to Frankie. Kitt seemed to look indignantly from Aubrey to Frankie and fidgeted a bit as Aubrey clambered onto his back.

Frankie respectfully approached Aida and extended his hand to her. Though not as surprised as he had been earlier, Aubrey still marveled at her gentle reaction to Frankie's touch.

This is just plain weird. Aubrey thought.

All his dealings with the two animals had been as

though they were merely living machines to be worked, fed, watered, and stored away. That's how his father had taught him. They weren't pets, like Scooter; they were farm implements, albeit living ones.

Frankie, on the other hand, treated them as creatures with feelings of their own. Seeing the amazing response he was getting from them, Aubrey decided that he would have to rethink his approach to them in the future. A slight tinge of guilt rippled through him, as he thought about all the times he'd treated them so impersonally, especially all the times he'd taken his anger at his father out on them. He leaned forward and stroked Kitts' neck, whispering, "Sorry, ol' boy, I'll do better, I promise." Kitt flicked his long ears with indifference.

Back at the barn, Frankie helped Aubrey unbridle his new animal friends and return the harnesses back to their respective pegs.

Aubrey gathered about half a dozen eggs the irritated hens had left behind into a small pail, and he and Frankie exited the tack room, hopscotching from stone to stone across the sea of black goo to the solid safety of the driveway.

Glancing at the Mickey Mouse watch on his wrist, Frankie realized he'd been there for over an hour and a half.

"Aw geez . . . I better head out," Frankie said reluctantly. "Momma's gonna be home soon, an' she'll get mad if I'm not there.

"Thanks for everything, Aub. I had a really great time," he declared. "Your farm is outta sight, man. Ya think it'd be okay if I came back, sometime?"

"Yeah, I hope so," he answered, wondering if his father would allow it. "I'll check with Paw, but I think me an' Maw can convince 'im. Especially since she already knows your maw."

"Thanks for comin' over," Aubrey said. "I had a real good time, too. See ya tomorrow, pal." He waved, as he turned uphill toward the house.

"See ya tomorrow, pal," Frankie said, and he waved back, as he headed down the meandering driveway.

Aubrey trotted lightheartedly up the opposite direction, whistling the theme to the *Andy Griffith Show* as he went.

For his own part, Frankie half-walked, half-skipped the country mile home in a giddy delirium. He couldn't remember when he had felt so good, or had so much fun. What a day! He'd ridden real live mules! The taste of chocolate chip cookies still lingered in his mouth, as he lightly shook the bag of sweet treasure he had so carefully stashed in the tack room, away from the probing beaks of curious chickens.

He reflected on the past two days. The loneliness of his life before Aubrey seemed a fast-fading memory. He felt very lucky to have met the good-natured country boy. He was glad that he didn't have to share his new friend with any of the other kids, except maybe his other new friend Tony. Life in the little town was definitely looking up.

His mother had told him that God puts people in your life for his own reasons. Surely God had led him to Aubrey . . . or Aubrey to him. He wasn't sure which, but right now, it didn't matter. He finally had a friend.

She had also mentioned that God takes them out of your life, as well, but Frankie wasn't thinking about that right now. The day was just too perfect to dwell on that aspect of the Almighty's plan. Today was about receiving his gifts, not losing them.

Before he knew it, he was opening the white picket gate to his own tidy home. Suddenly, the expansive front yard didn't seem so boring or useless to him. He imagined himself and Aubrey and maybe even Tony playing a thousand different games in it. He looked up at the old tree fort his uncle had built when he was a kid. Up to now, it seemed so useless. Tree forts were pretty boring after a while, even with such a friend as Solitude. Maybe his new buddies would help him fix it up?

Stepping into his house, he was overcome with mixed emotions. It seemed less lonely now. The emptiness that usually awaited him each day had somehow disappeared.

"It's okay," he felt Solitude whispering to him, *"I understand. Good for you, old pal. I'll always be here if you need me, but I really hope you don't. Goodbye, my friend. Fun will be here soon. You'll like him. He's a really great guy!"*

"Goodbye…and thank you," Frankie whispered back.

For the first time, he saw his own house through different eyes. It was not nearly as old as Aubrey's, but it wasn't new, either. There were family pictures on his walls, too, but not as many. Wallpaper covered the walls inside his house, too, but with brighter, more artistic patterns. The wall-to-wall carpet wasn't as elegant as the rug that covered Aubrey's living room floor, but it was comfortable. The furniture spoke of its own history, though not as long as the museum pieces in Aubrey's house. He felt a new appreciation for his home. He began to feel connected to a family he never knew.

He found himself studying the family pictures on the walls as though he'd never seen them before. These were his roots, his family, and yet he'd barely glanced at the smiling faces before.

There was his mother and his uncle Frank at different ages. Grandpa and Grandma McKinney seemed to be smiling just at him, evoking a warm feeling of belonging. His parent's wedding portrait hung next to his mother's graduation photo. There were pictures of his father in his army uniform, among pictures of other men in uniforms from other wars. There were even pictures of various family members posing with various family pets.

But who were all these other people? Who was that old man standing next to what appeared to be a young version of Grandpa, holding a little boy in a dapper suit and fedora, both men smiling proudly? Did he have family he didn't know about? He would ask his mother . . . someday. Right now, chocolate chip cookies called out to him from the bag he clutched in his hand.

He poured a tall glass of milk, then sat on the floor in front of the TV to watch *Gilligan's Island* and munch on Sarah's fabulous cookies, while he waited for his mother to come home. He had so much to tell her . . . and a lot to ask her.

OLD FRIENDS AND DADS

That evening, as Frankie pushed his peas around the dinner plate with his fork, too distracted to eat, he proclaimed, "Momma, I made a friend at school. His name's Aubrey Denton. An' he lives on a really cool farm, just down the road. An' he's just really cool."

Frankie hadn't made any real friends since they had moved to Haleyville. When he had asked his mother why the other kids acted funny around him, she would become quiet, as if the question hurt. But, at other times, she seemed to become irritated, as if the question was an insult.

After several failed attempts, he quit trying to make friends, convinced that there were none to be found in town, at least none that he wanted, or that wanted him.

Aubrey truly was a blessing to him. He'd made a friend without really trying, and those were the best kinds of friends to have.

"That's wonderful, hun," his mother replied.

After a few seconds, she added, "You know, I knew a girl named Betty Denton back when I was in high school. Do you suppose they're related?"

"I dunno," he said. "I'll ask him tomorrow."

He hesitated momentarily, then said, "There was a fight at school yesterday. Aubrey was in it. An' he won, too!"

"What? A fight?" she said, stopping her fork halfway to her mouth. "Why? I mean, how did it start? You're not mixing with a rough crowd are you, honey?"

If Aubrey was related to Betty, then he was also related to Buck Denton, too. She remembered Buck as a crude ruffian with a violent reputation. That wasn't the kind of friend she wanted for her son.

"No, Momma," he replied, cutting off any further protest on her part. "It wasn't like that at all. He was just stickin' up for Tony. Three big bullies were pickin' on him. But Aubrey jumped in an' whooped all three of 'em real good, all by hisself!"

"Who's Tony?" she asked, not sure she approved of this new development in her son's life.

"Oh, yeah, I forgot," he said. "He's another friend me an' Aubrey made today. He's kind of a little guy, an' the other guys were callin' him names an' shovin' him around." He became more animated, as he described what had happened.

"You shoulda seen it, Momma! Aubrey shoved all the other kids outta the way and then he just clobbered the creeps. It was great!"

He stopped momentarily; then, looking his mother straight in the eye, he added, in a more subdued voice, "I remembered what you told me about my daddy, an' I was going to do somethin', too, 'cause they were hurtin' someone that couldn't defend themselves. But Aubrey beat me to it, so . . . "

Shelley sat there for a long moment, a peculiar

expression on her face.

"You're so much like your father," she said, her voice wavering slightly. "You know I don't like fighting. It doesn't solve anything, but I can't fault you for wanting to help . . . what's his name . . . Tony? In fact, it makes Momma proud to know that you would want to. I just don't know about this Aubrey boy. Honey, if his father is who I think he is, then it might not be such a good idea to hang around him."

"No, Momma, you're wrong," he blurted, startled that he had been so bold with his mother.

Seeing her brow furrowing, he quickly added, eventually defending Aubrey, "I'm sorry, Momma. I didn't mean to say it like that. But Aubrey's different. He's really nice. He doesn't go around pickin' on people like some of the other big kids do. He hates that."

He added, "Just like my daddy did." Surely his mother couldn't argue with that.

"Besides, his mom is a really nice lady," he said. "She says she knows you. Her name is Sarah. And she makes the best brownies and chocolate chip cookies I've ever had."

He quickly added, "Um . . . except for yours."

"And just how do you know all that?" she grilled her son, eyebrows raised inquiringly.

"Um . . . I, uh . . . kinda . . . went over to his house after school today," he confessed, realizing that he'd done so without her permission.

"You 'kinda' went to his house?" she inquired, slightly irritated. "Frankie, you can't be doing things like that without letting me know what you're up to! What if you had gotten hurt, or something?"

Why do moms always think you're going to get hurt

playing with other kids?

"I'm sorry, Momma," he apologized. "I didn't think about that. I won't do it again, I promise. It's just that . . . well . . . but you're right, Momma. I shoulda waited until I told you."

"I'll let it go this time, baby. But you'd better tell Momma next time, okay?"

Frankie nodded, grateful that she would allow a next time.

Shelley certainly recognized the name Frankie had mentioned. Sarah had been a close friend of her brother's in high school. She recalled how Sarah always seemed to have a smile and a kind word for everyone she met. But it confirmed who Aubrey's father was, as well, and that caused her a little concern.

She felt a little ashamed that she had not looked Sarah up since they'd moved back to town. But her memories of Buck had been enough to keep her at bay.

Like everything else in her life, even this came back to Jack. She knew that Sarah, like every other girl in town, had had a crush on him. But unlike the girls who only pretended to be her friend, hoping only for a shot at stealing Jack's heart away, Sarah had been very respectful of their relationship. Never once did she let her infatuation show . . . at least not too obviously.

Sarah had become pregnant with Buck's child at the age of sixteen. It had been heartbreaking to see such a gentle soul go through the humiliation that the good people of Haleyville were so adept at dishing out.

If Sarah was Aubrey's mother, then perhaps it was okay to let her son befriend him. She had trusted Sarah back then, and she felt she could do so now. But she wasn't so sure about Buck.

"I love you so much," she said, a sadness in her voice.

"I love you, too, Momma," he said, a little confused.

Seeing her expression, he asked, "Are you okay?"

"I'm more than okay, baby," she answered. "I have you. Momma's proud of her little man. And I'm so happy that you've found a friend. You're right. Aubrey's mom is a sweet lady. Your daddy and I knew her back in high school. So did Uncle Frank."

The change in his mother's mood bothered him. In an effort to cheer her up, he started telling her about his wonderful day.

He described Aubrey's house as though it were a museum. He told her about Scooter, also, inserting, "Ya think I can get a dog?"

"We'll see," was her standard answer. It annoyed him, but he was too caught up to care, right now. He'd work on it later, for sure.

He nearly bounced with excitement as he told her about Kitt and Aida. She did her best to share his excitement and not to show her alarm at his escapade. She hadn't seen her baby this excited in a very long time. She could talk about being safe later. It had been too long since happiness had radiated from that sweet face. She wasn't about to spoil the moment.

Then his mood sobered as he said, "Momma . . . he had a black eye an' a busted lip when he got to school this mornin'. He said his father whooped him for fightin' in school."

Then he looked squarely at his mother and asked, "Is that what fathers do? Would my daddy have whooped me like that if I got in a fight?"

It took a second for Shelly to process what she'd just heard.

"Oh, no . . . darlin' boy, no! Daddies aren't supposed do that sort of thing. I promise you your father would never have hit you like that. He loved you too much to ever hurt you that way," she assured him.

"Baby, that wasn't a whooping Aubrey's father gave him—you know, like a spanking. Daddies sometimes have to do that."

He could sense the anger in her voice rising as she said, "It was a beating. It was a terrible, cowardly thing for him to do. A spanking is one thing, but a beating is quite another! Good daddies don't do that sort of thing."

She was becoming angry at the thought of the brute she remembered terrorizing his own son. To calm herself down, she said in a measured voice, "Tell me some more about Aubrey and that other boy, what's his name . . . Tony?"

"Oh yeah . . . Tony." Frankie could see the fire rising in her eyes and jumped at the chance to calm her down.

"They just moved down here from up North. He really likes Superman comics an' all. He talks kinda funny, though. But I reckon he thinks we talk kinda funny, too."

"Ya know what else happened today?" he added.

"Tell me," she replied, thoroughly enjoying her son's excitement. He hadn't been so talkative in ages. The brightness had returned to his eyes, and for that, she owed Aubrey and Sarah a debt of gratitude.

Frankie continued, with a perplexed look on his face. "Miss Shockley told Aubrey that he did a noble thing by stickin' up for Tony, and then she hugged him!"

"Miss Shockley?" his mother asked, amused. "What happened to Ol' Shock-face?"

"Well," he said, slightly embarrassed, "I reckon I shouldn't be callin' her that anymore."

"Why not, hun?" His mother was really enjoying his rambling.

"Well . . . Aubrey said she told him that she thought I was a good kid and a good friend to have."

Then he reflected, "An' all this time I thought she didn't like me."

"Baby, she's a teacher, so she has to be firm," she explained, smiling broadly. "You know . . . I had her for fifth grade, too. She's been teaching for a very long time.

"But she's also a woman. And what woman wouldn't just adore that face of yours?"

"Aw, Momma!" he said, turning beet red with embarrassment.

They laughed together for the first time in too-long a time.

But suddenly her laughter was cut short by a spasm of pain, as she clutched her chest. Alarmed at the sudden paleness in his mother's face, Frankie jumped up and went to her, gently stroking her back.

"You okay, Momma?" His voice was heavy with concern, bordering on panic.

Regaining her composure, she gasped more than said, "Yes, baby, Momma's okay. It's just a cramp." She didn't like lying to him, but she didn't want to scare him. She'd had a few of these fits of pain lately, and she was scared, herself.

"You're the best mom in the whole world, and I'm really glad you're mine," he said, wrapping his arms around her neck and laying his head on her shoulder. Still, he felt a little worried about her "cramp."

"And you're the best son any mother could ever have," she said, holding him close to her. "I'm so glad you're mine."

"Oh, I gotta tell you somethin' else," he said, returning to his seat. "Aubrey invited us to his church this Sunday. Us and Tony's family, too. Is it okay for us to go there this time, instead of our church, or isn't it?"

"Uh . . . well, yes, I suppose it'll be okay," she answered pensively, at first; then she said, a little more enthusiastically, "Yes . . . that would be nice. I'd really like to see Sarah again, and I'd love to meet your friends."

"Cool. Thanks, Momma," he piped, turning his attention back to his dinner. "This meatloaf is real good. You're a great cook."

"Why . . . thank you, sugar, and you're very welcome." *What a silver tongue you have. Just like your father.*

COMIC BOOKS,
BAPTISTS, AND MOMS

At last, Friday had arrived . . . the day the juvenile inmates were temporarily paroled for the weekend, and the hallways were buzzing with excitement.

During recess, Tony told Aubrey that his mom thought church was a good idea. *No surprise there!* He added, "She said she wants to meet the kid who actually wants to go to church."

"That would be you," he mumbled, pointing an accusing finger at him.

Frankie chimed in, saying how much his mother was looking forward to seeing Aubrey's mom again and meeting them, as well.

Aubrey was thrilled that he'd have friends to introduce to his Sunday school class. It was always a special time for all the other kids to show that they had friends. Finally it was his turn. His broad grin faded slightly when he noticed that Tony didn't seem as happy.

"Whutsa matter, Tony?" he asked. "You look kinda bummed out."

"Well, I told my mom and dad about how you stuck

up for me and whipped those guys, the other day," he said.

"My mom got real pissed off and said something about having a word with ol' man Pike." *As if that's gonna do any good.*

"My dad asked if I did anything to provoke 'em," he growled. "He always thinks things are my fault."

The other two boys exchanged knowing looks.

"They asked me about you," Tony said, nodding to Aubrey. "You know, like . . . did I know anything about you, an' all. That's when I screwed up and told them about how you live on a farm an' gotta do chores all day and that you don't get to watch cartoons or anything on Saturdays." He rolled his eyes.

"Then my dad starts saying stuff about how chores help build character and all that kinda crap," he said.

"So guess what? Now I gotta start doin' more of 'em. I gotta mow the danged lawn tomorrow, and every Saturday from now on, can ya believe that?" he griped, looking up at Aubrey and scowling, "Thanks to you!"

Aubrey burst out laughing.

"Aw heck, lil' buddy, it jus' might put some muscle on them skinny lil' arms of yours," he joked, wrapping his big hands completely around Tony's thin biceps.

"I wish that's all I had to do. I'll trade ya. You can come over an' slop the hogs, gather eggs, and help Maw hang the laundry, if ya want!"

"No thanks, ya big lummox!" Tony shot back, grimacing at the thought of the slave labor that he already had foisted on him. Then he grinned and punched Aubrey in the arm. Aubrey grabbed it, pretending to be hurt.

The school day ticked by one agonizing minute after another, finally ending with the clanging of the bell, releasing a mad stampede of liberated half-pints bursting through the big double doors to freedom, some racing for buses and cars, others sprinting short distances home, all of them eager to exploit their all-too-brief escape from their blackboard cells in the red brick prison dubiously referred to as school.

Tony managed to survive his new enslavement into Saturday chores, none the worse for wear. Of course, his cartoon schedule had been totally thrown off whack. He missed the *Bugs Bunny/Road Runner Hour,* as well as a Jungle Jim movie. But he managed to make it through the day, though more than once, he wished he could sell his family to cannibals on some South Pacific island. He would have sealed the deal for a Butterfinger bar.

Frankie showed more enthusiasm in doing his own chores around the house, out of gratitude to his mother. He had thought about skipping cartoons to show empathy for Aubrey, but he quickly reconsidered that rash choice as soon as Buckwheat started his antics.

Aubrey motored through his many tasks with a lightheartedness that caused his father and brother to give each other quizzical looks; however, his mother knew why her son was finally able to smile through his labors.

Sunday dawned bright and cheery, at least for most folks in town.

"Be quiet, ya stupid bird!" Tony spat through toothpaste at the mockingbird singing another bird's song outside his bathroom window. *What are you so danged happy about? You don't hafta go to church, do ya? I should still be sleeping! Oh well, maybe Baptists are different. I hate tryin' to stay awake . . . and I really hate singing church songs!*

After breakfast, he snuck back into his room to hide

comic books under his shirt.

He showed up at Aubrey's church, evading his mother to find his friends, grumbling about his slicked-back hair and bow tie and trying to keep the comics from falling out onto the ground.

Frankie managed not to laugh, thinking he looked like Alfalfa with blond hair, but Aubrey couldn't help himself.

"Shut up, ya big ox!" he growled.

"I'm sorry, lil' buddy," Aubrey said between chuckles.

"It's jus' that you look kinda funny all gussied up," he teased, causing Tony to turn a deeper red and getting a burst of laughter from Frankie.

Tony stuck his tongue out at Aubrey, getting even more laughter from the other two.

The boys wanted to sit to together, but to avoid embarrassing giggling and commotion, their mothers wisely chose not to let them. Instead, the boys had to endure standing up, then sitting back down, over and over through seemingly endless hymns, driving Tony crazy. He and Frankie both had trouble staying awake during Reverend Greene's interminable fire-and-brim-stone sermon.

Then the preacher called for the sinners to come forth and be saved . . . after passing the plate, of course.

Tony grumbled to himself, "I wish someone would come save me," earning a sharp elbow from his mother. *Geez, you got radar for ears?*

He had never seen such passion in any of the Catholic services he had been dragged to by his mother. He was used to being lectured in a monotone fashion and repeating chants or Hail Marys, not to mention all the kneeling.

Unlike Father Williams, Reverend Greene's face glowed bright red with holy indignation, and sweat streamed down his ample jowls, as he cajoled his flock from Satan's ravenous temptations. Wiping beads of righteousness from his furrowed brow, he promised eternal, fiery damnation to woeful sinners and salvation to the pious, whose sanctified place at Jesus' side was helped by their little envelope containing God's 10 percent for the week.

Afterwards, Tony seemed a little pale, as he met his buddies on the broad front steps of the brick church.

"You okay?" Frankie asked, seeing his face and wondering if he'd come down with something.

Tony shook his head, a mystified expression on his face.

"It's no wonder you're not afraid of anything," he said, looking up at Aubrey. "Do you Baptists get the crap scared outta ya every week like this?"

The other two boys roared with laughter.

Anxious to make their escape into the wonderful world of comic books, the boys began searching for their mothers.

"Hey, Momma!" Frankie called out, waving at his mother after finding her chatting with another lady.

Tony ran over to his mother, who was talking with Reverend Greene. After being introduced to the minister, Tony politely pulled her away and dragged her over to meet his friends and their mothers.

"Hi, I'm Shelley Albert, Frankie's mom," she said, introducing herself to Tony's mother, a petite, attractive brunette in an appropriate floral spring dress, her hair coiffed in the latest fashion.

"Oh, hello, I'm so pleased to meet you. I'm Kathleen

Carillo, Tony's mom."

The two women were engaged in conversation, when Aubrey's mother walked up.

Shelly immediately recognized Sarah and gave her a warm embrace, saying, "Oh my gosh, Sarah, it's been so long. How have you been? You look wonderful."

Sarah doubted that she looked wonderful, but she graciously accepted the compliment by exclaiming, "Shelley Albert, I do declare! Sweetie, you're as pretty today as you where back in school. How do you do it?"

"Careful, hun . . . this is a church," Shelley said. "Don't want the Lord striking anyone down for fibbing, now do we?"

Then Shelley laughed.

Shelley introduced Sarah to Kathleen, recalling their days in high school with affection.

Sarah had been a grade ahead of her. The changes that time had imposed on the woman were sobering. She looked much older than Shelley knew her to be, but her smile was as warm as ever, though slightly haunted.

Shelley smiled at the big, curly-haired boy standing awkwardly in front of her and said, "You must be Aubrey. Frankie has told me all about you. I'm so happy to meet you. You look just like your mother, you know that?"

Mom's a girl! Aubrey thought, but he replied, "Thank ya, ma'am. I'm right pleased ta meet you, too." He offered a gentlemanly hand, just as his mother had taught him.

"So this is my little hero!" Kathleen exclaimed, offering her hand to Aubrey, tactfully ignoring the fading bruise under his eye.

"It was really sweet of you to help Tony the other day, not that fighting is okay, mind you," she said, dutifully injecting the mandatory mother's disclaimer, "but I appreciate what you did. He told me about you, as well. He really thinks you're something, too."

Getting into a fight was sweet? But fightin's not okay? Aubrey mused, blushing at all the attention. *Moms are so weird.*

"Yer welcome, ma'am; I mean, I'm sorry that it was a fight, but . . . ," he said, trailing off, a little confused at being thanked for doing something he wasn't supposed to do.

"I'm sorry it was a fight, too, but you just did what your heart said was the right thing to do," she said.

Turning to Sarah, she added, "That's a brave little boy you have there!"

Sarah thanked her, but she insisted that she, too, didn't approve of fighting, especially at school.

She cast a proud glance at her son, then cast a furtive glance toward her husband, who was busy laughing with a couple of other men, not far away. *No doubt at a dirty joke,* she thought, *and at church, too.*

As their mothers fell into conversation, the three conspirators slipped around the church and raced toward the creek bank, Tony and Frankie clutching the treasures hidden under their shirts.

"Frankie looks so much like his father," Sarah commented. "I was so sorry to hear about Jack. He was such a good man."

Seeing the confused look on Kathleen face, Shelley said, "My husband died in Vietnam."

"Oh, I'm so sorry. I didn't know." Kathleen placed a sympathetic hand on Shelly's arm. "My cousin lost her son there, too."

"It must be hard to raise a boy on your own," she said. "I don't know what I'd do without Mike. You know how boys are." She rolled her eyes the way exasperated mothers do.

"If there's ever anything we can do, please don't hesitate to ask. Mike is really good with kids," she offered, though she wasn't really sure how good her aloof husband was with children.

"Thank you; I appreciate that," Shelley replied. "Boys can be a handful." There were certainly times when she felt that a man could relate to or could explain things to a boy better than a woman, or especially a mother, could ever do. There were times when a grown man's ability to intimidate an unruly boy could come in handy, as well.

But Frankie had never been that difficult to deal with; besides, she had a brother who adored him and affected all the male influence on her son that she felt he needed.

"My nephew, Chet, is a marine stationed in a place called Da Nang," Sarah interjected, deflecting the attention from a subject she knew Shelley had to be sensitive about.

"Your nephew: would that be Betty's boy?" Shelley asked, referring to Buck's older sister. She knew that Sarah was an only child.

"Yes, it would be," Sarah answered.

"Do you remember Keith Gordon?" she asked, referring to the timid, always harried projector boy with horn-rimmed glasses. Though he was constantly teased by the cretins and jerks in school, he kept a big, toothy smile, regardless . . . especially for Betty.

"No not really. Sorry," Shelley answered, trying vainly to place the name and face.

"Well, I suppose not," Sarah said. "He was easy to miss. He's a quiet sort of guy."

"Most of the kids thought he was a nerd, but he sure caught Betty's eye," Sarah continued. "Must've been the poetry he kept slipping into her locker. He's sentimental that way."

She smiled and said, "Anyway, they ran off and got married right after she graduated. He's a terrific husband and father. He treats her like a queen. They have a daughter, too. Her name's Cheryl; she's about Waylon's age. Chet's a bit older and the spitting image of his father, only built like a Denton. Cheryl looks just like her mother, but fortunately she's built more like his side of the family." Sarah chuckled, referring to the hefty build of the Denton women.

"They have a nice little place up in Kentucky," Sarah said. "He owns an appliance store. Imagine that!" She laughed.

What Sarah didn't say was that Betty had run away from home because she, too, had been a pregnant teenager. But, unlike her own brother, Keith had been quiet about it and chose not to humiliate the woman he loved. In fact, he had been thrilled at the thought of Betty bearing his child.

They had to leave Haleyville to escape Betty's abusive father, who surely would have beat her to a pulp and very likely would have killed Keith, as well. For years afterwards, Buck wouldn't speak to her. He resented her bitterly for leaving him behind to face a tragically dysfunctional home life all alone.

Only after their father had been sent to prison, did Betty try to repair the rift in the relationship with her brother. But, even then, it took years for the wounds to begin to heal. Ironically, their father's bloody death in prison helped the process, as he had given them something in common . . . a solid hatred for the old bastard. It was closure for them, in a morbid sort of way, but having hate and resentment in common made for a poor patch cloth.

Chet had played a big part in their eventual reconciliation. Every year, all through junior high and high school, he willingly spent a month out of his summer vacations on the Denton family farm, helping his uncle and cousins with the chores, keeping the family ties alive. Driving him down gave Betty the excuse she needed to visit her brother, her nephews, and Sarah.

Chet turned out to be every bit as tough and masculine as Buck felt a boy should be. But Buck had a way of pushing too often and too far, even with Chet, resulting in a few angry words between them. But Chet never backed down, earning him the respect of his irascible uncle. He often took advantage of that respect to shield his cousins from Buck's unpredictable temper.

Aubrey adored Chet, and each summer, he counted the days until his cousin came down. Buck even seemed to refrain from terrorizing his sons when Chet was around.

Sarah told them how Aubrey had become overwhelmed with worry when Chet joined the Marines. He quit watching war movies, and he cried himself to sleep for weeks after hearing that Chet was being shipped off to the war in Vietnam.

He knew his cousin was being sent into the same bloody mess that the network news so morbidly presented to the public every evening at dinner time, scaring mothers, worrying fathers, and boosting ratings. Eventually, she stopped letting her son watch the evening news, with all its sick, career-enhancing sensationalism.

She smiled as she told them how Aubrey faithfully wrote his cousin a letter at least once a week, as if his letters would keep Chet safe. He had sent his school picture and a picture of him with Scooter, as well as a short, crudely written, but heartfelt, poem he had composed just for his cousin.

Sarah didn't know it, but Aubrey had started his longest letter ever, telling Chet about Frankie and Tony, and also about how Frankie's father had died in Vietnam.

Chet always answered Aubrey's letters without fail, as if answering his cousin's letters would keep him safe. Aubrey lived for them, each one a treasure stashed safely away after reading them repeatedly. He had even sent little trinkets to him, some Vietnamese money, and a little bamboo stick puppet.

Chet sent a picture of himself standing next to a howitzer with a group of other young, shirtless marines, each one smiling their bravest and most reassuring smile for loved ones back home. Aubrey kept the picture under his pillow and held it in his hands when he said his prayers every night, asking Jesus to watch over Chet.

Shelley nodded and said, "I know what you mean. Frankie is crazy about his uncle Frank and worries about him running into burning buildings, too."

The mention of her brother's name elicited a sweet smile from Sarah.

"So . . . how is Frank doing these days?" she asked, with an obvious fondness in her voice.

"Oh, he's doing great," Shelley answered. "He's been with the fire department up in Nashville ever since he moved away. He loves it, too. You know how boys are . . . a fireman, a cop or a cowboy." So she teased, not bothering to add, "or a soldier." That was one thing she did not want her son to be.

"Of course he's doing great," Sarah said. "That's Frank for ya. But I would already know all that if he had stayed in touch . . . like he promised." Sarah huffed with feigned indignation.

But she knew why Frank hadn't called or written: Buck hated Frank. But then, Buck hated most people.

Sarah and Frank had been very special friends in school. They actually started out dating . . . sort of. Comfort dates, they had called them . . . but there had never been anything sexual between them. At first, that had bothered Sarah, making her feel undesirable, but when Frank confided his secret to her, it caused their friendship to bloom into something much more sincere and gratifying than a short high school romance could ever have been.

Shelley had always suspected that Sarah knew about Frank before anybody else, including herself. She had respected and appreciated the confidence with which Sarah had treated his secret.

That was before Buck had entered the picture. She had only dated him on the rebound, after having her hopes dashed for a romantic relationship with Frank. Back then, Buck was actually a fairly handsome young man, with charming, country-boy mannerisms—a charm, she would find out later, that he routinely used to seduce and shame other unwary girls.

Naively, she had given in to his advances. The passionate mistake in the back seat of an old Buick meant that neither she nor the father of her child would graduate from high school. Already her trap was closing in.

But he was a jealous and possessive lover and had felt threatened by her friendship with Frank, believing it to be more than it really was. He had warned Frank to stay away from Sarah . . . or else! Later Sarah would find out that the "or else" had really been aimed at her.

Buck's threat hadn't scared Frank, though. He had even offered to settle things man to man, but she begged him not to. Not wanting to make her life more difficult, he backed off for her sake. The nature of their friendship changed, much to Sarah's regret. But, as a true friend, Frank secretly offered his shoulder for her to cry on when her life came unraveled, just as she had done for him. Had Buck known, Sarah would have suffered severely.

She had grown up the daughter of very strict parents. Her only sibling, an older brother, had been killed in the lead-filled skies over Germany when she was just a small child. As she entered her teens, her mother clung tighter and tighter to her Bible, becoming ever stricter in her treatment of her budding young daughter.

Her home life became more intolerable when her father, a fundamentalist preacher at a small local church, died of a heart attack while railing fervently against the sins of makeup and rock 'n' roll one blistering summer Sunday. Her mother had found her secret stash of both "sins" and was sure they were what had driven him into his fatal frenzy.

After a shotgun wedding at the local courthouse, with only Buck's crazy Aunt Alice in attendance, her shamed and overly prideful mother disowned her and made arrangements to move to Georgia to live with her aging sister.

Her long, painful existence as Buck Denton's ever-suffering wife began, without a single soul to comfort her, except for Buck's only sister, Betty.

But, in spite of, more than because of, her upbringing, Sarah had a deep faith and conviction that the hypocrites and the sharp tongues she sat among every Sunday, could not shake. Very often, it was all she had to hold onto . . . that and her precious sons.

For her part, Kathleen talked about her teenage daughter, Maria, and her large Italian family back home in Jersey. She mentioned her husband's job as plant manager for the mattress factory outside of town, modestly omitting that they lived in the "rich" part of Haleyville, as evidenced by the shiny new Chrysler New Yorker she had driven to church in.

She lamented the conveniences of the big city, but she quickly praised the slower pace of life in the small town, preferring it to the hidden dangers and snares the big city held for her children.

The women chatted and laughed casually for a while. Shelley and Kathleen insisted that the others come over for tea, sometime. Neither showed any notice that Sarah had not made the same offer. Their intuition told them why, but they also insisted that Sarah take them up on their offers, on the premise that surely Sarah knew at least one home-style Southern recipe that she just had to show them.

"Oh, this is just wonderful," Kathleen nearly squealed. "I haven't had a tea party in ages. I can't wait."

Meanwhile, their sons had taken cover on the creek bank behind a towering sycamore tree. Frankie and Tony produced the comic books they had surreptitiously stashed under their shirts, knowing that their mothers would surely have confiscated them, had they discovered them. Tony had the biggest selection and insisted that Aubrey take half of them home to keep.

Aubrey graciously accepted, touched by the gesture and thrilled that, tonight, he'd be reading the first comic books he'd ever had. He'd be sure to keep them hidden from his father, but he'd let Waylon take a peek.

Not to be outdone, Frankie gave him two *MAD* magazines and then handed a couple to Tony, insisting that they keep them, as well.

Time whizzed by, as the boys chattered, imitating Superman and laughing at Alfred E. Newman. Aubrey seemed most interested in the Incredible Hulk, remembering what Tony had said about the raging green monster.

But, all too soon, Aubrey heard a familiar whistle and had to bring their secret meeting to a close. The boys stashed their illicit bounty of brain-rotting comics under their shirts and headed back to the church.

They found all three mothers and Buck standing together in the parking lot. Aubrey was surprised to see that his father was actually laughing with the women. Normally, he would hover impatiently several feet away, prodding his wife with sidelong looks to hurry up and end the conversation.

His naive, young eyes didn't notice the leering looks his father cast at Shelley and Kathleen, when he thought no one was looking. But his mother didn't miss a single lecherous glance.

As he approached, his father did something completely out of character. He reached out a huge, calloused hand and ruffled his son's hair affectionately.

"Hey son, Mrs. Carillo here told me what ya done," he said. "It was a good thang stickin' up for yer little buddy there." He nodded toward Tony, who stood looking wide-eyed at the giant man. "But, next time, take care of that sorta stuff after school, okay?"

"Sure, Paw," Aubrey replied awkwardly, hoping there wouldn't be a next time.

Frankie marveled at Buck's size, as well, but he was also aware of the man's brutal nature. Determined not let his apprehension get the best of him, he bravely stepped forward and extended his hand.

"Mr. Denton," he said, bolder than he felt, "I'm Frankie Albert. How are you doin' sir?"

"Well, howdy, Frankie Albert. Pleased ta met ya," he said, shaking Frankie's hand with his huge corn-cob-rough grip. "Ya know, I used ta know yer daddy, back in school." *And used to hate his guts!*

Sarah turned away, concealing a look of disgust. *Lord, forgive me.*

Seeing Frankie for the first time, Buck was somewhat taken aback, though he hid it. Looking down at the boy, he saw a miniature version of the only boy in town to ever beat him fair and square in a fight. After all these years, his humiliation revisited him in the face of the young boy standing before him.

He had hated Jack, but not so much for losing a fight to him. He hated him for the humiliating way Jack had treated him after the fight had ended.

Instead of gloating . . . instead of bellowing his victory and further beating Buck down with insults and jeers . . . Jack held his hand out to Buck, who was still on the ground, nursing a bleeding nose, and said, "Now that that's over with, ya think we can get along?"

Buck had slapped his hand away, mumbling, "Fuck you."

It was a kick in the teeth to Buck's ego. That's not how it was supposed to be done. When you beat a man, you beat him emotionally, not just physically. You tear him down. You make him ashamed to show his face around town. You make him flinch at the sound of your name. You make everyone understand that you won, not him. No debate, no questions. That's how his father had beat it into him, and that's how he was beating it into his boys, though he was having no success with Aubrey . . . thanks to Sarah.

Jack should have done that. Buck had started the fight; Jack merely finished it. He should have made Buck squirm. He should have trampled his dignity into the dirt. Buck would still have hated him, but at least he would have respected him, in his own perverse fashion. It would have made any revenge that much sweeter . . . and that much more necessary. But Jack had taken that away. Revenge would have seemed petty and hollow.

He felt more defeated by Jack's gesture of decency that he did by his own blood in the dirt or the bruises on his face.

Buck's father had taught him to despise such behavior as weakness. Respect meant people were afraid to cross you, afraid to do anything other than what you wanted them to do. To his father, and subsequently to him, peace was the absence of anyone big enough, or strong enough, to contradict your will. Jack had violated his peace. Jack had showed that he could be beaten.

When Buck was a sixteen-year-old sophomore in high school, his father beat his mother to death while in a drunken rage, trying make her understand how disrespectful she had been when she burnt the pork chops that night. When his father died in prison, Buck was sure he had died with the "respect" of his fellow inmates.

Being under eighteen, Buck was placed into the custody of his addled Aunt Alice, who spent her days talking to herself and asking Buck who he was more often than recognizing him. Because his father was more of a bootlegger than a farmer, he had inherited the family farm in a run-down condition.

He sent his crazy aunt off to a state hospital as soon as he turned eighteen and could sign the papers. He had never wanted the farm or the responsibilities that were thrust upon him, but he didn't know what else to do.

Sarah's pregnancy only complicated his life. The only upshot, in his eyes, was that she gave him two sons to help run the place, whether they wanted to or not.

Buck supposed that he respected his father's memory, though sometimes he wasn't so sure he wasn't confusing hatred for respect, or vice versa, since the two were always so closely juxtaposed for him.

Of course, he was pleased that Aubrey had won the fight, especially against three other boys. That would give him special bragging rights down at his favorite tavern. But the fight had taken place at school, and he'd be damned if he was going to let that bastard Pike think he couldn't control his boys. Waylon had been enough of a handful. Aubrey wasn't going to get away with embarrassing him in front of the principal or his teachers, as Waylon had.

Buck knew the fathers of the three boys his son had defeated. He saw them down at the feed mill every other weekend. He could relate to them. They were hard-working farmers, just like him. Hell, he'd tossed back a jar or two of moonshine with them at one time or another. They'd understand about boys getting into scrapes and scuffles. They'd respect him for his son's victory.

Ordinarily, when he got together with them, they

would engage in the usual small talk about livestock, sports, and how the slutty barmaid and her ample cleavage made Friday nights at The Tapped Out Inn so much more interesting.

But this week, he'd be gloating on behalf of his son. He'd be waiting for any of them to say a word. Then he'd gleefully remind them that his fifth grade son whooped all three of their sixth grade sons . . . at the same time. He wanted them to say something, maybe even challenge him. That might be fun.

He wasn't sure how he'd have reacted if his son had lost, though. But there was no doubt that Aubrey would have suffered a much worse beating, if he had.

Seizing the moment, Frankie boldly asked, "Pardon me, sir, but can Aubrey please come home with us for Sunday dinner?" Then, looking quickly at Kathleen, he added, "And Tony, too?"

He cast imploring eyes toward his mother, hoping he hadn't overstepped his boundaries by not asking her first, but he felt that he had to strike now, while Buck was in a good mood.

Buck managed not to glare at him, feeling he'd been ambushed by the boy and fighting back a resurging hatred for Jack. Giving either one of his sons permission to do anything fun was rare for him. Usually, he left it up to Sarah, who he had made sure understood his will, as it related to them.

But now, the other two women held him prisoner with their expectation. Sarah wisely did not meet his eye.

Much to Frankie's surprise and relief, his mother took up the invitation, saying "Oh…yes Buck, please. That would be so nice. It's usually just the two of us, and we'd love to have him over."

Just to keep from putting Buck on the spot all by himself, she added, "Tony, too, if that's all right, Kathleen?"

"Of course it's okay," Kathleen answered, looking up at the towering man, adding her pressure to his discomfort.

Buck looked from Frankie to his mother. She was another old thorn for him. He had never gotten the chance to date her, or, more accurately, to grope and to paw her perfect figure, then to rob her of her virtues and reputation by bragging about it around town.

It had been his favorite game until he knocked Sarah up and had been forced to marry her, bringing his self-perceived days as the town stud to an end.

He took perverse enjoyment in spotting his old conquests around town, seeing them quickly look away. Better yet, the cuckolded look in their husbands' eyes when they saw him leering at their wives, knowing that he'd been with them . . . and told the details to anyone who'd listen. It didn't matter how long ago it had been; Buck kept the memories fresh, just so he could enjoy their shame.

Now, he was relegated to the occasional, worn-out bar fly, too drunk to drive himself home, or to resist. The shame he had brought on Sarah was of no concern to him.

Shelley had always been so aloof . . . so into Jack, too good to give him a second glance. Just because she was Jack's, he had wanted to shame her that much more. He wanted to turn her from the girl all the other girls envied into the one they all laughed at. The same way he'd unintentionally brought that stigma onto Sarah's shoulders. Sometimes he hated Sarah.

Sarah fidgeted with her purse, not looking at her husband and expecting the worst, but she was surprised and relieved to hear him say, "Well . . . yeah, I reckon it'd be all right. . . this time. 'Bout time the boy got out an' started makin' some friends, anyway."

Looking down at his shocked son, he warned sternly, "Now you be on yer best manners, boy. Don't go embarrassin' me an' Maw." The implied threat hung heavy in the air.

Sarah reached over and gave her husband's hand a grateful squeeze, causing him to flinch at the uncharacteristic show of gratitude.

"Thanks, Paw!" Aubrey said elatedly, wrapping his arms around his father's ample girth in a rare moment of sentiment. "I promise I'll be good."

The big man's face flushed pink. He was unaccustomed to affection, especially in public. While it embarrassed him slightly, he had to admit that, somewhere inside, it felt just a little good.

He still felt that he'd been cornered into giving in by Jack's little brat and the scheming women, though.

"Okay, that's enough of that," he said, patting his son on the back and squirming to get away from all this politeness and sentiment. "Ain't no need ta git all mushy 'bout it!"

Sarah's eyes met Shelley's with a look that only a mother could understand.

After having their very lives threatened by their mothers, lest they misbehave, the ecstatic boys raced for the old Rambler before anybody could change their minds, calling out "Shotgun!" But all three ended up in the backseat.

Shelley thanked Buck, Sarah, and Kathleen, promising to have their sons' home before bedtime. Then she headed for the car, which was now rocking back and forth with three hyperactive boys jumping around inside and yelling excitedly.

Buck watched Shelley's well-shaped bottom, as it swayed inside her filmy, pleated skirt. Sarah watched her husband leer lustfully at Shelley.

FRIED CHICKEN AND COUSINS

Back at the Albert house, the afternoon was a blur of activity, as each boy tried to top the other with something new to do. They played a very short two-on-one game of pick-up-and-smear which Aubrey handily won, since even the combined efforts of Tony and Frankie could not bring him down. Nor could they escape his grasp, once he caught them.

Without warning, savage Indians were surrounding three cowboys, just like on *Rawhide*, but Rowdy Yates, Mr. Favor, and Wishbone, otherwise known as Tony, Frankie, and Aubrey, bravely fought them off, just before the Time Machine sent them spinning wildly back to the days of knights and dragons.

Then, out of the distant future, a siren's voice beckoned to them, announcing that a Tarzan movie was starting.

Aubrey had never seen one and was totally captivated by the Lord of the Jungle swinging through the trees, yodeling and battling hungry crocodiles, raging rhinos and sinister head hunters. He was especially impressed with Tarzan's ability to talk to the animals.

"Timba . . . umgawa!" the jungle man shouted, as he ordered the elephant to kneel. How did the ape man know elephant talk?

Aubrey elbowed Frankie and said, "Kinda reminds me of you, with Kitt an' Aida."

Afterwards, they were back outside, yodeling, climbing the big oak tree, and swinging from the tire swing.

"Umgawa!" Aubrey barked at imaginary elephants.

By mutual agreement, there was no Jane, just Tarzan and his jungle friend, who sometimes turned out to be an evil treasure hunter, capturing Tarzan, only to be defeated when Cheetah, Tarzan's loyal chimpanzee sidekick, brought all his animal friends to rescue the jungle man.

Frankie and Aubrey took turns being Tarzan, but Tony played a good Cheetah, since he was the smallest and could climb trees better than the other two. The chimp's defiance and troublemaking came natural to Tony.

Every so often, Shelley would stop what she was doing and just stand by the window, watching her son have more fun than she'd ever seen him have.

She made Frankie's favorite dinner: fried chicken, instant mashed potatoes, and sweet corn, along with sweet tea and her own special cherry cobbler. In the midst of it all, she noticed that she was really enjoying having the boys together in her home. It seemed to fill an empty spot in her heart. She would have to do this more often, for herself, as well as for Frankie.

Later in the evening, as the sun began to sink low on the horizon, the boys caught fireflies and gathered on the front porch to chow down on cobbler.

"So where was your bruda dis morning?" Tony asked

Aubrey, his New York accent muffled by a mouthful of cobbler.

"Well, Waylon don't go ta church no more," he explained. "He says it's borin'. That always makes Maw a little sad, too. She talks ta Jesus a lot about him."

"Your mother talks to Jesus?" Tony snickered.

"Don't laugh at folks that pray, Tony!" he admonished sternly, causing Tony to nearly choke on his cobbler.

"Sorry, Aub," he apologized meekly.

Aubrey shrugged and went on, "She also spends a lot o' time prayin' fer Chet, too."

"Who?" Frankie asked.

"My cousin, Chet; he's a Marine, an' he looks just like John Wayne in his uniform!" He beamed with pride.

Aubrey's mood changed slightly, as he reflected, "Sometimes I hear Maw out on the front porch prayin' an' beggin' Jesus ta protect Chet. He's jus' like another son, ta her. He's my favorite cousin, too."

"He always calls me his lil' buddy," he said, casting an affectionate glance at Tony, who smiled broadly at the compliment.

"An' he writes me letters all the time. He taught me how ta ride my bike an' how ta swim, an' he took me ta the picture shows, too."

He had to stop and swallow the lump that was growing in his throat.

"I sure hope Jesus looks after him," he squeaked, barely audible. "It'd sure hurt Maw an awful lot if sumpthin' happened to him." The devastation it would cause him was unthinkable.

"He's in Veet-nam, fightin' commonists!"

"What's a commonist?" Frankie asked.

"Heck, I dunno," Aubrey answered, "but Chet says

they're really bad people."

"My father was there, too." Frankie added somberly. "I bet they're the same creeps that killed him."

"Your dad died in the war?" Tony asked, dumbfounded, a spoonful of cobbler frozen halfway to his mouth.

"Yeah, Momma says he was a hero and that he saved a bunch of folks' lives when he died." His mood was slipping into darkness.

"I can believe that!" Aubrey said emphatically, looking his friend square in the eye, trying to lift his sudden change in mood. "Maw said he was a really cool guy in school, too."

"She did?" Frank asked.

"Yep, she did," Aubrey assured him. "She said he was that kinda guy, always stickin' up fer the underdog."

Tony and Frankie looked at each other.

Shelley had been listening to the boys chatter from her chair in the living room, not far from the screen door. She had to choke back a lump in her own throat.

"What's Waylon like?" Frankie asked, not knowing what else to say.

"Waylon's the best brother a guy could ever have." Aubrey said sincerely, his mood changing back.

"Ya know how I said that him an' me got into it the other night?" Aubrey asked.

Frankie nodded back.

"Well, that's a flat out lie," Aubrey said. "He ain't never hit me. In fact, he's whooped a couple kids that did. Heck, he's even took whoopin's from Paw that shoulda been mine. I seen him cry after I got a whoopin' a couple times, too."

He choked.

"Him an' Paw don't see eye to eye 'bout that sorta stuff," Aubrey went on. "He thinks Paw whoops me too much. I do, too."

"It must be nice to have a big brother." Frankie said. The conversation was becoming too serious for his liking.

Tony sat speechless. He'd been spanked on more occasions than he cared to recall, but somehow, looking at the brownish-purple crescent under Aubrey's eye, he knew that the "whoopin's" Aubrey spoke of were more than mere spankings on the bottom. He felt his affection for his oversized protector grow, tempered with sympathy and a slight feeling of disgust toward Aubrey's father.

While his own relationship with his father left something to be desired, it certainly was far better than Aubrey's, and unlike Frankie, he actually had a father at home, however on the sidelines he might be.

"Yeah!" agreed Tony emphatically, hoping to cheer things up. "All's I got is a bossy ol' sister that keeps tattling on me and won't let me watch what I want on TV." So he grumbled, breaking the somberness in his usual fashion. The other two boys laughed gratefully.

"I don't have a brother or a sister, or any cousins, but I got the coolest uncle in the world," Frankie proclaimed.

"He's a fireman, and he drives a Corvette," he bragged.

"All my uncles are goobers," Tony said. "Except for my Uncle Marty; he's cool. He's got a Harley chopper."

"A whut?" Aubrey asked. Tony said some of the strangest things, sometimes.

"A chopper!" Tony exclaimed. He nearly added some comment about living on another planet, but, remembering whom he was talking to, he decided to explain.

"It's a big motorcycle that's been customized with

long forks, a sissy bar, and ape-hanger handlebars."

Aubrey had no idea what Tony was talking about, but he chose not to show it. Instead, he just gave a false, "Ohhh!" as if he had understood.

"Me an' Uncle Frank built a model Corvette, just like his real one. Wanna see it?" Frankie asked.

"You bet!" Tony blurted, jumping to his feet, nearly dropping the empty cobbler dish. "Models are far out! I didn't know you built 'em, too. Right on!"

"Heck yeah, man! Me an' Uncle Frank built a bunch of 'em. Come on, I'll show ya!"

"I ain't never built a model before," Aubrey lamented, the last one to scramble to his feet. "I always wanted to, though." He clearly had some catching up to do. He'd ask Waylon about choppers. Waylon knew about everything that was cool.

The boys poured into the house, not noticing Shelley at first, but then Aubrey skidded to a stop and turned to her, saying "I thank ya kindly, Mrs. Albert. Dinner was great, an' that cobbler was really sumpthin' else. You sure can cook!"

Not to be outdone, Tony added his flourish of compliments, and Frankie added, "Yeah, thanks, Momma. It was great."

"You're welcome, sweetheart," she replied. "I'm really glad you boys could come over. We'll have to do this more often, okay?"

Cheers of "All right!" and "You bet!" rang out. Frankie flashed the biggest smile his mother had seen in a very long time.

"Come on, y'all!" he said loudly, as he turned for the stairs.

Just as the door to his bedroom slammed shut,

Shelley gave into a spasm of pain, clutching her chest. *Please God . . . for Frankie's sake . . . please!*

Later that night, Frankie cuddled contentedly next to his mother on the couch and watched *The Wonderful World of Disney.*

Down the road, Aubrey wrote about the day in his letter to Chet, then settled in to secretly read his new treasures. The Hulk was really incredible, but ugly.

Across town, Tony lay in bed, staring through his window at the stars he was still fascinated at being able to see so far away from the big-city lights. He thought about his friends and how different their lives were from his, the obstacles they faced, and the privileges he had. A rare thought crossed his mind. *God . . . if you're really out there . . . thanks for my new friends.*

SCHOOL'S OUT
FOR THE SUMMER

At last, the long awaited month of May came around, and that meant only one thing . . . summer parole for the imprisoned urchins.

Every kid in town had plans for the summer. Some stayed home. Some would visit aunts and uncles with obnoxious cousins or doting grandparents. Still others were lucky enough to be packed into the family station wagon and headed for the Grand Canyon, Disneyland, or some other tourist destination, driving their parents crazy by asking every half hour if they were there yet or begging to stop so they could pee.

For Frankie, Aubrey, and Tony, more free time meant more time to play and share cool things with each other. More time for fun.

One Friday, Buck shocked Aubrey by letting him "goof off" and spend the night at Tony's house, since the crops were still growing and no urgent chores needed to be done.

The next morning, the boys watched the old 1950s

version of *The Three Musketeers* movie on the Carillos' combination color television and stereo console. Totally awed by the sword fighting and heroics of the swash-buckling defenders of the Crown, they immediately dubbed themselves, "The Haleyville Musketeers."

Even though d'Artagnan wasn't really an official Musketeer, he had the coolest name, so Tony got dibs on it, while Frankie settled on Aramis. Aubrey thought Porthos was just fine. Since there were only three of them, they decided that Athos had been killed by the evil Cardinal Richelieu's minions or that he was somewhere on a secret mission and would show up whenever one of the others had been captured or temporarily killed.

All summer, armed with homemade wooden swords, the three gallant heroes would find themselves in one sinister ambush after another, as an endless stream of the cardinal's lackeys would lie in wait for them behind every tree or around every corner.

If one brave Musketeer went down, the other two would flank him, fighting off the pressing hoards, as the fallen comrade would take a bite of the magical Musketeers bar that restored life; then he would count to ten and leap to his feet, just in time to stand fighting over another companion who had just been skewered by invisible pikes, swords, or arrows.

"All for one, and one for all!" they shouted, whenever they greeted each other and shared a secret handshake that Tony came up with.

They spent every available minute they could, or that their parents would allow, with each other. Only the chores their parents made them do, and which Tony particularly despised, would tear them from each other. Otherwise, they were inseparable.

Maria considered them totally insufferable, though, especially when they would chase each other through the den, yelling, while she was trying to watch *The Flying Nun* or some other equally important program.

Eventually, each boy's parents began to see the changes the friendships had brought about in their sons and were content to simply accept the mayhem and enjoy the laughter.

Shelley no longer saw the melancholy little boy that used to sit, gazing absently out the window, or moping about the house, bored and fidgeting for something to do.

Kathleen noticed a more cooperative attitude in her son and fewer temper tantrums over petty issues. Tony insisted that his mother stop using "baby talk" when she spoke to him, as well. Only slightly saddened by this, Kathleen was happy to see her son start to come out of his self-imposed cocoon and evolve into a normal, energetic little mischief maker.

Sarah was elated as Aubrey's self-esteem blossomed. His newfound eagerness to get his chores done quickly so he could have more free time suited Buck just fine.

For his part, Buck felt an easing of the tensions between him and his son, as well as between him and his wife. He even let Frankie and Tony visit the farm regularly. A happy benefit from this was that by letting his son play more often, he actually got more work out of him, and it got done more quickly because the other two boys joined in to help, often competing to get the chore done. They helped fill a growing gap Waylon was leaving, as he spent more time with Irene and less time at home.

At first, Buck watched Tony and Frankie closely—especially Frankie—looking for any sign that they were looking down their noses at his home or his family. He was surprised to see that they were, in fact, fascinated by life on the farm and took no notice of the Denton family's "place" in the minds of the people in town.

They turned Aubrey's chores into games to see who could gather the most eggs or lift more bales of hay. Slopping the hogs became an adventure involving grunting dinosaurs or some other mythical, ravenous beast. Weeding the garden became a search for gold or lost treasures.

Tony started deliberately going after more of the heavy-lifting chores, determined to build muscle on his tiny frame. Buck was amused at his first strenuous efforts, but the wiry boy's determination impressed him, and eventually he began to notice his skinny arms become hard with muscle.

Sarah enjoyed the laughter of boys ringing out from every corner of the farm. Whether in the side yard or from the barn loft, it was all music to a mother's ears. It was music that had been absent on the Denton farm for far too long. She was especially pleased that the boys continued to go to church, though she suspected ulterior motives, but it was still church, and that's what counted.

But it was a sad tragedy that, every now and then, Aubrey would show up with another black eye or a bruise somewhere else. Usually, it happened on Saturdays, after his father had visited the tavern the night before. His buddies understood and never embarrassed him by bringing it up. But they knew the truth, and they hated Buck for it. They never let their contempt show, though, fearing it would mean the end of their visits to the farm. That was something they were not going to allow to happen, if for no other reason than for Aubrey's sake. The farm was really far out, too.

But one of these days Buck would be sorry, each one swore . . . or at least hoped.

Shelley and Kathleen always knew when it happened, too, because their sons would come home a little depressed. They too, were careful to never let Aubrey, or his mother, see their reaction.

Even Tony's father had begun noticing the bruises. The disciplined businessman and former naval officer felt outraged at the thought of a grown man, especially one as big as Buck, punching a small boy with a closed fist.

Slowly he began to become introspective about his relationship with his own son, feeling that perhaps it was lacking in some areas. But, as usual, he held his opinions and comments to himself, ever the stoic father figure.

To Tony, that was pure bullshit. He wondered if his father cared about his friend . . . or even about him, for that matter.

But the hearts of young boys are resilient, and personal dramas could not overshadow a wonder-filled summer. Any time they spent together was a blessing, but, without a doubt, they had the most fun at Aubrey's farm. His knowing that helped him through the pain.

He had learned to play his father's moods to his advantage, and in a rare moment of generosity, Buck gave him permission to teach his pals how ride a mule.

Initially, he was sure that allowing Aubrey and his friends treat his mules like riding horses would make them more difficult to handle behind a plow. But after only a couple of weeks with the boys, the plow team showed a spring in their step and an easier disposition than they had shown in years. Aubrey told him that it was probably because they got more exercise. But when his father wasn't around, he told his mother that it was just as probable that "playing" with the boys made the mules happier than just working all the time.

At first, Aubrey just led them by the reins, as he had done for Frankie. But as the mules and the boys became more comfortable with each other, he let them take the reins themselves, showing them how to use them and how to control the animals with the heels of their feet.

Frankie picked it up fairly easily and was content to simply ride them at a walk or a canter, sometimes at a full gallop. Kitt seemed particularly drawn to Frankie and would wait patiently for him to scramble up onto his back. Aubrey was still amazed at how gentle the normally irritable beast was around Frankie.

He had told his mother about the strange connection. She said that maybe Frankie was a "whisperer," explaining that some people just have a natural connection with animals and can communicate with them on a different level. She said it was a special gift from God that not too many people had. Since he considered his friends a gift, anyway, he had no problem accepting that they may be gifted, as well.

After quickly figuring out how to get onto the mule's back, Tony took to bareback riding instantly. His small size made it easier for him to stay in place, though it made his thighs ache at first.

Always the one to push the envelope, one day he got brave enough to try standing up on the mule's back, as he had seen trick riders do in the circus. Much to his everlasting delight, he found the broad, muscled backs an easy place to stand upright and even figured out how to guide them by moving his feet. Even Buck was impressed by his spunk and agility.

Of course, Scooter joined the fray whenever she could, becoming their loyal mascot, even joining them when they swam in the creek. But she had to slow her pace, weighed down with a litter of puppies, much to the delight of the boys . . . and very much to Buck's chagrin.

As he gained strength and confidence with the mighty draft animals, Tony became determined to never be bullied again. One day, over peanut butter and jelly sandwiches with grape Kool Aid, he asked Aubrey to teach him how to fight.

Aubrey was reluctant, explaining that he didn't like to fight and that he only did it when he had to. But Tony argued that Aubrey's size gave him that option, while his own small size took it away from him and gave it to the bigger boys.

Aubrey had to admit that Tony had a point. He then rationalized that if Tony could take care of himself, then he wouldn't have to keep such a close eye on his feisty little friend.

So, from time to time, Aubrey showed him some of the moves that Waylon had taught him. By summer's end, Tony had morphed into a solidly muscled scrapper with catlike reflexes, often challenging the other two to wrestling matches, sometimes even winning. He was nothing at all like the scared boy he was when they first met.

As he watched or participated, Frankie benefitted from Aubrey's tutoring, as well. He realized that getting punched wasn't the worst thing in the world but that being afraid was. While Tony grew stronger physically, Frankie grew stronger emotionally.

OL' BEN

One bright Saturday afternoon, Shelley asked Frankie to go with her to Ben's Garage. Ben Ivey was a dear friend and the only person she knew she could trust to fix the rattles and squeaks her old rust bucket elicited . . . and not to charge her an arm and a leg.

Shelley pulled into the parking lot at Ben's place. Numerous cars in various stages of disassembly or repair sat waiting for attention. Parts and pieces were scattered here and there, waiting to be put back in their respective vehicles or to be thrown onto the rusting scrap heap behind the building.

Frankie was fascinated by mechanical things and loved visiting Ben.

"Well, as I live and breathe," called a raspy voice, as a grizzled old man hobbled toward them, a heavy limp in his left leg, "if it ain't Shelley Albert! How have you been, darlin'? It's been a 'coon's age."

"Hi Ben, how are you? It's so good to see you, too," Shelley responded with a hug.

"I'm sorry I haven't come by sooner," she apologized, nodding toward Frankie, who was busy peering into the guts of a torn-down engine block, "but things have been kind of hectic lately."

Ben cocked an eyebrow at her and said, "That's no excuse, girl. Hell, if ya don't wanna see me, at least have pity on that old car of yours. How long has it been. . . two months?" He was exaggerating.

"Oh, come on, you ol' coot." Shelley parried back. "It's only been a few weeks. You must be getting senile."

"Hell, as crazy as most folks around here think I am . . . who'd know the difference?" he laughed.

Then he turned to Frankie and asked, "So . . . how's my little gearhead doin'?"

"I'm doin' great Uncle Ben, how 'bout you?" he answered.

"Old and cranky, lil' buddy, old and cranky," he chuckled.

"As usual," Shelley chided playfully, getting an equally playful growl from him.

Though he didn't like to let on, Ben really looked forward to these visits. Like them, he had no living relatives in town. He had no living relatives anywhere that he knew of. He was an orphan, and like Jack, he was raised by nuns in a Catholic orphanage.

He had been one of Jack's favorite people, and Jack had been one of his. In fact, Ben regarded Jack as the son he never had. The orphan's bond fostered a relationship few others could relate to.

When Jack was playing football, Ben never missed a game, even frequenting practices, just to watch from the bleachers. On Saturday mornings, he would walk down to the barber shop on the square, just to hear the old men raving about Jack's skills on the field the night before, his speed, the receptions, and of course, the touchdowns. Then the crusty old mechanic would walk away, grinning like a Cheshire cat and mumbling to himself, "That's my boy."

Jack and Shelley's brother had been best friends, and Ben had taught them everything about cars that their eager minds could absorb. All through Jack's sophomore year, the three cobbled together a hot rod out of an old junkyard wreck, laboring tirelessly into the evenings and on weekends to complete it.

Jack tore up the streets and the back roads with it, showing only his taillights to anyone foolish enough to pull up to the line and challenge him.

"Can I see it?" Frankie asked eagerly.

"Well, it is yours, so I reckon ya can," Ben answered, knowing exactly what the boy was talking about. Frankie asked to see his father's creation every time he visited Ben. It did the old man's heart good to see the interest he showed in cars.

They walked over to a corner of his garage, where a tarp was draped over a boxy shape. Ben slowly, lovingly began pulling the tarp back, first revealing a fenderless front tire, then progressively the rest of a gleaming roadster.

It was a masterpiece of mechanical simplicity and power. It glistened jet-black, with wicked flames streaking down each side of the car from the firewall. Whitewall tires complemented the red, wire-spoked wheels finished with chrome hubcaps. No hood obstructed the view of the brilliant red flathead V8, dressed in chrome heads with white headers and topped by three double-barrel carburetors under a bulbous chrome scoop. The chrome radiator and bullet-shaped headlights sat atop a solid axle, dropped to within inches of the ground, giving the car a predatory stance. Inside, bloodred tuck-and-roll leather upholstery highlighted the two-seater, while surplus aircraft gauges were placed strategically in the homemade wooden dash. Everything about the machine screamed fast and cool . . . really cool.

"Is it really mine, Uncle Ben?" Frankie asked breathlessly. He knew the answer. He'd asked before . . . many times. He just couldn't believe that his father and uncles had actually built such a thing, and he especially couldn't believe that it would be his, or rather, that it already was his. Someday, he'd bring Aubrey and Tony to see it, but, right now, it was something special that only he and Uncle Ben . . . and his mother . . . shared. He didn't know why; maybe it was just because his father's hands had built and driven it.

"You betcha buddy. It was your pop's, so, of course, it's yours . . . when you get old enough," he declared, giving a wink to Shelley. He didn't mind answering the oft-repeated question. "Hell, I damn sure couldn't drive it, what with this bum leg an' all, and ain't nobody else gonna touch it. That's for sure. All I do is keep it clean."

Ben had stored the hot rod for Jack when he went off to the army. It was his only tangible connection he had with Jack. His heart broke a little every time he uncovered it. The memories were too real. But this was Jack's boy, and by God, he'd damn sure see to it that the boy would get it in top shape. So he affectionately cared for the car, polishing it inside and out and regularly cranking the engine over to keep things loose. But he could never drive it; that would hurt too much . . . and not his "bum" leg, either.

The old wrench master tended to be caustic with most people, but he had a definite soft spot for Shelley and her brother. But little Frankie held the biggest, most special spot in the ex-dirt tracker's heart.

Ben had been particularly shaken by Jack's death. He had shut his shop down for weeks, as he emptied one bottle of Jack Daniels after another, staring at the hot rod, sitting under its tarp, right where Jack had left it in his care.

Shelley had dropped by to visit once during that time, only to stop outside the door, as she heard the old man alternately wailing mournfully from the depths of his soul, and then instantly flying into a rage, cursing Jack for getting his "damned fool self" killed, scattering tools and car parts across the garage.

That is when it really hit her. Jack had meant a lot to other people, too. The funeral was the first time anyone could ever remember seeing a tear in Ben's eye, but he growled menacingly at anyone who approached him or tried to comfort him . . . except for Shelley and Frank. With them, he wept openly.

The only other time she saw him get sentimental was when she brought a newborn Frankie to the garage to meet him for the first time. She remembered, with a smile, how brightly Ben's face lit up, as he gingerly held up and then hugged the infant as if he were his own grandchild. She remembered how he had hugged Jack and then her, nearly bursting with pride. She remembered the lone tear trickling down sun-cracked cheeks when they announced the baby's middle name . . . Benjamin.

Of course, the warmest reception she received when she returned to Haleyville was from Ol' Ben. He was, for all intents and purposes, her only family in town.

He had been one of her brother's staunchest defenders when the rest of the town had turned against him. He had actually chased people away from his garage, refusing to work on their cars, if he heard that they had said anything bad about Frank.

It hurt his business, but he didn't care. He was getting old and had everything he needed, including a healthy stash of money in the bank. He only continued working because he loved cars. He didn't care much for people, though, saying that most of them sat on their own shoulders, heads firmly lodged up their asses.

"Ya can't fix what's broke in some people," he used to quip, "at least not without crackin' their heads open!"

"So how's that lawn mower runnin'?" he asked Frankie.

On their last visit, Frankie had told him that it wouldn't start when he pulled the cord. As usual, the visit turned into a lesson in mechanics. Ben quizzed him as to what the mower was or wasn't doing, how it smelled and sounded, and so on, finally deducing that the problem came from the spark plug.

Ben delighted in teaching Frankie, just as he'd taught his father. Frankie soaked everything up like a sponge, just like his father. It was like having Jack back in his shop, again. It gave the old man something to live for.

Frankie listened closely, and later that same day, the lawn mower was running like a champ, thanks to the new spark plug Ben had given him.

"It's runnin' just fine," Frankie beamed, proud that he had fixed it all by himself. Shelley was equally as proud, seeing her husband's abilities bloom in his son.

"There's a big ol' Baby Ruth bar in my desk drawer that needs some tunin'," he told Frankie. "Think you can handle it?"

Because of the nickname his Uncle Frank had given

him, Ben kept a box of the candy bars in his desk drawer, just for Frankie.

"You bet I can!" he answered, racing toward the tiny room in the corner of the shop that served as Ben's office.

"Now, darlin', tell me what this old bucket o' bolts is doin'," Ben said, returning his attention to Shelley and the Rambler.

Meanwhile, Frankie easily found the candy bar. He scrambled up on the bar stool Ben kept in his office and began to look at the wall full of black-and-white glossy photographs. There were images of a much younger "Battling Ben" Ivey standing in front of a scarred and dented Hudson Hornet, highly modified for racing, with the number thirteen hand-painted on the side. In most of them, he was holding trophies and getting kisses from scantily clad young women.

The old man had started his lifelong love affair with cars as a teenager, when he got his first beat-up old Ford Model A. Soon his natural abilities got him noticed by some of the local moonshine runners, and before long, he was modifying Ford coupes to outrun Federal revenue agents. The magic he worked on their flathead V8s and swapped-out Cadillac engines, gained him a reputation among dirt-track racers, as well.

The natural progression was to drive a car of his own, and for years, he raced against such legends as Junior Johnson and the great Fireball Roberts.

Then, one hot summer evening, less than halfway through the feature race, seven cars out of a field of twenty-five clashed in a metal-crunching, bone-breaking convergence just out of the second turn. One man lost his life; another lost an arm. Ben lost his racing career to a crushed left leg.

Frankie thought Ben was the toughest man he knew. He jumped off the stool and walked over to the home-made bookshelf, where Ben kept his Chilton manuals, and pulled down the one for Plymouth 1950 through 1955. He liked to open the manuals to the first part of each section where they showed the front end of the cars, according to the year they were made. He tried to memorize each one and liked showing off his knowledge to Aubrey and Tony by identifying the different makes and models as they passed on the street.

"Frankie!" he heard his mother call to him nearly a half hour later. "It's time to go."

" . . . that worthless brother of yours to stop by some time," he heard Ben saying playfully to his mother.

"I sure will, Ben," she said, reaching into her purse and pulling out her wallet.

"Young lady . . . " Ben said sternly, "you put that thing right back where it belongs. Don't make me get onto you about it, again. Your money ain't no good in this here shop!"

"But, Ben . . . "she tried to protest.

He held his gnarled, permanently grease-stained hand up, saying emphatically, "I thought your parents raised you better than to argue with your elders."

Then he grinned and said, "The usual fee will do just fine."

Shelley reached up and gave him the usual warm hug he charged for his services, adding a kiss on his whis-ker-prickled cheek. "I love you, you cranky old fart."

"I know ya do," he said. "Ya just can't help yourself, can ya?"

Turning to Frankie, he said, "I hear you got a birth-day comin' up."

He never forgot Frankie's birthday. Even when she and Jack lived on some army base hundreds of miles away, Ben would send a small package. It was Ben who gave Frankie his bicycle last year.

"Sure do; how'd you know?" he teased.

"Smart-ass!" Ben growled. "You better get in that car before I take that tire iron after your scrawny butt." He snarled playfully, lurching toward Frankie, who easily dodged him.

"Come by for dinner, sometime," Shelley offered, as usual, and as usual, Ben said he would, but as usual he never did. He felt awkward outside his little wrench-twisting world, even among friends, and dinners seemed way too formal for his curmudgeonly ways. His lonely, old easy chair and TV tray in his lonely, old house was fine with him.

But, from time to time, Shelley would bring a plate of dinner to him, always under his protests, but always with his gratitude, especially when it was spaghetti. The plates were always returned sparkling clean and with a big hug and an admonishment to not go to so much trouble over a crotchety old man.

BIRTHDAYS AND FIREWORKS

As with all boys their age, birthdays were a big event for the Musketeers. Frankie's and Aubrey's birthdays were both during the summer break, only seven weeks apart. Tony's birthday fell in the middle of February. He hated that it was so close to Valentine's Day.

Aubrey's birthday came in late June. It would be his first birthday party that included friends, instead of just family, so Sarah put special efforts into making it a good one for him. Shelley had picked him up, then dropped him and Frankie off at the Carillos' house in order to arrive early and help Sarah decorate the house with paper streamers and balloons. She also wanted to help make Aubrey's day as special as they could.

Sarah confided in Shelley that she was probably just as excited as Aubrey about the party. As a young mother, she had envisioned this sort of thing for her children every year. But the reclusive existence Buck imposed on his family meant that social gatherings at their home were nonexistent.

He had scoffed at the decorations, but the women refused to let him put a damper on the day and shooed him out of the house, ignoring his grumbling about wasting good money on stuff that just gets thrown away.

Everyone arrived before noon, and the boys were given peanut butter sandwiches with strawberry Kool-Aid and were herded outdoors until everything was ready. Kathleen joined the other mothers in the kitchen, while Maria sat on the front porch swing, flirting with Waylon, who suddenly came up with manly things to do, like restacking the firewood to show off his country-boy muscles to the cute city gal.

Aubrey took the opportunity to show his buddies the litter of puppies Scooter gave birth to just a few days earlier.

Frankie was fascinated with the squirming little critters, all wrinkled and soft, eyes not yet fully opened. Two of the pups were solid rust-colored, just like their mother. Aubrey said that he figured the sire was old man Waller's dog, since the remaining three looked like him.

"I wish I had a dog," Frankie lamented. "Momma says they're a lot of work, but I still want one."

"Maybe she'll let you have one of these," Aubrey suggested.

Finding homes for the puppies was a priority for him. Buck had threatened to drown any of the helpless little creatures that they couldn't give away.

At last, Sarah called the boys in. She had outdone herself by making a three-layered chocolate cake with cherry-flavored frosting and "Happy Birthday Aubrey" scrolled across the top in white icing. After the obligatory round of "Happy Birthday," Aubrey blew the twelve candles out with such gusto that the nearest two candles tilted slightly.

The boys fidgeted, as the mothers cut and distributed

huge slices to each boy.

"Tony, sweetheart, do you want to stay inside and wash dishes with Mommy, while Frankie and Aubrey go outside?" Kathleen asked, in that deathly sweet tone that all sons fear.

"Uh . . . no . . . Mom," Tony answered carefully.

"Well, then wait for everyone else." Her steely smile bore right through him.

He laid his fork down and didn't touch it until everyone, including his mother, had picked theirs up.

Sarah and Shelley each stifled a snicker. Frankie and Aubrey yanked their own hands back, as if the fork had suddenly turned into a poisonous viper. Maria and Waylon took their cake back out to the porch, because cake tastes better in a porch swing to flirting teenagers.

"I sure hope Irene doesn't hear about this." Sarah whispered to the other two women. She would have a serious talk with her oldest son about trifling with a girl's feelings.

After cake and ice cream, it was finally the best part of the day . . . time to open gifts.

The birthday boy nearly squealed as he opened the present Frankie gave him. It was his first plastic model ever, an F-4 Phantom jet fighter, just like the ones in Vietnam. Shelley gave him a model paint set and a tube of glue.

Tony gave his "Big Galoot" friend a Superman T-shirt and a dozen brand-new assorted comic books, the later drawing a raised eyebrow from Buck.

Waylon gave his brother an Old Timer pocket knife, which delighted Aubrey. Whittling was a favorite pastime of his.

"Now, don't be cuttin' yer fingers off jus' ta get outta

chores," Waylon playfully admonished his brother.

Buck gave his son a new pair of work boots.

Kathleen gave him a new shirt, and Maria gave him a paint-by-number set of The Attack on the Alamo.

Sarah gave him a new Bible, with his name engraved inside. His old one was beginning to fall apart. But not to be too stuffy, she also gave him Monopoly and Mouse Trap board games to share with his friends on rainy days.

After presents were opened and proper thanks were given under Sarah's approving eye, the boys raced off to the barn to play in the hay loft.

Soon the U.S. Cavalry called on them to track wily Apaches among the craggy boulders on the hillside in front of the house. Hide-and-seek came a little later, as the sun began to sink behind the trees, offering more places to hide. At dusk, they frolicked amongst an unmatched firefly show.

That evening the Musketeers gathered on the front porch around a fold-up card table beneath the single, dangling lightbulb. Frankie and Tony showed their pal how to put his model airplane together, using the instructions only when they really had to. For his part, Aubrey was absorbed by the illustrations and studied them intently, fascinated at the precision of the drawings.

Shelley brought out her Kodak Instamatic and took pictures of the three happiest boys in the world. Tony sat on one side, Frankie on the other, with Aubrey in the middle, proudly displaying his new jet fighter. The plane was covered with gluey fingerprints, painted a crazy camouflage pattern, and brandishing torn decals, but it was a masterpiece to them. She was sure there was as much paint on the boys as there was on the model.

That night, Aubrey lay in bed, wearing his new

Superman T-shirt and gazing lovingly at the plastic jet fighter basking under the lamp light on the nightstand next to his bed.

The military jet caused his thoughts turn to Chet. This was the second birthday Chet had missed, but his Vietnamese-style birthday card, with five bucks inside, had arrived just two days before. The card stood next to the model jet, and a one dollar bill from the money Chet had sent was folded neatly beside it, waiting to be dropped into the offering plate at church the following Sunday.

Aubrey hopped back out of the bed and knelt beside it to say an extra special prayer for his cousin.

America's birthday fell bright and sunny between Aubrey's and Frankie's own birthdays. The three families gathered on the shores of Lake Owen, along with almost the whole town, to picnic, to swim, and to watch the fireworks display the local chamber of commerce promised for later that evening.

It seemed that being away from the school environment made the boys more socially acceptable to the other children in town, at least for the day.

They played in a softball game, in which Aubrey hit a home run every time he went to bat. Tony managed to steal three bases, much to the chagrin of the bigger boys. When it was Frankie's turn at bat, he didn't live up to the nickname his uncle had given him, but in the outfield, he never dropped a fly ball that came his way.

However, he was unbeatable in the swimming races, winning a blue ribbon and a free banana split at the Dairy Queen.

They joined in on a few other games, but for the most part, the three boys kept to themselves. They still didn't trust the motives of the same kids who had shunned and teased them at school the rest of the year.

Even Buck had a good time and didn't cast his usual wet blanket over the day. He figured that since he couldn't get anything done at home, he might as well make the best of it. Besides, there were a lot of women and young girls running around in Bermuda shorts and tight pedal pushers, so at least there would be entertainment.

To everyone's surprise, he insisted on being the grill master, cooking hamburgers and hotdogs for the boys and steaks that he had grudgingly brought from his own freezer for everyone else. He grumbled and fanned at the constantly shifting cloud of hickory smoke he had to endure, but he wouldn't let anyone else near the grill, and they were content to let him have his way.

The boys raved about his "great" hamburgers, and Tony complimented the hot dogs, saying they were "better than any ol' stadium dog."

Their compliments seemed to bring out his good side, because he did something he had never done before . . . he played football with all the boys, including Waylon. The lightheartedness of his laughter sounded foreign to his sons, but it was welcomed by them and their mother, nonetheless.

Maria was smitten by Waylon's country-boy mannerisms and good looks, but her hopes were dashed when Irene came by to say, "Hello," and then, casting a wicked eye at her, she walked off with Waylon on her arm.

But her long, blonde locks were noticed by the other teenage boys, and soon she was surrounded by suitors, all vying for the attention of the cute "Yankee" girl. Kathleen watched her flirtatious daughter like a hawk, sharply eyeing any boy foolish enough to look her way.

After several "Oh mother" moments, Maria cleverly led her entourage of drooling school boys a safe distance away from scowling maternal eyes.

The only shadow on the day was that Mike had to fly to Pittsburg on business and couldn't be there.

"What a surprise!" Tony said sarcastically, when he found out. Kathleen was not happy about it, either. The relationship between her husband and his children bothered her, especially when it came to Tony. She confided her worries to Shelley and Sarah over yet another glass of the special "Mother's Punch" she had brought just for them.

The boys, and Buck, to some degree, wondered why the women were so giggly, but they were liberally giving permission for them to run off unsupervised, including Buck.

Later that evening, under the colorful bursts of sky-rockets, Buck embraced his wife and told her that he loved her and that it had been one of the best days of his life. The red, white, and blue of the fireworks reflected off the unseen, single tear that rolled quietly down Sarah's cheek until it melded with the sad smile on her lips.

She speculated that the ice-cold Pabst Blue Ribbon beer might have helped a little, too. She knew better than to think that Buck had somehow magically changed, but she was grateful, nonetheless, and she whispered a silent prayer of thanks for the brief moment of serenity.

And then it was Frankie's birthday. The day before his big day, the boys were walking back to his house after taking a dip in the creek.

"All right...Uncle Frank!" Frankie shouted, as he spotted the bright red Corvette convertible sitting in

front of his house. He broke out in a dead run, followed closely by the other two, who were just as anxious to meet the legendary Uncle Frank, the fireman.

Not bothering to use the steps, he leapt up on the porch and nearly took the screen door off of its hinges while opening it. Uncle Frank was sitting on the couch, and he barely managed to get to his feet before the soon-to-be eleven-year-old slammed into him, arms crushing his waist.

"Hey . . . Bambino!" Uncle Frank wheezed, as he caught his breath.

Uncle Frank was a baseball fanatic and had given Frankie that nickname at birth, saying he thought Frankie looked like Babe Ruth. Frankie hadn't always been particularly fond of the nickname, thinking it a baby's name, but once he realized who "The Babe" was and how much his uncle admired him, he changed his mind. At least his uncle wasn't calling him "Babe."

"I knew you'd come!" Frankie said, breathlessly.

"Now when have I ever missed my Bambino's special day?" he asked. "I wouldn't do that for anything. I told the chief that he was going to have to keep Nashville safe all by himself for a few days, because I had something more important to do!"

Uncle Frank always made Frankie feel like the most important kid in the world.

"What'd ya bring me, Uncle Frank? More models, I hope."

"Well, you'll just have to wait and see, won't ya?" his uncle teased.

Looking up at the two boys who stood panting in the doorway, he said, deliberately pointing at the wrong one, in turn, "You must be Aubrey, and you must be Tony."

A chorus of "No, I'm Tony" and "I'm Aubrey" corrected his feigned mistake.

"Of course, I know who you are! You're all the Bambino talks about whenever I call."

"Bambino? Who's that?" Aubrey asked, with a puzzled expression.

"You don't know who the Bambino is?" Tony fairly shouted at him, incredulous that his friend didn't know the greatest baseball player that ever lived. And then, much to Uncle Frank's delight, Tony proceeded to give his friend an abbreviated lesson about Babe Ruth.

"Not bad, Tony," Uncle Frank complimented, when he'd finished.

"Aw, heck, Mr. . . . um . . . " He stopped, not knowing how to address his buddy's uncle.

"You boys just call me Uncle Frank, too, okay," he offered. "I don't care much for the 'Mister' stuff."

"Cool!" said Tony.

"Yes sir, Mr. . . . er, I mean, Uncle Frank," Aubrey stammered, blushing at his gaffe. "Thank ya kindly."

"It's my honor, kind sir," he said, bowing at the waist to Aubrey.

"Wow, jus' like Robin Hood!" Aubrey gushed, getting a laugh from everyone in the room.

"Well, I've been called a lot of things before," Uncle Frank chuckled, "but never Robin Hood. That's a new one."

"But you help folks that's in trouble, jus' like him, dontcha?" Aubrey declared.

"Boy, you sure know how to schmooze a fella." Uncle Frank replied. "Are you going into politics when you grow up?"

"Oh, no sir, I could never do that," Aubrey said,

taking Uncle Frank seriously. "They shuck n' jive people, an' break their promises all the time. That ain't honest."

Uncle Frank burst out laughing and said, "Sis, you didn't tell me the Bambino had such witty and virtuous friends. I'll have to be sharp around these guys."

"Did you know that your mother and I were best friends in high school?" he asked Aubrey.

"Yes sir, I do," he answered politely. "She told me that you was the nicest guy in the whole town and a good friend to her. I thank ya fer that, too."

"Wow!" Uncle Frank exclaimed. "You're Sarah's boy all right. She was always real big on manners. But I'll tell ya what . . . you don't have to say 'sir' to me, either. It makes me feel old. I'll straighten it out with your mom, so you don't get in trouble. Okay?"

"Yes sir . . . I mean, yep," Aubrey said. "That'd be fine, um . . . Uncle Frank." Aubrey grinned, not accustomed to being able to address an adult so casually, but clearly pleased about it.

"So . . . Tony . . . tell me more about the Babe," he implored, as he led the boys out onto the front porch for some general guy talk.

Out on the porch, the talk quickly came around to firefighting, and Uncle Frank accommodated them with dramatic accounts of fires and rescues, always attributing the heroic parts to his fellow firemen, never building himself up as the hero. But the boys knew he really was one.

Frankie's mother called Sarah and Kathleen to ask if the boys could stay for cheeseburgers, as was the tradition whenever Uncle Frank came to town, because, as he boasted, "Nobody burns 'em like a fireman." She also talked their parents into letting them stay overnight.

Sarah was particularly pleased to hear that her old friend was in town.

"You are a glutton for punishment, aren't you girl?" Uncle Frank commented, as the boys went crazy at the news, racing out the door and into the front yard, whooping and yelling like the wild Indians they watched on TV.

"It's not punishment, big brother. It's a joy that I don't want to miss out on."

Frank detected a note of sadness in her voice.

"What does the doctor say?" he asked knowingly, his own mood becoming suddenly serious.

"He said . . . " She had to catch a lump as it rose in her throat. After a heavy pause, she continued, "What he said wasn't very good, big brother. He said that my case was somewhat unusual because of how rapidly the cancer has spread and that, at this stage, it has metastasized to my lungs and it's inoperable. I guess that's why I get so short of breath and have coughing fits sometimes."

"He said if I had caught it earlier, it might be different. Apparently, it will continue to progress rapidly . . . even with medication. How fast? He wasn't sure."

Pausing briefly, she went on, "He said that I had some options, like radiation therapy or a fairly new procedure called combination chemotherapy, but there were no guarantees it would be successful or do anything other than postpone the inevitable. He said that any time I might gain would not be pleasant . . . for me and for anyone around me. I could end up spending what time I might gain sick and bedridden."

"I just can't put Frankie through that. It seems the best I can hope for is medication for the pain; at least with that, I can try to have as normal a life as possible . . . for Frankie."

"Oh Frank . . . ," she said, bursting into tears and falling into her brother's arms. "What's going to happen to him? I can't stand the thought that tomorrow might be the last birthday I spend with my baby!"

Her sobbing became uncontrollable. Frank gently guided her into the kitchen, in case the boys came back into the house.

"Sis, don't you worry about Frankie," he reassured her, fighting to hold back his own emotions. "Our Bambino will be taken care of; I swear to you, he will."

He embraced his sister closely, gently rocking her back and forth, as her grief convulsed through her. "Besides, you haven't gone anywhere yet, so . . . "

No one slept much that night. The boys were too high strung with excitement and spent the night telling jokes and playing card games. Uncle Frank joined them around midnight to tell ghost stories. One story nearly caused Tony to pee in his pants.

Afterwards, he joined Shelley on the front porch swing. She was determined not to miss a single moment of this night. Moments like this were priceless, even if late in coming.

"I'm trying real hard not to be angry with God, Frank," she said, after a long silence, laying her head on her brother's shoulder, as they swung back and forth in the evening breeze.

"I know he has a reason for this, but I can't understand it, and I just can't accept it," she protested.

Frank didn't believe it was the will of an Almighty power to deprive a boy of his mother or to deprive a mother of watching her son grow to be a man, but he respected her beliefs.

"I suppose he just needs another angel, sis," he said, choking back a sob of his own. "I just think we need you more down here."

A tear rolled down his cheek and fell gently onto her soft, blonde hair.

Feeling it, she looked up at him, and, smiling a tear-stained smile, she kissed him lightly on his wet cheek.

"At least he's blessed me with a wonderful brother to look after my baby boy," she said, laying her head back on his shoulder, sniffing back more tears. "I don't know what I'd do without you, big brother."

"Hey, do you remember when . . . ," Frank said suddenly, with false cheerfulness, as he began taking his sister down pleasant memory lanes not traveled in years. Soon he had her laughing and recalling memories of her own, including those of Jack and the trouble he and Frank used to get into in school.

"How's ol' Ben Ivey?" Frank asked, as the conversation progressed.

"Still the adorable, cultured gentleman he's always been," Shelley answered sarcastically. "We just saw him last week."

"Really? Trouble with your car?"

"No" she recounted. "He has talked me into letting Frankie take the Number Three bus from school on Fridays. It drops him off right across the street from the garage. I pick him up when I get off work. He's teaching him the same way he did you and Jack. You should see the way Frankie's eyes light up when he sees that dirty old garage; you'd think he was at Disneyland."

"I think he inherited his father's mechanical abilities, too," she said. "He's always fixing things, or at least tearing them apart. I seem to recall a certain brother of mine doing the same thing," she spoke playfully.

"Yeah, Dad was always putting things back together, wasn't he?" Frank mused. "Ya know, I think I'll swing by to see the old geezer tomorrow. Mind if I take Frankie?"

"Huh! Just try keeping him from going when he finds out where you're headed. Ben really loves Frankie, and vice versa."

"That doesn't surprise me. Jack was his favorite."

"Oh, don't be so modest," Shelley said. "You and Jack both were his favorites. You know what a kick he got out of helping you two build that old jalopy." Shelley was recalling how much of their time the hot rod took to build.

She lost count of how many nights she had spent sitting off to the side of the shop, watching them hammer, wrench, and weld on the homebuilt car. But she never begrudged her favorite three guys the time. She loved all three.

"He really misses you; I can tell," she said.

Somewhere along their nostalgic adventure, the noise of rambunctious boys upstairs faded into snores of contentment. But she and her brother watched a beautiful sunrise dawn on a very special day.

Shelley woke the groggy, late-nighters and fed them breakfast and then asked Frank to drive Tony and Aubrey home. He had to take her old Rambler, since his Corvette couldn't hold them all. The boys gazed disappointedly at the sports car, as they pulled away.

But they returned as quickly as they could, with their mothers in tow and carrying the gifts they had for Frankie.

When he arrived with his mother, Aubrey made a

quick detour to the garage, carrying a box, before coming into the house.

Sarah was excited to see Frank, and he was elated to see her, though somewhat shocked at the change that time and Buck had made in her. He tactfully avoided any outward expression of his surprise, though.

In school, she had been an attractive girl, in a plain-Jane sort of way. Her mother's extreme religious beliefs forbade her to wear makeup or poodle skirts. Back then, she had been well shaped and stood slightly taller than most of the girls in school. More memorably, she always had a smile ready to give freely to anyone who needed one . . . even those who didn't deserve one.

Frank had thought of her as a rose waiting to bloom but never able to do so. The serenity she projected had made her well liked among most of the other girls. He suspected that it was because she posed less of a threat to them than the other prettier girls who shunned them. But Sarah had never put too much emphasis on fashions she couldn't indulge in, anyway.

Most of all, she had been one of the few people in town who had stood by him in his time of need. Buck had not been at all kind in his reaction to her loyalty, though.

Looking at her now, he saw that she was only slightly heavier, certainly not fat. She showed signs of a hard life, without the niceties and luxuries most other women had on their vanity tables and in their marriages.

She still wore no makeup and kept her hair tied back in the kind of desperate bun that hopeless women wore. Her clothes were nondescript, and her general appearance was that of a house maid, not that of a cherished wife. Instead, she wore the austere uniform of a farmer's wife, with its lack of soft lace and delicate perfumes.

Sarah's vanity table, passed down from Buck's grandmother, sat unused in the corner of her bedroom, its mirrors hazed over with dust from neglect. What did she have in her life to look pretty for?

He resented Buck for having put one of the sweetest, most loving girls he had ever known into a hateful cage of hardship, neglect, and abuse.

"Well I'll be doggone, if it ain't Sarah Pickard," he said enthusiastically, using her maiden name, as he reached out and drew her into his arms.

"It's good to see you, girl," he fawned. "You're a sight for sore eyes. How ya doin', Dumplin'?"

"Still the sweet talker, I see," she said, returning his prolonged hug.

"Hello, Frank. How long has it been?" She didn't bother to correct him on her last name.

"If you can remember," she goaded.

"Ooooo! That stung," he answered defensively. "Obviously it's been way too long. Tell me all about everything. Catch me up.

"How is the sweetest girl in Haleyville doing?" he asked flirtatiously, giving Sarah a last squeeze before releasing her.

"Oh don't be so silly, Frank," Sarah protested. "You exaggerate."

"No, my dear, I don't," he reprimanded. "You are one of the very few good things about this backwater burg."

"You have no idea how far the memory of that sweet smile of yours has carried me over the years," he winked. "When I get depressed, I just picture those pearly whites of yours, and things get better."

Sarah blushed a bright pink. Such compliments never

echoed in her home.

"I, uh . . . I owe you an apology, Dumplin', for not staying in touch, or at least not looking you up the few times I've been in town," he started to explain. "It's just that . . . "

"Oh hush!' Sarah responded. "You don't have to apologize. I understand."

A knowing look passed between them. "But we're here now, aren't we? Let's just go with that, okay?"

If ever there had been a woman for me, it would have been you, he lamented.

The two former classmates engaged in a long string of "Do you remember so-and-so?" and "Whatever happened to . . . ?" They mutually avoided any mention of Buck. Why toss a turd into the punch bowl?

Shelley joined in, whenever they mentioned someone she remembered or when Jack came up. But, for the most part, the focus was on Sarah, making her feel special for the first time in a very long time. Buck would have exploded with insane rage, had he known.

Tony and his mother arrived a little later. And after introductions, all four adults became caught up in small talk and memories, bringing Kathleen up to speed about their shared past. Before long, she felt as if she'd known them for years, even relating some of her own high school memories for them, as they sat on the back porch sipping more of Kathleen's special "punch."

Outside, the boys were once again running wild in the front yard, giddy with excitement. Frankie could barely contain himself and had to be run out of the house numerous times by his mother.

Finally, after what seemed like forever, she called them in. After a quick round of "Happy Birthday" and shoveling cake and ice cream into their mouths, it was Frankie's turn to open presents.

He dove in enthusiastically. Despite her limited budget, his mother managed to afford a G.I. Joe with all the accessories, including the official authentic footlocker.

Uncle Frank brought several models of cars, airplanes, and ships. He also gave Frankie a pup tent. It would never hold all three of them at the same time, but he had no doubt that they would try.

A couple of days earlier, Uncle Ben had sent a brand-new, red tool box, with an assortment of essential tools in it, as well as an envelope containing eleven dollars, one for every year, as was his custom.

Tony gave him a baseball glove, which was a big hit with Uncle Frank.

Following precedent, Kathleen gave him a shirt for the upcoming school year. Tony suspected that he was going to get the same when his birthday came around.

Just as she did with her own son, Sarah gave him a new illustrated Bible, with his name embossed inside the front cover. Oddly, Frankie found that he really appreciated the gift. She also gave him the Operation board game.

But as wonderful as all those were, the best gift of the day came from Aubrey.

He handed Frankie a small, hastily wrapped gift. Opening it, Frankie held up a small, crudely carved wooden image of a dog.

"I whittled it myself!" Aubrey declared proudly.

"Wow, Aub. This is really cool. Thanks," Frankie said, as enthusiastically as he could. He knew Aubrey didn't have money for fancy gifts.

"Is this Scooter?" he asked.

"I bet you thought that was all, huh?" Aubrey grinned impishly.

Seeing the confused look on Frankie's face, he said, "Wait here."

He ran out the back door and returned with a medium-sized, unwrapped cardboard box.

"I had ta hide it in the garage; sorry it ain't wrapped, but . . . " he trailed off as he placed it on the table in front of Frankie. The package shook slightly.

The birthday boy started to bend the folded flaps back, but before he got to the third one, up sprang a miniature copy of Scooter, rust-colored and complete with floppy ears and a long. thin tail, whipping to and fro.

"*A Puppy!*" he shouted.

"Momma, I got a puppy!" he exclaimed, jumping up and down ecstatically, taking the equally excited little creature out of the box and immediately being drowned with wet puppy kisses.

Then he paused, looking at his wide-eyed mother. "Its okay, isn't it, Momma?"

Aubrey suddenly realized that he hadn't asked Frankie's mother if it was okay. "It's okay, ain't it Mrs. Albert?" he pleaded guiltily, looking at his mother and getting a scornful look. She had assumed that he had cleared the gift with Shelley.

After a short moment of surprise, Shelley laughed and said to Frankie, "Yes, it's okay, sweetie."

She then turned to Aubrey and said, "That was a precious thing for you to do, Aubrey. Thank you."

She walked over and gave him a hug and gave a wink of approval to a slightly embarrassed Sarah.

Also feeling a little embarrassed, Aubrey said, "Aw,

it ain't nuthin'. I seen how much Frankie likes playin' with Scooter, so I figured, 'Why not?' B'sides, Paw was wantin' me ta git rid of 'em. He says puppies is nuthin' but trouble an' he wants ta git Scooter sprayed . . . whutever that is. I reckon I shoulda asked ya first though, huh? I'm sorry."

"That's okay, darlin'," she replied. "I'd have said yes, anyway."

"And it's 'spayed,' sweetie," she corrected, chuckling at his mispronunciation. "It means getting her fixed so she can't have more puppies. It's probably best for her health, too."

"So . . . ," Uncle Frank asked his nephew, "what are you going to name it . . . her . . . him?"

"He's a 'him,' Mr. . . . I mean, Uncle Frank," Aubrey answered awkwardly, still not accustomed to calling someone "uncle."

"Okay," Uncle Frank asked Frankie, "what are you going call *him*?"

Frankie thought for a moment, and then said, "I think I'll call him Rusty, 'cause of his color."

"That's a good name," Uncle Frank agreed. "Looks like a redbone hound."

"Is that right?" he asked Aubrey.

"Yep, mostly, that is," he replied. "Waylon calls him a Heinz 57, 'cause he's probably got fifty-seven different kinds o' dogs mixed in!" He laughed.

Uncle Frank laughed and excused himself, as he slipped over to the armchair close by.

"Hey Aubrey," he called, as he reached into a large paper bag he had hidden behind the chair, "would you and Tony come here for a second, please?"

From countless telephone conversations with

Frankie, he had learned that Aubrey was fascinated with airplanes and had just built his first model of one not long ago. Aubrey stood in silent amazement, as Uncle Frank pulled a large, flat box containing a B-52 bomber kit out of the bag and handed it to him.

"Whoa!" was all Aubrey could say, as he examined the artwork on the huge box, his mouth agape.

Uncle Frank had also learned that Tony was a big superhero fan and that he liked to draw, so he pulled a stack of brand-new superhero coloring books and some colored pencils—because only little kids used crayons—out of the bag and handed them to Tony, who stood speechless, for once.

The boys couldn't believe it. Getting gifts on someone else's birthday was unheard of . . . but completely cool.

"Holy Crimeny!" Tony yipped, getting a stern look from his mother.

"Oh Frank, you shouldn't have . . . ," Sarah and Kathleen protested in unison.

"Nonsense," he protested. "I used to hate going to birthday parties. It didn't seem fair that one kid got all the good stuff." Then he winked.

That was not all Uncle Frank had up his sleeve. He had seen how the boys pored over his Corvette, oohing and aahing at every little detail, saying, "I bet this is the fastest car in the world!"

So he decided to surprise them by announcing that he was going to give them each a ride in it.

At first, their mothers protested, but he reassured them that he had cut his driving teeth on the country roads around Haleyville and that he would keep a safe speed. Besides, it was a Corvette, for crying out loud. How many chances did the boys have to ride in a

Corvette . . . with the top down?

Then he grinned at Sarah and Kathleen, saying, "Afterwards, I'll take you two pretty ladies for a ride, too." Shelley rolled her eyes at her older brother's flirtation, but it was enough to melt any resistance.

Frankie, being the gracious host, insisted that his friends go first. Besides, he'd ridden in his uncle's car before.

Tony immediately jumped up, yelling, "Me first . . . me first!"

"Tony!" his mother admonished. "Don't be so rude. Let Aubrey go first."

"That's okay, Mrs. Carillo," Aubrey said, a little apprehensively. "Tony can go first; I'll wait."

"Well, now that we've settled that . . . shall we?" Uncle Frank asked and nodded to Tony.

"*Yahoo!*" Tony yelled, as he sprinted through the door and leapt off the porch, racing toward the shiny, red sports car.

They were gone for only fifteen minutes, and when they returned, the wiry, little guy was absolutely bouncing with excitement.

"That's was so far out!" he yelled, as he clambered out of the convertible. "Nothin' but flat out cool!"

He turned to Uncle Frank, who sat waiting for Aubrey to get in, and asked "Can we do it again?"

"Tony!" his mother scolded.

"I know, Mom," he protested, "but it was just so boss!"

"I'm gonna be a race car driver when I grow up!" he declared.

His mother shot a raised eyebrow at Uncle Frank, who sheepishly looked away, whistling.

Aubrey was a little slower getting in. Uncle Frank

noticed his apprehension and did what any considerate man in his position would do. He floored the gas pedal, sending gravel flying and the tail end of the car sliding sideways.

Aubrey assumed a white-knuckled grip on the dashboard handle in front of him, as Uncle Frank wove through turn after turn on the country roads that surrounded Haleyville.

When they returned, Aubrey's eyes looked like saucers amid his pale face. Uncle Frank couldn't stifle a grin.

"Whatsa matter, Aub?" Tony teased.

"Did ya finally find somethin' that scared ya?" he goaded.

"Shuddup, ya squirt!" Aubrey growled back, still a little pale. "I ain't never been in no fast car before."

Getting out of the car, he turned to Frank and said, "Thank ya kindly, Uncle Frank. It sure was, ah . . . excitin'. This is some kinda car."

Then he turned to Tony and scowled, "At least I had the manners to say thank you!"

Tony stammered, looking from Aubrey to his mother's reproaching glare, and finally to Frank, who played along, with eyebrows raised in expectation.

"Um . . . gee, uh, sorry," he said, flush with embarrassment. "Thanks a bunch, Uncle Frank. It was awesome."

"You're quite welcome, Tony," Frank responded formally. "Maybe I'll take you for another ride, next time I'm in town."

Glancing at Kathleen, he added, "That is, if it's okay with your mother."

His mother stood there in the typical mother's pose, crossed arms and pursed lips feigning annoyance at her son, but then she said, "I suppose it wouldn't do any harm . . . if he can remember his manners."

"*Yes!*" Tony shouted, jumping up, his fist jabbing the sky.

"Well, I guess that leaves you, Bambino!" Frankie's uncle beckoned.

Without hesitation, Frankie handed Rusty to his mother and jumped into the fabulous machine.

"This is the birthday boy's ride," Frank told to the onlookers, "so don't fret if we're gone for a little while." He exchanged a knowing look with his sister.

"You're so awesome, Uncle Frank!" Frankie declared, as the Corvette zoomed through one curve after another.

"Thanks for everything," he said, then thoughtfully added, "Especially for treatin' my friends so nice."

"My pleasure, buddy."

Uncle Frank always put little Frankie at ease with his smooth style and big brother-like attitude. "Hey, ya wanna go see ol' Ben?"

"Heck, yea!" Frankie barked, totally surprised by the suggestion.

Frankie felt like a prince riding in style through town. He recognized several kids from school, as they gawked at the rumbling sports car. He could see the envy in their faces. A couple of them even waved at them as they passed.

This is what cool is like, he thought, casually waving back, like some movie star. *Uncle Frank is one awesome guy!*

NOW, LISTEN TO ME, LORD!

Uncle Frank stopped the car just before reaching Ben's parking lot, and, with a mischievous grin, he said to Frankie, "Hold on tight and watch this."

He downshifted into first gear, then punched the gas pedal to the floor. The engine roared its presence to the world, causing the rear tires to spin, loudly squealing and smoking. As soon as the car gained traction, he turned the steering wheel toward the parking lot, causing the rear of the car to swing around until he was facing straight into the garage. Then he let off the gas and rolled casually up to the open bay doors and stopped, a cloud of tire smoke and dust whirling behind him.

Uncle Frank hopped out of the car, Hollywood-style, without using the door, and leaned against the front fender, his arms crossed and still grinning broadly.

"You crazy sumbitch!" Ben shouted, as he hobbled out of the shop toward them.

"Godammit, I shoulda known it was you," he scolded, as soon as he got close enough to see that it was Frank.

"Ain't you a bit old to be actin' like some damned juvenile delinquent?" he barked, half-laughing, as he embraced Frank, with a hearty pat on his back.

"Damn good to see ya, son. I see ya brought the birthday boy with ya, too," he said, ruffling Frankie's hair. "Happy birthday, hot rod."

"Thanks, Uncle Ben, and thanks for the tools. They're really cool. Now maybe we can build that go-cart you were talkin' about."

"You betcha, sport. Startin' next Friday; how's that sound?"

"Far out!" Frankie exclaimed. Ben didn't know what to think about this new "hippy talk," as he called it, but then, they had some goofy sayings back when he was a kid. *The Bee's knees?*

"It's great to see you, too, old man," Frank said affectionately. He really had missed the cranky old coot. Ben was like a second father to him. The best memories he had of Haleyville included Ben. Along with Sarah, Ben had kept his spirits up when it seemed the entire town was against him.

He had been terrified of being rejected by his friend and mentor when his dirty little secret came to light. He could never forget his relief when Ben accepted what he was without hesitation or judgment, saying, "Hell, I've hopped on more than a few whores in my time, an' I damn sure don't want any of these local idiots sayin' a damn thing about it. It ain't none of their bidness. What you do behind closed doors is up to you."

He cherished how the old man had taken the edge off of the moment by adding, "Just don't be wearin' no dresses 'round here. They'd show yer ass if ya bent over a fender, an' I don't reckon that'd be a pretty sight."

Frank had laughed so hard his side hurt.

"I reckon firefightin's a lucrative livin', ain't it?" Ben

said, running his hand along the curves of the Corvette.

"This is one damn fine car you got here, boy," he complimented. "A bit fancy for my tastes, but I hear these babies can haul some serious ass."

"I'll bet you could make her go faster, though," Frank flattered.

"Well, of course, I can. But then . . . so can you, right?" he returned.

"Yeah, but it would just get me more tickets," Frank replied.

"Aw, who gives a damn about tickets?" the ex-racer quipped.

"I'll have to take you for a spin, sometime," Frank offered. "Show you what she can do."

"Excuse me?" Ben retorted. "You? Show me? How 'bout I show you what real drivin' is?"

"Actually," Frank answered, "I'd kinda like to keep it in one piece."

"Yeah? Well, I reckon I do tend to break 'em, don't I?" he admitted, chuckling. "I bet it'd be fun, though."

Frank noticed a man he recognized from school inside the garage.

"Hey, Harlan," he waved.

The man turned away without acknowledging him.

"Hey . . . you rude sumbitch!" Ben called after his employee. "The man said hello. Ain't you got any manners?"

Harlan turned and gave a weak wave, then turned back to what he was doing.

Ben shook his head, saying, "Don't pay any attention to him. He's just ignorant. People in this town are so damn narrow-minded that if they fell onto a pin, they'd be blinded in both eyes."

Ben's racing career had taken him far beyond the borders of Haleyville, to tracks near big, sinful cities. He'd seen and done things that would mortify the good, pious townsfolk. Frank's sexuality meant nothing to him, but the town's attitude about it pissed him off.

Frank brought Ben up to date on the events of his life, while Frankie ran off to claim his Baby Ruth bar. Ben beamed like a proud uncle, while Frank talked about life as a firefighter in the big city.

Inside the office, Frankie was sitting at the bench, scanning through yet another Chilton's manual and looking out the dirty office windows, at his real uncle and the old man he called uncle. He saw Ben clap his uncle on the back and shake his hand, as if congratulating him about something. But then, just a few minutes later, he saw Ben throw his greasy rag down on the ground as hard as he could and then kick it in anger. He could almost hear the string of foul language issue forth, as Ben ranted and then retrieved a white hanky from his back pocket to wipe his eyes.

He was surprised. He'd never seen Ben so worked up. What had Uncle Frank said to upset him that way? He climbed off of the bar stool and wandered back through the shop.

Harlan was busy cleaning car parts as Frankie passed by, but he stopped long enough to give him a sidelong sneer that frightened Frankie a little. He knew Harlan didn't like him, but he didn't know why.

"It just ain't right," Frankie heard Ben say as he approached.

"What's not right?" he asked.

The men looked at him, surprised to see him standing there.

"Uhh . . . the price of gasoline, squirt," Ben recovered quickly.

"You'd think it was gold, they way them Ay-rabs keep jackin' it up," he lied. "Hell, ethyl's all the way up to twenty-eight cents a gallon, the greedy bastards."

Frankie knew that the price of gasoline wasn't what upset the old man, but he didn't press it.

His uncle looked down at him and gave a reassuring wink. "Come on, Bambino. We've been gone too long. Your mother is probably beside herself with worry."

"You okay, Uncle Ben?" he asked, seeing the redness in Ben's eyes.

"Yeah, squirt, I'm fine," he answered. "You run along, now. And give your momma a great, big hug for me . . . ," he said, cutting his words off, lest the lump in his throat betray his feelings.

"Ben . . . it was great seeing you again," Uncle Frank interjected, seeing the old man's distress. "I promise it won't be so long, next time. I got some ideas for the 'Vette I want to run by you."

"Anytime, son, anytime," he said, sticking his hand out, then pulling Frank into an embrace.

"You tell my Shelley girl I love her," he whispered into Frank's ear, in a rare spoken expression of his affection for her.

"I will, Ben," Frank whispered back. "She loves you, too . . . so do I."

"Now you boys get outta here before you get me in trouble with your momma," he said to Frankie. "See ya Friday?"

"You bet, Uncle Ben," Frankie answered.

Ben watched as they drove off. After they were out of sight, he turned and slowly walked back to his garage.

"You still workin' on that?" he shot sourly, as he walked up to the bench Harlan was working at.

"I cain't believe you let that queer hug you," Harlan said acidly.

Ben spun him by the shoulder to face him.

Whap!

Harlan's face stung, and his head swam, as he stumbled backward, falling to the ground.

He lay sprawled out on the dirty floor, a shocked expression on his face.

"Whut the hell didja do that for?" he sputtered.

"You're fired, goddammit!" Ben roared, "Get the hell outta my shop, you ignorant sonuvabitch!"

"If I ever hear you say anything about that boy again, I'll take a jack handle to your stupid ass."

Shaking with rage, he continued, as tears welled up in his angry eyes, "That man risks his life every goddamn day, pulling folks he don't even know out of burnin' buildings. What the hell do you do with your life, you fuckin' idiot? Get drunk and sweep a goddamn floor? You ain't nuthin'. Hell, he's ten times the man you'll ever be.

"Ya know, I only hired you in the first place because I felt sorry for your retarded ass. Get out, I said!" he ranted, taking a step toward the startled man still splayed on the floor.

"Don't ever come back, either. I'll mail your fuckin' check to you."

Harlan scrambled backwards without taking his eyes off of Ben until he felt he was a safe enough distance away from the raging madman to clamber to his feet.

"You ain't heard the last of this, old man!" he threatened, as he made a dash for the open bay doors.

"Bring it on, hillbilly," Ben shot back. "Let's see what

you got!"

Harlan got into his rusty pickup truck as fast as he could and gave Ben the middle finger as he tore out of the parking lot.

"Stupid bastard," Ben grumbled to himself, as he walked over to the chain that controlled the bay doors. Rolling both doors down, Ben closed his shop early for the first time in years.

He walked into his tiny office, slumped down into his tattered leather chair, and leaned forward, placing his elbows on the cluttered desk and his craggy face into his calloused, oil-stained hands. Not since Jack's funeral had the old man cried. Now he let a flood of silent tears flow freely down the lines in his face, like tiny rivers coursing through myriad canyons of time.

After a while, he sat upright and opened the top drawer to his desk. Reaching to the back of the drawer, he retrieved the Bible that the good sisters at the orphanage had given him decades ago. Staring at it for a long time, he ran his hand over its cracked leather cover.

Religion hadn't been a part of his life since he'd left the orphanage at the age of thirteen. But he still held a fairly strong belief in God, despite the best efforts of the nuns to beat it into him, one knuckle rapping at a time.

In his heart, he knew that God was much more than someone, or something just to be feared and chanted to. Nor was he to be used as a battering ram, or as justification for narrow-mindedness and persecution, the way some folks did.

The one thing that had stuck with him was how the Bible described Jesus as a friend to the lowlifes and the sinners and a refuge of widows and orphans, like himself. Ben admired how the Son of God condemned the self-righteousness of the self-holy and how he cherished the poorest and least among them over the pious and the wealthy. Jesus was his kind of guy. It's too bad folks can't quit ruining his P.R. with all their stupidity.

Ben didn't need the rules and regulations of men eager to control the minds of others. He knew the whole reason for Jesus walking among his flock was to free those minds from ritual slavery and superstitious fear. But, as usual, mankind had got it all wrong . . . again and again.

Holding the dusty old Bible to his forehead, he began to pray the way they had taught him in the orphanage.

"Dear heavenly Father . . . ," he started out stiffly, but then stopped. It had been so long since he'd prayed that he'd forgotten how, and he didn't want to sound like some phony tithe-chasing preacher.

Instead, he began a one-sided conversation with the Lord. He knew God would understand, even without the formalities. After all . . . he is God.

Holding the Bible to his chest, as though hugging a child, and tilting his tear stained face to the ceiling, he began again . . .

"Lord...Ben here. It's been a long time, I know. Too long; I know that, too. I know an old foul-mouthed curmudgeon like me has got no right to bend your holy ear or to ask anything from you. And I sure don't deserve any favors, given the things I've said and done in my time. But this ain't for me, Lord. This is for my Shelley and for little Frankie...and big Frank, too.

"I hope you'll overlook all my many transgressions just long enough to listen to me. I remember the sisters telling me that you would, if I just ask with a sincere heart. I believe you will, too, so I'm holdin' you to it. I've never been more sincere about anything in my whole useless life.

"Lord, I don't pretend to know your reasons, and normally I wouldn't be questionin' 'em, either. But right now, Lord...I'm at a loss as to why you'd do such a thing to such a beautiful human being...and to such wonderful little boy. Neither of 'em have ever done anybody any harm. Truth be known, Lord...I think it's pretty rotten, the way they've been treated by others who claim to be doin' your will. I suppose that's one excuse for me not sitting amongst 'em on Sunday mornings.

"Lord....as you know, I never had a family of my own, but Jack, Shelley, Frank, and the boy are the closest I've ever come to one. You know my heart and how much I love them....and need them. That's another solemn truth. I really do need 'em. You already took Jack from us. Ain't that enough?

"I know it ain't about me, but if this is about punishing me for all my sins....you're doing a damn fine job of it. Why can't you just send me to Hell, where I belong, and leave them alone?

"I know you don't make deals....like ol' Satan does, but if you could make an exception this time, I'll take my punishment like a man and gladly roast in Hell for all eternity; just don't take her. Would you at least consider it? Please?

"Hasn't that little boy suffered enough, Lord? You took his grandparents away before he even got a chance to know them. Then you took his daddy from him. Now you're gonna take his momma, too? I thought you were a God of compassion.

"I gotta tell ya, Lord. I'm more than a little angry with you right now. But don't hold that against them. Hold it against me.

"I know I ain't likely to change your mind, but, for her

sake, and especially for little Frankie's sake, could you at least make it to where she doesn't suffer too much? He's gonna have a hard enough time believin' you love him, as it is. Seeing his mother in pain won't help that any.

"I read, in this here Bible, that even your own son questioned your motives at least once…in Gethsemane, so it ain't like this is something new. I admit that I used to be pretty bitter about how you chose to bust my leg up. But I realize that if you hadn't, I might not even be alive, today. I wouldn't have come back to this shabby, little town and opened this dirty, little garage. And then I never would have met Jack and Frank. I never would have been blessed to have Shelley and little Frankie in my life, either. So I'll take this opportunity to thank you for makin' me a gimp. But that doesn't mean I'm any happier about what you're doing to my family.

"I s'pose I'd better stop talkin' now; otherwise, I might just say something I'll regret. For what it's worth, I still believe in you, Lord. I still have faith in your promises, too. I just wish you'd show some of that mercy and compassion I've read so much about.

"I don't know what else to say, Lord. You're doin' one heckuva a tap dance on this old man's heart, but you're really gonna tear that little boy's heart to shreds. I hope you have a good plan for him."

Hesitating for a long moment, he finally said, "Amen," and he added, "Thanks for your time, Lord…I hope I haven't wasted it."

He knew he had violated all the rules of prayer the nuns had hammered into him, but he didn't believe God followed them, either. He felt as if God just wants to hear from his children, from time to time. Probably more than once every decade or so, though.

FIRECRACKIN' FIREMAN

Frankie and his uncle rode back home in silence. Frankie noticed a strange look in his uncle's eyes that he couldn't understand.

"What's wrong, Uncle Frank?" he inquired.

Frank felt like kicking himself. This was his nephew's day, and he didn't want anything to spoil it.

"Aw, I was just getting' a little bummed about having to go back home, that's all," he lied.

Frankie wondered what was so secret that both Uncle Frank and Uncle Ben had to hide it from him.

"When ya gotta go?" he asked.

"The day after tomorrow," Uncle Frank answered.

"Well, can'tcha stay longer? Please!"

"I really wish I could, Bambino."

He was scrambling for a way to salvage his nephew's day. Then an idea occurred to him.

"But the guys at the station get out of hand without their new, um… assistant fire chief," he announced, his usual smile returning to his face. He had planned on making the announcement later, but now seemed a good time, instead.

"Assistant fire chief?" Frankie shouted. "Wow! That is so cool! Wait'll the guys hear that!"

"Well, you and Ben are the first to hear about it," he confided. "I haven't even told your mother, yet. Maybe you and your buddies can help me celebrate. Since I wasn't able to come down for the Fourth of July, I brought some fireworks, if that's okay with you."

"Okay?" Frankie yipped. "It's more than okay. It's great! Wow!"

"That is so awesome," he proclaimed.

"What kind did ya bring? Bottle rockets?" he inquired excitedly.

"Yep, and a whole lot more." Uncle Frank answered, listing all the different fireworks he had brought.

But as he drove, his heart weighed heavy, dreading the task ahead of him. He had insisted that his sister let him be the one to break the news of her illness to Frankie. She reluctantly, but gratefully, accepted his offer. It certainly was not something he looked forward to doing.

When the Corvette pulled up in front of his house, a very excited Frankie leapt out of the convertible without using the door, as he'd seen his uncle do at Ben's garage, anxious to tell his buddies about the fireworks.

But, first, he ran up on the front porch, where the three mothers had gathered over iced tea, to hug his mother, as Ben had asked. He told her the news about his uncle's promotion and, of course, about the fireworks.

Aubrey and Tony were playing near the old tire swing, alternately chasing and then being chased by Rusty. The excitable puppy now sported a temporary collar Shelly had fashioned from an old, black belt of hers, while her son and her brother had been away, joy riding.

"Hey, fellas!" he shouted as he flew off of the porch

toward them. "You won't believe this…."

He told them about the fireworks, eliciting a chorus of whooping and hollering. When they had calmed down, he told them about his uncle being made assistant fire chief.

"Wow!" the other two breathed, as they turned awestruck faces at the tall, muscular man striding toward the porch to join the ladies. He seemed a real-life superhero to them. Especially Tony, who was now thinking about becoming a fireman when he grew up.

The sun was beginning to set, when Uncle Frank called the boys over to his car and opened the trunk. Inside, several brown paper bags took up what space the car's hardtop roof had spared. In exaggeratedly careful movements, Uncle Frank delicately began handing the bags to them one at a time, issuing dire warnings to be very careful how they handled them.

Feeling that Uncle Frank had entrusted them with something special and taking the fireman very seriously, they slowly carried their dangerous cargo to the porch and gingerly set them down, as if the packages might explode at any moment. Each boy breathed a sigh of relief when they had accomplished their dangerous mission.

Of course, none of them considered that the very same bags were in the trunk when they were being jostled around country roads earlier that day. If they were going to explode, that would have been the time.

Uncle Frank came striding up with the largest bag, seemingly oblivious to the danger. Suddenly, he stumbled forward, dropping the bag, and then threw his arms up in front of his face, as if to ward off an explosion.

The boys panicked and dove to the ground, screaming

warnings at Uncle Frank and covering their heads, just like the soldiers in the war movies.

When no explosion ensued, they slowly looked up to see Uncle Frank still standing and laughing.

"Gotcha!" he shouted, pointing at them.

"Why you…" Tony growled, leaping up and running at the laughing man. Aubrey and Frankie joined him, trying to tackle the overgrown prankster. Finally, they succeeded in bringing him down and then promptly swarmed him, as their mothers sat, laughing at the spectacle.

The fireworks show Uncle Frank put on for them was spectacular. It was even better than the Fourth of July, because it was their private show. Some of the nearest neighbors stepped out of their homes to watch, and apparently one of them called the sheriff.

Jimmy Bryant, the sheriff's deputy showed up about halfway through the display, delaying it briefly, while he checked Uncle Frank's credentials. Once he was satisfied that the big-city fireman knew what he was doing, he promptly joined in on the fun himself.

After the show, Uncle Frank pulled the boys aside and secretly gave each one a small bag of Black Cats and Lady Fingers, as well as punks to light them. He then warned them, in a hushed voice, not to let their mother find out and to be very careful with them. They each made a solemn promise to keep his secret.

That evening, amid a chorus of chirping crickets, beneath a warm, star-strewn August sky, the guests bade a final happy birthday to Frankie and thanked Shelley and Frank for a wonderful day.

Aubrey and Tony declared their admiration for Uncle Frank and assured Frankie that he really did have the coolest uncle in the world. Frankie thanked his friends for coming and for their gifts.

Aubrey and his mother stayed a few minutes longer than the Carillos, which gave Frankie a chance to give thank Aubrey for giving him Rusty. The puppy now lay sleeping on the couch. It was a habit Shelley would have to nip in the bud.

"Aub …" he began, not sure how to put his feelings into words, "thanks for Rusty. I've always wanted a dog of my own.

"You're the best friend I could ever have," he said, patting his friend on the shoulder. "I wish you were my brother. Then we could be together all the time."

"Yeah…me, too," Aubrey replied, shuffling his feet in the cool evening grass.

"But best friends is the next best thang, ain't it?" he said, giving Frankie their secret handshake.

Meanwhile, Sarah was talking with Shelley and Frank.

"This was a wonderful day….for both of us," she said "Frankie's such a fine young man. I'm so proud of him." She spoke as if Frankie were her own son.

"Thank you, sweetie," Shelley said. "Aubrey's a great little guy, too. I just adore him."

She added, "You have done well by him."

"Well, I've tried to raise respectful boys."

"I would say you've succeeded," Frank assured her. He then reached out and drew her into a warm hug.

"It was wonderful seeing you again, Dumplin'; really it was. I hope we can do this more often, now that our boys are such good buddies and all."

"I sure have missed you, Frank," she replied, returning his hug. "Thank you for everything. Congratulations again on the promotion, I'm real proud of you, too.

Please stay safe, okay? I'll be praying for you."

Shelley laced her arm in Sarah's and walked her out to the pickup truck.

"Sarah…can you come by tomorrow after dinner?" she asked pensively. "I have something important to talk to you and Kathleen about."

"Sure I can," she replied, sensing the urgency in Shelley's voice. "I'll even bake some brownies, too." She winked.

"Oh, that's so sweet," Shelley said.

"Frankie just goes on and on about your brownies, but you don't have to bother," she protested politely.

"It's no bother at all, hun," she said, giving her hand a pat and calling out for Aubrey, as she got into the beat-up truck.

Shelley, Uncle Frank, and Frankie waved at the sputtering vehicle, as it disappeared into the night.

"Well, this was quite a day, eh, Bambino?" Uncle Frank chimed.

"It was the best birthday ever!" Frankie declared, stretching his little arms wide to hug his mother and his uncle.

"Momma…" he asked, as they walked back up the flagstone path to the house, "can Rusty sleep with me?"

"Yes, baby, at least until we get a bed for him," she agreed, adding, "A dog is a big responsibility, you know. You're going to have to clean his messes and feed him and…." So she began instructing him, as they mounted the steps and went inside.

Shelley had shot several rolls of film that day, wanting to capture every memory she could on film. Frank offered to have them developed, knowing how painful it would be for her to go through them later. He promised to have copies made for Frankie's friends, as well. Their discussion on this ordinarily mundane detail lent an air of finality to her situation. Both knew it was probably the last birthday she would ever celebrate with her son, but neither wanted to acknowledge it.

Later that same evening across town, Ben sat in his office, still ruminating the news he'd been given. Suddenly he heard the out-of-tune coughing of an engine he'd heard a hundred times before. Looking out the grimy office window, he saw Harlan's dilapidated old Chevy pickup pull to a stop on the dark street in front of the garage. The parking lot lampposts provided the only light to silhouette Harlan's next move.

As he watched, Harlan lit something on fire and threw the flaming object toward his garage, miscalculating the distance he needed to throw the homemade firebomb.

Instead of hitting the building, it landed on a pile of old tires and bounced sideways, spinning in the air before smashing and exploding in a brilliant sweep of orange flame in the empty gravel lot, illuminating the night.

Shaking his head in disgust, but seeing no immediate urgency, Ben picked up the phone and called the fire station…then he called Sheriff Tanner.

HARLAN GETS A HOLIDAY

The next day dawned as bright and beautiful as any morning could. Frankie clambered downstairs, with Rusty hot on his heels, both driven by the heavenly aroma of pancakes and bacon.

Uncle Frank sat at the kitchen table, sipping coffee, as Frankie's mother, with her usual perfect timing, placed a stack of steaming hot of flapjacks at Frankie's place at the table, and the same in front of her brother. It was followed by a plate piled high with crisp, thick-cut, country bacon for everyone to dig into.

"Whoa!" Uncle Frank said to Frankie, as he plowed ravenously into his breakfast. "Slow down, hot rod. You act like you're starving."

"Mo, I'mfh..." he started through a mouthful of pancakes. But he saw his mother's reproachful look and stopped talking long enough to finish the food in his mouth and wash it down with a gulp of cold milk.

He gave a "sorry, Momma" look and continued, exclaiming excitedly, "No. I'm gonna teach Rusty some tricks!"

"Baby, he's just a puppy," his mother interjected. "Give

him a little time."

"Oh, I don't know," Uncle Frank protested lightly. "He looks like a smart, little fella. I'll bet he could learn to fetch easily enough. But your mom is right. Give the little guy time to be puppy."

"Yeah, I s'pose you're right," he agreed, tossing a strip of bacon to the hopeful pup.

"Frankie, don't feed him at the table," his mother said gruffly.

"Sorry, Momma."

Then it occurred to him that they had no dog food. "What's he gonna eat then?"

Shelley fetched a saucer and a bowl from the cupboard. Placing a few small strips of bacon and a chunk of pancake on the saucer and pouring a small amount of milk into the bowl, she set them down in front of the bouncing puppy.

"This probably isn't too good for him, but it'll do for now. Maybe you and Uncle Frank can run down to the store and get some real dog food."

"Can we, Uncle Frank?" he implored.

"Sure thing, Bambino; you can drive," he said, straight-faced, as he took another bite of syrup-drenched pancakes.

"Wha…" Frankie's eyes widened, and his mouth fell open.

Shelley nearly dropped the plate she was setting for herself.

"What did you say?" she demanded.

"Just kidding," Frank chuckled, "I had ya for a second there, didn't I? Besides, your feet wouldn't reach the pedals!" He winked at Frankie.

Shelley rolled her eyes and shook her head, as she

sat down. She really loved her brother's sense of humor. Most adults took themselves way too seriously, she thought, but not Frank. He was never afraid to laugh or to act like a kid.

Uncle and nephew rode into town, cracking jokes and laughing. Frankie loved the way everybody turned to stare at the bright red sports car, beaming with pride every time he saw that a kid from school recognized him.

Suddenly, their attention was drawn to the old fire engine sitting in front of Ben's place, the single red bubble on the roof flashing its warning. It was the very same prewar engine that Frank had climbed on many times as a kid, when the volunteer fire department had open house. The bright red machine had been an inspiration for him to become a firefighter, as well as the heroes who manned it.

Next to it sat Sheriff Tanner's patrol car, its own red light flashing. Frank noticed that someone was sitting in the backseat, but he could not tell who it was.

"I wonder what's going on?' he asked himself out loud.

"I dunno," Frankie answered, thinking the question was directed at him. "I hope Uncle Ben's okay."

"Let's check it out," Uncle Frank said, wheeling into the parking lot and stopping a safe distance from the commotion.

They were relieved to see Ben standing nearby and talking with the sheriff and with what Frank assumed was a fire investigator. He and Frankie got out and headed to the cluster of men. As he walked toward them, he noticed a wide, burnt patch in the gravel, near the pile of tires.

"Howdy, Ben," he said, as he approached them.

He introduced himself and Frankie to the sheriff and the investigator, informing them that he was a fireman, too.

"What happened here?"

"That damned fool Harlan tried to burn me out last night," Ben scoffed.

"You're kidding me," Frank answered incredulously.

"Nope," Ben responded. "But just like everything else he ever did….he fucked it up. I was just tellin' the chief here that I saw the whole thing."

He recounted what he saw to Frank, who just stood there, shaking his head. Frankie couldn't believe what he was hearing.

A few minutes later, Sheriff Tanner walked back to his car and opened the rear passenger's door, revealing a harried-looking Harlan sitting with his hands cuffed behind his back.

"Harlan," he started, "you really stepped square into the shit this time. Ben told me that he fired ya, and he told me why. Ya know…he's about the last person in town that was willin' to hire you. Good gawd almighty, boy. What the hell were you thinking?"

"He shouldn't a hit me," Harlan spat.

"Maybe so, and maybe you should've kept that dumbass comment to yourself, too. But not you! Oh no! You had to say something ignorant….as usual. And then you just couldn't let it go, could you?"

"I got a right to say what I want," Harlan insisted.

"Yep, ya do. But does it always have to be something stupid? Harlan….Ben saw the whole thing from his office."

"So," Harlan sneered arrogantly.

"So? So it means that since somebody was in the

building you tried to torch, it ain't just attempted arson…
its attempted murder, too," the sheriff informed him.

"What? Murd…aw, hell no!" Harlan shot back, his
voice becoming shrill.

"I wudn't tryin' ta kill 'im. I just wanted to rattle the ol'
bastard," he protested. "That's why I used a little co'cola
bottle, an' not a big 'un."

"Well, thanks for the confession," Sheriff Tanner,
grinned at him. "Looks like you're gonna be a guest at
Brushy Mountain for a spell."

Then he chuckled, "By the time you get out, you'll
have a better understanding of what it's like to be a
homo. Try not to drop your soap in the shower too often.
When you do take a shower, that is." He finished speaking, wrinkling his nose at Harlan's pungent body odor.

"What the…? Fuck you, Earl. I ain't no queer," Harlan
yelped a bit too defensively.

"Shut the hell up, Harlan!" the Sheriff ordered, his
tone hardening. "You're 'bout a fat hair away from a
good sound beatin' with my night stick. Do yourself a
favor and for once, for just once…keep that dumbass
mouth of yours shut…while you still got teeth." He finished speaking, slamming the door shut and walking
around to get in the driver's seat.

Earl liked Ben…a lot. The no-nonsense engine wiz-
ard kept his squad car faster than anything else in the
county…and he could handle his whiskey, to boot. He
didn't like Harlan…at all, and was grateful that finally
he'd be rid of the bigoted troublemaker for good. Still, he
shuddered to think about what might have happened if
the moronic menace had succeeded.

Stupid jackass! he thought, scowling at Harlan in the
rearview mirror.

Meanwhile, Frank was still talking with Ben, apologizing profusely to his old friend, convinced that it was his fault.

"Ben…I'm so sorry I brought this on you."

"Frank…" Ben said sternly, "don't you fret one minute about it. You didn't do a damn thing except be who you are. Harlan's a goddamned idiot with a brain smaller than a boll weevil's. You can't help that. He'll have some time now to think about what comes out of that sewer hole he calls a mouth. But if I know Harlan, the lesson won't take. I swear to God I don't know why ever I hired the dipshit.

"Besides," he finished, "the moron didn't do anything but burn gravel. That's the story of his life, just one fuckup after another."

Secretly, though, he wondered if his talk with God had anything to do with the results of the failed attack.

He and Frankie left Ben with their well wishes and stopped at the Piggly Wiggly to complete their original mission of getting some dog food. Uncle Frank treated Frankie to a bottle of grape Nehi.

Later that day, Aubrey and Tony showed up to play. Frankie told them about what had happened at Ben's place. But since Frankie's regular visits to Ben were his own private thing and neither of them had been to the garage, their interest was marginal, except for the fire truck. Fire trucks were always cool.

They played with his new G.I. Joe for a while, and then they set up the pup tent. They ran themselves ragged, chasing Rusty and vice versa, until Shelley called them in for a lunch of bologna-and-cheese sandwiches.

That afternoon, after his buddies went home, he and Uncle Frank opened one of the model car kits and started building it.

Dinner time came and halted their construction. After dinner, Uncle Frank stood up and stretched, saying, "Ya know, I feel like a drive before the sun sets. How 'bout you Bambino?"

"You bet!" was the obvious reply. Frankie scrambled from the table and ran upstairs to brush his teeth.

Frank walked over and wrapped his arms around his sister from behind, as she began washing dishes.

"We'll be back after a while," he told her, adding softly, "he'll be okay. I promise."

"Thank you," was all she could bring herself to say.

Frankie raced back into the kitchen.

"I'm ready!" he declared.

"Then let's get rollin'," Uncle Frank replied, just as enthusiastically. He really hated the task ahead, especially right after the joy and happiness of the day before, but it was something he couldn't and wouldn't burden his sister with.

THE END BEGINS

Shelley was still washing dishes, as Frank's Corvette rumbled off into the early evening. As soon as the sound of the engine disappeared, she broke down, sobbing. In a flash of anger, she slammed a plate onto the floor, scattering shards of broken ceramic across the floor and scaring Rusty out of the kitchen with a yelp.

She had barely cleaned the mess up when the doorbell rang, announcing Sarah's arrival. Wiping the tears from her face and straightening her dress, she tried her best to assume a pleasant expression.

But Sarah could see right through her efforts and inquired worriedly, "Shelley, what is it, darlin'?"

Her voice cracked, as she said cryptically, "I'll tell you as soon as Kathleen gets here. I don't think I can say it twice."

That really peaked Sarah's concern, but she didn't push it. The sound of Kathleen's car in the gravel out front meant that it wouldn't be long, anyway. A few minutes later, Shelley was serving tea to her worried friends, her hands trembling.

Over the past few months, as their sons had forged a

strong bond, so had they, growing closer with each visit. Sarah and Shelley had grown especially close, their common ties binding their hearts together.

For Sarah, just having someone she could trust and talk to was something her soul had yearned for. Although she almost never wore makeup, she would occasionally show up with rouge caked on a little too heavy, trying to hide the bruises. But the other two always knew, and, inevitably, she would end up crying her eyes out on one's or the other's shoulder.

"Why do you stay with him?" Kathleen had asked on one occasion.

"Buck has his moments," she had defended. "He wasn't always so mean. In fact, he used to be a real charmer. I think the burden of trying to make the farm work and the pressures of being a father just got to him. He didn't have a very good example to follow, you know."

They were all excuses, she had known, but what else could she have said? She had needed excuses to justify her life, however miserable it might have been.

"Mostly, though," she had continued more honestly, "I stay for my boys. They're my special gifts from God. I can't imagine my life without them. But if I ever tried to take them from Buck, well…" The women had known what the consequences would have been.

Kathleen too, had laid her soul bare, expressing the frustration of leaving everything she knew and loved behind, only to move to a town full of prejudices and devoid of the conveniences and luxuries she'd taken for granted back home. At first, she hadn't been able to understand how having one of the nicest houses in town had set her so far apart from the people of the town. She had tried to warm up to the local women at the beauty parlor or the grocery store, but none had seemed very receptive. Maybe it had been her accent? Or the way she had dressed? Eventually, though, she had begun to understand that the problem lay with them and not with her.

Now she and Sarah sat wondering what news could be so dire as to have Shelley in such a state of anxiety.

"Thank you for coming. I really needed you to be here," Shelley said, trying to work up the nerve to tell them the bitter news.

"I, ah….I don't know any other way to say this, so here goes," she hesitated, taking a deep breath.

"I have, uh…I have cancer…breast cancer, to be specific," she managed to force out. "It's, um…it's… terminal."

"Oh, my God!" Kathleen gasped, clasping a hand over her mouth.

Sarah froze, mouth agape and teacup in hand. After a brief second, she set the cup down and rushed to kneel at Shelley's side, embracing her. "Oh my Dear Lord!" she exclaimed, her voice starting to crack. "How could this happen?"

Kathleen joined Sarah, dabbing at her running mascara. The women rocked together gently, their eyes spilling their heartbreak down their cheeks.

After a few minutes, Shelley pulled herself together enough to whisper a croaking, "Thank you."

She patted Sarah's shoulder with one hand and squeezed Kathleen's hand with the other. The two women remained kneeling by their friend, as they each tried to regain control of their emotions. She had important things to say and didn't want Frankie walking in on such a scene.

She looked into her friends' eyes, Kathleen's smudged with eyeliner and Sarah's red and puffy. She knew she could count on them.

Reading their obvious questions in their faces, she went on.

"A while back, I felt a tiny lump, but I didn't think much about it. I really should have, though. Maybe if I had…" She trailed off.

"Anyway, my doctor said that if I hadn't delayed getting a mammogram done, he would have found it in time to get treatment…or at least a mastectomy," she shuddered. However repulsive that may have been, it could have saved her life.

"But not me. Oh, no. I couldn't fathom anything so terrible happening to me. That sort of thing only happened to other women who didn't take care of themselves, or to older women. So I didn't do anything. Cancer was the furthest thing from my mind. Finally, it started hurting every time I so much as put my bra on, so I finally went to a clinic in Huntsville, a couple weeks ago. But, by then, it was too late. It had spread, and now….it's inoperable. I was such a fool for not paying attention to it sooner." So she tearfully berated herself.

Steeling herself, she continued, "I asked the doctor if he thought that it could have been genetic; I was afraid cancer might be something Frankie could inherit. He said that all the current research says no but that nothing was sure.

"He said breast cancer research lags behind other research, like research for lung cancer, and is still in its infancy. They just don't know a whole lot about what causes it….or how to treat it."

She gave a sardonic grunt, saying, "Infancy?

Somehow, that doesn't sound right in the same sentence as breast cancer.

"He said a lot of women have died needlessly because of simple ignorance brought on by idiotic social stigmas that keep people from talking about women's breasts, as if it's some kind of taboo. I guess that would include me, wouldn't it?

"You know, it's funny that society can highlight them with fashions and even bare them in magazines. But we just don't seem to be able to talk about them in a non-pornographic way. Look at what I'm doing right now. Them? They're breasts, for God's sake. They're not 'tits' or 'boobies' or playthings to be ogled at. They're just breasts. Every woman has them. Why can't we talk about them without giggling or feeling embarrassed?" So she ranted.

Her friends nodded their agreement, realizing their own embarrassment, as she talked about it.

Kathleen reached up and stroked Shelley's tear-dampened face.

Clearing her throat, Sarah acknowledged the eight-hundred-pound gorilla in the room.

"Did he, um…say how long you had?" she asked, knowing the question had to be asked, but wishing it wouldn't be answered.

"Yes, he was able to answer that question. I guess he's seen enough cases to know that with a little more certainty," she answered, somewhat sarcastically.

"He said that I had a year, maybe more…maybe less," she managed to say, before her chin wrinkled and more silent tears flowed.

"Can't anything be done?" Kathleen asked. "I mean… modern medicine and all."

She repeated what she had told Frank, adding, "I don't want my last days with my baby boy to be in some sterile cancer ward.

"I told my doctor that," she said.

"He tried to convince me otherwise, but, eventually, he acknowledged my reasons," she finished, somewhat defiantly.

"He said he'd prescribe pain pills when I needed them. And he assured me that I would need them, especially toward the...end."

After what seemed an eternity, Sarah asked yet another poignant question, "What's going to happen to Frankie?"

"Frank is going to..." she choked on the words she was loath to say, "Frank is going to take him...when... when the time comes.

"Oh... my baby, my sweet little baby!" she sobbed.

Sarah knew that the time would also come when Shelley would become bedridden and would need help with even basic personal hygiene tasks.

"Shelley, sweetheart, at some point, you're going to need special care."

Her bluntness got Shelley's attention.

"But don't you worry one bit. Whatever you need, I'll be here for you, I promise."

Then, looking at Kathleen, she added, "We'll be here."

Kathleen nodded gratefully.

"What about Buck?" Shelley asked. "Surely he won't like you spending too much time with a dying woman."

"To hell with Buck," Sarah countered defiantly, "he doesn't have a say in this."

When she could finally speak, Kathleen told them that she had a cousin who worked in the cancer clinic of a major hospital up north. She said that she would get all the literature on the subject that she could.

"She told me once that a cancer patient's diet had a great deal to do with how they reacted to treatment. I'll call her and make a list of what you should eat and drink, okay, hun?" she said, desperately searching for hope.

"We're going to take good care of you…and Frankie. I swear on the Rosary," she said, making the sign of the cross as she said it.

Shelley was overwhelmed with the outpouring of love and support. "Will you two promise me something?" she asked.

"Anything you want," Kathleen said, getting a nod of agreement from Sarah.

"Will both of you please go get examined…as soon as you can," she beseeched them.

"Yes, darlin', we will," Sarah promised.

"Of course, we will," Kathleen agreed.

"There's a new women's clinic in Memphis. I'll make an appointment for both of us tomorrow," she said, looking at Sarah.

"I'll take care of everything. Don't you worry. It'll be nice to have someone to ride with," she said with a smile, knowing that Sarah didn't have the financial resources to afford expensive medical procedures, like the new mammograms.

Sarah smiled back gratefully. Normally, she would have declined such an expensive offer, but she realized that she was genuinely frightened at the horrible prospect of going through what Shelley was suffering.

ROOT BEER BY THE
LIGHT OF THE MOON

Meanwhile, as the women shared their grief, Uncle Frank and his unsuspecting namesake cruised to the A&W Drive-in for a root beer float. Frank was working up the courage to do something he knew would shatter his nephew's innocent world.

He had to tell him that God, in his infinite wisdom, was going to take away the single most important person in his young life, because, among the wonders God had created, he had also placed snakes in the grass. God's divinity was revealing some of its more perverse and perplexing facets.

Briefly, he toyed with the idea of putting the hurtful task off until a better time, but when would the time be better? He was here now, and he wasn't sure that he would have the nerve to do it later. His sister's symptoms were only going to get worse, and he owed it to Frankie to be honest with him.

"Whatsa matter, Uncle Frank?" he asked, spooning the floating ice cream. He could tell his normally jovial uncle had something on his mind.

"Wanna take a night cruise?" Uncle Frank asked, as he put his empty cup on the tray next to the drive-in squawk box and started the engine with a roar, causing Frankie to grin broadly. He didn't want to break his heart in such a public place.

"Heck, yeah; where to?" Frankie replied eagerly.

His innocent enthusiasm caused Frank more than a little distress.

"Ya know, Bambino….back when I was a kid, I used to like to go down to Lake Owen whenever I had something on my mind. Ever been there at night? It's pretty cool."

"Naw," he answered. "Momma takes me there sometimes, but it's always during the daytime."

"What's it like at night?" he asked. "I bet it's spooky, huh? Some of the kids say that there's a monster that comes out at night down there, you know, like the Gillman in the movie, *Creature from the Black Lagoon*."

"But I don't believe that," he finished, bravely.

"Well, you're right; there are no monsters," his uncle reassured him.

"There's nothing down there but teenagers doing what teenagers do in the moonlight," he absentmindedly mused.

"What're they doin'?" Frankie's curiosity begged.

"Uhh…we'll leave that one for another time, okay buddy?" his uncle answered, dodging the subject, for the time being. It suddenly occurred to him that it would be up to him, not the boy's own mother, to have the birds-and-the-bees talk with him. The thought gave him a knot in his stomach.

A short while later, they pulled up to the picnic area,

and Uncle Frank doused his headlights, as the tires crunched loudly through the gravel parking lot, dotted with cars, whose steamy windows hinted at the activities inside.

The memories they brought back to him were mixed, some good, others not so good. It was in this very same dusty lot that his life had changed forever.

Putting sufficient distance between them and the adolescent breeding ground, he pointed his car at the silent lake and came to a stop, killing the disruptively loud engine. Moonbeams shimmered on the lake's sparkling surface.

Under different circumstances, the scene would be beautiful, but, now, it looked only forlorn and heartbreaking.

He pivoted halfway in his seat to face his nephew. The full moon supplied plenty of light to show the clueless boy's innocent face.

"Frankie…" he started. "Buddy, I…ah…I got something to tell you, and it's not good."

Frankie stopped sipping on his half-empty root beer and looked at his uncle.

"What is it, Uncle Frank?" he inquired sheepishly. If his uncle said it wasn't good, he wasn't sure he wanted to know.

"It's about your momma. She, ah . . . ," he hesitated, raising Frankie's alarm.

"What about my momma?" he demanded sharply, panic beginning to emerge.

Taking a deep breath, his uncle continued, "Frankie, uh…your momma is sick." He spoke bluntly, not knowing how else to approach it.

"Sick?" the boy asked urgently. "Whaddya mean she's

sick?" His heart started thumping in his chest.

The thought of his mother being anything but perfectly well had never crossed his mind. How could she be sick?

"Well, she…uh…has a real bad sickness…in her chest," Frank said, trying to find a way to describe a horrible disease to the boy.

"Is it like a bad cold or sumpthin'?" Frankie ventured hopefully.

"No, buddy, I wish it was, but…"

His nephew looked at him in confusion and fear.

"Frankie…you've heard of…um…cancer, haven't you?" he continued, hoping it wouldn't be too traumatic for him.

"Uh-huh," he answered weakly. "Mr. Pauley talked about it in health class last year. He said it was really bad and that people die…."

Then the realization hit him, and he squeaked in a constricted voice, "M…Momma has ca…"

Frank could hear the heartbreak in his nephew's voice. The moonlight glinted on the tears beginning to well up in his eyes.

"*No!*" Frankie suddenly shouted, throwing his cup to the ground outside the car.

"*You're lyin'!*" he screamed at his uncle.

"*My momma is not gonna die!*" he yelled, as he yanked open the door and bolted from the car, running into the darkness.

Frank leapt out after him, calling for him to wait.

The devastated boy ran randomly into the night, stopping only after he tripped on an unseen tree root and fell face first onto the thick, newly mown grass.

His uncle slid to a stop next to him and fell to his

knees, scooping up the hysterical boy in his arms.

Frankie thrashed and punched at his uncle, as he tried to hold him close.

"You lie! You Lie! You lie!" he repeated, until he broke down into convulsing spasms of utter despair. His uncle rocked him back and forth, crying almost as hard, himself.

Interminable minutes passed, as uncle and nephew poured out their grief, each clinging tightly to the other.

"Ca...ca...can't the... doctors f...fix her up?" Frankie asked, sucking in deep sobs, as he tried to speak.

"I really wish they could, Bambino," his uncle answered through his own sobs. "I truly wish to God they could. I'd gladly give my own life for hers, if it would mean that she could stay here with you. But the doctor said that she was too sick."

"Does it hurt her?" he asked meekly, afraid of the answer.

His uncle would spare him that truth, saying, "Just a little. It makes her tired, but that's all." The lie was monumental, but he had broken his nephew's heart enough for one night.

"I seen her napping a lot," Frankie reflected sadly. "But she said she was just tired from work." His little chin wrinkled, as he fell back into tears for his mother.

"I'm s..sc..scared, Uncle Frank," he sputtered between sobs.

"I know you are, little buddy," he said, trying to comfort the grieving boy. "But you got be brave for your her."

"I'm always here for you, if you need me," he said, gently wiping the stream of tears from Frankie's cheeks. "But you gotta be there for her. She's really going to need you."

The boy laid his head on his uncle's chest, and, after a long, painful silence, he said, sniffing, "I'm sorry I called you a liar an' for hittin' you."

"Don't apologize, Bambino," his uncle said soothingly. "I understand. I feel the same way."

"She's your mom, but she's also my sister," he choked.

Frankie felt a twinge of guilt for not thinking about his uncle's feelings.

Frank cradled his grieving nephew for a while longer, until Frankie lifted his head and wiped his running nose and tears on his sleeve, saying, "I wanna see my momma."

"Me, too, little one; me, too," he sighed.

Walking back to the car and holding his nephew's hand, he doubted that he would ever come back to this miserable place again, now that it held yet another bad memory for him. Leave it to the hopeful lovers, whose lives had not yet been wracked by the pains of reality.

He remembered that he had said that there were no monsters. But he had lied. There were monsters, just not the Hollywood type, eventually slain by the hero, but, yes, there were monsters.

They rode in silence for a while, each one lost in his own grief. Eventually, Uncle Frank spoke, "Bambino, your momma is going to need you to be very strong for her. Ya think you can do that, buddy?"

"I'll try to," he answered, in a distant voice, "if I can."

Then he vowed with a measure of determination, "No… I mean, I will, for sure. She's my momma."

"Uncle Frank," he asked after a few quiet minutes, "why does God wanna take my momma away from me?"

It was the second time he'd been asked that stabbing question, and he could only give the same answer, "Well,

Bambino, I reckon he needs another angel in Heaven."

His anger at God was growing, though, in the back of his mind, he wondered if, somehow, this was retribution for his own sins. *Can't you just punish me, God?* he pleaded silently.

"She'll make a good one, won't she?" Frankie replied sullenly, sniffing back his tears.

A lump formed in his uncle's throat as he choked out, "She'll be the best one up there!"

Pausing to gather his emotions, he continued, "But she's not there yet, buddy, so let's make her as happy as we can until then, okay?"

"Yeah," was all Frankie could squeak out. He was trying his hardest, but his little heart had been shattered into a million tiny pieces, and he wasn't sure he could keep it together when he saw his mother.

As they pulled up to the house, Frankie saw the pickup and the Chrysler parked out front. He panicked, thinking his friends were there. He didn't want them to see him crying like a baby.

"What are they doin' here?" he asked his uncle desperately.

Sensing his nephew's apprehension, Frank said, "Relax, buddy. It's just their moms. They're here to help your momma. She's going to need all the help she can get from now on. She needs friends, too, just like you do, and they're a couple of really nice ladies."

"Yeah, they are," Frankie breathed a sigh of relief, saying sadly, "Good. I'm glad she's not alone. I like their moms. You're right; they are really nice ladies."

"Did you know that I went to school with Aubrey's mom?" he asked, attempting to take some of the edge off of Frankie's mood.

"Uh-huh, Momma told me," he answered hollowly. His tone told his uncle that the attempt was futile.

As soon as the car came to a stop, Frankie's resolve to be calm dissolved instantly. He fumbled the door open and made a stumbling dash up the path for his mother, yelling, *"Momma! Momma!"*

The women fell silent as soon as they heard the rumble of Frank's car approaching. Shelley drew a deep breath, dreading what she knew was coming.

"Well, I guess it's done," she whispered.

"What's done?" Kathleen inquired.

"Frank insisted on telling Frankie for me; God bless him," she said, her voice cracking under the agony she felt in anticipating her son's reaction.

"Oh, sweet Jesus," Sarah mumbled softly, her own heart breaking for the boy and for Frank. It had to have been an agonizing task for him.

"We should go," she said, glancing at Kathleen.

"No, please stay," Shelley implored. "I think we're all going to need you both for just a little while longer."

Hearing her son's desperate cries as he ran up the path, she gasped quietly, "Oh, no… my poor baby."

The screen door flew open with a slam. Frankie raced to his mother, as she rose from her chair. Flinging his arms around her waist, he buried his face in her stomach, crying, "Momma….Momma….please don't die!" His muffled plea brought the other mothers to tears. "Don't leave me, Momma! Please don't leave me!"

Gathering all her strength, she fought back her own breakdown. She wanted to be strong for him.

"Frankie…" she started, gently prying him away and sitting back down to face him. "I love you more than anything in the world. You know that, don't you?"

Unable to speak, he nodded, tears streaming down his cheeks once more.

"Then you know that Momma will always be with you...right here." She placed her hand over his heart. "Don't you ever forget that, baby."

So far, her wall was holding up, but she could feel the cracks beginning to weaken it. "No matter where you go, or what you do, Momma will always be with you. I promise, angel boy."

Frankie looked up at her, sobbing, "That's what Uncle Frank said you were gonna be, Momma...an angel."

Kathleen rushed out of the room for the front porch, struggling to hold back her own meltdown.

She bumped hard into Frank, just as he opened the screen door. He caught her by her shoulders, as she rebounded off of him.

"Are you okay?" he asked.

"No, I'm not," she sobbed, momentarily startled.

She collapsed into his arms in tears, counting on them to hold her up.

"It's just not fair," she whimpered. "Why her? And that poor little boy!" Her tears flowed freely.

Frank just gently wrapped his arms around her, as she laid her head against his chest, his shirt still moist from his nephew's tears. He, too, was speechless.

But, what about me? he thought. *I'm hurting, too.*

Everyone's focus had been on Frankie, but his sister's imminent death was tearing him apart, as well.

Frankie and Shelley were all he had. No uncles or aunts, no cousins, no grandparents. No spouse to lean on, no one else at all.

But he had to shove his feelings back down into the armor-plated hole he had created for them and rivet the door shut. Right now, they needed him. Later, he would allow his heart to be shredded in private.

"We'll be okay," he whispered hoarsely, the implication slipping out unintentionally.

Kathleen gently pushed away, embarrassed at her reaction.

"How thoughtless of me," she said, wiping at her tears. "I'm so sorry, Frank. I'd forgotten that you're hurting, too."

She raised her hand and stroked his face sympathetically. "I know how much you really love your sister… and how much she loves you."

"They're all I've got, Kath," he said, struggling to keep the desperation from cracking through his tenuously held-together bravado. It wouldn't do any good for his sister or his nephew to see him break down, though that is exactly what he so desperately wanted to do.

"You're such a wonderful brother," Kathleen soothed. "I'm sorry. I don't mean to be blubbering so much. It's just that I've grown very fond of her and of Frankie, too."

"No need to apologize. She's lucky to have friends like you and Sarah. I really appreciate all y'all have done for her….and Frankie."

Kathleen smiled and said, "I must look an awful sight."

Then she prattled, "Oh, look at your shirt, the mascara…I'm so sorry, Frank."

"Don't worry about it," he said. "That's what I get for wearing a white shirt."

"Besides, it'll give the guys at the station something to talk about," he joked glibly.

Kathleen dabbed at her mascara-streaked face with an already soaked tissue.

"I need some air. I'll be all right in a minute," she said, as she walked to the porch swing and sat down.

Frank smiled as brave a smile as he could muster, nodded, and went into the house.

Sarah and Kathleen stayed for a short while longer, before leaving the grieving family to themselves. Both women cried earnestly and freely in the privacy of their cars.

Sarah was particularly overcome with grief and spent nearly half an hour sitting in her pickup after she'd pulled up outside her home. Buck finally appeared on the porch, wondering why his wife was still sitting in the truck. She eventually got out, after wiping the tears from her eyes.

Even in the dim light of the dangling porch bulb, he could tell she was very upset.

"What's the matter?" he asked, in an uncharacteristically gentle voice.

She relayed the sad news to him, struggling to maintain her emotions.

"Yer shittin' me! Now that jus' ain't right!" he declared, drawing his wife close in a consoling hug. Though crude and uncultured, the big man had his tender side. It was the side Sarah had fallen in love with, those many years and tears ago. It was the side she lamented seeing so rarely. Softly, she began sobbing again.

"My God, Kath. What's wrong?" Mike asked, startled at seeing her normally perfectly appointed face streaked with makeup.

"It's Shelley, Mike," she croaked, her voice dry from sobbing the whole way home.

"Shelley? What happened?"

Kathleen told him the news, stopping several times to

regain her composure.

"Holy Mother of God!" he exclaimed, embracing his wife, as she broke down yet again.

THAT'S NOT FAIR!

Uncle Frank left the next day after lunch. He half-heartedly suggested a picnic, but neither Frankie nor his mother where up to it. The previous evening still weighed heavily on them.

"Bambino…" he started, as he sat in the convertible, "I'm counting on you to be the man of the house." He clapped Frankie on the shoulder.

"He already is," Shelley said, smiling down at her son.

"He's strong, just like his daddy," she proclaimed.

Frankie couldn't meet her loving gaze. He wasn't as sure about it as she seemed to be.

"I will be, Uncle Frank," he assured his uncle, with as much confidence as he could muster.

Shelly leaned down and kissed her brother on the cheek.

"Now you be careful, ya hear? Don't be drivin' like a maniac," she admonished, playfully.

"Oh, how you wound me, little sis!" he protested. "I am a superb driver!"

"Mm-hmm!" she replied skeptically, although she knew it was true.

Both adults were making every effort to lighten the mood and reassure Frankie, but he could see through the charade.

"Uncle Frank…please come back soon, okay?" he begged, a desperate sadness in his voice.

His uncle winked, saying, "You just try to keep me away!"

With that, he started the engine and waved them good-bye. As soon as he was on solid pavement, he punched the accelerator, his tires spinning as he fishtailed onto the road. He would drive some of his frustration away on the winding country roads between Haleyville and the Interstate….cops be damned.

Shelley shook her head and said, "That brother of mine…"

Frankie just stood there, feeling strangely alone, and watched the car disappear down the road. Then he turned and wrapped his arms around his mother. No tears this time, though. He had promised that he would be strong, and he was determined to do just that.

Sarah sent Buck and Waylon into town on an errand so she could have Aubrey to herself. Waylon had taken the news bravely, but she could tell that it bothered him deeply, too. Sarah suspected that her older son had a teenage crush on Shelley.

"Aubrey!" she called from the front porch. "Honey, Momma's gotta talk to you about somethin'."

Looking up from playing with Scooter, he saw the somber expression on his mother's face.

"Whut is it, Maw? Did I do sumpthin'?" he asked with concern, as he approached her.

"No, darlin' boy," she answered. "You haven't done anything wrong. In fact, you've been a little angel."

He felt relieved, but was still concerned.

She paused, trying to figure out how she was going to explain Shelly's illness to him.

"I am so proud of the way you've been such a good friend to Frankie. He's very lucky to have a friend like you."

His mother was acting strangely. He knew most all of her moods, but there was something different in her voice that he couldn't put his finger on.

"What's the matter, Maw? You don't look so good."

"Well, honey…come have a seat with Momma," she said, motioning him to sit beside her on the steps.

"I got some bad news about Frankie and his momma," she started.

His young mind raced to imagine what it might be. Were they moving away? Had he done something?

She went on, "Aubrey, honey, Frankie's momma is sick…real sick."

He felt relief that he hadn't done anything wrong and felt guilty for feeling relieved. His concern for his friend instantly eclipsed everything else.

"What is it, Maw?" he asked, dreading the answer.

It took effort, but she explained the nature of Shelley's illness to him. She had to struggle to keep her composure when she reached the point of telling him that Shelley was ultimately going to die.

"Aw….no…that cain't be right!" he said, choking up. "She's too nice a lady fer that."

"Frankie needs his maw," he whimpered. "Cain't Jesus help her?"

"Oh, sweetheart," was all she could say. She drew him into her arms, as he started to cry and began to rock him gently, her heart breaking for him.

After several long minutes, he looked up at her and asked, "What's he gonna do when she's gone? He's gotta live somewheres."

Then he ventured, "Can he live with us?"

"Honey child," she said, looking into his puffy eyes, "I sometimes wonder how you can keep such a big heart in such a little chest."

She patted his heaving chest.

"But, no, darlin', he's gonna be living with his Uncle Frank when his momma's gone."

Aubrey stared back momentarily, and then he said, in an even sadder voice, "You mean he's gonna be leavin', huh?" He broke out into a new round of tears.

Sarah hadn't anticipated this reaction, and her heart broke anew for him.

Across town, on a tree-lined street in Haleyville's "good" neighborhood, Kathleen opened the door to her son's room and stood for a moment, watching him as he lay prone on the floor, carefully penciling in the colors in one of the books Uncle Frank had given him.

"Tony? Sweetie, can I talk to you for a minute?"

"Yeah, sure Mom," he replied.

"Look what I've done so far!" he said excitedly, as he spun into a sitting position and presented the book to her. "It's the Green Lantern."

"That's lovely, dear . . . ," she started.

"Yeah, Frankie's uncle is awesome!" Tony beamed, interrupting his mother.

"Sweetie," she insisted, "I need to talk to you about something."

"Oh, okay Mom, sorry," he apologized lightly. "What's up?"

"It's about Frankie and his mom," she said.

The sullen tone in her voice finally got through to him. "Gee, Mom. You don't look so good. Is something wrong?"

She took a deep breath, walked over to his bed, and sat down. "Come here and sit by me, Anthony. I have some bad news to tell you," she said, patting the mattress beside her.

Anthony? This must be real serious. "Did something happen to them?" he asked.

"Well, yes and no," she answered, evasively. Seeing his eyebrows rise, she hurried on, "Frankie's okay, but it's his mom. She's really sick."

"Sick?" he asked. "Whudya mean 'sick'?"

"Real sick, darling. She has, um…she has cancer," she blurted, not knowing how else to say it.

"Cancer?" he asked, his brow furrowing, as he tried to grasp the magnitude of the announcement.

"Cancer?" he repeated more urgently, his eyes widening. "Isn't that what Uncle Sal had?"

His father's brother had died five years ago. Memories of his uncle were vague, but not the memories of the sadness that his death caused his family, especially his father.

"Well, yes," she answered, "but Uncle Sal had a different kind of cancer." She wasn't sure why she had made that distinction. She'd have to explain it to him, but not right this minute.

"Is she gonna die, too?" he preempted her explanation, as he turned his gaze to the floor.

Taken aback by the directness of the question, she hesitated and then said, "Yes, I'm afraid so."

An awkward silence followed, while she struggled to control her feelings and fought for the next thing to say to him. He lifted his watering eyes to her and managed to say in a weak voice, "That's not fair, Mom." Then suddenly he reached to hug her, burying his face into her breast.

"No, darling, it's not," she, too, began to cry. "It's not fair at all."

Mother and son sat in silence, both agonizing for their friends.

Then Tony asked, "Mom, what's Frankie gonna do? I mean, when she, um…you know…dies? Where's he gonna live? Do ya suppose he might wanna live with us?"

"Sweetheart, that is such a wonderful thought," she said, "and I truly wish that he could. But he's going to live with Uncle Frank in…Nashville."

"Wha…but…he's…?" his chin wrinkled, as he realized that Frankie would be leaving Haleyville, probably for good.

Kathleen felt that she had not handled things very well.

"Hopefully, that won't happen for a very long time. But he's really going to need you and Aubrey to stick by him. That's what friends are for."

"I know, Mom, I will . . ." he said, straining to keep from crying more.

"It's just that . . ." he couldn't continue, so he turned away and shoved his face into the pillows on his bed.

As if the heavens, themselves, cried for the three children, a late-afternoon summer rainstorm stirred up and began depositing its multitude of tears throughout the quiet, little town.

The next meeting of the Musketeers was subdued. No one felt like playing, and none of the boys knew how to broach the subject with one another. Frankie was afraid he'd start bawling, and his buddies felt as if they were being nosey.

Nobody said anything, as they sat leaning against the old oak tree in Frankie's yard, facing away from each other. Finally, Tony broke the ice.

"Um…I'm real sorry about your mom," he said to Frankie, who was idly petting Rusty.

"Yeah, me, too," Aubrey offered.

"Thanks fellas," Frankie said softly, still stroking the puppy.

"Your mom is a supernice lady," Tony said.

"Yeah, she really is," Aubrey added, not knowing what else to do but to agree with Tony.

"She's a great mom," Frankie whispered, struggling to keep from crying.

Aubrey felt the pain in his voice and moved over to squat down beside him, putting a reassuring hand on his shoulder.

"Um, ya know…" he whispered into Frankie's ear, "it's jus' me an' Tony. An' it's okay if ya cry fer yer maw. I dun some cryin' fer her myself last night, truth be known."

Frankie turned his watering eyes up at the boy. Aubrey was the bravest, toughest kid he knew, but he was also the most caring person he knew. He simply nodded at his big friend and let his tears flow.

After a few, long, awkward minutes, he looked up at his friends, expecting to be embarrassed by his tears. But, instead, he saw the other two boys quietly shedding tears of their own.

For some reason, the sight of the huge Aubrey and of the much smaller Tony sitting there with tears rolling down their cheeks struck him as funny. He began to giggle lightly; then he laughed out loud in earnest.

"You should see you two goobers!" he laughed bravely through his tears.

"You got a snot rocket hangin' down!" he said, pointing at Tony.

"Why you . . . ," Tony growled as he wiped his nose on his sleeve and leapt for Frankie. All three joined in on a free-for-all wrestling match, shoving their sadness into the special little pouch all boys keep handy for such painful and embarrassing emotions.

No mention was made after that initial acknowledgement. Whenever the subject would come up, they referred to it as "that thing" and quickly passed it by. There was nothing a young boy could do about it, so they just did what young boys do. They played to forget their troubles.

Together, they escaped into their fantasy worlds, pretending to defeat monsters and armies as only a superhero could, leaving the real monsters of the world for the grown-ups to fight. Their childhood was racing by, its innocence already cracked and tarnished by reality, and the boys were determined to enjoy every moment they could for as long as they could.

NEW BEGINNINGS

However awful the news of Frankie's mother had been, the summer had otherwise been a triumph for them. Neither of them could remember when they'd had so much fun or had so many adventures. It had truly been a summer of wonders for each of them.

But as summer always does, it began to fade into autumn, and that meant only one thing... the beginning of a new school year.

For the first time in his life, school was not a harbinger of humiliation and self-doubt for Aubrey. It had always been an agonizing experience for him. There were things that he knew he should be learning but that he never seemed able to do so.

Frankie had given him his copy of *The Call of the Wild,* after tiring of reading it to him during sleepovers. He loved reading about Buck, the sled dog, even though the brave animal shared a name with his not-so-inspiring father.

Even the comic books were surprisingly helpful in improving his reading and comprehension skills, though his mother might not agree. He began to realize that if he really wanted to know or to understand something, then reading about it was important. Gradually, reading became easier for him.

His desire to know more about the world around him grew. His vocabulary grew, as well, though he still managed to mangle pronunciations.

Help came from surprising sources. Dividing candy bars, M&Ms and other things between the three boys helped him comprehend fractions and division.

He found that building models taught him that instructions were very important and could be quite helpful when they were followed.

To his own surprise and delight, he had begun understanding much of what had been so elusive to him before, just in time to graduate from the fifth grade.

No longer intimidated by the specters of classrooms full of snickering kids and hovering teachers, he beamed with pride, as he walked into school, officially a sixth grader. He looked forward to a much better year, this time around.

"Howdy, Miss Shockley!" he called cheerfully across the crowded hallway. "I made it ta the sixth grade!"

"Yes, you did, Mr. Denton," she acknowledged, waving back. "I'm very proud of you. How was your summer?"

"It was real good, ma'am. Thank ya fer askin'," he answered politely.

"That's great," she said; then she asked, with a reassuring smile, "Would you please come by my classroom before recess. I'd like a word with you."

"Sure thang, Miss Shockley," he answered, wondering what she could have on her mind.

"Aubrey's got a girlfriend! Aubrey's got a girlfriend!"

Tony teased, as they walked away, seeing Miss Shockley's smile.

"Huh?" Aubrey asked, puzzled; then, realizing what Tony was saying, he yelped, "Oh man! That's gross. She's a ol' woman!"

"Yer jus' sick!" he said, reaching to grab Tony.

The smaller boy easily evaded his grasp, but he spun around and accidentally collided with another, larger boy.

"Oops! Sorry, man," he said, as he started to bounce back.

"'Sorry' didn't cut it, shrimp!" the boy barked, shoving Tony backwards into Aubrey. "You stepped on my new Converse All Stars, ya punk. I oughta kick yer ass!"

"You ain't kickin' nobody's ass," Aubrey growled, as he moved forward to step in between Tony and the threatening sixth grader.

But Tony shoved his way in front of Aubrey, his fists balled and ready at his side.

"I said I was sorry. It was an accident, an' if that ain't good enough, then tough shit!" he growled, every bit as menacing as Aubrey.

Striding up like a pissed-off banty rooster, he added, "If you ever touch me again, I'm gonna shove my fist down your fricken' throat! Got it?"

Aubrey and Frankie were shocked, and they looked at Tony, as if they'd never seen him before.

The other boy stepped back, confused and not knowing what to think about the little hellcat that stood glowering at them, teeth gritted and fists cocked and loaded.

"Uh, yeah….um…it's cool, man," the boy said, looking around for an escape route. As he walked away, he cast a glance back at Tony, unsure of what had just happened.

"What're you two goons lookin' at?" a grim-faced Tony demanded of Frankie and Aubrey.

Without taking his eyes off of Tony, Aubrey asked, "Hey, Frankie, ya ever seen that movie 'bout them body snatchers from outer space that hatch fake people from giant bean pods?"

"Yeah," Frankie whispered back. "Maybe we should check out Tony's house."

"What?" Tony shot back.

"Yooz guys act like ya never seen a guy stick up for himself before," he said; then he lightly sucker-punched Aubrey in the stomach and bolted away before Aubrey could respond.

"Ooof! Come back here ya lil' twerp!" Aubrey wheezed, as he and Frankie leapt into hot pursuit.

When they finally caught up to him, Aubrey said, "Whut the heck was that all about? He coulda cleaned yer clock, man!"

"Yeah, he coulda," Tony answered, "but he didn't. Did ya see it?"

"He backed down…from me!" he boasted.

"You were right, Aub. I really get it, now. It don't matter how big you are. What matters is how you are big. Jus' like how a little dog can make a big one run away."

He had fretted all summer about how he would handle himself when the first bully came along. He knew the bullies would come along. They always did.

All the times he had spent wrestling, pretending to battle monsters and savages, and then wrestling some more had helped to prepare him for the onslaught of bullies and thugs that always prowled the hallways and the playground. Apparently, Aubrey's coaching had paid off. Superheroes had to know how to fight, and now he felt as if he did, even though no real fighting had occurred.

Helping Aubrey with chores on the farm had put solid bulk on his once-soft and weak frame. Pitching bales of hay and shoveling manure had added sinew and muscle to his arms, legs, and back, and he had discovered fearlessness on the back of a mule. His self-confidence had mushroomed to the point of near cockiness as he strutted down the hallway, his newly muscled chest puffed out.

However, up until just now, he hadn't been sure that he had the nerve to back up his bravado when the moment of truth came.

But the moment had presented itself, and he had stood his ground. He no longer doubted himself. Someone bigger than him had backed down from him. That had never happened before. Though he wasn't anywhere near ten feet tall, he sure felt like it, and he felt bulletproof, to boot, even though his stomach was doing flip-flops as the adrenaline wore off.

He imagined a cape hanging from his shoulders, gently flying behind him in the breeze.

"That was really sumpthin', lil' buddy!" Aubrey congratulated, pounding him on the back. "I'm doggone proud o'ya!"

"Yeah, me, too!" Frankie offered. "That was far out!"

The Three Musketeers headed off down the hall, laughing and joking.

Frankie and Aubrey ended up in separate classrooms and only saw each other during lunch and at recess. Tony's classroom was closest to the playground, and he got there first, so he waited for the other two just outside the double doors.

It had been a couple of days since he'd faced down the sixth grader, so he was not paying attention when the boy walked up behind and grabbed him, pulling him into a gap between the school building and a portable classroom, accompanied by another boy.

"Where's yer bodyguard now, ya jerkoff?" the boy Tony had faced down goaded, shoving him against the wall.

"Yeah, where's yer gorilla, Carillo?" the second one taunted.

"Hey," he continued, looking at his cohort, and then snickering, "Get it? Carillo's gorilla." He laughed, impressed with his own limited wit.

The two bullies took turns shoving him back and forth.

This time, there was no audience—probably, Tony thought, as he was being shoved, to keep anyone from rescuing him, as Aubrey had done the year before. This time, though, Tony was not as intimidated as they had thought he would be.

Much to their surprise, he went completely wild, screaming, *"I'm gonna kill you, you sonuvbitch! I'm gonna kill you!"* as he flew into them, swinging his fist and swearing a blue streak, getting a few good punches and kicks in before being overpowered by the two larger boys.

Frankie walked through the doors leading to the playground, just in time to see Aubrey dash into the place where Tony had been dragged. He quickly followed and saw a melee of fists and feet, as Aubrey dove into the ruckus, grabbing shirts, hair, or anything he could get his hands on.

Then he saw Tony's black high-top sneakers scrambling at the bottom of the pile. This time, there was no hesitation, no soul searching, no moral justification. His friend was in trouble, and that's all that mattered. Instantly, he joined the fray and began tugging on a fistful of blond hair and an ear, as he dragged one of the attackers off of his friend as easily as he'd tossed bags of feed in Aubrey's barn.

Within seconds of finding Tony being double-teamed, Aubrey and Frankie had evened things out very nicely. Aubrey had the biggest attacker in a headlock, with the boy screaming, "*I give! I give!*"

"*No! He's mine!*" Tony screamed, as he swiped Frankie's hand from the other boy's hair. With the speed and agility of a cat, he leapt on the boy's chest and started pounding his face as hard and as fast as he could until Aubrey pried him off, saying, "Let's git outta here b'fore ol' Pike shows up."

Tony thrashed at the shocked and whimpering boy, as Aubrey pulled him off, landing a glancing kick to the boy's mouth, leaving him bleeding and crying.

"*Ya sonuvabitch! I'll kill ya!*" he yelled back at his attackers, as they turned to make their escape.

"What was that all about?" Frankie demanded, as the boys snuck around the building to another entry.

"Well, I come outa the doors and heard some racket over between the buildin's," Aubrey explained, between heavy breaths. "I didn't know it was you, Tony; I jus' seen two guys whoopin' up on one, an' so…" Then he shrugged.

"I coulda handled 'em!" Tony declared, giving each of them a sharp look, before adding, "But thanks, anyway, guys."

Then he raised his right fist, as if clenching a sword, and yelled "All for one, and one for all!"

All three joined in the salute. This time, it really meant something. It hadn't been just a game. They really were Musketeers, weren't they? They had fought a real fight, side by side, in defense of one of their own. That's what friends do for each other, isn't it?

"I reckon them buttholes know better'n ta mess with ya, now, huh?" Aubrey proclaimed, patting Tony hard on the back, nearly knocking him over, but getting a huge grin, in return.

"Did you see ol' Tony here? He was like a ferocious tornado!" he said to Frankie.

"Yeah, it was awesome," Frankie declared, his own adrenaline still flowing and feeling proud that he'd stepped up to the plate when he needed to.

Their victory celebration was short-lived, though. As soon as they stepped into the hallway, an agitated Principal Pike roared from just yards away, *"You three... stop right where you are!"*

They froze in their tracks, giving each other the *"Uh-oh, we're busted"* look.

"So..." he started. "What do we have here?" The portly, middle-aged man circled the boys like a wolf assessing his prey, looking for weakness and waiting to pounce.

The three boys noticed a teacher helping the bloodied aggressors through the clinic doorway just up the hall. The boys appeared to be milking their situations for all the sympathy they could get, whimpering like babies... until they looked up and saw the Musketeers grinning maliciously at them.

Tony stuck his tongue out at them, earning a sharp,

"Hey boy, I'm talkin' to you!" from Principal Pike.

The burly principal herded the Musketeers toward his office, casting warning glances at the children in the crowded hallway, as they parted, allowing him to escort the battling desperados to their doom.

Tony and Frankie knew that they would be in trouble when they got home, but it would be a lecture and a grounding, at worst. But they were genuinely worried about how badly Aubrey would be punished.

Just as they had expected, Aubrey showed up the next day with a fresh black eye, and, this time, he had a limp in his right leg.

"My paw thinks I'm gittin' too big fer jus' a smackin'," he explained in a whisper to Frankie. "So now he kicks me, too."

He fell silent for a moment, then softly vowed, "One o' these days, he ain't gonna hit me no more!"

"Oh, an ya'll cain't come over fer a while, neither."

HE'S A WHAT?

That afternoon, when school let out and as Frankie was on his way to catch the bus, a pudgy boy with stringy black hair and thick freckles called out to him. An even chubbier boy with dark brown, curly hair stood next to him.

"Hey….wudn't that you I seen ridin' in that there red Corvette?"

Thinking he was going to hear envious praise, Frankie smiled and replied, "Yeah. Sure was. That's my uncle's car. Cool, ain't it."

"Yeah, the car's cool," the boy sneered. "Too bad yer uncle's a goobersmoochin' homo."

"What did you call him?" Frankie demanded, stunned at what he had just heard. His mood shifted instantly toward rage.

"I said...yer uncle's a goobersmoochin' homo. My daddy said so," the boy shot back. "Whut? Are you deaf, or sumpthin'?"

"You take that back!" Frankie shouted, as he threw down his books and started to advance on the boys. He didn't need Aubrey or Tony, this time. His own rage was

237

quite sufficient.

"Frank Albert!" Mr. Pike shouted from the school-house steps, stopping Frankie.

"What do you think you're doing, boy?" he said, as he strode over.

The two other boys ran as soon as they heard Mr. Pike roar.

"They called my uncle a homo!" he defended, his fists still clenched.

"Did they, now?" Mr. Pike inquired with a marked lack of outrage at the comment. "Well now, that don't give you the right to go and start another fight!"

Another fight? Frankie thought, his anger mounting. *I didn't start the other one.*

"Son, you've been nothin' but trouble, ever since you hooked up with that Denton boy," the principal said sourly. "I think I need to have a talk with your momma."

"You leave my momma alone!" he shouted.

Mr. Pike was taken aback by Frankie's harsh reply. "Son . . . ," he started angrily.

"I'm not your son!" Frankie spat.

Mr. Pike reached for him, but Frankie dodged his grip and dashed off toward the buses, as they stood waiting for their cargo. Seeing the principal in hot pursuit, he decided that the bus wasn't the best place to get cornered in.

Instead, he headed off the school grounds in a dead run, knowing the overweight Principal could never keep up. His house wasn't all that far away. Besides, a good run might do him some good.

The boy's words echoed in his head. He had said that his father had told him Uncle Frank was a homo. That just couldn't be true. Everybody knew that homos were sissies and weaklings. That's what all the kids said. He'd even seen some cartoons of homos that had been torn out of girly magazines and shown around school. They wore lacey shirts, had wavy, slicked-back hair, and talked with a silly lisp.

Uncle Frank was no sissy. He was a fireman, an assistant fire chief, in fact. And he certainly wasn't a weakling. Uncle Frank was the strongest, coolest guy Frankie knew. He was fearless, and even Frankie had noticed how the girls stared, all dreamy-eyed, at his uncle.

But that fat kid had gone too far. Nobody had talked about his family that way and had gotten away with it. Frankie swore he'd make that fatso take it back….and he wouldn't need Aubrey to help him.

As he stomped angrily along the rural road, he began to realize that his anger had totally dispelled any fear or apprehension he had. He began to understand that when something is worth fighting for, fear doesn't matter. Even his responses to Mr. Pike were fearless. He didn't care what that old bald-headed jackass said or did.

Uncle Frank is a hero. He ain't a homo. The boy's words rang in his ears, stoking his rage. *I'm gonna smash that tub of lard in the face! I'll teach him to call my uncle a homo.*

By the time he reached home, he had calmed down enough to realize that he was probably in a lot of trouble for yelling at Mr. Pike the way he did. He still didn't care. He was sure his mother would understand and take his side.

She didn't need this kind of trouble, as sick as she was. Now he dreaded telling her for entirely different reasons, and it was still another hour or so until she got home.

He reached into the big ceramic apple cookie jar and

retrieved a handful of oatmeal raisin cookies his mother had made for his after-school snack. He poured a tall glass of milk and settled on the floor in front of the television to watch *Gilligan's Island,* while he waited for his mother to get home.

But the day's events still distracted him. The fight at recess and then yelling at Pike? Yep, he was in trouble.

When his mother finally got home, he greeted her at the door, timidly hugging her and saying, "Momma…I gotta talk to you about somethin'."

The nervous tone in his voice told her that his "somethin'" wasn't going to be good.

"What's the matter, baby?" she asked, as she set her purse on the credenza in the foyer.

"Um…I think I'm in trouble with Mr. Pike," he started, nervously. "I kinda yelled at him."

"You did what?" she replied, her eyes wide with surprise.

"This fat kid called Uncle Frank a homo, an' I was gonna make him take it back, but Mr. Pike . . . ," he chattered urgently.

"Whoa…stop," she ordered. "What did you say about Uncle Frank?"

"I didn't say anything, Momma," he defended. "This other kid did. He called him a homo. He said his daddy told him so."

Shelley was stunned. *Oh, dear God, it's starting all over again.*

He could see that she was upset. Had he been wrong about her taking his side? He was sure that he had gone too far by yelling at the principal, but he was defending his family.

"I'm sorry, Momma," he apologized. "I know I

shouldn't a yelled at Mr. Pike. It's just that he said he was gonna call you, an' I didn't want you getting' all upset, 'cause I know it's not good for you."

Shelley realized that her son had misinterpreted her reaction, and she was touched by his protectiveness.

"Baby, that's not it." It was time to unveil a family secret and tell him the truth about his uncle.

"Frankie, we need to talk," she said cryptically, leading him into the living room.

"Momma…what's a homo?" Frankie asked apprehensively, as he followed. "I mean…I know it's bad, 'cause I hear other kids calling each other that sometimes, when their mad at each other or teasin' somebody. But…what is it?"

Shelley closed her eyes for a second to gather her thoughts. Now he was sure that he'd gone too far. They sat on the couch, and she took his hands into hers.

"Darlin' boy, Momma's not sure how to tell you this, but…." She hesitated, then took a deep breath. She decided that the direct approach was best.

"Well…to answer your question…the correct term is 'homosexual,' not 'homo.' That's an ugly word that's meant to hurt people."

"Now…." she continued, "a homosexual is a person that prefers the company of their own gender. It's like… men who prefer to be with men and women who want to be with other women."

Frankie was totally confused. He thought his mother was going to be upset with him for yelling at an adult, especially a school principal. But she was talking about the name the fat kid had called Uncle Frank and not even mentioning his having yelled at Mr. Pike.

"What's wrong with that?" he asked, innocently. "I'd

rather hang around Aubrey and Tony than some silly ol' girl any day. Does that mean I'm a…uh…homosexual?"

She was doing a miserable job of explaining it to him. But the suddenness of it, along with the anger she was feeling, made the task more difficult. She had intended to have this conversation with him at some point, but she had hoped it would happen at a more convenient time.

She hadn't even had the "birds-and-bees" talk with him yet, and now she was forced into a "birds-and-birds" explanation. Her brother had volunteered to fill in for his father and have the conversation about the "facts of life" with him, but now she knew that option was gone.

That her son was being exposed to the hateful, ugly side of the subject meant that her task was going to be that much more tedious. She feared that her son's opinion of his uncle would change for the worse.

"No…no…no, baby. There's much more to it than that," she said, struggling to come up with a way to explain a complex subject that even most adults couldn't, or wouldn't, understand.

"You know how a boy and a girl can become boyfriend and girlfriend?" she asked.

Frankie nodded, as the wheels in his head began to rotate.

"Well…that's how it is with homosexuals. It's like boyfriend and boyfriend," she said, hoping he would grasp what she was saying.

He did. "Momma…that's not right…is it?" he asked. "I mean…don't boyfriends and girlfriends go on dates an' kiss an' stuff?"

"Yes, baby, they do," she replied; a short answer was all she could muster, as she groped for something better.

"You mean homosexuals do that, too?" he asked, incredulously. His face screwed into a mask of confusion.

"Um…yes, honey…they do." Yet another short answer to a long question.

"*Yuck!* That's…aw, that's just gross!" he declared disgustedly.

"No, baby. It's not gross; it's just different." Then she thought of an approach.

"Would you kiss any of the girls at school?" she asked, hoping for the right answer.

"Heck no! That's gross, too."

That was the right answer. "Darling, right now you think that. But trust Momma. In a few years, you'll think differently. You'll want to be around them all the time. You know how Waylon always wants to be with Irene?"

"Yeah. Aubrey thinks it's goofy. So do I," he quipped.

"Well, someday, you'll meet a girl, and you'll feel the same way." *At least I hope it's a girl.* The realization of what she had just thought sickened her. She suddenly felt like a hypocrite.

"Anyway," she hurried on, "sometimes a boy will feel that way about another boy, or a girl might feel that way about another girl."

"Momma…I don't understand. That just dudn't sound right. I mean…don't boyfriends and girlfriends get married and have kids, like you and my dad?"

"Yes, baby, they do, but…"

"Well, two boys or two girls can't do that? Can they?" he interrupted.

"No, Frankie, they can't. It's not the way things normally happen." This was getting deeper than she had anticipated. She had to try something else.

"Sweetie, your father and I got married because we

loved each other and wanted to spend the rest of our lives together. We loved each other, because we made each other feel special and important. He wasn't just another person. When your father held my hand, or hugged me, it felt good and right. He was the only person I wanted hugging me. That's how one homosexual feels about another. It's about love and other special feelings."

She had to be very careful not to let the discussion get too sexual. Her son wasn't ready for that aspect, just now.

"I don't really understand how one man can feel that way about another, either, baby," she tried to explain. "It just happens. It's just something we should accept. It doesn't hurt you or me in any way. In fact, the people it always ends up hurting the most are the homosexuals themselves. That's because there are a lot of people out there who feel threatened by a different kind of love that they can't understand, and so they hate it and ridicule it. It doesn't make sense, but that's how it is. Some people are so fearful they feel like they have to do God's job and judge what other people do or how they live.... or love."

Frankie understood that part. He felt judged by other kids who had fathers at home. He also knew how other kids judged Aubrey and his family for not having as much money as others had. Even Tony was judged for being little and having a "Yankee" accent.

"I think I understand, Momma, but why did that kid's daddy say that about Uncle Frank? Is he a ho....?" A sour thought struck him. He'd never seen his uncle with a girlfriend, or even heard of him having one. Aubrey's mother was the closest thing to a girlfriend he'd ever heard about Uncle Frank having, and everyone insisted that they were just friends.

Shelley saw the sinking expression on his face.

"Does Uncle Frank wanna be with other men?" he asked, in a voice that sounded as if it had come from the bottom of a barrel.

His tone struck her deeply. Her answer could destroy her son's image of his uncle, if she wasn't careful. Honesty, she knew, was the best and only way to handle it. If he felt she was lying to him, it could damage his trust in her, as well.

"Honey, let me tell you a story, okay?" she began, as she took both of his hands into hers. "A long time ago, Uncle Frank had a friend named Robby. He was a really nice boy, and they were best friends all through school. For years, they did everything together. You never saw one without the other. Robby would spend the night here, and Uncle Frank would spend the night at Robby's house. They played on the same baseball and basketball teams, and so on.

"Then one night, when they were in high school, they went out to Lake Owen to drink some beer that they managed to get their hands on. They did that a lot, like all the other boys in town.

"Anyway, on that night, Robby was behaving differently. After a few beers, he told Uncle Frank that he loved him. At first, Uncle Frank didn't understand what Robby was saying. But when he finally did, he got really mad at him, and they got into a terrible argument. Uncle Frank called Robby some awful names and told him that he never wanted to see him again. That really hurt Robby pretty badly."

"Darlin', what I'm going to tell you next is pretty

harsh," she warned, "but you need to know the whole truth. About a week later, Robby's mother found him in their garage, dead. He had hanged himself. A couple days after that, Uncle Frank got a letter in the mail. It was from Robby, telling him how sorry he was, but that he couldn't help the way he felt. He apologized for bringing shame on our family. He said that even though Uncle Frank didn't love him the same way, he hoped he would remember the good times they had together and wouldn't forget him."

Shelley had to pause for a moment. The memory of how devastated her brother had been still stung. Frankie was taking in all that his mother said, his eyes fixed on the patterns of the fabric on the couch. After a strained pause, she continued.

"That really hit your uncle hard, baby. For a long time, Uncle Frank would go from being very sad to being very angry and back again, in a matter of seconds. I used to hear him crying in his room at night. That's about the time he and Aubrey's mom became such good friends. I think she really helped him get over Robby's death… and," she hesitated, "I think she helped him admit to himself how he had really felt about Robby."

"He loved Robby back. He just didn't know it, huh?" Frankie asked intuitively.

"Yes, he did, baby," she answered. "For a long time, it was hard for him to admit it to himself. He had treated Robby badly, and it broke his heart. He blamed himself for Robby's death. He really missed him." She was grateful that Frankie had such insight.

"He tried to keep it to himself, but one day, another boy at school said something really ugly about Robby. Uncle Frank lost control and beat the boy up pretty badly. Badly enough to where the other boy had to go to the hospital. After that, almost everyone in Haleyville turned against him. Well, everyone but your father and Uncle Ben, that is….and, of course, Sarah."

"They loved your uncle very much…in a different way, that is," she added, hoping it didn't confuse him.

"Like the way I love you, or…" she ventured, "the way Uncle Frank loves you. Like family."

"My dad knew about it?" he asked.

"Your father and Uncle Frank had become best friends even before I met your daddy. He knew about Uncle Frank, but he didn't care."

"You mean a homosexual, don't you?" he replied.

After another strained pause, she answered in a matter-of-fact tone, "Yes, Frankie. Your uncle is a homosexual."

"So that fat kid's daddy was right, huh? Uncle Frank is a homo," he said, a little more angrily than he'd intended.

"No!" she defended. "That boy's father was using an ugly, hateful word to teach his son to be just as hateful as he is."

Frankie felt he had been left out of something very important. He even felt a little betrayed. Didn't his mother and uncle trust him enough to tell him something so important? Did they think he was just a stupid little kid who wouldn't understand?

"Momma….I've heard some of the older boys talk about what queers do to each other, does Unc…"

"*Frankie!*" she snapped sharply. "Don't you ever let me hear you use that word again, especially when you're talking about my brother!"

She immediately regretted being so harsh.

"I didn't…mean…to…call . . . ," Frankie muttered.

His eyes flooded with tears, as he squeaked out, "I'm sorry, Momma."

His chin sunk to his heaving chest. Now his mother was angry at him.

"Oh, no…no…no, baby boy," she said, reaching to embrace him.

"Momma's sorry. I didn't mean to get so upset," she assured him. "It's just that I used to hear so many of the people in town call him that. It hurts me, too.

"I'll tell you what, sweetie. Let's use the word that Uncle Frank prefers. Let's use the word 'gay,' okay? It isn't an ugly word, like 'homo' or 'queer.' Honey, don't be angry with Uncle Frank. He loves you more than you'll ever know."

"Why were people so mean to him? He didn't do anything to them, did he?" he asked, after calming down slightly. "Were they mad at him cause of what that other boy did?"

"People will hate what they don't understand, or what they feel threatened by," she said, rocking him in her arms.

"Why do they feel threatened by hom…I mean gay people?"

The depths of his confusion grew deeper, but the comfort of his mother's embrace helped.

"Well, sweet boy, maybe some of them are afraid that they might be the same way, and they can't deal with it," she answered honestly. "But I think that it's mostly because they aren't at peace with themselves, so they can't be at peace with others."

"Momma," he said, in a barely audible voice.

"Yes, baby?"

"I think I need to talk to Uncle Frank."

She thought about his request and said, "I think that's a good idea."

The rest of the evening crept by in silence. Conversation was minimal, and no more was said about Uncle Frank or homosexuality. Neither had much of an appetite, nor did Frankie have any interest in television. Long before his usual bedtime, he kissed his mother good night and retreated to his room. Uncle Frank's old room, he realized.

After he'd gone to his room, Shelley called Sarah and told her what had happened.

"My God!" she declared. "Is there no end to the evil the people in this town do to each other? Aubrey told me that Frankie wasn't on the bus this afternoon and that he saw him walking as the bus passed him by."

"I wish I'd never moved back here," Shelley spat, but then she realized what that might be saying to her friend.

"Oh…I'm sorry, Sarah. I didn't mean…"

"You hush up, girl," Sarah comforted. "I completely understand. I wish I could get away from these idiots, too.

"Frankie's going to need somebody. It's still early enough for me to talk to Aubrey," she offered.

"There's no need to involve him. He's still innocent, so…" Shelley started to object.

"Innocent?" Sarah snorted. "Honey…my boy lost his innocence the first time his father beat him like a dog!"

Shelley could hear the resentment.

"I think my Aubrey can handle this, especially if he knows how much Frankie is going to need him.

"You call your brother, okay? He's got a huge chore ahead of him, and he needs all the preparation and support he can get."

"You're an amazing woman, Sarah," Shelley said. "I don't know how you do it, but I'm glad you're my friend."

"And I'm grateful to have you in my life, too, sweetie," Sarah replied. "Tell that brother of yours I send my love, okay?"

"Of course, I will. Thanks again, and, Sarah, I love you."

GREAT EXPLANATIONS

As soon as Shelley finished talking to Sarah, she dialed her brother's number.

"Sonuvabitch!" Frank barked, after hearing what his sister had to tell him.

"Those motherfu…" he caught himself.

"I'm coming down this weekend," he told her.

Then he hesitated, adding, "And sis…I'm sorry."

"For what? Being you?" she admonished. "Don't ever apologize for that again, you hear me, big brother?"

"I love you, sis…and Frankie, too. Please tell him that for me, will ya?"

"You bet, but he already knows that…and so do I. I'll see you Saturday, hun."

Meanwhile, Sarah knocked lightly on Aubrey's bedroom door. "Aubrey, are you still awake?" she asked loud enough for him to hear, if he was, but not loud enough to wake him, if he wasn't.

"Yes ma'am," she heard him answer.

She opened the door and stepped into his room, ducking to dodge the giant B-52 hanging from the gabled ceiling. She remembered how much fun he and

Frankie had putting it together. Buck had even helped his son hang it up for display after congratulating the boys on a good job of building it.

"Sweetheart," she started, "Momma's got something to talk to you about."

The last time his mother had something to talk to him about, it was bad news. He wondered if that was the case, this time.

"Is it about Frankie's mom?" he asked furtively, half afraid of the answer, as he put the comic book down and swung his legs off the bed into a sitting position.

I have got to find a better way of approaching him with bad news, she thought, seeing concern sweep his face.

"No, darlin', it's not about his mother," she assured him. "But it is about Uncle Frank." Sarah sat on the bed next to him.

Completely confused, he asked urgently, "Whut is it, Maw? Did Uncle Frank get hurt or sumpthin'?" He was alarmed at the thought of Uncle Frank getting hurt…or worse.

"No, honey, Uncle Frank is fine." She liked the way he had taken to calling Frank "uncle." In the depths of her heart, she wished it were "dad", or in Aubrey's case, "paw," but "uncle" was good, too.

"You remember telling me about Frankie not being on the bus today?"

"Sure, Maw. He looked perty mad, too."

"Well, sweetie…he had good reason to be angry."

"Why is that?"

"Aubrey," she started cautiously, "have you heard any of the other kids use the words 'homo' or 'queer'?"

"Yes ma'am, I have," he answered. "They ain't very nice words, neither. Are they?"

He didn't tell her that he'd heard his own father use those words.

"No, darlin', they're horrible words," she continued. "Well, it seems that one of the kids in school called Uncle Frank one of those words in front of Frankie."

"Whut? Who?" he demanded angrily. "I'll teach 'em ta…"

"No…you won't, Aubrey," his mother said firmly. "Don't let hate beget hate, son. The reason I'm telling you this is that Frankie is going to need a good friend over the next few days."

"Why, Maw?' It's just name callin', ain't it? Frankie's tougher'n that. I seen it."

"Honey, let me tell you a story about Uncle Frank, okay?" she implored. After getting a nod from him, she told him the same tragic story Shelley had told Frankie, including her part in helping Uncle Frank come to terms with himself.

Afterwards, Aubrey sat in thoughtful silence for a few minutes; then he asked, "Maw, didn't the Bible say that men layin' down with other men is wrong?"

Her son's uncanny knowledge of God's Word never ceased to amaze, or delight, her.

"Yes, darlin', it does. But remember…those aren't Jesus' words. They come from a disciple…Paul, isn't it?"

"Yes, ma'am, but…"

Holding her hand up, she cut him off. Now wasn't the time for a technical debate about the Bible. "What Jesus did say was that we should love and forgive others and that we shouldn't judge them."

"That's right. He tells us that we should pay attention to the big ol' plank in our own eye, before we point at the little bitty splinter in our brother's eye, an' that we shouldn't be judgin' other folks 'cause that's His and His Father's job, an' if we do that, they're both gonna be mighty angry with us."

The way he spoke of Jesus and God in the present tense, as if they were standing in the room, made her heart soar.

"He tells us that it's okay ta hate the sin, but it ain't okay ta hate the sinner. That's jus' wrong." He paused for a thoughtful moment.

"I see what you mean, Maw. Uncle Frank cain't help bein' the way he is, but it don't make him a bad man… and it don't mean Jesus dudn't love him just as much as he loves me an' you. Does it?"

"Child…you are your mother's delight," she said, wrapping her arms around him and kissing him on the forehead. "You'd make a jim-dandy preacher, you know that?"

"Ya think so? I hadn't thought about it, but…" He let the thought trail off into his mind.

"Maw?" he asked, suddenly sullen.

"Yes, darlin'. What is it?"

"Them folks that said all them bad thangs 'bout Uncle Frank. Did any of 'em go ta our church?"

Sarah thought for a second. She didn't want to taint her son's faith, but then she knew that it didn't come from the people or the world around him. It came from within, and he was strong enough to endure the trials life had thrown at him so far.

She knew that the hypocrites who professed Jesus with their tongues, yet denied him with their actions, could not damage her son's faith. He was a true Christian. He was an angel in the form of a living, breathing little boy.

"Yes, son. I'm afraid a few of them did…and some

still do."

"Was Reverend Greene one of 'em?" Aubrey had to know if the shepherd of the flock he was in was a good and true shepherd of the Lord.

"No, darlin'. He came later." Sarah realized that she had not yet broached the subject with her minister. Did he know the history of some of his flock? How would he react? What would his advice be?

"Good," Aubrey said. "I think I'm gonna talk to him about it. He's a good preacher. I bet he'll know how ta help Frankie and his maw."

"Honey," Sarah said pensively, "you might not want to do that."

"Why not, Maw? He's our preacher. If ya cain't turn ta yer preacher...who can ya turn to?"

He had a point! She couldn't say no. Her twelve-year-old son was going to approach his minister about a subject most of the adults in his congregation dodged, denied, or condemned. The pride she felt at that moment for him was immense. God had truly blessed her with a son any mother would cherish.

Buck was her trial, but Waylon and Aubrey, especially Aubrey, were her rewards.

The next day, Shelley let Frankie stay home from school and took half the day off from work, herself, in order to go to the school and have a face-to-face meeting with Principal Pike.

The principal did not fare well in the meeting.

Like a mother lioness defending her cub, she blasted the man for his obvious bias toward her son. She became truly angry when he said, "That Denton boy is a bad influence."

A threat to go to the county school board and a promise to tell "that Denton boy's" parents what he had said about their son were enough to scare him into promising to back off her son and his friends in the future.

She thought she saw a tinge of fear in his eyes when she mentioned Aubrey's parents. She suspected he knew about Buck's temper and reputation. Everyone else in town seemed to, so why not him?

She wondered how Jack would have handled the situation. She doubted if Pike would have been so condescending to him. She wondered if Pike would have come away without a black eye.

She didn't really expect the man to change his ways, though. Men like him rarely do. Especially when confronted by mere women. Their authority over helpless children is a drug to them. They guard their little fiefdoms with vigor and jealousy.

It's usually all they have in life.

As she was leaving, she encountered Miss Shockley in the hallway. The elderly woman could see her distress. Tactfully, she was able to get Shelley to tell her what was going on.

The teacher was appalled, but not surprised, at Mr. Pike's attitude. She was aware of Frank's history in the small town. The treatment he received offended her, too. Small-mindedness always did.

"I've dedicated my life to countering ignorance," Miss Shockley said. "But I can't counter the malice that these children learn at home. A parent's ignorance scars deeper than any enlightenment can counter."

"Frankie is a good boy," the teacher complimented. "You've done very well by him. I can only imagine how difficult it has been for you having to raise him on your own."

Then she added, "I don't care what that ex-jock, jack-ass of a principal says; your son's friend, Aubrey, is wonderful little boy. He has such a big heart. There's no way he can be called a bad influence. Roy Pike is an ass; it's just that simple."

Realizing that she had just insulted her boss in front of a parent, she said, "Oh dear, I shouldn't have said…"

She had outlasted many principals, and Pike didn't scare her, but proper decorum was still important.

Shelley laughed out loud and put her hand on Miss Shockley's arm, saying, "Don't fret. I agree wholeheartedly."

The two women said their good-byes and parted ways, with Miss Shockley imploring Shelley to send her regards to Frank and to reassure him that some of the people in town had minds larger than dried peas.

"Mr. Henderson…Mr. Bennett! You boys stop running!"

A warm smile spread across Shelley's face as she heard the infamous teacher call out, resuming her role as the most dreaded teacher in the school.

Out on the playground, Tony asked Aubrey where Frankie was. Aubrey told him what had happened, and Tony flared, "Who called Uncle Frank a homo? I'll kick his ass!"

Aubrey was amused at the little guy's audacity and impressed with his loyalty to Frankie and to Uncle Frank.

"So it don't bother ya that Uncle Frank is that way?" he asked.

"Bother me?" he answered incredulously. "Why should it bother me? Heck, I got a cousin up in New York that's gay. His name's Julian, but sometimes he goes by Julia. He's in college, and sometimes he even dresses up in women's stuff and goes to the special clubs for guys like him. Some of my relatives don't like him, but he's always been supercool with me, and he's really funny, too."

Then he added, "You don't suppose Uncle Frank dresses up like that, do ya?"

"Yeah…right!" Aubrey chortled. "I can just see Uncle Frank in a dress…muscles an' all!"

"Holy crap!" Tony laughed. "That would be hilarious. But naw; I guess you're right. He's too big for that kinda stuff. Plus he ain't a sissy. Julian's a little guy, like me, and a bit of a sissy, so it works for him."

"Maw told me that I can get off at Frankie's stop this afternoon, so I can talk to him. Wanna come along?" Aubrey offered.

"I can't. I have to have permission from my mom," he answered, slightly dejected.

Then he said, "To heck with that. Frankie's my pal… and a Musketeer. I'll call Mom from his house. I'll get grounded, but it's worth it."

Tony liked pushing the envelope, so defying his mother in this instance was not a stretch.

That afternoon, the juvenile counselor and the scrappy conspirator got off the bus in front of Frankie's house. Frankie was pleasantly surprised to find his buddies standing at his door when he opened it. He had spent the whole day ruminating over his uncle and what it meant.

"Maw said you wudn't feelin' well, so we thought we'd stop by an'…" Aubrey started.

"Who called Uncle Frank a fag?" Tony demanded, throwing diplomacy out the window.

"I'm gonna kick his ass!" he repeated the threat.

Frankie was taken aback. He hadn't told anyone but his mother, yet his pals seemed to know all about it.

"How do you know?" he asked, stepping aside and waving them in.

Aubrey punched Tony in the arm and said, "Big mouth!"

Frankie led them to the kitchen, where he offered them milk and cookies. Both boys accepted them gladly.

"Yer mom called mine last night an' told me all about it," Aubrey told him, dipping his cookie into his milk.

Frankie's face flushed pink with embarrassment.

Sensing his distress, Aubrey quickly added, "It don't make no difference ta us about Uncle Frank. We still think he's a great guy."

"It ain't anybody else's business," Tony interjected. "So he goes on dates with other guys. So what?"

Tony's complete acceptance took Frankie by surprise, just as it had Aubrey. "Does that make him less of a hero when he's draggin' somebody out of a fire? No... it doesn't. An' I'll bet the person he's draggin' out doesn't care, either."

"But haven't you heard about the stuff hom...I mean gay guys do with each other?" Frankie asked.

"Yeah, sure I have." Tony answered. "I don't believe most of it. I think it's gross, but hey...as long as it ain't me, who cares?"

"Well..."Aubrey started, "the Bible does say that it ain't the normal way folks should behave, but after Maw talked to me, I spent all night thinkin' 'bout it an' prayin' ta Jesus about it. An' ya know, the Bible just barely mentioned it, an' it wudn't Jesus who said anything about it, anyway. He's more concerned about how we treat each other. Folks that pass judgment on others are takin' his job away, an' that makes him mighty upset. I think I'll listen ta Jesus, an' ignore all them hippo-crits.

"Besides, I know in my heart, without any misgivin's, that Jesus loves Uncle Frank as much as he loves you or me. I think we gotta be better than the folks that say bad stuff and try ta forgive 'em, like Jesus tells us to. 'Cause it's like he said to his father while he was on the Cross . . . "Father, forgive 'em, for they know not what they do."

Frankie and Tony were spellbound by the adolescent preacher and his miniature sermon.

"Dang Aub, that was awesome," Tony complimented. "You know your Bible better than most grown-ups. You gonna be a preacher when you grow up?"

That was the second time that suggestion was made. The prospect of sharing the Word of God really appealed to him. He would have to think seriously about it.

"Yeah, Aub," Frankie added quietly, "that was a pretty cool thing to say. Thanks guys. Ya'll are great."

"Anyway..." Tony said, "who called Uncle Frank a fag? I'm serious. I wanna kick his ass."

"Didn't you hear what I jus' said?" Aubrey demanded.

"Yeah, I heard ya. Forgive 'em," Tony protested. "That don't mean they can't be taught a lesson."

"You jus' don't get it, do ya?" Aubrey shot back. "It made me perty mad, too. I wanna smack somebody, too. But Maw says that's jus' hate begettin' hate."

"Yeah, well, if ya let 'em get away with it, then the whole school's gonna do it," Tony responded.

"All the kids in school know about what you did to those chumps last year," Tony went on. "I'm just sayin' that we if cornered the creep and told him that if he ever said it again, then we'd clobber him, and then maybe that would get around, too."

"I ain't no bully! I ain't gonna go threatenin' some-body littler than me," Aubrey objected, assuming that the guilty party was smaller. A natural assumption on his part.

"He ain't smaller than you, Aub," Frankie confessed absently. "He's a big, fat sixth grader with greasy, black hair. And his buddy is even fatter, with curly, brown hair."

"His buddy? There was more'n one of 'em?" Aubrey's forgiving temperament was beginning to dissolve.

"Just two of 'em," Frankie answered. "I was gonna pound his fat face, but Pike stopped me, an' they ran away."

"Ya see, Tony?" Aubrey said. "They're scum-suckin' cowards, jus' like the ones that picked on you. But I don't wanna get into trouble fer fightin' at school."

The other two understood their big friend's reluctance.

"Yeah, I guess you're right," Tony capitulated. "But what if we catch 'em away from school?"

"That's different," Aubrey allowed, with a grin.

"Hey guys," Frankie said, "um....Momma told me that Uncle Frank is comin' down this weekend to talk to me about all this."

"Good," Aubrey said. "I really like him. Ya think I might be able to talk ta him, too?"

"Sure, I suppose. Why?" Frankie inquired.

"I dunno. I jus' feel like talkin' to him...about stuff."

Aubrey felt compelled to tell Uncle Frank that God's love embraced him, too, regardless of who or what he was.

"Hey, ya think he can take us for some more rides in his 'Vette?" Tony asked, hopefully.

"Dang it, Tony, cain't you ever be serious? He ain't comin' down fer fun, ya know," Aubrey scolded.

"Geez, Aub, relax. I was just asking," Tony replied dejectedly.

"Aw, shoot. I'm sorry, lil buddy," Aubrey apologized. "I didn't mean ta bark atchya. It's just that, well…you know."

"Yeah, I know. It's okay," Tony said.

"But I get first dibs on the fat kid!" he impishly added, sucker punching Aubrey in the arm.

"Hey…it's time for *Gilligan's Island*," Frankie reminded the boys, tired of the depressing seriousness of the subject.

"Cool," Tony said. "I just have to call my mom and get grounded, okay?"

His precursory acceptance of his imminent punishment amused his friends.

"Yer sumpthin' else; I tell you whut!" Aubrey chuckled.

Initially, Tony was right. His mother was furious with him for not getting permission first and grounded him for two weeks, but after he explained everything, she called Shelley to confirm what had happened. Hearing the whole story, she forgave her son and only took one Saturday morning's cartoons away from him.

When she told Mike, her husband's only comment was, "Well, I never would have guessed. But I suppose things like that matter more than they should down here, don't they? That's too bad. Frank's a good man."

What if it was your brother? she thought, irritated by his seeming complacency.

The next day at school, Frankie pointed out the boy who had called his uncle that awful name. Aubrey knew who he was and assured his friend that the kid was really a wimp who liked to pick on smaller kids, and that he would be easy to scare. No fight would be necessary.

The plan the boys had come up with was for Frankie to lure him away from the watching eyes of the teachers monitoring the playground by challenging him to a fight behind the building.

Andy, the loud-mouthed kid, was more than happy to oblige, especially considering his chunky sidekick was there to back him up, should Frankie prove to be more than he appeared.

"So you think it's okay ta go callin' other folks hateful names, huh?" Aubrey growled from the shadows, as the three boys came around the corner.

The satisfied sneer melted from Andy's face, when he saw Aubrey standing there, fists clenched.

"Yeah . . . ," Tony added from behind the two corpulent bullies, "especially if they're smaller than you, huh?"

Seeing that they were outnumbered and surrounded, the chunky kid turned and ran, leaving his cohort alone to face the Musketeers.

"Uh....my daddy said . . . ," Andy stuttered. Even though he was bigger than Tony and Frankie, and heavier than Aubrey, he knew Aubrey's reputation, and his fear grew rapidly.

"Your daddy is an idiot!" Tony taunted, advancing menacingly toward the now-sweating boy. His own reputation for being a fireball had spread, as well.

Aubrey's assessment of the boy proved true, as Andy began to whimper and stutter, "I....I... didn't...m... mean nu...nuthin'. I'm sorry." He cast his eyes from Aubrey to Tony and, finally, to Frankie.

Tears began to leak from his frightened eyes. "Yer un...uncle's car i...is really co...cool," he pleaded.

Just the mention of the word "uncle" was enough to set Frankie off. He leapt toward the frightened boy, screaming, "You take back what you said!" Spittle flew from his mouth, as he raged forward.

A surprised Aubrey was barely able to catch him before he reached the blubbering boy. Thinking quickly, he said "You better take it back…I cain't hold him much longer."

"I ta…I ta…I take it b…back, I…promise!" Andy yelped, staggering back into Tony, only to be shoved forward by the feisty little Italian.

"Get offa me, ya creep!" Tony shouted.

Andy was paralyzed by the unexpected turn of events. Again, Aubrey seized the moment.

"If I hear 'bout anybody else sayin' stuff about our Uncle Frank, I'm comin' after you! Ya hear?" he threatened, still holding a flailing Frankie at bay.

"No!" Frankie screamed. "I want to kick his ass!" The emotions of the past two days began to boil over into an insatiable rage. Aubrey had to genuinely struggle to keep a hold on him.

"Look!" Tony shouted, pointing at Andy's dampened crotch, "He pissed in his pants! You scared the piss out of him." He began to laugh at the much larger boy.

"You say anything ta Pike or the teachers, I'll get-cha, too. Now git outa here b'for I let him go!" Aubrey threatened further.

Seeing the blood in Frankie's eyes, Andy dashed aside, giving Tony a wide berth, and ran back out onto the playground, not stopping until he was safely in the building.

"Why didn't you let me go?" a furious Frankie demanded of Aubrey, after the boy had fled and Aubrey had released him.

"Because ya didn't need ta fight him. Didn't ya see

how scared he was?" Aubrey argued back. "We dun whut we planned, didn't we?"

"Yeah, Frankie. Didn't ya see how he pissed in his pants? That was great. He'll never bother you again," Tony assured. "If he says anything, we'll tell the whole school about it."

Frankie slowly began to recover his composure, although he still trembled from the adrenaline.

"Okay…you guys are right," he capitulated. "It's just that when I think about what he called Uncle Frank…. well…"

"It pissed us off, too, ya know," Tony chimed in. "Why do ya think we're here?"

Frankie nodded and said, "Thanks fellas."

"All for one…and one for all!" Tony said, raising an imaginary sword.

"All for one…and one for all!" the other two joined in, their own imaginary swords raised as well.

This time, Mr. Pike was nowhere to be seen.

That afternoon, on the bus ride home, Aubrey confided in Frankie that he hadn't liked ganging up on Andy but that he realized that it had been necessary.

Frankie agreed and thanked him for being there for him and that he was glad Aubrey had stopped him.

The following Saturday morning, Frankie heard his uncle's car rumble up to the house, as he was watching a *Road Runner* cartoon. Ordinarily, interruptions to his Saturday ritual were annoying, but this time he wasn't really watching the cartoon, anyway.

He was just killing time, waiting for his uncle to arrive. But now that Uncle Frank was here, a knot began to grow in his stomach.

He got up from the floor, went to the front door,

and slowly opened it. Ordinarily, he'd be halfway to his uncle's car before the screen door closed behind him. This time, he just stood there.

Uncle Frank was retrieving his overnight bag from the passenger seat. A million thoughts rushed forward in Frankie's mind, causing the knot to grow.

Uncle Frank turned from locking the white picket gate behind him and saw Frankie standing behind the screen door, looking at him.

Neither uncle nor nephew moved for several strained moments. A crack began to form in Uncle Frank's heart. Normally Frankie raced out to meet him. Now he just stood there, looking at him as if he were a convicted criminal or a mangy dog.

Frankie saw a look of despair begin to overtake his uncle's face, as the two stood staring at each other.

Shelley had heard her brother's car, too, and had come from the kitchen, drying her hands on a dish towel. The sight of her two most beloved people simply staring at each other was crushing. She had feared that a chasm would form between them, and her already-tattered heart just couldn't take that.

But her fears proved unfounded, as Frankie threw the door open and flew off the porch, wailing desperately, "Uncle Frank…Uncle Frank!"

Frank dropped his bag and crouched down to inter-cept his nephew in an equally desperate embrace.

"Oh Frankie…my Bambino!" he whispered hoarsely, as he held his nephew close.

"What have I done?" he added guiltily. "Can you for-give your ol' uncle?"

"You didn't do nuthin, Uncle Frank," Frankie sobbed. "You didn't do nuthin."

Shelley had to turn away. Retreating to the kitchen, she gave her two men their private moment, while she regained control of her own emotions.

"I love you, Uncle Frank," Frankie declared, through sniffs and sobs. "I don't care what anybody says."

Frank had dreaded this moment ever since his sister had called him. He had feared a much worse reception. He had feared revulsion from his namesake. His stomach, too, had been in knots, and the bags under his eyes revealed that he hadn't been able to sleep well, either.

The world be damned; only his sister and his nephew mattered. The thought of Frankie rejecting him was more than he could stand. The relief he felt at Frankie's reassurance was overwhelming. He, too, began to cry.

The two embraced for several minutes, as if they'd been apart for years, rather than weeks. Finally, Frank stood up, his nephew still clinging to him. Retrieving his bag, he carried Frankie in one arm, the boy's face still buried in his uncle's shoulder, up the front steps and into the house. Shelley was standing inside, waiting, and she gave her guys an all-encompassing hug.

After everyone had recovered from the initial moment, Shelley greeted her brother. "Hey, bubbie, are you okay?"

"Yeah, I'm fine…I suppose."

"How's Charlie?" she asked, her arm locked in his.

"Oh…he's okay," Frank stammered, then added, "Truth is, sis, he doesn't know about all this."

"Do you think it's fair to keep it from him?" she asked. "I know he cares about you."

"I'm sure it's not fair, but…well, I just don't think it's…"

"Hey, don't worry about it, right now, okay?" she

soothed.

She told them that she had catfish fingers and fries for lunch and that they had better eat them before they got cold.

After lunch, Frank and Frankie wandered out to the back porch to talk. It felt both private and nonconfining. Shelley brought them lemonade and cookies and went back into the house, leaving them to their discussion.

"Um…Bambino, your mother told me that you wanted to talk to me," Uncle Frank started nervously, "I don't know where to start, buddy. I'm really sorry I embarrassed you at school. I never intended for anything like that to happen, ya know."

"You didn't embarrass me, Uncle Frank." The boy reassured. "Me an' Aubrey an' Tony took care of the creep that called you a ho…" he stopped himself from repeating the word, knowing it would hurt his uncle, "um…I mean that name."

"It's okay, buddy," he tried to reassure his nephew. "I've heard worse. It's only words." His own words were brave, but words still stung.

"Frankie…I know it's hard for you to understand, but . . . ," he hesitated, searching for a way to explain a complicated adult emotion.

Frankie seized on the hesitation and said, "It's okay, Momma an' Aubrey talked to me about it."

"Aubrey?" Frank responded, a little surprised.

"Yeah," Frankie continued, "he said what you are doesn't keep you from lovin' me, so it shouldn't keep me from lovin' you back. He said that Jesus still loves you, too, no matter what, an' that if Jesus does, then I should, too. He said it isn't really your fault; it's just how God made you, even if the Bible does say it's not the way things normally are."

"Aubrey said all that, huh?" Uncle Frank mused. "Wow. That's…um….that's really something. He's quite a kid, that Aubrey."

"Yeah, he's pretty cool, huh?" Frankie said, taking a bite from his cookie and washing it down with lemonade.

"He helps me a lot. An' he knows a whole bunch about Jesus an' the Bible. He said his mom thinks he oughta be a preacher when he grows up; so do Tony an' me. That'd be cool, huh?"

Uncle Frank sipped his own lemonade, wishing he had something stronger to add to it. Maybe there was hope for the world if kids like Aubrey were in it. He was grateful to Aubrey for softening the blow and making his task a lot simpler.

That his friends were so accepting no doubt helped Frankie, too. A few plastic models and coloring books seemed paltry thanks for what they had done for his nephew….and for him.

"So…where do we start? You have questions, don't you?" Uncle Frank asked.

"Um…well, yeah," Frankie said, and shifted slightly in his seat.

"Momma said that you, uh…like bein' around other guys instead of girls. You know, like on dates and stuff," he said, squirming uncomfortably. "Why is that? Don't you like girls?"

Breathing deeply through his nose, Frank said, "Well…yeah. I guess that's, uh…I guess that's right. I like girls well enough, for friends, but, uh…I just feel more comfortable around guys. Not just any guy, either, just certain guys that are like me. Does that bother you?"

The "stuff" part of Frankie's question nearly panicked him. As far as he knew, Shelley had not yet had the dreaded talk with her son, as it relates to "straight" sex. In fact, Shelley had hinted at having him have that "birds-and-bees" talk with his nephew. He was sure that she'd probably change her mind, now. How was he going to explain the sexual aspect of homosexuality, without it sounding repulsive or disgusting to an eleven-year-old boy?

The thought of his sister not being able to rely on him for such things hurt him deeply. How was she going to feel about her son ultimately living with his gay uncle?

He feared that if he attempted to explain, he'd flounder and destroy Frankie's innocence and the trust he had in their relationship. That would be a loss that he didn't think he could handle.

"A little bit, maybe, 'cause all the stuff I heard homo… uh, gay guys do. I mean…I don't understand it, but . . . ," Frankie replied, hesitant and confused.

"Uncle Frank?" he started, nervously changing the direction of his questions. "I really like bein' around Aubrey an' Tony more than any ol' girl. I have fun with them an' we share secrets, an' all. I feel good when they're with me. Does that mean that I'm a ho…I mean a gay guy, too? 'Cause if you're one, does that mean that I might be one, too?"

Frank felt like a deer in the headlights of a speeding semi. This was unexpected. But, at least, he had an immediate answer.

"No, Bambino. Wanting to be around your friends at your age doesn't mean you're a, ah…gay guy. It means you're a normal eleven-year-old boy who hasn't found out what girls are all about, yet. That won't happen for a little while, yet. Then you'll start to understand.

"Well…as much as any guy can understand girls, they can be mighty hard to figure out, ya know. But don't you worry about it, kiddo. Just enjoy being who you are and hanging out with your buddies. Things will get complicated for you soon enough. Don't rush it, and don't fret about stuff you can't do anything about."

"Well…you were a kid like me, too, weren't ya?" Frankie asked. "An' you liked to hang around with your buddies. Right?"

"Yes, of course, I was, and, yes, I did like to hang around with my buddies, but…"

"Well then…how did you get gay?" Frankie interrupted.

"Little man, you have no idea how many times I've asked myself that same question." Frank answered. "But, first, let me assure you that it's not something that you get from your family, like blue eyes and black hair." He reached over and ruffled Frankie's hair.

That his nephew didn't flinch, or pull away from his touch was reassuring.

"Maybe Aubrey's right. Maybe God just made me this way," he speculated. "But, ya know, there are some people out there, including doctors called psychiatrists and psychologists who say that it was because of the environment that I grew up in."

"Huh?" Frankie asked, becoming more confused. "What do ya mean?"

"Ya see Bambino, Grandpa Robert and I didn't get along real well. I mean, we didn't hate each other and fight a lot, or anything like that. Well….we did have our differences, but…

"Anyway, we just didn't seem to like each other very much, so we didn't do the kind of stuff that dads and sons do together. You know…like camping, fishing… building models, that sort of stuff. I caught lectures instead of baseballs.

"My father didn't spend time with me showing me what it means to be a man, or a father, or anything like that. As long as I stayed out of trouble, he was happy. My father didn't give me someone I could look up to, respect, and be proud of. Just someone whom I obeyed and got an allowance from." He paused.

"You mean…like how I'm proud of you an' respect you?" Frankie interjected.

An overwhelming feeling of love washed over Frank. "You really feel that way?" he asked, incredulously.

"Of course, I do," Frankie answered in a matter-of-fact tone, as if neither the question nor the answer were necessary. "You're my uncle."

"Thank you, Frankie. You don't know how good that makes me feel."

"Anyway . . . ," Frankie began again, "some doctors say that might have something to do with it. They think that having a good, strong father to help him through the tough spots is important to how a boy grows up and thinks about himself and the world around him."

"So it might be Grandpa Robert's fault?"

"Well, no, I don't want to go blaming him; besides, it isn't that simple. Some of the doctors also believe that an overbearing mother might have a lot to do with it, too. And believe me, buddy, Grandma Emma was very overbearing."

"What's that mean…overbearing?" Frankie asked.

"It means a mom who is too protective of her son and wants to run his life for him." A tinge of bitterness crept into his voice.

"When I was real little, Grandma Emma would freak out if I fell down and scraped my knee. She always wanted to pick out my clothes and dress me in the morning and things like that."

That would drive me nuts! Frankie thought.

Uncle Frank continued, "As I was growing up and going to school, she would get real mad when I got in trouble, along with other boys, for doing things like pulling pranks or stealing watermelons from ol' man Griggs's watermelon patch.

"And, boy howdy, if I got in trouble at school, she would go ballistic. But she didn't get as mad at me as she did at the other boys, and even their parents. She caused a lot of embarrassment for me, and I lost a lot of friends because of her.

"She didn't want me to do anything that might get me hurt or in trouble, or even dirty, like catching frogs or wrestling with my buddies. She got real upset when I joined the football team. She thought it was dirty and brutal.

"She was right; it is dirty and brutal, but it's what boys do. She just couldn't get around that, though.

"Ya know…she didn't even like ol' Ben teaching me about cars. She thought all that stuff was beneath the son of a lawyer."

"My grandpa was a lawyer?" Frankie asked. "You mean like Perry Mason?"

"Yep, he sure was. Of course, not exactly like Perry Mason, but close enough. Your momma didn't tell you that?"

"No, she didn't, but that's far out. Wait till the guys hear that."

His uncle could see the wheels turning in Frankie's

head, as he said, "But…I didn't have a dad to go campin' an' fishin' with, an' Momma got upset when I got hurt or when I got in trouble, so…

"Trust me, little one," Uncle Frank chuckled, "your mother is not overbearing. She's a great mom. As far as the camping and the fishing go, there's a world of difference between not having a dad around at all and having a dad that doesn't seem to care."

Frankie thought of all the times Tony had commented on his father being like that.

"And, buddy, I'm not saying that those are the reasons that I'm, uh…gay, or that they're even right." Using the word for the first time to describe himself to his nephew felt very awkward.

"I'm just saying that there are doctors and other people out there, who are trying to understand what makes people behave the way they do. I don't think anyone has the real answer, and they may never have it, either. Some things just are the way they are, and that's all the explanation we'll ever get. I mean…does anyone understand what makes a man fall in love with one woman, and not another?

"But, to tell you the truth, I prefer Aubrey's explanation better. God just made me this way. That means I don't get to blame other people; I just have to accept it… and so do they."

"Oh, yeah . . . ," Frankie said, "speakin' of Aubrey, he asked me if it would be okay if he talked to you, too."

"Uh…I don't know," Uncle Frank said, totally surprised. "His mother might not want me to. I know his father wouldn't." He had anticipated Frankie being ashamed and wanting to hide his uncle's sexuality, but it seemed that the opposite was true.

"That's okay. It was his momma that told him all about you," Frankie informed him. "Him an' Tony still think you're pretty cool, too. I think he just wants to tell you that Jesus still loves you."

Good ol' wonderful, Sarah. He should have known he could count on her to make things right. *I should have married that girl,* he thought.

But what kind of life would it have been for her? A gay husband? It would have been better than her being a battered wife, though. Wouldn't it?

No, she deserved better than either one of those alternatives. She deserved so much more.

"So Tony knows, too, huh?" *So much for his nephew being ashamed and secretive about it.*

"Yeah, 'course he does," Frankie said, casually. "He's my friend, too. But don't worry 'bout him, either. He has a cousin up in New York that's that way, too. He said his cousin sometimes likes to dress up like a girl."

After an awkward pause, he looked sidelong at his uncle and asked, "You don't do that, do ya?"

"No, Frankie . . . ," his uncle laughed, feeling more at ease with his nephew. "I don't wear dresses. I'd be one ugly girl, don't ya think? Besides, Bambino, not all gay men do that, just some who have a different way of expressing themselves."

"Whew! Good, 'cause that would really freak me out," he laughed back.

In the kitchen, Shelley heard them laughing and whispered a quick prayer of thanks. Her biggest fear had been that her son would not understand or accept her brother's sexuality and that their relationship would suffer irreparable damage.

"Got any more questions?" Uncle Frank asked.

"No . . . ," Frankie answered pensively, "not really." The questions rolling around in his young head were questions he didn't really want answered, because he just couldn't see his uncle doing the things that some of the other kids said gay men do with each other. He was content to be in denial, even though he didn't realize that he was.

It was okay with him if his uncle was more comfortable around other men. That was something he could relate to. He trusted what his uncle had said about not being a "gay guy" himself, just because he felt that way, too.

He believed that he would start liking girls more when he got older, too. In fact, there was a cute little blonde girl at school he liked looking at. He was relieved to know that being gay was something that he wouldn't inherit, either.

His answer told his uncle that there were questions, but his reluctance to ask them was actually a relief.

"Well, that wasn't as bad as I thought it would be," Uncle Frank confessed.

"What do ya mean?" Frankie inquired.

"Um…truthfully? I thought you might be ashamed of me, little buddy," Uncle Frank answered, surprised at the sudden lump in his throat.

"I thought you might not want to be around me, maybe even hate me."

Frankie got up to hug his uncle. "I could never hate you or be ashamed of you, Uncle Frank."

Frank was unable to do anything but hug his nephew and choke back a sob.

Shelley had ventured to the screen door that led from the kitchen to the back porch. Seeing the two most important people in her life embracing brought tears of joy to her eyes. Relishing the sight, she waited for them to end their moment, before making her presence known.

"How are my guys doing?" she asked cheerfully.

"We're doin' great, Momma," Frankie answered, for both of them.

"Are you okay with everything, baby?" she asked him.

"Yeah…I'm okay. I guess I'll do some prayin' about it, like Aubrey says."

"Oh yeah . . . ," Uncle Frank started, eyeing his sister with playful accusation, "what's this I hear about you talking to Sarah about me?"

"Um…I just thought that . . . ," she stammered, not sure if her brother was really angry or just teasing.

"Relax, sis," Frank smiled, to her relief. "I'm glad you did. Between her and Aubrey…and Tony, too….my job was a lot easier than I'd thought it would be."

"Frankie tells me that Reverend Aubrey wants to talk to me," he added, winking at Frankie.

"I reckon I oughta get that over with. I hope he's not too harsh on me. Would you call Sarah for me? I don't think Buck would appreciate me calling her."

"Oh…to hell with Buck," Shelley snapped. "But you're probably right. I'll give her a call."

LIL' PREACHER BOY

Sarah made up a "woman-thing" excuse, and later that evening, she and Aubrey came by to visit with Frank. Meeting her at the door, Frank wrapped her up in a bear hug, lifting her off the ground.

"Frank...put me down. My son is watching," she protested mildly, feeling a little wicked at being in the arms of another man, however innocent it might have been.

"Oh . . . ," he responded, putting her down. He then reached down and gave Aubrey the same hug, getting a yelp of surprise from him.

"Well, someone seems mighty cheerful," Sarah observed, after greeting Shelley and Frankie.

"I got good reason to be cheerful, Dumplin'!" he said. "Not the least of which has to do with this boy of yours." He set a somewhat-befuddled Aubrey back on the floor.

"Whut'd I do?" he asked, confused but not unhappy.

"You helped my Bambino past a really hard spot; that's what," Uncle Frank answered. "But I hear you have a few words to say to me. I think Frankie's mom just might have a few more cookies and lemonade that might help that."

"They're already out on the back porch, waiting. You boys go on out," Shelley said to Frankie and Aubrey. "Uncle Frank will be right out. Okay?"

"Sure thang, Mrs. Albert," Aubrey responded eagerly.

"Aubrey, honey," Shelley started, halting him in his tracks. "I'm Uncle Frank's sister, and I don't know why I haven't said something before, but it sounds a little silly when you call him 'uncle,' and then call me 'Mrs. Albert.' Do you suppose you could do me the honor of calling me 'aunt'? That would make me feel so good."

She felt that only family cared as much, or did as much, as the mother and the son standing before her did and had done.

"Well…'course I can," he answered solemnly. "That'd be nice…if it's okay with Maw." He looked at his mother.

Sarah gave a smiling nod of approval. Aubrey and Frankie raced each other for the back door, and for the cookie treasure that awaited them.

"Ya know what, Frankie?" Aubrey asked, stuffing a chewy peanut-butter cookie into his mouth. "I reckon that makes us kinda like cousins, huh?"

"Well…yeah, I s'pose it does," Frankie replied, after washing down his own mouthful. "That's far out!"

Aubrey nodded his agreement, his mouth too full to talk.

Back in the kitchen, Sarah said to Shelley, "That was very sweet of you. He adores you, you know. He says you're the prettiest lady he's ever seen. Of course, he always adds 'after you, Maw.' But I know he's just being polite."

"Oh, Sarah, hush," Shelley protested. "You're embarrassing me."

"Well, it's true," Sarah reiterated. "Calling you 'aunt' and Frank 'uncle' means the world to him. He doesn't have that sort of family here in town. It's amazing how he's bloomed since he and Frankie became best buddies. I am so grateful for that."

"Honey, I adore him, too. He's done Frankie…and me, a world of good, as well."

"If we can get past this meeting of the Mother's Mutual Admiration Society, I'd like to squeeze in a word or two….before I talk with Reverend Denton," Frank chimed in.

Turning to Sarah and grasping her hands in his, he said, "Sarah, I don't have the words to tell you how much I appreciate you for all you've done for sis here, for Frankie, and for me. I've got a bucketful of regrets here in Haleyville, but you, Dumplin', are not one of them; quite the opposite. This nasty, little town could learn a lot from you and your son."

They held each other's gaze for a long moment, their eyes saying what their words could not…at least not openly.

Shelley stood quietly by and let them share their moment. Without knowing it for sure, she felt that she understood their relationship. She, too, wished that it had developed differently.

Finally, Frank released Sarah's hands and said wistfully, "Well…I guess I'd better face the good reverend's music, eh?"

Sarah chuckled and said, "Don't worry. He promised not to be too rough on you."

"Wish me luck," he said, turning from the women and heading for the porch.

"Well, Reverend," Frank said to Aubrey, as he walked out onto the porch, "I'm ready."

"Reverend?" Aubrey replied. "Yer joshin' me, ain'tcha?"

"If you mean that I'm making fun of you, then....no, I'm not," he reassured Aubrey. "I would never do that. I am teasing you, though. But just a little. So...Frankie tells me that you'd like a word with me. What's on your mind, sport?"

"Ya'll want me to leave ya alone?" Frankie asked, looking from one to the other.

"Naw, that's okay," Aubrey said. "I ain't gonna say nuthin' you cain't hear. B'sides, you'd bug me 'til I told you anyways."

Uncle Frank had to smile at the country boy's candor.

"I ain't got a whole lot ta say, Uncle Frank," Aubrey started. "I jus' wanna ask ya some questions and let ya know that I don't hold nuthin' against ya fer bein' who ya are. An' I promise ya that Jesus don't hate ya fer it, neither. In fact, I b'lieve he understands ya and loves ya better'n anyone else. After all, him an' his father made ya.

"He knows what's in the hearts of folks, good or bad. An' I'm bettin' that the good you do, fightin' fires and rescuin' folks sets a whole lot better with him than the ugly stuff some folks might say about ya. An' I won't ever judge ya, 'cause that jus ain't right, an' I don't wanna make Jesus mad at me fer doin' his job. I ain't smart enough fer that, an' that's fer sure. But I do pray fer ya. I hope that's awright."

Frank was genuinely touched by Aubrey's humble sincerity.

"Aubrey....I don't believe I've ever had anyone represent Jesus to me better than you just did. You really do have him in your heart, don't you?"

"Well…'course I do. You do, too. Ya jus' might not recognize him."

The adolescent minister went on, "Did ya ever have a time when you was runnin' into a burnin' buildin' that you thought somebody was watchin' over ya?"

"Uh…yes, as a matter of fact, I have, many times," Frank replied. He was dumbfounded by Aubrey's insight.

"Well…there ya go," Aubrey said, as if it should be as obvious as water being wet.

"I'm perty sure ya learned this in Sunday School," he went on, "but Jesus didn't hang out with the preachers… he hung out with the folks that needed healin' in their hearts, like the prostitutes and the tax collectors. In fact he, uh…whut's the word?…oh yeah…he admonished the doctors to heal themselves first, meanin' the preachers, before they tried to heal the sick, meanin' the sinners."

It took Frank a minute to overcome his speechlessness.

"Aubrey…man, oh man! Frankie told me you were thinking about becoming a preacher. Quite honestly, I think you're already there. You just don't have the formal training. I'm thinking that maybe you don't need it, either. I hate to see some other men's notions get in your way."

Aubrey glowed under Uncle Frank's praise.

"So what questions do you have for me, big guy?" Frank was a little more apprehensive about Aubrey's questions now, but he felt comfortable with him. Besides, answering Aubrey's questions might help Frankie understand a little bit better.

Aubrey asked some of the same questions Frankie had asked, plus a few more. Fortunately, just like Frankie, Aubrey didn't delve into the sexual aspects, much to Frank's relief.

The fireman and the schoolboy found themselves engaged in an exchange of ideas, philosophies, and moralities that far transcended what Frank had expected from a twelve-year-old. It cemented his belief that Aubrey was just as special as his mother, if not more so.

To his credit, Frankie stayed up with them as best as he could, even interjecting an occasional comment, question, or opinion.

Before long, the cookies and lemonade were all gone, and the boys became boys again, talking about model airplanes and firecrackers. Eventually, they were sitting in awe, as Uncle Frank regaled them with embellished tales of heroism from the fire station, his fellow firefighters always the heroes, of course.

The evening wore on, and, all too soon, it was time for Aubrey and his mother to go home. They all said their good-byes on the front porch. Shelley excused herself and went inside, while Frankie and Aubrey walked to the pickup truck.

"Thanks again, Sarah," Frank offered. "You really are a gem."

He leaned down to kiss her on the cheek.

At the same time, she reached up to kiss his cheek.

By sheer coincidence, their lips met briefly.

"Oh . . . ," Sarah gasped, pulling back, her face flush with embarrassment.

"I'm sorry . . . ," Frank stammered at the same time, his own face burning.

Then, like two teenagers, they both began to giggle. Frank drew her into a warm hug.

"I miss being around you and talking with you, Dumplin.'"

"Me, too," was all her fluttering heart would let her

say.

"Well, I'd best be going," she finally managed to say, reluctantly pushing herself away.

"You take care of yourself, ya hear?" Frank insisted.

"And Sarah . . . ," he said, "please call me, if you ever need to...or just want to. Buck doesn't have to know. I mean, it's not like we're up to anything. I just need a friend....and I think you do, too."

"I will, Frank. I promise."

It was a promise that she intended to keep. Frank could never be her lover, but he could be the friend she had so desperately missed all these years.

He waved good-bye, as the truck rattled away, then turned to go inside.

Shelley had chanced to see the unexpected kiss through the screen door.

"Be careful, big brother," she said to him, when he came into the house. "She may appear tough on the outside, but she's been through a lot and I'd hate to see her get hurt."

"Wha..?" he asked, puzzled. "Oh, that? Don't worry, sis. That was an accident. A pleasant one, mind you, but just an accident. She's married, and I'm gay. I don't think that formula works too well."

Meanwhile, Sarah's thoughts whirled in her head. She felt a love for Frank that transcended anything physical and that was certainly different from the way she felt toward Buck.

As if he had read her thoughts, Aubrey said, "You like Uncle Frank a lot, dontcha, Maw?"

Uh-oh! she thought. *He saw that kiss.*

But before she could fashion a response, he said, "Me too. Ya know what I like best about him?"

"Uh…no, honey. What?"

"The way he always makes you smile an' feel good."

Then he added somberly, "Paw don't do that."

She didn't know how to respond to that. She could clearly hear the difference of nuance in his voice when he spoke of each of the men. One made her happy, the other hurt.

The next morning, after church services and true to his word, Aubrey sought out Reverend Greene and asked him if he had a few minutes to answer some questions about Jesus and about their church.

"You're in luck, my boy," Reverend Greene answered cheerfully. "I was planning on doing some fishing in the creek over there. Care to join me?"

It was a favorite tactic of his with his male parishioners who came seeking his council. It helped them relax. And he really did like fishing, whether he caught anything or not.

Aubrey was the star of his Sunday school class, sometimes even leading the lesson. Mrs. Arnold, his Sunday school teacher, had bragged profusely to the minister about him. So Neal Greene was more than happy to spend some time with the blossoming prodigy.

"I'll ask my Maw," Aubrey chirped. *Wow! Fishin', too.* he thought.

Of course, Sarah gave her permission. Buck had no authority when it came to her son's spiritual education. She had established that long ago, when Waylon was just a tyke. Buck had gladly capitulated. He wanted little to do with matters of the Almighty. Just sitting in church taxed his patience with the "Bible thumpers."

Reverend Greene assured Sarah that he would drive Aubrey home afterwards. When the last of his congregation had left, he had Aubrey wait on the porch of his parish house, while he changed into his "nonpreacher" clothes, as he called them.

Fetching a couple of fishing rods, his tackle box, and a can of bait worms he'd dug up the day before, he and Aubrey ambled down to the nearby creek for an afternoon of fishing for Jesus.

After some small talk about school and home, Aubrey dove headlong into the reason he was there.

"Reverend . . . ," he started, "do you know about Frankie Albert's uncle?"

"Do you mean him being a fireman?" the reverend asked, as he fished.

"No, sir. I mean him bein' a, uh…"

Now that he'd started the question, he found it harder to ask than he had thought it would be.

"Well…him bein' a gay guy," he finally blurted.

"Well, yes…I'd heard something about it. Why do you ask, Aubrey?" the reverend inquired, concern lacing his voice. "Has he said anything, or done anything, to you that makes you uncomfortable…like maybe touch you?"

"No sir!" Aubrey shot back in irritation at the suggestion. "He ain't never done nuthin' ta me! He's been like a uncle ta me. Him an' Maw are best friends from high school."

The minister was taken aback by the fierceness of Aubrey's objection. "I'm sorry, son. I thought…"

"No, sir, Reverend. I'm sorry," he interrupted, contrite at his outburst to his minister.

"I didn't mean ta git so upset. Its jus' that Uncle Frank is…" He hesitated and directed his thoughts back to his original question.

"I reckon that's what I want ta talk to ya 'bout. You

know, folks thinkin' the worst about others and sayin' hateful thangs that they shouldn't be sayin.'" Even in his apology, he could make adults think about what they had said.

"That's okay, son. I should have let you explain before I jumped to any conclusions," the admonished minister said, noticing that Aubrey had referred to Frank as "uncle." "Now, what's your question?"

"Well, Maw explained to me all about whut happened when he was in school, with that other boy an' all. An' about how a lot of the folks in town were real hateful to him, callin' him ugly names an' stuff."

He hesitated briefly, then said, "Includin' some of the folks that go to our church, here.

"My question is, Reverend, how can someone claim to love Jesus an' claim ta believe in what he teaches, an' then turn around an' be so hateful to someone who cain't help bein' what God made 'em ta be? That jus' don't sound right to me."

The minister had anticipated a hundred other questions a twelve-year-old might ask, like, "Why did God take my grandma?" or even, "Why is there war?" But he had not anticipated such a damning question on the hypocrisy of some Christians from such a young boy. Especially questions implicating those who sat in his own church, nodding agreement and shouting "amen" and "hallelujah" every Sunday morning.

He knew Aubrey was hanging on his answer, and he wanted it to be a righteous answer. He knew it had to be direct enough for the boy to understand; he just didn't know how to come up with one. Instead, he defaulted to an honest one.

"Aubrey...son, I just don't know how to answer that,"

the preacher lamented. "I know I have some of those kinds of folks in my flock. I know that some of them drink or gamble, or worse. And I know that some of them use God's Word as a bludgeon to beat down other folks who don't act the way they think they should.

"I try to reach them, to help them correct the error of their ways, but the sad truth is…some people are just too set in their ways to admit that they may be wrong. It breaks my heart. I pray constantly on it."

"Hmmm," Aubrey mused for a brief moment. "I reckon they're no different when they sin by judgin' others than Uncle Frank is by bein' a gay guy. They jus' cain't help themselves, huh?"

"Well, not exactly, son," the minister offered. "You see…I personally believe that Frank, or…Uncle Frank, is less guilty in his sin than they are in theirs, if that's possible." His beliefs on the subject had alienated him from the mainstream Baptists, and, ironically, they had landed him in the backwater town he now ministered to.

"Reverend…Maw told me to say 'gay" an' not 'homo' or 'queer,' like other kids do. Why is that? Don't 'gay' mean happy? Does that mean they're all happy about sinnin' like that?"

Aubrey was really pinning the minister down.

"Yes, the word does mean happy, and yes, many of them do appear to be content with who and what they are and don't consider it sinning. But many of them fight a terrible battle within themselves. They feel afraid that the rest of the world will hate them and hurt them for what they are. It's an awful dilemma for them. So I suppose they use the term to soften the emotional blow. But I could be wrong.

"Believe it or not, Aubrey," he went on, "I've had

many conversations with homosexual men and women about this very subject, before I came to Haleyville, of course. What I've come to believe is that, a lot of times, they don't really understand it themselves. It causes a lot of guilt and shame, and even self-hatred.

"It has caused an awful lot of them to turn against God and Christians, too. Worse than that, it has caused a lot of them to cast their own hatred against anyone who isn't like them, or who doesn't accept or condone their... um...lifestyle, as they like to call it."

"Maw says that's just hate begettin' hate," Aubrey interjected.

"Yes, it is," the reverend responded. "Your mother's a wise woman Actually, my boy, you've hit upon the real reason many people, not just homosexuals, have turned against God.

"I'm sorry to say that way too many Christians and non-Christians seize upon certain parts of the Bible that suit them and disregard the other parts they should be paying attention to. All too often, the part they seize upon is the part that they feel gives them the authority to condemn others. They consciously choose to judge and condemn others.

"But I believe that homosexuality is a subconscious response to something deeper, some irresistible drive, perhaps. Of course, there are plenty of folks out there who think otherwise and who believe that they choose to live the life they do out of perversion, or even rebellion to society, or to their family.

"Over the years, I've learned that those who judge others, be they Christian or not, tend to be unhappy people with injured souls, looking for someone or something to blame for their own unhappiness. In my opinion, Christians who do this are just going through the motions of their professed faith, but don't really live the spirit….the way you seem to do. Do you understand what I'm saying to you?"

"Mm-hmm," Aubrey nodded, not wanting to interrupt his minister. In his heart, he was glad that Reverend Greene felt they way he did. It would be difficult for him to receive truth and blessings from a man who contradicted what Aubrey knew in his heart that Jesus taught.

"Reverend . . . ," Aubrey started, "it ain't just some Christians that seem ta hate folks like Uncle Frank. Other folks that don't go ta church do, too. Why is that? They ain't got no Bible reason fer it, like them misguided Christians do."

"Son, people tend to hate and fear what they don't understand," the reverend explained. "I think some people hate homosexuals because they fear they might become one of them, as though it's some kind of infection, which is just plain silly. You are what you are. You can't 'catch' homosexuality, just like you can't 'convert' to it, either, like you can to Christianity.

"I think one of the best explanations was one I read about a couple years ago in a magazine that talks about human psychology."

"Do you know what that is?" he asked, not wanting to go over the boy's head.

"Yes, sir, I do. Maw explained it to me a while back."

"Good. Well, what the article said was that we humans have a part of our brain that reacts on a very primitive basis. It's the part that makes us run from danger and that sort of stuff. Are you following me?"

"Yes, sir."

"Well, that part of the brain—it's called the 'basal ganglion. Some call it the lizard brain," he said, getting a slight chuckle from Aubrey.

"Anyway, that part of the brain perceives danger or threats, to us personally and to our species. And since homosexuals can't have babies, which is the whole reason for God creating men and women, the 'lizard brain' sees homosexuality as a threat to the continuation of our species...of humans. Does that make sense to you?"

"Yes, sir, it does," Aubrey answered. "It's like bein' stupid without knowin' it, huh?"

"Well...it's a little more complicated than that, but I think you're on the right track," Reverend Greene said, and chuckled in response to Aubrey's country-boy simplicity.

"We humans have come a long way since the Lord created us, but we still have a long way to go. And there are some things we may never understand....like what causes homosexuality."

"Yes, sir, it's like God tells us...his ways ain't our ways, and we cain't possibly understand his mind. I really 'preciate you talkin' ta me like this, Reverend. Maybe you should talk to Frankie, too. I think he's kinda confused about it and dudn't have nobody ta talk to but me."

"Well, son, he could do a lot worse. I think you have a pretty good handle on it. You do my heart good, boy," he said, smiling at Aubrey. "A minister needs to know that his words mean something and that he really does have a lamb or two in his flock, not just a bunch of goats."

Aubrey chuckled at that and said, "Preacher, I learned a lot about the Bible in Sunday school . . .an' from yer sermons, too," he added quickly.

"I know whut the first words in the Bible are, but Maw

me taught what the last words are, too," he proclaimed.

"This is the Word of God. Keep it perfect. Don't add to it, an' don't take away from it," he recited, in his own juvenile fashion.

"That don't seem too hard to understand ta me. How come folks are always tryin' ta tell others what is or ain't in the Bible?"

The tip of the minister's fishing pole bobbed up and down. But all thought of the creature struggling at the end of his line was set aside. Instead, he was caught up in the irony of being fed fishes of wisdom from the twelve-year-old basket sitting in front of him and quoting a part of the Bible most people don't even know exists.

"Aubrey," he began, "have you read where Jesus says, 'Let those who have the eyes to see and the ears to hear be blessed'?"

"Uh-huh."

"Do you know what that means?"

"Sure do," Aubrey said, proudly. "Maw told me all about it. It means that not everybody can understand what Jesus is talkin' 'bout, when he teaches his father's Word an' stuff. She said that those who can understand have a special blessin', right?"

"I couldn't have said it better, son," Reverend Greene said. His amazement at Aubrey's intuitiveness grew with every word the boy said.

"Does it mean anything else to you?" he asked.

"Um…Preacher," Aubrey said, nodding to the frantically bobbing pole, "I think ya got a bite."

"Huh?" the preacher responded. Then grasping what Aubrey was talking about, he grabbed his pole and reeled in a big, fat catfish.

"It means that I should try to remember that just

because someone don't git the same thang outta whut the Bible says that I do, it dun't mean they're stupid… or wrong."

"Your mother taught you that?"

"Well, yes, sir, but I kinda felt that way, anyway."

He paused, then added, "Preacher, I know you talk to the Lord, 'cause that's whut preachers do, but, sometimes, when I'm prayin'…well, it just feels like maybe Jesus is talkin' back to me. I mean…it's like I can actually hear his voice. Like he was right there in the room with me or talkin' like me an' you are, right now. I know that sounds kinda crazy, but…."

"There's nothing crazy about that, at all," Reverend Greene reassured him. "In fact, it's the blessing Jesus was talking about, Aubrey. You have that blessing."

An inspired thought came to him.

"Aubrey, I have a small group from the congregation that I study the Bible with every Wednesday night. We pick a topic or a verse and share our opinions and understandings with each other. They're some pretty smart folks, too. I learn a lot from them. It helps me compose my sermons.

"I'm telling you this because I'm wondering if you'd like to come to a meeting, sometime, and get to know these people. I'm sure they'd love to meet you."

Aubrey was stunned. His minister was inviting him, a dumb, little boy, to sit with him and the smartest folks in church and talk about God and the Bible.

"Uh…I 'preciate that, Reverend, but . . . ," he slowly stammered, "I, uh…I don't reckon I'd be much good. I sure don't know as much about the Bible as ya'll do."

"My boy, it's not about knowledge; a lot of people can quote the Bible verse for verse, but few understand….I mean, really understand in their hearts, what God's Word means," the reverend explained. "I believe you have that rare gift, and it would be a shame…almost a sin…not to nurture that."

Now Aubrey really felt uncomfortable. *It might be a sin not to meet with these folks?*

Seeing his discomfort, Reverend Greene chuckled and said, "Aubrey, son, you don't have to do anything you don't want to. When I said 'almost a sin,' well, that was just a figure of speech. Of course, it's not a sin. I'm sorry if I made you feel uncomfortable.

"I'll tell you what…why don't you talk to your mother about it. See what she says, okay? I can see that she has had a lot to do with your spiritual upbringing, so I'd love to see her come, too."

"Sure, Reverend," Aubrey answered. *If his mother was there with him, then…*

"It looks like you might have a bite there, yourself," the reverend said, pointing to Aubrey's bobbing fishing pole.

"We've done enough talking, so unless you have more questions for me, let's do some fishing, okay?"

"That sounds good to me," Aubrey declared, grabbing his pole and cranking on the reel. Between Uncle Frank and the good reverend, he'd had enough serious talk for a while. Besides, he'd found out what he wanted to about his minister.

That evening, after dinner, as he was helping his mother wash dishes, he told her about his conversation with Reverend Greene and about the invitation. Sarah's eyes watered with pride, as she happily gave her permission, saying what a wonderful opportunity it was for him.

He told her what his friends and Uncle Frank had said about him becoming a preacher when he grew up and that he thought it might be a good thing to do. The thought of her youngest son becoming a minister made her heart leap with joy.

Later that night, mother and son prayed together in happy gratitude for all the blessings they'd received. Then she lovingly tucked him into bed, saying, "Momma loves you so very, very much. You are the greatest gift God could ever give me."

"I love you, too, Maw. God dun me a big favor makin' you my mother."

GIRLS, GLORY, AND GUNS

Autumn moved briskly toward winter, as Halloween approached. Frankie managed to find a way of living with his mother's illness, one day at a time. He cherished every single moment with her, even if it was just helping her wash dishes or folding laundry. He wanted all the memories he could gather. He knew he would need them later, after she was gone.

He still cried himself to sleep more nights than he could count, though. The lurking specter of being without his mother weighed heavy on his small shoulders, and the burden grew with each passing day.

It was a heavy burden for a young boy to bear, but Uncle Frank called him more frequently, and that helped.

His friends also helped him cope with his feelings.

Between Tony's sharp wit and Aubrey's serenity, he was in good hands.

They reminded him of a song he'd heard on the radio, about getting by with a little help from his friends.

Meanwhile; back in school, Tony's reputation had begun to spread.

He had taken on one of the bigger boys, who'd made

the mistake of teasing him about his size, and had sent him squealing away with a bloody nose.

That was enough to give other potential tormentors pause to think about crossing the little titan.

Usually, all it took was a threatening snarl, backed up by a deadly glare.

Some of the girls even began flirting with him, waving and batting their eyes at him or sitting close to him in the lunchroom.

Unfortunately, the flirting usually happened in front of Aubrey and Frankie, much to his dismay. But, secretly, he enjoyed the attention, especially from a certain little auburn-haired cutie named Cindy.

For the first time in his life, he walked the halls of his school without fear, and that felt wonderful.

With some after-school help from Frankie and Tony, Aubrey made surprising progress with his schoolwork and started getting better grades than he'd ever gotten before. His self-confidence grew, as well. Waylon began teasing him about being the "smart kid" in the family.

Of course, his mother was elated.

At one of the Wednesday night Bible study sessions she and Aubrey had begun attending, Reverend Greene had casually called him a good fit for the Baptist Seminary College. She had dismissed it as a well-intended compliment, but now she could hope for the possibility.

His father paid little attention to the improvement, even becoming annoyed if it was brought up. Sarah reasoned that Buck felt threatened by anyone who he felt was "better" than him, including his own son.

Aubrey also began to be noticed by the girls. A very shy, raven-haired girl named Lisa began smiling at him in the lunchroom and on the playground.

Tony wasted no opportunity to rib him about it, teasing "Aubrey's got a girlfriend!"

At first, Lisa's attention bothered Aubrey, but her green eyes and delicate smile started getting his interest. He often caught himself searching for her in the hallways. He was beginning to have feelings that thoroughly confused him.

"Why does she always smile at me?" he asked Frankie, when Tony wasn't around to tease him about it.

"Doggone it, Aub! Are you daft, or sumpthin?" Frankie asked, exasperated by his friend's cluelessness. "She likes you, dummy."

"Naw...uh-uh!" he shot back. "Naw, she don't."

"Don't go gittin' that started," he warned.

"Yeah...she does, Aub," Frankie crooned. "She likes ya, man. Ain't no gittin' around that."

He deliberately failed to mention the little blonde girl that had been catching his own eye.

"Oh, man," Aubrey lamented, "I don' want no girl likin' me!"

"I didn't say ya had to like her back," Frankie said. "But ya know...she is kinda cute."

"Yeah...I reckon she is, at that," he answered. Seeing Frankie's grin, he blushed bright red.

"I think you like her back," Frankie teased, getting a growl from his big friend.

"Hey...I got an idea," Aubrey said, changing the subject.

"Let's go git Tony. I finished that battleship last night. I think I'm ready ta go ta war with ya'll."

"Did ya make sure it floats right?" Frankie asked, as they walked to their bus.

"Yep. I put some clay in the bottom and then floated

it in the kitchen sink ta check it out."

"Cool. Tony said he was done, too. I've been done for a week," he bragged. "We were just waitin' for you."

Tony had concocted the idea that each one of them should choose a different nation's navy from World War II and build a fleet of plastic models from their respective choice. Then, he gloriously suggested they could take them down to the lake and have their own naval battle. They could use their BB guns to sink the other guys' ships, and whoever had any ships left floating after the other two guys' navies were sunk…would be the winner and rule the high seas of Lake Owen. It was a supremely popular idea with the other two boys, and the Musketeers embarked on a miniature arms race with each other.

Tony and Frankie earned the money to pay for their naval buildup by mowing lawns or doing odd chores for neighbors. Their efforts didn't go unnoticed by their parents, who thought they had merely developed an obsessive interest in model warships.

But Aubrey had no such option, since his father refused to pay him or to let him try to earn it, otherwise. Frankie mentioned it in a conversation with Uncle Frank, and within a week, Aubrey received a crisp twenty-dollar bill inside a greeting card that was signed, "Happy sailing, Commodore!"

Two dollars from it went into the offering plate that following Sunday.

They kept their ultimate intentions secret when their parents asked about all the little ships, fearing they would forbid the battle to take place…because they might put someone's eye out with the BB guns.

The next Saturday, after cartoons, Tony asked his

father to drive them to the lake, not really expecting him to do so.

Much to his surprise, his father agreed to ferry the pint-sized admirals and their armadas.

Mike guessed what their intentions might be when he saw each boy with a BB gun and several boxes of carefully packed model ships, but he decided not to comment.

In fact, he found it rather humorous and almost wished he could join them. Lately, he had begun to take notice of his son's change in attitude and was curious about it, so he went along quietly.

Tony sat riveted in his seat, lest his father start asking questions.

Aubrey and Frankie sat in the backseat, pinching each other, to keep themselves from bursting out laughing.

When they got to the lake, they found a good spot for their pending battle, a small, calm, shallow cove, where no one was swimming.

They carefully carried their boxes and guns from the car, down to the water's edge.

After an impromptu christening speech by Tony, they carefully launched their fleets in that small, calm, shallow cove.

The warships scattered into a chaotic flotilla, bobbing randomly on the still lake water, awaiting the coming battle.

Each one of the boys had picked a color to distinguish his fleet from the others, lest one boy accidentally sink his own ship.

Aubrey chose grey, since the models already were that color and he didn't have to buy the paint. Frankie chose tan, for no special reason, and Tony chose red, because it made him look unafraid and bold.

They each loaded their "cannons" with the tiny, brass antiship projectiles and made ready to fire.

"You boys watch what you're doing," Mike advised lightly, concealing a grin. "Don't point those things this way, you hear?"

"Yeah, Pop, we know," Tony answered glibly. "We might put our eyes out!" Rolling his eyes, he turned away, thinking, *What do you care, anyway?*

"First one to sink all the other guys' ships wins!" Frankie declared; then, he started the battle by yelling, "Ready…aim…fire!"

With that, the Great Sea Battle of Lake Owen began.

The carnage was gruesome!

Tiny chunks of styrene flew about, as imaginary captains barked orders to their heroic, fighting sailors, who died valiantly trying to save their ships.

It was a titanic contest between powerful warships, some of which had never met each other in real life, slugging it out over dominion of the lake.

The mayhem was epic in scope, with each boy admiral adding his own sound effects of explosions and dying men's screams.

Within a half hour, the mightiest gathering of plastic battleships, destroyers, cruisers, and aircraft carriers the world had ever seen lay at the bottom of the shallow, muddy waters.

Only Aubrey's cracked and punctured Japanese battleship *Yamato* was still afloat, but it, too, was beginning to show signs of sinking.

"Hey!" Tony protested. "The Japs ain't s'posed to win, ya know!"

"Yeah…and the Americans ain't s'posed ta lose,

neither!" Aubrey goaded back. "But they did!"

Picking up a large, flat rock and lifting it over his head, he heaved it at the floundering little boat, landing squarely amidships and shattering it, amid cheers from all three boys.

"That was so far out!" Tony yipped.

"Hey, Pop . . . ," he called, but, seeing his father napping in the car, he said dejectedly, "Never mind."

"I reckon yer paw was tired," Aubrey offered cheerfully.

"Naw," Tony lamented, "he just doesn't care about any of the stuff I do. Ya remember the time when we got into that fight?"

"'Course I do." Aubrey answered, remembering his punishment more than the fight.

"Well...I thought I was going to get a whippin', too," Tony said. "But, instead, Mom was the one who got all upset about it. Pop just looked at my shiner and told my mom that I had to learn how to defend myself. And then he went back to readin' his danged ol' newspaper. He thinks I'm a wimp."

"Well, he don't know Tony the Tiger like we do then, does he?" Aubrey bragged about his friend.

"He ain't never seen ya ride a mule, or he sure wouldn't think that."

Unknown to the boys, Mike had actually watched them, as they ran excitedly up and down the bank, vying for the best advantage point to sink their opponents' vessels.

He chuckled when he realized that the three boys were being extra careful not to point their guns where they "might put somebody's eye out."

The sight of his son having such tremendous fun

had touched him and had triggered a need for some introspectiveness in him. As they returned to the car, he pretended to be asleep in order to catch what they said without them feeling restrained.

But his son's razor-edged comments cut him deeply. He had no idea Tony felt that way. Had he really failed his only son so badly?

He had actually been proud of Tony when he saw the black eye and heard what had happened. But being a manager of people, accustomed to avoiding or resolving conflicts, he responded neutrally—too neutrally, apparently.

Obviously, he had handled it all wrong.

His son's words hurt him. They made clear that his lack of fatherly input had caused more harm than good.

His stomach soured at the thought of his failure.

He had always excelled at whatever he applied himself to. He had been class president in college, and he had climbed the corporate ladder rapidly. He had even excelled as a naval officer, earning several commendations.

Unfortunately, it seemed he had not applied that excellence to the most important responsibility a man can possibly have...being a good father.

I'm a fricken' idiot! he berated himself.

The thought of failing at such a vitally important task delivered an emotional sucker punch he had not seen coming.

He was going to have to work on that...starting right now.

Pretending to wake up, just as the boys opened the car door, he jumped slightly and rubbed his face awake.

"I just had the weirdest dream," he said, to neither

boy in particular, "something about a mule."

Aubrey laughed, as he climbed into the big sedan, and said, "Heck, Mr. Carillo, that wudn't no dream. We was jus' talkin' 'bout how good Tony here is when he rides my paw's mules."

Tony gave him a sidelong look of disapproval, thinking his father would belittle the feat.

"Tony rode a mule, huh?" his father asked, puzzled.

Here we go. Now I'm gonna catch crap for doing something stupid or scary, Tony thought.

"Wow, son, that's, um…that's really impressive!" his father complimented.

"Is it true what they say about mules?" he asked his surprised son "You know, that they're harder to ride than horses?"

Tony was dumbstruck.

"Um, I dunno, Pop," he answered, bewildered. "I never rode a horse before. I guess it could be."

"Yes, sir, Mr. Carillo," Aubrey said, coming to the rescue, "it can be if ya got a hardheaded one that dudn't wanna be rode. But ours don't mind it much."

Then, clapping Tony on the back, he added, "You oughta see him. He's even stood up on their backs while they're runnin', an' that ain't easy!"

Now Tony was sure that his father would berate him for taking such a risk, but, much to his surprise, Mike said enthusiastically, "Whoa! That's terrific! I had no idea, son. I sure would like to see that sometime…if it's okay with you."

Tony's eyes were as big as saucers, and his mouth hung open.

"Sure ya can, Mr. Carillo," Aubrey answered for him. "In fact, this Sunday'd be good, if that's okay." He knew how dejectedly Tony had spoken about his father's attention and felt that this might be an opportunity to help his friend.

"Sounds like a plan, Aubrey; thanks."

"So . . . ," Mike went on, changing the subject, "now that I have all three of you together, tell me about the fight the other day."

The three boys froze, feeling a clever trap had just been sprung.

"I hear some chumps jumped you from behind, son. Is that so?" he asked.

Then, without waiting for an answer, he said, "And you boys jumped in to help him, right?"

"Um . . . ," Aubrey started.

"Don't worry boys," he chuckled, playing on their apprehension.

Then he said to Tony, "I didn't want to say anything in front of your mother, son; you know how she is about that sort of stuff.

"But, actually, I'm very proud of the way you stuck up for yourself."

Then he nodded to Aubrey and Frankie, saying, "And I want to thank you boys for standing with him, too."

He hesitated for a moment, and then added, "Now, don't get me wrong, boys. I'm not saying that fighting is okay or that it's the best way to solve all your problems, but sometimes a man's gotta do what a man's gotta do, right? Especially when it comes to your friends and your honor. Those are two very important things in a man's life.

"Hopefully, you've made your point, and you won't have to do it again," he added.

The boys were stymied.

Tony pinched himself to see if he was dreaming. His father had just referred to him as a "man."

"So who won the battle?" Mike asked, pointing to the lake.

"Huh?" Tony replied, gathering his wits.

"Oh, that! Aubrey thinks he won, but I say he cheated!" he teased from the front seat, knowing that there really was no need for Aubrey to cheat, since he was the better shot, by far.

"Did not!" Aubrey protested. "You jus' cain't shoot worth a darn, that's all. You need lessons, boy."

"I can too shoot," Tony said, pouting and crossing his arms.

His father looked at him sideways and smiled. Here was opening for him to get closer to his son.

"You know…I used to do some competition shooting in the navy," Mike revealed. "Maybe I can show you a thing or two, son."

"You were in the navy?" Aubrey asked, an awe in his voice.

"Sure was," he bragged, in typical navy swagger.

A collective *"Wow!"* issued from Frankie and Aubrey. Tony looked at his father a little differently than he had just this morning.

"What did ya do, Pop?" he asked. "I mean, I knew you were a sailor, but…"

He stopped, rolling a thought around in his head, then asked, "Did ya fight the Japs?"

Mike heard the awe and newfound respect that resonated in his words.

"No, son; that was a little before my time. But I did serve in the Korean War."

Then, a multitude of lights suddenly flashed on in

his mind, and he remembered how awestruck he had been when his own father had returned from Germany after the war. He remembered how his father had seemed larger than life, with his medals and war stories.

He was only thirteen at the time, and he remembered the pride he had whenever he would brag to the other kids about how his dad had won the war, almost by himself.

"My dad fought the Krauts!" or "My dad fought the Japs!" were bragging rights all the sons of the warriors boasted.

The sons whose fathers didn't come home were given special respect.

It had never occurred to him that his own son might crave that sort of image of his father, too. He felt that he had cheated him by not sharing some pretty important things with him. He realized that he had not given him someone to look up to, just a paper image of a father. He had denied his own son the thing a son needs most…a hero for a father.

Instead, he had merely been a presence in his son's life, and apparently not a particularly positive or significant one.

Like a Klaxon bell going off in his head, he realized that what he'd been wanting from his son all along was the kind of respect he had for his own father. The kind of respect a boy has for his father when he sees him as larger than life, even heroic.

It would be a challenge to earn that respect, but earn it, he would.

He now understood his son's obsession with comic book heroes. While he didn't consider himself a failure, he could no longer look at himself as being a successful "dad."

That was a badge of honor he had not yet won, the medal he now found himself yearning for.

"I was on a light carrier called the U.S.S. *Bataan*," he told them. "We launched fighters to take on the MIGs that the enemy sent, as well as bombers to support the marines fighting on the ground."

"My cousin Chet's a marine," Aubrey announced.

"He's over in Veet-nam right now, but Maw told me that the war was gonna be endin' soon an' he'd be comin' home sometime around Christmas. She's been mighty worried 'bout him."

"That's great news, Aubrey. I hope it's true," Mike said cheerfully, but he knew the politics of the war and had also heard the old "be-home-by-Christmas" promise firsthand, himself.

"So he's a devil dog, eh?"

Seeing the confused expression on the boy's face, he added, "That's what they call each other, sometimes. They usually called us navy boys 'squids' or 'swabbies.' After he finished speaking, he earned a hearty laugh from the boys.

Tony was awestruck, enraptured by the thought of his very own father heroically fighting enemy airplanes on the high seas, bullets and shrapnel whizzing by, just like a John Wayne movie.

"Awesome, Pop!" Tony declared. "What'd ya do? Were you a fighter pilot?"

"No, son; nothing that glamorous," he said. "I was just a signal officer. I helped guide the planes back to the ship after a mission, that's all." He was modestly playing down the importance of his part.

Mike glanced into the rearview mirror and noticed Frankie sitting sullenly quiet.

"I know about your father, Frankie," he said, as sympathetically as he could, remembering the friends he'd lost to war.

"I'm real sorry for your loss, buddy. I know this may sound a bit silly to you, but I'd like to say 'thank you' for what he did."

Thank me for what he did? He got killed and left me without a dad! That's what he did, Frankie thought, but he simply nodded back.

Mike sensed his thoughts, and explained as he drove, "Frankie, as an ex-war fighter myself, I know what your dad went through every day and every night. It was hard, scary, and very dangerous. I don't know how it happened, but you can bet he was a real hero, buddy.

"I just wanted you to know that some of us are grateful for the sacrifices others make for us. Since I can't thank him, thanking you seems the next best thing. Your dad was one of the best."

Mike had seen the news casts of long-haired war protesters spitting on returning soldiers. He had seen news reporters painting them as butchers and drug addicts, in their quest for the personal glory of an anchor spot on the evening news. He had come to despise such people as witless idiots.

He especially despised the self-impressed celebrities who had managed to dodge the draft yet who had still degraded the young men who had no choice but to do a dirty job for their country, a job they were obviously too cowardly to do themselves.

"Thank you, sir," Frankie replied meekly.

"Look, I know that sometimes a fella needs to talk to someone about things that a moms or girls just don't understand," he started, painfully aware that his own son was hearing this for the first time, too.

"I know you have your Uncle Frank, and he's quite a guy, too. But if you ever just want to talk about stuff, whatever it is, I hope you'll think about talking to me… you, too, Aubrey."

Then looking at his own son, he said, "Tiger, that goes especially for you. We have some catching up to do. I'm sorry if I haven't acted much like a dad for you. I promise I'll try harder from now on." He had used the nickname he'd heard Aubrey use.

Tony was confused by his father's behavior. Such a confession in front of his friends was astounding to him, but, gratefully, he beamed back, "You bet, Pop!"

He liked being called 'Tiger' by his 'dad.'

"Aubrey, you said that Tony doesn't shoot very well, right?"

"Um, I didn't meant ta say anything . . . ," he answered pensively, thinking he'd insulted his friend.

"Relax, buddy. You're right. He probably doesn't."

Tony looked stricken. *I knew it!* he thought.

"It's okay, son," Mike said, seeing his son's face. "It's my fault. I never taught you how, did I?"

"Um…no, Pop. But…."

"No buts about it. I dropped the ball," Mike confessed. "So…how about some of those lessons Aubrey was bustin' your chops for?"

"Lessons?"

"Yes…lessons. You know what those are, don't you?"

The other two boys could see where Tony got his sarcasm.

"'Course I do, but…."

"There ya go butting in again," Mike teased; then he went on before his son could respond, "Here's the deal....I'll teach you how to shoot. It's that simple. You too, Frankie...if you want? Aubrey seems to have a handle on it, but you two might need a little help, ya think?"

"Yer right, Mr. Carillo," Aubrey answered.

"My paw dun taught me how, an' he's a real good shot," he went on.

"Hey, maybe I can talk ta him an' ask if ya'll could do them lessons at our place," he offered. He would need his mother's help to get his father's permission, but it was worth a try.

"Well, you mentioned that Sunday would be a good time to check out Tiger's riding skills. Maybe we could cook off a few rounds while we're there?" he said, grinning over at Tony. "If it's okay with your parents, of course."

"That'd be perty cool," Aubrey said, "I'll ask Paw. He gets a kick outta watchin' Tony ride, so maybe he'll say okay."

As they rode on, Frankie fell silent, while Aubrey and Tony chattered on. He had pondered both of his friend's relationships with their fathers many times.

He knew Aubrey's father was a terrible example of what a dad should be. He could never reconcile how someone like Aubrey, so kind and thoughtful, could have such a tyrant for a father. How could his friend have such a sympathetic heart for others, when his own heart was routinely stomped on by his father?

It didn't make sense to him that Aubrey would be so ready to defend the smaller, more helpless among them. He could easily be the biggest bully in school. No one would, or could, stand up to him. He could clobber anyone with one hand tied behind his back.

Yet he was the kindest, gentlest kid he knew. He

was always polite around adults and kindhearted to all animals, including kids. How could he have such peace inside when he suffered such violence on the outside?

Aubrey was a real hero, too, Frankie thought.

Tony's father was a bit of a mystery to him, though. All he had ever seen when he visited Tony was a man sitting in his easy chair, reading the paper, making an occasional, mumbling comment. Not one to be particularly feared, or really noticed, for that matter.

He knew Mike made a good living for his family, from the nice things that filled their nice house and the nice car they were riding in.

It was what the TV said a father should be like, wasn't it?

Ozzie Nelson, Ward Cleaver, and Mike Carillo.

Why was Tony always so negative when it came to his father? He had the "normal" family. He didn't get beatings like Aubrey, and at least his father was alive. Tony didn't know how good he had it.

And now it sounded as if he were going to have it even better.

Frankie felt sorry for one and envied the other.

"Well, how about those shooting lessons?" Mike asked Frankie, as he pulled up in front of his house.

Snapping out of his ponderings, Frankie said, "Um… sure, Mr. Carillo. I'll ask Momma and call ya'll tonight."

He gathered his empty box and BB gun and said goodbye to his buddies and Mr. Carillo; then he bounced through the gate, leaving his thoughts for another day. Shooting lessons? Now that's cool.

That night, Mike had a long, heartfelt talk with Kathleen about how he'd been so negligent to his children.

Confessing to his wife broke down the wall he'd so carelessly, even callously, built around himself.

His apology to her brought forth a river of remorse and repressed tears that had a cleansing affect on his soul.

It reminded him that to be a real man, you had to be able to cry over the important things, like your family.

As she cradled her tearful husband, Kathleen shed tears of her own, rejoicing in the change. He promised her, and himself, that he was going to become a better, more active father for his children.

Every promise he had ever made paled in comparison to the vital importance to this one.

He would not allow himself to break it.

READY, AIM, FIRE!

With a little persuasive help from his mother, Aubrey had gotten permission from a very reluctant Buck to allow Mike and the boys to shoot their guns on his farm. The following Sunday, after church, Mike arrived at the Denton farm with Frankie and Tony.

The boys could barely contain their excitement. After greeting Buck and Sarah on the front porch of the farmhouse, Mike returned to his car and opened the trunk.

Reaching in, he pulled out his old competition single-shot .22 caliber rifle. The boys were ogling the weapon, when they noticed a scope in the velvet-lined case.

"Cool, a scope too," Frankie observed.

"My paw says that if ya need a scope, you ain't such a good shot," Aubrey said, almost apologetically.

"Maybe so," Mike agreed, "but, with a scope, you can hit a squirrel in the eye at the length of a football field."

He didn't want to embarrass Aubrey, so he continued, "But you're right, Aubrey; you need to learn without a scope first. A scope will only make you a better shot at a further distance; that's all."

Buck had agreed to let them shoot, but he declined to participate, claiming he had better things to do than play with guns all day.

"Make sure ya clean up all yer damn shells," he said to Aubrey, but Mike knew whom the jab was intended for. He bristled at the insult to a former naval shooter, but he wasn't going to give Buck the satisfaction of reacting to it.

Buck's refusal to join in reminded Mike of all the opportunities to spend time with his son that he had passed up. But he had done so tactfully, in a way that he had mistakenly thought wouldn't hurt Tony's feelings.

Buck's rudely flippant way of rejecting his son only served to further sour his opinion of the man.

He knew of Buck's abusive attitude toward his family and his abrasive personality. Kathleen had told him about the times she had seen bruises on both Aubrey and Sarah.

He regarded him as a frustrated blowhard, afraid of the world, but determined to show otherwise. Only a coward smacked women and children around. But it was a judgment best kept to himself, for Aubrey's sake.

He showed the boys how to set up the store-bought targets on bales of hay borrowed from the barn, making sure that the hill was behind the bales. Then he meticulously showed them how to hold the rifle properly and how to line the sights up.

The lessons went well, even for Aubrey. Of course, he already knew the basics of handling and shooting accurately, but when Mike showed them the different positions to fire from, he became more interested.

He had seen soldiers in the movies firing from the prone position and was eager to learn how to do it right.

He was surprised to find that the sitting position helped him to steady his aim.

As expected, Aubrey had the best scores of the three, regularly getting bulls-eyes, but Mike turned out to be an excellent instructor. It didn't take long for Frankie and Tony to begin racking up tight patterns, as well.

Soon, several empty ammunition boxes lay at their feet, amid piles of spent shells.

Frankie had taken to it particularly well, seeming almost a natural at it. By the end of the day, he was shooting almost as well as Aubrey.

"You'll be outshootin' me, before too long," Aubrey complimented, without a trace of jealousy.

"Hey, I just had an idea," he said. "But I'll have ta tell ya 'bout it later…in case it don't work." He teased everyone's interest, including Mike's.

But, for Tony, the best part of the day was that his pop, his own father, was the hero and was spending time with him, instead of reading the papers and watching sports on TV, the way he usually did.

After expending all the ammo, Mike had the boys pick up all the brass shells that littered the ground around them and return the bales of hay to the barn, denying Buck any reason to complain. He told them that he'd show them how to clean a rifle some other time.

Then he asked the boys about the mules he'd heard so much about. "I might even try riding one, myself, if that's okay."

As it turned out, late afternoon was the time the mules were normally taken to the pond to be watered. Usually, Aubrey or his brother would mount one and lead the other by the reins down to let them drink their fill.

This time, though, Aubrey and Frankie fetched them

from the barn and led them next to one of the boulders. It was of ample height to allow Mike to scramble up onto Aida's bare back, while Aubrey climbed onto Kitt.

Tony was snickering, amused at the way his wide-eyed father grasped Aida's mane for dear life, not having a saddle or stirrups to help him in his folly.

"Ya better relax, Pop!" he shouted, laughing. "If he thinks you're scared, he'll throw you off."

"Thanks, son," Mike answered nervously. He'd only ridden a horse once or twice in his life, and, even then, they were tame stable horses, well accustomed to strangers on their backs.

Aubrey grabbed Aida's reins and started toward the creek, Tony and Frankie following on foot close behind. But Aida sensed Mike's nervousness and did exactly what Tony said he'd do.

In a flash, his father was flying in an arch, from the mule's back to the ground, thankfully softened by the tall grass stalks and thick clover.

Tony fell down laughing, as his father gingerly clambered to his feet and brushed off the dirt and the grass.

After reassuring himself that his father was all right, except for a bruised posterior and bruised pride, Tony got a boost from Frankie and climbed, as nimble as a cat, onto the big animal's back.

Leaning forward, Tony patted Aida on the neck, as he reached for the reins and said, "Let's show 'em how it's done, ol' girl."

Without hesitation, he dug his heels into Aida's side, and the mule launched forward, like a thoroughbred. Tony seemed a mere fly on the huge animal's back, but he had no trouble staying on the unsaddled animal.

Mike flinched, fearing for his son's safety, but he was

genuinely surprised and impressed at how well Tony handled the animal.

A lump of pride swelled up in his chest for his boy. He decided right then to find a riding school and sign Tony up.

Inside, he berated himself for not seeing these things sooner. How much had he missed out on? He didn't want to think too hard about it, right now, though.

That was the past; he was watching the future stand up on the galloping beast's back with no saddle, beaming with pride and waving at him.

"I gotta admit," Buck said, as he walked up to Mike.

"That boy of yers is one helluva horseman," he complimented. "If he can do that good with mules, I reckon he can do a lot better with the real thang."

"Thank you, Buck," Mike replied. Then, returning a fatherly compliment, he said, "You know, your son is a damn good shot. He says you taught him. You did a good job. Do you take him hunting often?"

"Yep, all the time. We gotta keep the squirrels an' rabbits down 'round here. Else they'd eat us outta feed fer the livestock; plus they spread rabies," he answered, turning even hunting into a chore for his son.

"I reckon shootin' them lil' fuckers on the run sharpens yer eye perty good, though, don't it?"

"Yeah, I guess that's true," Mike replied, his distaste for the man returning.

"I really appreciate you letting us come out today. This really means a lot to Tony and to me," he said. Offering an olive branch, he stuck his hand out to shake Buck's rough paw.

"Hell, it ain't no thang," Buck responded, shaking Mike's hand. "I reckon even city boys need ta know how ta shoot." He had finished his statement with a slight sneer.

Asshole! Mike thought, as he watched Buck amble away. He understood why Aubrey preferred to visit, rather than be visited. He felt sorry for the boy.

Tony was still standing on the mule's broad back as he trotted back to the waiting group. As he got close enough, he yelled, "Catch me, Pop!" and leapt from Aida's back into his father's arms.

"That was absolutely awesome, son!" his father proclaimed proudly, hugging him close before setting him down.

"Mr. Denton is right; you are a good horseman!"

"My paw said that?" Aubrey asked, with a mix of surprise tinged with a little hurt. He could do all the same things that Tony could; in fact, he had taught him how. But his father had never said anything so complimentary about him. "I reckon he's right."

Sensing Aubrey's reaction, Mike said, complimenting him, "You know, Aubrey, you are one heck of a shot. Those were some real tight patterns. I bet you'd make a good marine sharpshooter."

"Thank ya, Mr. Carillo, but I think I'd druther fly airplanes. That'd be more fun."

Son, the movies got it all wrong. There is no fun in war! Just ask your cousin when he gets home.

"I'll bet you'd make a good pilot, too," he complimented, getting a grateful smile in return.

Turning his attention back to his son, he asked, "How do you control her without reins, son?"

Then he added, "To tell you the truth, I was a bit nervous, even with them."

"Yeah, we saw that," his son teased, grinning impishly

at his father.

As Aubrey and Frankie rode the mules down to the pond and then back to the barn, Tony proceeded to explain that he could guide the huge beast with subtle nudges from his knees to the animal's side and with foot pressure when he was standing on her back. Keeping his balance was just a natural thing to do, but he also assumed that being as small as he was helped some.

"I'll tell ya what, buddy," Mike said to his son, "we won't say anything to Mom about you standing up, but I'm sure she'll be just as proud as I am to hear about the rest. Oh, and if it's okay with you, we'll keep my short ride our little secret, okay?"

Tony's heart was doing backflips. His once-complacent, unapproachable father was now his playful dad. And now they had their first secret between them. That's what friends do, he thought.

"Is keeping our secret worth a root beer float?" he coyly blackmailed his dad.

Mike was caught off guard by the request, and he raised a pensive eyebrow, but then he chuckled, "I'll do you one better. How about root beer floats for everybody?" He looked from one boy to the next.

Cheers of "Yeah!" and "All right!" rang out, as the three sharpshooters raced for the car. Aubrey stopped short, saying, "Aw, shoot! I gotta ask my maw!"

Mike said, "That's okay; I'll ask her for you. I'd like to say good-bye to her, anyway."

He walked up to the old house, climbed the creaking stairs, and knocked on the weather-beaten door.

Sarah answered the door, wiping her hands on the kitchen towel she held.

"Oh, hi, Mike," she said, cheerfully. "You boys all

through?"

"Yeah, we are," he answered. "At least with the cow-boy stuff."

Letting a little chuckle escape, she continued, "It's so nice of you to spend time with the boys. They need that sort of thing."

Sarah knew about the strained relationship between him and his son. It did her heart good to see him emerge from his stoic cocoon and bloom into an involved father. She only wished her own husband would do the same.

She was also happy for the influence it could have on Frankie. Shelley had confided her worries about Frankie's emotional well-being, since he didn't have a male presence at home. The episode with her brother only served to raise her concerns.

But Sarah's most tangled feelings were for her own son. Buck was a brutal father. Not a "dad," by any measure. All Aubrey had known was hardship and ridicule from him. She was elated that he now had another positive male role model to look up to, in addition to Frank. But she was saddened that it wasn't his own father.

"Would you mind if I took Aubrey to the A&W for a float?" he asked.

Sarah gladly gave her permission and expressed her gratitude. She'd smooth it over with Buck by cooking his favorite meal: fried chicken and mashed potatoes. She knew her irascible husband's weaknesses.

Of course, the root beer floats were a huge hit. Mike engaged the boys in idle chatter, until the sun began to set. They talked about everything, including how they called themselves the Three Musketeers. When Mike explained to them what a real Musketeer was, the boys were elated, but they were a little confused that the weapons of choice had been swords and not muskets.

Mike sorted that out for them, too, explaining how long and difficult it could be to reload a musket in real life and that sword fights always looked better on the silver screen.

From then on, whenever the Musketeers gathered, they alternated between their wooden swords and their BB guns to defeat the villains of the world.

For his part, Mike couldn't remember a more rewarding day. All the accolades and awards he'd won in the business world and even his cherished navy medals seemed so unimportant now, even somewhat silly.

The greatest reward came after he'd dropped Aubrey and Frankie off, when a drowsy Tony laid his head in his father's lap and said, "Thanks, Dad," as he dozed off to sleep. Mike took a long, circular route home, not wanting the moment to end.

I can do this, he proclaimed, as a swell of joy rose in his chest.

Later in the evening, Kathleen reaped in the benefits of a "born again" father and husband. Her special "punch" stayed in the refrigerator. She had something else to help her sleep well tonight.

HOLIDAYS AND MALAISE

As the holiday season approached, leaves began painting their autumn colors in broad strokes on the hillsides around Haleyville.

First came Halloween, a very special holiday for rambunctious boys everywhere. Aubrey had been trick-or-treating only a few times, since living out in the country didn't really accommodate going door to door, and Waylon had lost interest in it after getting into middle school and discovering girls.

Frankie's interest had waned somewhat over the past couple of years, since his mother was the only one he had to go with. But Tony was still in the spirit of things, so his enthusiasm infected the other boys.

Naturally, the costumes of choice were to dress up as the Three Musketeers. But where would they get them? Frankie mentioned the dilemma to his mother.

After calling the other two mothers, she assured him that he and his friends would have better costumes than any ol' store could offer.

All the mothers showed their flair for creative sewing by making the best Musketeer costumes Haleyville had ever seen. Kathleen drove all the way to Memphis to find patterns, dragging a reluctant Maria with her, and she insisted on buying all the best materials. She even had her sister in New York mail three pageboy wigs purchased from a theater supply house for the boys to wear.

For two weeks, they alternated the sewing sessions between homes, deliberately driving Buck up a wall with chatter when it was Sarah's turn to host a session. Kathleen's new portable Singer sewing machine easily made professional-looking seams.

Shelley put special effort in what she was sure would be the last costume she would ever make for her son, often coming to tears over that awful thought.

Sarah and Kathleen were always ready with a joke or a juicy bit of local gossip to bring her out of her funk.

The boys were supremely pleased with their new costumes, though Aubrey was a little apprehensive about the lace cuffs and frilly shirt.

Tony set him straight by telling him that they didn't have blue jeans and flannel shirts back then.

Frankie had hoped Uncle Frank would come down and take them trick-or-treating, but his uncle explained that Halloween brings out the crazies, some of whom like to start fires, so his fire station had to be on alert for the inevitable trouble.

But he did promise to come down for Thanksgiving, instead.

Trick-or-treating was fun enough for a while, but after they had filled their pillow cases with candy, they became bored with the routine.

It was time for some adventure.

Living out their costumes and characters, the Musketeers proceeded to rescue young Cinderellas,

Snow Whites, and ballerinas from the clutches of juvenile vampires, white-sheeted ghosts, or evil astronauts, whether they wanted or needed rescuing or not.

One mother, who was escorting her Frankenstein-costumed son from door to door, was startled when the boys jumped from behind a bush, brandishing their wooden swords. She yelled at the lace-frilled heroes, saying that they would "put somebody's eye out!" with their swords, prompting Aubrey to ask his buddies, "Have ya'll ever known about anybody puttin' their eye out with a stick fer real?"

"No, but my mom thinks everything can put your eye out!" Tony replied.

The three intrepid vigilantes boldly chased off dastardly pumpkin smashers from their mission of destruction. Feeling brave, they confronted a roving band of pranksters brandishing rolls of toilet paper and cartons of eggs in their hands, with vandalism on their minds.

Three oddly dressed boys with wooden swords running at them surprised the would-be vandals, causing them to run away and opt for another street to wreak their havoc on.

They had saved the neighborhood! Hip-hip hurrah and tallyho!

Exaggerated sword fights with imaginary castle guards and repeated rounds of "All for one, and one for all!" punctuated the evening.

At least until the sugar high subsided.

Later that evening, three mothers found three boys clutching bags of sugary treasure, amid scattered wrappers, snoring contentedly on three couches.

After Halloween had passed, Tony wanted to continue to dress up and to play Musketeers, but Aubrey didn't want to risk ruining his beautiful costume.

"Ya only dress up on Halloween!" he declared. "Otherwise, it looks goofy!"

The weather changed and brought autumn's chill to the air. Shelley's illness progressed at a discouragingly rapid pace, though not as cripplingly as she had feared.

For that, she was grateful, but she needed Frankie's help more often than she liked, as her strength slowly eroded away.

He never complained, and he made every effort he could think of to make things easier for his mother. His young, naive heart held out the hope that if she didn't have to work so hard, maybe she'd be strong enough to get better.

As word of her condition spread, she began to see the kinder side of Haleyville.

Ladies in her Bible study group brought prepared dishes of food to her house, as well as the latest gossip.

The pharmacist at the Rexall Drugstore gave her generous discounts on her medication, helping her cover what her meager insurance wouldn't.

People who had previously taken little notice of her were now greeting her fondly. Though she appreciated the kindness, she couldn't help wondering if they would do so if she weren't dying.

One rainy Saturday, she heard a knock on her door and sent Frankie to answer it. He opened the door, and, to his utter amazement, he saw Miss Shockley standing there.

"Hi, Frankie," she said. "How are you doing?"

"Uh…I'm doing fine, Miss Shockley," he answered warily, wondering if he had somehow gotten into trouble at school and didn't know about it.

"Is your mother home?" she asked, with a warm smile on her aged face.

"Um…yes, ma'am, she is," he said. His mind was racing, wondering what she wanted.

"Who is it, sweetie?" his mother called from the living room.

"Um…please come in, Miss Shockley," he offered, as politely as he could, stepping aside to admit her in, as one would step aside for a lioness suddenly in one's presence.

Sensing his apprehension, she chuckled and said, "Don't worry, Frankie. You're not in any trouble. I'm here to see how your mother is doing; that's all."

She added, "She was a student of mine, a long time ago. Did you know that?"

"Oh," Frankie said, breathing a sigh of relief. He then led her to the living room and announced, "It's Miss Shockley, Momma."

Before he could explain, Shelley started to get up from the couch, saying, in complete surprise, "Well… hello, Miss Shockley."

"Is there something wrong?" she asked, casting a pensive glance at Frankie.

"Oh no, no, no, dear. I just wanted to stop by and visit one of my favorite students," she said cheerfully. "Please, don't get up."

"Oh, and please call me Aggie. You're a little old to be calling me Miss Shockley, don't you think?"

"Um…well, of course," Shelley answered, dumbfounded.

"Please…have a seat," she said, motioning to the large overstuffed chair next to the couch.

"Would you like some tea? Frankie was just going to

make some for me."

"That would be delightful, dear," she accepted.

Shelley sent Frankie off to the kitchen to fetch tea and cookies.

"I can tell by the look on your face that you're a little confused, right now," Aggie said.

"Just a little…um, Aggie." It felt strange calling her by her first name. She had always been Miss Shockley to nearly everyone in Haleyville, because nearly everyone in Haleyville had been her student at one time or another.

"Well…that's the price I pay for being the most feared, um…battle-axe, I think that's what they call me….in school," she confided, with a knowing smile, and apparently without regret.

"Young children need consistency, even at school. But you know," she continued, "I wasn't just being nice. You really were one of my favorites."

"I was?" Shelley replied, astounded that the elderly woman even remembered her.

"Oh, yes. I'll never forget when you…." Aggie began recounting some of the things Shelley had done to earn her favor.

The two women enjoyed a long, pleasant chat that included memories of Jack and compliments on what a good boy Frankie was.

Inevitably, the subject of Aubrey came up. It was a subject that brought a tear to Aggie's eyes. She had a growing soft spot for him.

By the time Aggie left, Shelley felt she had found another friend in town whom she didn't realize she had.

Frankie had excused himself and retreated to the safety of his room. She was, after all, still Miss Shockley to him. After she left and he felt it was safe again, he came back downstairs to watch TV with his mother.

"Aggie . . . I mean, Miss Shockley . . . says that you have a really good teacher this year. Mrs. Delgado, is it?"

"Uh-huh. She's really nice, too. She's from Texas, and she likes to read stories to us about history and stuff. It makes it more fun to learn things than having to read about it in the books ourselves. She sometimes does funny voices when she reads, too. She's got pure-white hair, kinda like an old person, but she doesn't look old."

"I like her," he said, adding hopefully, "Maybe you can meet her sometime."

"I'd love to, honey. She sounds great," she replied, with as much hope as she could muster.

At work, her boss showed his sympathy by reassigning her to office duties, getting her away from the dirty, arduous work of the production line.

He even fought with the company's insurance providers on her behalf, to keep her covered, going so far as threatening to change providers if they refused. Seeing his sizable commission in jeopardy, the insurance agent capitulated.

Much as she appreciated his efforts, she knew they were only temporary. Week by week, it was becoming more difficult to show up for work.

At her doctor's recommendation, Shelley began taking short walks to keep her strength up.

On days when she had the strength, the walks were actual journeys along the streets she had grown up on, reliving memories of her childhood and teen years.

But on days when she didn't have the energy or when the weather was bad, she sat on the front porch swing and took metaphoric journeys down sun-sparkled memory lanes.

On these walks, she could shape the memories to suit her moods, some happier than they really had been, others disproportionately sad.

She replayed her life over and over again, hopelessly desperate for a different outcome, but always ending with the same harsh reality.

She wanted to share some of her better memories with her son, so one Saturday morning in mid-November, she decided to pack a picnic lunch.

She gathered Frankie and Rusty into the old Rambler and drove to Sweetheart Falls, a popular place for romancing couples at night and a favorite place for swimming during the hot summer days.

The well-used, pothole-pocked dirt road to the falls peeled off the main road to Lake Owen and wound through thick woods.

Eventually, it emptied into a broad, natural amphitheater at the base of a rushing waterfall that plunged forty feet over the towering bluff above.

The near bank had been worn into a muddy, sandy beach by thousands of feet over the years.

To the right, the falls thundered loudly. A spindly trail wove its way next to the plunging water and up to the top ledge, where only the bravest dared to jump from. There were several points along the trail for the less courageous, or foolhardy, to jump into the roiling waters below.

Behind the cascading falls, the force of the water had hollowed out a small, open-faced cave. It was a favorite spot to leap through the falling water into the churning pool below, white with foam and swirling with eddies and currents.

Over the millennia, the falls had carved out a pool the size of a basketball court, relatively deep at the plunge and gradually sloping up to a muddy shore at the opposite end near the outlet of the pool, where it emptied into a stream to finish its journey through the reeds and into the lake beyond.

On this crisp, cool autumn day, no swimmers were around. Frankie, his mother, and Rusty had the whole place to themselves.

"You know why I brought you here?" she asked him, as he picked up a rock and tossed it into the pool.

Rusty darted to and fro, exploring the cacophony of scents left by previous visitors and the local wildlife.

"Um, for a picnic?" he gave the obvious, though sarcastic answer, wondering where she was going with her questions.

"Well, yes, but that's not all," she said, chuckling to herself at his wit.

"This is a very special place for me, honey," she remembered.

"This is where your father asked me to marry him."

Her face glowed with the warm memory of the spring day when her heart's desire was fulfilled.

"I was sitting on that boulder, right there," she said, nodding to a large, foot-worn boulder near the water's edge, as they walked toward it.

"He knelt down right here," she said, pointing to the sacred spot on the ground. She knelt down and touched the spot he had proposed to her on, her heart pounding in her chest and a tear forming in the corner of her eye.

"We named it 'Proposal Rock.'"

"Your daddy was so romantic," she lamented, gathering her emotions.

"You know, he would never let the other boys use bad language around me!" she mused.

"Your Uncle Frank used to give him a hard time about how mushy he was. But he was always a perfect gentleman."

Her gaze wandered back in time, as if she could see him kneeling in front of her.

Not wanting the mood to grow somber, she said, "You know…. your father was the only boy brave enough to dive headfirst, off of the top up there."

She pointed to the highest point on the falls to dive from. Frankie looked in awe at the height, amazed that his father had the guts to do so.

She spent the afternoon telling her son about all the amazing things his father had done, or could do. She told him more about the bond of friendship between his father and his uncle. She told him how her brother had reluctantly introduced them after Jack had pestered him endlessly to do so.

She told him of how his father had stood beside his best friend at a time when everyone else turned their backs on him, even telling old friends not to come around if they couldn't accept his uncle for who and what he was.

She told him how his father was a man of honor and loyalty. It seemed the more he learned about his father, the higher the bar was being raised.

Shelley continued to regale her son with as many stories about her time with his father as she could. Most were happy, even mushy, but some were more poignant.

Caught up in her revelations, his mother told him of the time, back when they were still in high school, that Aubrey's father had been picking on a smaller, much weaker boy.

He had made the poor boy miserable on a daily basis with his cruelty. Eventually, the boy ran away from home, too ashamed to face his peers. The boy's parents pleaded desperately with any student they came across for hints or clues where he might be. Fortunately, after only a week, he returned home, but not to school.

That was the last straw for Jack. He caught Buck in the gym locker room and smashed his nose flat, warning him to leave the poor guy alone….or else! Word spread through school like wildfire, humiliating Buck and scalding his delicate pride.

Later that night, she and Jack were at the A&W Drive-in, hanging out with all the other teens that cruise the parking lot in an endless circle of souped-up cars and pickup trucks.

Naturally, Jack's black and flamed Deuce coupe ruled the cruise, with its rumbling headers and reputation for shutting down all challengers.

Then Buck showed up, eyes blackened like a raccoon from the broken nose his bullying had earned him. He had let his cohorts goad him into seeking revenge.

Confident he would win, he confronted Jack.

A vicious fight ensued, egged on by the action-hungry high school audience. By the time it was over, Buck lay on the ground, stammering, "I give…I give!" through a badly bleeding mouth.

Jack came away with a black eye and a fat lip, but Buck never picked on another person, where Jack could find out about it.

That his own father had beaten up Aubrey's father made a few things much clearer to him. Now he understood why Buck always seemed sour toward him.

Whenever he and Tony would help Aubrey out with his chores, Buck would inevitably give him the dirtiest or most difficult ones.

Aubrey told him that, one time, his father smacked him across the face for asking why he always gave the worst chores to Frankie.

What Shelley couldn't know at the time was that the same night had brought an epiphany to a newly pregnant Sarah Pickard.

That night, Sarah saw Buck's violent, cruel side. She knew then that her future was going to be bleak, being tied to Buck Denton, the town bully.

She vowed right then that no children of hers would grow up to be as mean as their father. It was a vow that would cost her, physically and emotionally, but one she was determined to keep.

By the time the sun started to shrink behind the surrounding hills, Frankie had learned a great deal about his father and even some things about his grandparents, all of whom he'd known only as a toddler.

All this new information was intriguing to him, but it only drove home the finality of his mother's disease. In the depths of his mind, he wanted to tell her to slow down and not to tell him everything at once. That way, she'd have to stick around longer to tell him more.

Seeing the glow on her face whenever she spoke of his father made him ask her more about him just to see her smile. He soaked up every image he could of his mother laughing and having fun. He found himself in conflict over whether knowing what was going to happen was good or bad.

On one hand, if he didn't know, then times like this would be different, maybe happier, but less important.

On the other hand, knowing that she was not going to be around much longer added to the importance of the memories they were creating, crowning each with a golden mantle of love.

Finally, though, he decided that being sad because of what he knew was better than regretting what he did not know. It gave him a perspective that would otherwise be missed.

Even at his young age, he knew that he would regret not knowing about it later on. He knew there would be times when he would say to himself, "If only I'd known!"

Knowing also made him admire his mother's bravery in the face of her own death. He wasn't sure which would be harder to face, a death like his father's, where you never knew if or when you might die and at least had a chance of making it out alive, and if you did die, it would be quick.

Or would a death like his mother's be harder to face, knowing that you were going to die, that there was no help for it, and that it was going to be drawn out and painful in the end.

He knew it must be terribly hard for her to know all this and still wear the smile she always had for him. A smile that kept the closing darkness from consuming all the happiness she had built in their home.

He decided his father's death was more merciful.

In either case, he knew that he was the son of two very brave people. The pressure to be just as brave weighed heavy upon him.

"Well, darlin," she said, as she started to get up, "I suppose we'd better head back home. It's starting to get chilly, and we don't need to catch colds, do we?"

"I don't mind catchin' a cold, Momma!" he declared.

"That way, I can stay home from school," he said, as he began folding the blanket and packing the basket, insisting on doing all the work.

He loaded up the car and opened the door for his mother. The gesture was not unnoticed by her. She thanked him and kissed his cheek, calling him a gentleman, "Just like your father."

On the ride home, Frankie thought about the things his mother had told him. She had given answers to questions he had not yet thought to ask, and she had raised questions he was not yet ready to hear the answers to.

But all in all, he was grateful for what she had told him. It only made his love for her grow stronger, if that was possible.

Just like all children his age, he hadn't given much thought to his mother's life and her feelings.

She was Momma.

She had always been there, and she always would be. Even when she was gone from this world, she'd still be Momma, and she'd still be here with him.

Since learning about his mother's illness, he had tried hard to prepare for her not being around, but he was never able to fully accept it.

That he would be leaving Haleyville and his friends only served to make the inevitable more difficult to face.

He felt that he, too, was facing a certain kind of death, a death of the spirit, a death of innocence. Everything he had grown to love was going to be left behind. Everything familiar would become history. His life, as he knew it, would end when his mother's did.

BUCKSHOT AND BUCK

Soon, Thanksgiving was upon them.

The trees were bare of all their leaves, and frost blanketed the morning lawns, but the autumn sun melted it away in time for front-yard football games that sprang up around town.

True to his word, Uncle Frank showed up two days before Thanksgiving Day, this time in a red-and-white Nashville Fire Department station wagon. The reason was evident, as soon as he opened the rear door to reveal more sacks of groceries than Frankie had ever seen.

"I assume we're getting together with the Dentons and the Carillos," he stated, more than asked, after unloading the car with Frankie's help.

"Well, yes," Shelley answered, surveying the mass of brown paper bags covering the kitchen table, "but we'd only planned a small get-together."

"Bah humbug!" Uncle Frank barked, in a phony British accent, adding, "Oops, sorry; wrong holiday, mate. Make that 'balderdash!' or whatever the Pilgrims would say. We're gonna have a Thanksgiving feast to remember!"

Walking over to the phone and scanning the list of

phone numbers Shelley kept on a pad nearby, he started dialing. Before she could ask him what he was doing, she heard him say, "Hello, Sarah, how's my favorite girl doing on such a fine day?"

A couple seconds later, he said, "Yes, as a matter of fact, this is Frank. How'd ya guess?" He went on to announce his grand plans, complete with enormous amounts of food and desserts, especially pumpkin pie, followed by college football, assuming the local channel carried it.

Three days earlier, Aubrey had called Frankie with some exciting news.

"Hey...guess whut," he started. "Ya 'member that idea I said I had when Mr. Carillo was givin' us shootin' lessons that time?"

"Well . . . ," he went on, before Frankie could respond, "I asked my paw if I could invite you an' Tony fer our Thanksgivin' hunt....an' Maw helped me convince him ta say yes."

"Thanksgiving hunt?" Frankie asked, trying to catch up to his excited buddy. "What's that?"

"Well...huntin' is when you take a gun and ya shoot animals," Aubrey answered sarcastically.

"I know what hunting is...smart ass," Frankie retorted.

"I know ya do," Aubrey chuckled. "I was just messin' with ya."

"Me an' Waylon an' Paw always go squirrel huntin' the day before Thanksgivin'," he explained.

"Anyways, Paw said it was okay, so I was wonderin' if ya wanted ta go?"

"Whoa!" Frankie exclaimed. "Hunting? You mean with real guns?"

"Well, of course with real guns," Aubrey said, amused at Frankie's reaction. "Ya cain't hunt 'em with BB guns. We got a couple .410s me an' Waylon used ta use. You an' Tony can use them."

"Heck yea, I wanna go!" Frankie nearly shouted. "I gotta ask Momma, but if your mom said it's okay, I'll bet mine will, too."

Shelley had serious misgivings about Frankie being out in the woods with a gun and with Buck, but, after some gentle persuasion from Sarah, she reluctantly agreed, under the condition that her brother would accompany them.

Convincing Buck to let Frank come along was difficult, but Sarah had traversed the minefields of her husband's ignorance often enough to eventually convince him that homosexuality wasn't contagious…or a threat to him. Her manipulating the last point had touched a nerve, causing Buck to declare, "I ain't afraid of no goddamn queer!"

Tony was even more excited, and Kathleen had similar misgivings, but after Mike insisted on going himself, she agreed. Mike had to admit that he was a little excited, too. But, knowing how much Buck and Frank disliked each other, even hated each other, he had apprehensions about them being in the same proximity with firearms.

Frankie had called his uncle with the exciting news as soon as he had hung up with Aubrey and got his mother's okay. Not surprisingly, Uncle Frank had something special for his nephew.

After all the groceries had been unloaded and the guests had been invited, Uncle Frank bade Frankie back out to the car with him. Reaching behind the front seat, he retrieved a long, flat box, with the word "Revelation" emblazoned across the top. Frankie knew immediately what was in the box. He'd seen that name on the shotguns they sold down at the Western Auto store.

"Wow! Did you get a new gun?" he asked, excitedly.

"Nope, you did," Uncle Frank answered, as casually as giving him the time of day.

"Wha . . . ," Frankie said, his mouth falling open.

"Me?" he asked, incredulously pointing to himself.

"Yep, you," Uncle Frank responded, still nonchalant.

"No way!"

"Yes way," his uncle continued to reassure him.

"Now let's go see how your mother handles it," he said, grinning and handing the box to Frankie.

Frankie could feel the weight of the gun and started to run, but he caught himself, recalling what Tony's father had said about running with a gun in your hands. Instead, he cradled the new gun, box and all, in the crook of his arm and quickly, but gingerly, walked back to the house.

"Momma...Momma!" he shouted eagerly. "Look what Uncle Frank got me!" He had announced Frank's gift before he was even through the door.

"What's that, sweet . . . ," Shelly started to inquire, but she stopped as soon as she saw the box. She, too, knew what was inside.

"Frank...you didn't," she scolded, as soon as her brother walked through the open door.

"Yes, I did, sis," he responded, as bravely as he could.

"But Frank...he's just . . . ," she protested.

Uncle Frank stopped her with a hand held up between them.

"He's not 'just' anything," he defended. "He's a grown boy, and it's about time he had his own gun...a real one, not just a BB gun."

He rushed on, "I had one when I was his age…and so did Jack." He knew the last point was unfair, but he needed any leverage he could get. He hadn't asked her about it because he knew she would be against it. All mothers were against letting their baby boys have real guns.

Shelley stood with her arms crossed and one eyebrow cocked, as she watched her son open the box and handle the gun under careful supervision from his uncle, his eyes wide with wonder at this giant step into manhood.

Frank made the point to her that he was going to be making decisions like this in the future for her son. Reluctantly, she caved into the inevitable. After all, her precious son was growing up, whether she liked it or not.

Frankie was fascinated with the sleek, bolt-action .410 gauge shotgun, its dark mahogany stock accented by the blue-black barrel. It felt light in his hands, but heavier than the .22 caliber rifle Mike had used to teach them. He brought the butt of the shotgun up to his shoulder, but Uncle Frank reached out and gently pushed it back down.

"We're indoors, Bambino," he admonished lightly, casting a glance at his sister.

"I brought some shells. How 'bout we step out in the backyard and cook off a few…just to get you used to it?"

"Whoa…really?" Frankie replied, giddy with excitement.

"If it's okay with your mom, that is," Uncle Frank asked, more than said, still looking at Shelley.

She knew it was something that all boys in this part of the country went through, usually at a younger age than her son's. And she knew that her brother had hunted rabbits and squirrels in the very woods that surrounded their house. But she had no love of guns or the evil they could be used for….like war.

"Oh…all right," she capitulated, adding unnecessarily, "Just be careful."

"Don't worry," Uncle Frank said glibly. "We won't put anybody's eye out."

I bet Granma Emma said that a lot, too, Frankie thought, as he and Uncle Frank walked through the kitchen, onto the back porch, and into the yard.

Being as far from town and as close to the countryside as they were, gunshots were not a cause for concern to the neighbors. Uncle Frank opened the box of slender, red, plastic shotgun shells and took three out.

He carefully showed Frankie how to load them into the magazine and how to operate the bolt to eject them.

Then he took aim at a large knot on the side of a giant hickory tree behind the house and fired.

The blast surprised Frankie, causing him to jump. He had not expected it to be so much louder than the crack of the smaller .22 caliber he'd fired before.

"It's got a loud bark, doesn't it?" Uncle Frank asked, seeing the surprise on his nephew's face.

"Yeah," Frankie answered, "it sure does."

"Well, it has a bit of a kick to go with its bark, too. So be careful and hold onto it," Uncle Frank warned, handing the shotgun to Frankie.

"Hold it nice and snug to your shoulder, or it'll kick worse."

Just as Mike had done, he showed Frankie how to hold the gun and take aim. "Whenever you're ready, take a breath, hold it, and just squeeze the trigger; don't jerk it," he said, again repeating the same instructions Mike had given.

Frankie was confident he could handle it. As he squeezed the trigger, the shotgun roared its might at the same knot Uncle Frank had assaulted a moment earlier. Frankie was surprised at the recoil and nearly dropped the shotgun.

"Bites a little harder than a .22, huh?" Uncle Frank mused, a smile on his face.

"I'll say it does," Frankie gasped, trying not to appear intimidated.

Uncle Frank told him to cock the bolt and fire again. After that, he let Frankie reload and fire several more rounds of ammunition, just to get used to handling the gun.

"We'd better save some ammo for the hunt," he suggested, much to Frankie's disappointment.

"Pull the bolt back and leave it open," he instructed. "That's how you should carry it until you get ready to use it. Then you can load it and put the safety on."

"After the hunt, I'll show you how to clean it."

"Clean it?" Frankie asked.

"Well…yeah. You gotta clean your gun after you use it," Uncle Frank explained. "If you don't, all the burnt powder will foul up the works and ruin your gun."

Frankie gently cradled the gun in the crook of his arm and headed back to the house, his uncle's hand resting approvingly on his shoulder.

This was a proud moment for uncle and nephew, but for different reasons.

Frankie had fired his own gun—and a shotgun, at that. He couldn't wait to tell Tony and Aubrey.

As soon as the gun was safely in its box, he was on the phone, bragging to his friends.

For his uncle, it was a bittersweet moment. This should have been Jack's moment, and it saddened him that it wasn't. But he was elated that he could be there for his nephew. It gave him a feeling of fatherhood he never thought he'd have.

It also saddened him to realize that he'd have many more such moments that should belong to his sister. He pushed those thoughts aside. This was Frankie's moment, and he wasn't going to allow it to be spoiled.

The morning of the Great Thanksgiving Squirrel Hunt arrived.

The Carillos showed up in time for morning coffee, followed shortly by Sarah. While the three mothers and Maria gathered around Shelley's kitchen table to plan and prepare for the next day's feast, the men and the boys left for the Denton farm.

Sarah reassured Shelley and Kathleen that their sons would be perfectly safe. Aubrey had been on dozens of hunts like this, she told them, and, the night before, he had promised her that he would keep a close eye on his buddies.

Waylon had decided to spend the day with Irene, as he did with all his spare time lately, so he wouldn't be going on this year's hunt.

Aubrey had been less than enthusiastic about hunting alone with his father. Not that he was afraid of being hurt, but he knew his father would find fault with something that he did or didn't do. Having Frankie and Tony along was exciting for him. Having Uncle Frank and Mike along was a relief...to him and to the mothers.

The cadre of rookie hunters marched through the gate at Aubrey's house and up onto the front porch, where Aubrey and Buck stood waiting.

You didn't have to go very far to be in squirrel country, around Haleyville. In fact, they probably could have bagged a few from the porch, but there wasn't any adventure in that.

"That sure is a perty gun." Aubrey complimented, when Frankie proudly held out his new treasure for his inspection.

"Man, this is so far out!" Tony declared, when it came to him.

"Check this out, Dad," he said to his father, handing the gun to him. "Ya think I can get one, too?"

"We'll have to see, son," Mike answered. "Your mother's still a little skittish about the .22."

"You're right, Aubrey. It is a fine-looking weapon," Mike complimented, using the warrior's vernacular for guns.

"Nice lines...good balance," he said, assessing the shotgun and holding it to his shoulder. "I'd like to fire it sometime, if you don't mind."

"'Course I don't mind, Mr. Carillo. Heck, you can fire it right now, if ya want," Frankie offered proudly.

"Well...maybe after we hunt," Mike replied. "Wouldn't want to scare all the squirrels away, would we?"

"Now, you boys remember what I told you about your safeties being on and being mindful of where the barrel was pointed, don't you?" he asked his son and Frankie.

Mike insisted on a brief gun-safety lecture to the boys, showing them how to hold their rifles while walking and how to pass through or over fences and so on.

Buck made a show of being bored with the lesson, saying, "Me an' my boys been huntin' these woods all our lives; I think we know what to do."

Aubrey's face burned red with embarrassment.

Mike's patience with the uncultured hulk began to wear.

"Well, if you don't mind, Buck, my son and I haven't hunted here before," Mike said. "In fact, this is his first hunt ever, and I'd like him to know the safety rules." Mike spoke firmly, his irritation growing.

"I think Frankie needs to know too, Buck," Uncle Frank joined in, getting a dirty look from Buck.

To lighten the mood, he said to Aubrey, "I'll bet you know where all the best squirrel holes are, dontcha?"

"Yeah, you bet!" Aubrey chimed in, realizing what Uncle Frank was trying to do.

"My paw knows all these here woods like the back o' his hand, dontcha, Paw?"

Huffing and rolling his eyes slightly, Buck said sourly, "Damn right I do, boy. Some of us hunt these woods 'cause we hafta, not jus' fer fun."

Buck barely disguised his contempt for Frank. He had been at the vanguard of the ridicule the town had dished out and was presently wondering why he'd allowed himself to be conned into this ridiculous hunt, with a damned Yankee and a faggot.

"Yeah, well those of us who do it for fun prefer to do it safely," Mike said icily.

"Now how about using some of that backwoods expertise of yours to show us where the game is, as you claim to know," he challenged with a glare.

The ex-naval officer in him was maintaining control, while the father in him wanted to knock the big buffoon on his ass for trying to embarrass him in front of his son.

Buck stood assessing the city man and decided not to push any further. "This way," was all he said, as he dismounted the porch and led them into the thickets and underbrush that bordered the nearby woods.

Mike was surprised at how silently the big man maneuvered through the leaf-strewn forest. Buck's stealth was natural, and Aubrey's movements mimicked his father's. His own footsteps and those of the other three sounded like a herd of buffalo among the dry twigs and leaves beneath the trees.

After only a few minutes, Buck turned to the group and asked gruffly, "Do ya'll want to shoot 'em, or scare 'em?"

The tone of his voice told Aubrey that he might be losing his temper soon. *Oh please, Paw, not today! Please?* he begged silently.

Mike spoke up, an edge in his own voice, "It's like you said, Buck. You've been hunting these woods all your life. We haven't. Instead of griping at us, why don't you teach us city slickers how it's done?"

He glared at Buck, with no intention of backing down.

Buck had seen the look before, on the faces of men who had reached the end of their patience with him and given him the fight they thought he was looking for.

Often enough, he had come out on the losing end of the deal. What he saw in Mike's eyes told him that the city boy just might be able to take care of himself.

Tony and Frankie gave each other scared glances. Aubrey looked at the ground in shame.

Frank's mind raced to find a way to diffuse the situation. But he, too, was becoming fed up with Buck's attitude, and he could most certainly hold his own. Buck had seen him do so more than once, back in high school.

"Aw… hell," Buck sputtered, feeling outnumbered. "I cain't expect ya'll ta know whut you never done before."

"Aubrey…you show them boys how ta walk, an' I'll show these two," he said, nodding toward Frank and Mike.

Aubrey felt relieved. His father had backed down. It was something he wasn't accustomed to.

Quickly, he motioned Frankie and Tony over to show them how to roll their feet on the side from heel to toe as they stepped, avoiding noisy footfalls.

"That's how the Injuns dun it," he explained, turning a potentially tense situation into a game of Indian hunter. His father showed the other men the same, with less humor.

"Now this is how ya flush the tree rats out!" Buck explained, when he'd finished instructing the other two men.

"Aubrey, go yonder, 'round that big hickory!" he said, as he moved behind a tree and propped his rifle up in preparation to fire.

With the silence of a shadow, Aubrey circled wide, disappearing into the woods to get away from the noisy hunting party and to get behind the tree his father pointed to.

"Now ya'll stay still, ya hear?" Buck whispered to the group. Pressing his rifle to his shoulder, he concentrated on the large, lower branches of the towering tree. Aubrey reappeared on the opposite side of the big hickory tree, making considerably more noise than he had been previously making.

Distracted by his reappearance, the other hunters were startled when Buck fired his semiautomatic rifle three times. They were just as surprised to see three big red fox squirrels drop from the branches like rain, each with a bullet to the head.

"What the…?" Uncle Frank blurted, fully impressed. "How did you…?"

"Ya weren't watchin' too close, were ya?" Buck snorted.

"Squirrels watch what's movin'," he explained impatiently. "I sent my boy around the tree to distract 'em, while I stood still."

"They picked up on him an' fergot about me bein' here when they went ta hide from him. Git it?" he finished somewhat sarcastically.

"Still," Mike chimed in, "that's some damn good shooting."

He had to admit that Buck was an expert shot. Hitting three small, fast-moving targets in as many seconds was a feat he doubted he could pull off.

Too bad you're such an asshole.

Aubrey and his father bagged a total of eight squirrels, while the other two men managed only one kill each. Frankie and Tony didn't hit anything and didn't care one bit.

They'd been hunting for the first time in their lives and several "almost" shots were good enough. Several of Frankie's shots were at nothing more than a leaf or a stray hickory nut dangling in the open. He was more interested in firing the shotgun than he was in killing squirrels.

Mike and Frank gave their kills to Buck, since neither one knew how to properly clean a squirrel, nor did Kathleen or Shelley know how make squirrel stew.

Aubrey assured them that his mother made the best squirrel stew anywhere.

"I'd like to try some, if it's all right with her," Mike requested.

"Yeah, me, too," Uncle Frank added.

Frankie and Tony were less enthusiastic.

They had been given the job of retrieving the furry little critters when they fell from the trees. Seeing them up close and dead made them very unappetizing. Frankie actually felt sorry for them, while Tony struggled with having to handle a dead animal.

Aubrey told them he'd show them how to tan the pelts, but neither boy was very enthusiastic about the prospect.

"Me an' Chet made a squirrel-skin blanket fer Aunt Betty, one year," he bragged.

Tony didn't think his mother would be too thrilled about that, but then she did have fur coats, so....

That evening, as shadows overtook everything, the hunters were gathered on the front porch of the Albert homestead, drinking hot chocolate and engaging in posthunt small talk.

Mike told the boys that he'd be showing them how to clean their guns that evening. Uncle Frank showered them with praise, especially Aubrey, who merely stood there, blushing and shuffling his feet in modesty.

Back at the farm, Buck had gone around to a shed in the backyard as soon as they returned to the house, claiming that he needed to skin and to clean the squirrels before they "went bad"; plus he had some evening chores to do.

But the adults knew, and the boys guessed, that he had reached the limit of his social graces and simply didn't want to be around anybody. That was just fine with Mike, who was straining to maintain civility with Buck.

For her part, Sarah was glad he had chosen to stay

home. She and Aubrey were able to relax.

"So..." Shelley teased through the open door, "do you big, strong hunters want to see what's on the menu for tomorrow?"

"Squirrel?" Uncle Frank asked, getting a loud round of laughter from everyone.

TURKEY DAY

Early the next morning, Kathleen and Maria knocked on the Alberts' front door, each laden with a clothes-basketful of cookware and food.

"Our guys will be along shortly," Kathleen explained. "Where do we put this stuff?"

Shelley led them to the kitchen, where all three began unloading the baskets.

A short while later, Sarah showed up, with Aubrey in tow, each of them loaded down with boxes of utensils and food, as well.

"Buck's not coming. He's putting on his usual holiday pout," Sarah said sourly, rolling her eyes, but then added happily, "And I don't care. I'm not going to let him spoil it this year, the old stick-in-the-mud."

Aubrey's expression seemed to reflect her feelings as well. No further explanation was needed by the others, and no one seemed displeased about the announcement.

In fact, an air of relief wafted through the room.

Still, Shelley sensed a tension in Sarah's demeanor.

The women chased Frank and the boys out of the kitchen so they could begin cooking what promised to be a feast fit for a king, or for several kings.

One of the luxuries Frank had provided his sister with was a brand-new color television console, complete with a stereo record player and an eight-track tape deck.

While the women were working their magic in the kitchen, he and the two boys started watching the *Macy's Thanksgiving Day Parade*.

Aubrey had seen only a few small parts of it before, and only in grainy black-and-white. Being able to watch the whole parade in living color was a real treat for him.

He was particularly fascinated with the giant, floating balloon figures. His favorites were Underdog and Bullwinkle the Moose.

Toward the end of the parade, Tony and his father showed up, bearing beer for the men, wine for the women, and grape Nehi for the boys….and, of course, Sprite for Maria.

Tony seemed more contented than he usually did, as he snuggled up next to his father on the couch to watch the festivities.

Kathleen caught a glimpse of the scene through the kitchen doorway and stopped short. It was a sight she had prayed for. She wasn't sure what had happened over the past few weeks to draw the two men in her life together, but she was grateful for it and wasn't about to question it.

Despite his prankish nature, Tony was a good kid, with enough spirit and energy to more than make up for his lack of size.

When he wasn't with Frankie or Aubrey, he spent hours running around the house and the yard, acting like Superman or some other comic book hero.

Kathleen had worried that he was relying too much

on comic book characters for his male role models, instead of his own father.

But whatever had happened, it was obvious that they had turned a corner together.

Sarah saw her standing there, looking wistfully into the living room.

"You okay, hun?" she asked, laying a hand on Kathleen's arm.

"Oh, I'm fine, sweetie," she replied, gently patting Sarah's hand.

Still gazing at her son and his father, she said, "In fact, I feel just wonderful. I've never seen Mike and Tony so together like this before. I don't know what it is, and I'm not going to ask. I'll just thank the Lord." A slight tremor in her voice hinted at her emotions.

"Mike's a great guy," Sarah complimented, "and a wonderful father, too."

"I envy you. Tony is lucky to have a dad like that."

"Sarah," Kathleen started, "Aubrey is the most wonderful boy I have ever met. I've never seen such a polite and thoughtful boy. I wish Tony was more like him." Then she smiled.

"You've done an amazing job, considering..." she stopped, then went on, "I'm sorry. I meant..." She hesitated again, then settled for, "Well, I just love that boy of yours!"

"It's okay, Kath. I understand," Sarah replied, smiling. "I know, more than anyone, what my boys face. It's been tough, but they're all I got in this world. They're gifts to me from the good Lord, an', honey, there ain't no way I'm gonna let anybody ruin that."

"I wonder how Jack and Frankie would have gotten along," Shelley said from a few feet away, drawing the two women's attention back into the kitchen. "I think they would have been good together."

"Jack would have been the perfect dad," Sarah proclaimed, "I mean….he was such a good man, you know, the way he cared about others."

"Trust me, sugar, a few years with a good man is a whole lot better than a lifetime with an asshole!" she finished, turning her attention back to candied yams she was preparing, embarrassed and surprised at what she'd just said.

Conversation fell silent. The others had ever heard Sarah use such strong language before. Shelley and Kathleen exchanged looks of surprise, but they understood Sarah's dilemma.

Even though he wasn't in the house, Buck had still managed to cast a pall over the room.

"So….where's Waylon?" Shelley asked, seeing that Sarah seemed even more agitated about Buck than usual.

"He's spending Thanksgiving with his girlfriend," Sarah answered.

"That's where he spends all his free time, these days. I can't blame him, though. I wish I had someplace to get away, too."

Without intending to do so, she had allowed her envy and frustration to bubble to the top. Realizing it only made her feel worse, she stopped what she was doing to collect her emotions, but without success.

Suddenly, she hurried out the kitchen door onto the back porch and began to sob quietly to herself.

The other two women rushed after her, leaving a confused Maria alone in the kitchen, peeling potatoes.

"Sarah, honey, what's the matter?" Shelley asked, as she walked up behind Sarah, though she had a good idea about what was bothering her.

Kathleen wrapped her arm around her from the other side.

"Oh, I…I'm just being… silly!" Sarah declared between sobs.

"Look at me," she said, wiping her tears with her apron. "Blubbering like a school girl… feeling sorry for myself because my life isn't perfect."

"Honey, you've got all the right in the world. Go ahead and let it out," Kathleen soothed, as she hugged Sarah.

"But it's like I said—you have done wonders with your boys," she said. "They're such treasures. I would call myself the best mom in the world if mine turn out as respectful and considerate as yours have." She was trying to get Sarah to focus on something good.

"Thank you, Kath. You're a sweetheart," Sarah said. "You're right. I am blessed. I should be ashamed of myself. I have two wonderful boys, and that's all that really counts. I just can't help wondering how my life would have been with someone else, that's all."

An awkward silence took hold for a few seconds, all three women thinking how different their lives would be, had they married different men.

Breaking the silence, Shelley said, "You said that Waylon is spending time with his girlfriend. Is it serious?"

"Well, he says it is," Sarah answered; then she added sternly, "And you can bet your bottom dollar I sat the boy down for a long talk about foolin' around before he was married."

Her emerging smile turned into a chuckle, as she said, "You should have seen the poor boy squirming while having to listen to his mother talk about sex. It was priceless." She laughed.

"Well, when your boys get married, I just know you're going to make a fabulous grandmother!" Kathleen declared.

"Not too soon, I hope," Sarah responded. "But I have to admit that grandbabies are a dream of mine…. eventually."

"Mom!" Maria called from the kitchen.

Kathleen said, rolling her eyes, "I'd better see what she wants. I swear that girl is allergic to anything domestic."

Before returning to the kitchen, she reached up and placed a gentle kiss on Sarah's wet cheek and squeezed her arm, saying "You're wonderful all by yourself, sweetie."

Sarah smiled her thanks.

"Why do you stay with Buck?" Shelley blurted out, without really intending to get so personal.

"Oh, geez…I am so sorry. It's none of my business. I should keep my mouth shut," she admonished herself.

Caught off guard by the question, but unperturbed, Sarah responded, "No need to be sorry, dear. I've asked myself that question a thousand times. The only answer I ever come up with is that I've stuck around for my boys. That really is the truth ya know, but it's not like I have much of a choice, either."

She paused briefly, then turned to face Shelley.

"I did leave Buck once, back when Waylon was a baby." She had felt a need to open her heart.

"It was one of the first times he hit me. I took Waylon and went to Betty's place in Kentucky. Chet was just a little guy, too. But I let myself be talked into coming back. Betty said she didn't think it was such a good idea, but my head was screwed on kinda crooked, back then," she explained.

Turning away, she continued in a haunting voice, "Buck was okay for a while, picking flowers for me and all. I thought that maybe he had changed."

"But then, one day, he took me down beside the barn and showed me a big, long hole he had dug."

She shuddered visibly, saying, "When I asked him what the hole was for, he told me it was for me, the next time I tried to take his son from him."

"Then he reminded me of what I was," she continued.

"He told me, in no uncertain terms, that I was his wife and the mother of his child, whether I liked it or not. I was a mere possession, and one he didn't seem to care too much for, other than cooking, cleaning, and raising his child. I should have left town right then and there, and run as far from him as I could."

"But I was young and scared, with no place to go. My father was gone, and my mother was in Georgia, not that she would have welcomed me, anyway. I'm an embarrassment to her, you know." She spoke sourly.

"And it was for sure that none of the good people of Haleyville gave a tinker's damn about a tramp married to a Denton!" she added bitterly.

"Ya know…the evil bastard kept that hole neat and clean for years. I guess it's some sick reminder of his ownership, or a threat."

"My own sons have played in it over the years, not knowing what it really was."

She then elaborated morbidly, "Do you have any idea how it feels to look out your window and see your children playing in what was intended to be your grave?"

"No, I guess you wouldn't, would you?" she said, seeing the shocked expression on Shelley's face.

She continued, "I think Waylon figured it out a couple years ago, though. He and Buck had a real bad fight."

"I heard Waylon say 'grave' before he and his father came to blows," she explained.

"Needless to say, he didn't fare too well in that contest. But he was my hero. Still is."

"I sent him up to stay with Betty for a couple months," she explained. "But after a while, Buck realized that he and Aubrey couldn't run the farm without him, so he called Betty, demanding that she send him home."

"You should have seen the look on his face when Keith got on the extension and told him that he was he was out of line for talking to Betty like that and that he'd better not do it again."

She grinned and said, "It was the first time Keith had spoken so boldly to Buck, and it really threw him off. I can only imagine how Keith was feeling, God love him."

"But then, bless her heart, Betty spoke up for Waylon and really laid into Buck for doing such a sick thing and that he should be ashamed of himself. She told him that Waylon wasn't going anywhere until he promised to fill the hole in and give Waylon more freedom. She even threatened to send him to Keith's relatives in Arkansas, unless he did. Thank God for Betty."

Shelley was at a loss for words.

Just then, Frank stepped out onto the back porch.

"Are you all right, Sarah?" he asked, genuinely concerned. "Kathleen said you were upset about something."

"What's up, Dumplin'?" he inquired, using his pet name for her to try to cheer her up.

"Oh Lord," Sarah said, "now look what I've gone and done. This is Thanksgiving. It should be a happy day, not a day for crybabies like me."

"It's Buck, isn't it?" he asked, knowing full well it was.

"Thank you Frank, really," she said. "But don't worry. I'm just like those ol' mules of ours. I do what I'm expected to do and don't expect too much in return. I've gotten used to it." She was resigned to her fate.

"Damn it, Sarah," Frank protested. "You're not some damned mule. You deserve better than that idiot. Yeah, I know, he's your husband, but…" He trailed off.

Then he asked pointedly, as he looked into her eyes, "He hits you, doesn't he?"

He didn't need an answer. The looks on the women's faces were enough.

"That chicken shit sonuvabitch!" he growled.

"Frank!" Sarah said, with surprising firmness. "My choices, no…my mistakes….put me where I am and they keep me there. It's my cross to bear, no one else's."

Softening her tone, she continued, "But thank you for caring so much. You're a good man. You always have been." She felt a familiar, deep stab of regret.

Frank wrapped his arms around her to comfort her. For a few minutes, the old best friends stood in silence, one's heart breaking for the other, and the other's heart slowly, but surely, crumbling into ruins of disappointment and disillusionment.

"Ya know, Dumplin'," Frank said, holding her at arm's length, still looking firmly into her puffy eyes, "and I mean this with every fiber of my being….if you or your sons ever need a safe place to go, I have plenty of room up in Nashville. I promise you nobody would harm you there."

"You're such a sweet man, Frank," she said, cupping his strong face in her hands. "But I could never impose upon you like that. Thank you for the offer, though." The politeness she had groomed in her sons kept her from screaming, *"Oh, God, please take me away from all this!"*

"It's not just an idle offer, Sarah. I mean it," he protested. "It would never be an imposition, either. Just keep it in mind. Please promise to call me if you ever need me. It'll break my heart if you don't."

"God love ya, Frank. You're so sweet," she complimented, as calmly as her heart would let her.

She stood gazing into his eyes, remembering how disappointed she was that he had never been more than just the best friend she had ever had.

Turning to Shelley, she gently took her hands into her own and said, "Since I've already bared my sordid past, I have a confession to make. I hope you won't think too badly of me afterwards."

"You, too, Frank," she said, imploring him to understand.

She paused, then said to Frank, "Back in school, before I met you, I was head-over-heels in love with Jack."

"It's a secret I've kept close to my heart all these years. I've never spoken to anyone about it, before now. I was always green with envy whenever I saw him with you, but I knew he would never look at someone as plain as me, you being so pretty and all." She held her hand up when Shelley started to protest.

"But even though I was sorry for myself, I really was happy for you. I thought you two made a beautiful couple. I even voted for you for Homecoming King and Queen, ya know." She smiled. Shelley silently returned the smile.

"When I heard about his death, I was devastated. I

couldn't function. I felt like I was the widow, too. I was useless for days. Buck and the boys thought I had come down with something. Of course, I couldn't tell them the real reason; I couldn't even cry if they were around. It was torture. I know it was wrong, but even though he was your man, I held the memory of Jack dear to my heart for years."

"I'm telling you this now because I've been feeling guilty about it for so long, especially lately. After all, he was your husband, not mine. I have no right to such feelings."

"It's just that, well…at first, I liked the idea of Jack's son being so close by. It was like having a part of him near me. But then I got to know you better, and I realized that I was coveting something that belonged to you…the memory of him."

"Getting to know you helped me get over my feelings, and I've let them go, now."

She paused to try and make sense of what she was saying.

"I know all this sounds pretty strange. He was never mine to miss or to pine for."

She looked down in shame, then raised a solemn face and said, "I've grown to love you like a sister, and I don't want to hide anything from you. You're a wonderful a person, and Jack made a great choice when he picked you."

"Please don't be upset with me," she pleaded. "But I wouldn't blame you if you are. I don't mean to be presumptuous, but like I said, you're the sister I never had."

A sly smirk crept across Shelley's face.

"Sarah, Sarah, Sarah!" she said, playfully. "You silly girl. I knew all about your crush way back then. I can still see it in your eyes whenever we talk about him."

Squeezing Sarah's hands, she went on, "Now, how can I be mad at someone for doing the very same thing I did?"

"I fell pretty hard for him, too, ya know! Half the girls in school had it bad for him. I'm just the one who got lucky, that's all."

"Sweetie, don't punish yourself for something you're not guilty of," she concluded.

"Ah-hmm!" Frank cleared his throat to remind the two women that he was still on the porch.

"What about me?" Frank asked, feigning hurt feelings.

"Oh, I like you way too much as a man to think of you as a brother!" Sarah flirted.

Frank blushed, and for once, he didn't have a snappy comeback.

Rolling her eyes at him, Shelley continued, "Jack noticed you, Sarah."

Sarah seemed truly surprised at that.

"Really, he did. He liked you a lot, too. He thought you were a nice girl. Not like all the others."

Sarah could only return a stunned look.

Then looking at Frank again, Shelley donned a grin that would make the Cheshire Cat envious.

"You know, he wanted me to fix you up with ol' Frank here!" she said, poking him in the chest. "He thought you two would make a good couple."

Frank coughed his embarrassment and said, "That is true, Dumplin'. They twisted my arm to take you out... but only the first time," he added quickly.

"All the other times I did it because of you and the way you made me feel about myself," he said. "You'll probably recall that I was going through my own personal hell, at the time."

"But if things had been different…" he smiled warmly at her.

Finding that her feelings weren't as secret, or as sinister as she thought, lifted a huge stone from her shoulders. She had already been forgiven by the woman whose husband she had coveted for so long.

Forgiveness was something she was not accustomed to getting. She gave out more than her share, that's for sure, but receiving it was a strange feeling.

She embraced Shelley in a tearful hug of joy. Frank wrapped his long arms around both women.

This really would be a day to give thanks, she thought.

Meanwhile, back in the living room, just as the parade had ended, a knock was heard at the front door. Frankie dashed to answer it.

"Uncle Ben!" he shouted. "Awright!"

"Hey, Momma, Uncle Ben's here," he announced loudly toward the kitchen.

Shelley came into the foyer, a pleasantly incredulous expression on her face, followed closely by an equally surprised Frank.

"Ben…how wonderful," Shelley gushed. "I'm so happy to see you."

"I don't believe it," Frank declared. "What natural disaster pried you out of that dingy ol' shop?"

"It's called Thanksgivin', ya smart ass," he growled playfully.

"Hi Shelley, how ya doin', darlin'?" he said, embracing her warmly. "It got a little lonesome around the shop, whut with Harlan not bein' there to throw tools at. I hope you don't mind me bargin' in like this."

"Barging in? Well, I never. I've been trying to get you to come to dinner for years," she admonished.

"Of course, I don't mind. I'm so tickled that you're here. Come on in; there are some folks I'd like you to meet."

After introducing him to everyone as someone very special to her, she fetched a cold beer from the refrigerator and shooed him into the living room, along with the men and the boys, warning all of them to stay out of the kitchen.

"I've heard a lot of good things about you, Ben," Mike offered, breaking a short, but awkward, silence.

"Well...I wouldn't be in too big a hurry to believe 'em," he said. "As I hear it, most of the townsfolk think I'm a real SOB." He winked at Mike.

"I'll say," Frank chided, laughing.

"But, seriously, you won't find a better wrench man this side of the Mason-Dixon Line," he complimented.

"Back in school, ol' Ben here helped me and Jack build a real sweet Deuce coupe. He still has it down at his shop."

"Really?" Mike asked. "I'd love to check it out, sometime. I've always thought that old-school hot rods were the best. I helped my cousin trick out a '37 Chevy, back when I was a kid."

"Ah, so you're a gearhead, too?" Ben asked.

"Nah, not really. Mostly I was just free labor for handling tools and other odd jobs."

"Well...that counts. Just ask Frank," he teased.

"What the..." Frank protested indignantly. "I did my part, you old coot."

"Yeah, ya did," Ben admitted. "Actually... you did lay down some pretty good welds. Yer paintin' wudn't too bad, either."

The conversation centered on cars for a few minutes, while Mike searched the channels for a college football game on TV.

Tony was the color commentator, as he explained all the positions and plays to Aubrey, who'd only been to a couple of local high school games with Waylon, and Waylon had only gone to meet girls, so not much had been explained.

Aubrey decided to cheer for the opposite team that Tony cheered for, just to agitate him. That Tony was a very animated fan helped Aubrey's mission a great deal. By the time the game was over, he had several fresh bruises on his arm where Tony punched him after being goaded over a touchdown or a bad play.

"That boy of yours gets pretty worked up, dudn't he?" Ben said to Mike.

"Yes he does," Mike answered exasperatedly. Then he suggested a game of football in the back yard.

The boys tripped over each other in the rush to get out of the house.

Aubrey and Uncle Frank squared off against Mike, Tony, and Frankie. Ben chose to be the referee, saying he didn't want to hurt anybody. Uncle Frank and Mike played quarterback, while the boys did all the running and tackling.

Tony was fast, but Aubrey was surprisingly agile, and once he got his hands on Tony, there was no moving forward for the smaller guy. Frankie stuck to blocking, since he was not very fast, nor was he very good at catching the ball.

Rusty played mascot, chasing anyone who ran, and even managed to drag down Tony once.

Of course, Aubrey took the opportunity to chide his friend for being tackled by a half-grown dog.

The game ended when Shelley stepped out onto the front porch and hollered, "Anybody hungry?" triggering a stampede toward the house.

Aubrey yelled, "We won!" just to irritate Tony, not really sure if his side had won or not.

Naturally, Tony protested vigorously with, "Not in this life, you didn't!"

The two boys kept goading each other, even after they sat down at the table, until Sarah intervened.

"Will you two monkeys please stop all that chatter? It's time to say grace," she said, ending their chatter with a firmness they understood.

A huge turkey dominated the table, surrounded by platters and bowls occupying every available inch of space, heaped with every good thing about Thanksgiving dinner.

More dishes of holiday cuisine were scattered on the countertops in the kitchen.

The three mothers had chosen a specialty of their own to cook.

Sarah had made minced-meat, cherry, and blueberry pies, with extra pumpkin pies on the side.

Kathleen had made her grandmother's secret stuffing and a large pan of cinnamon cornbread.

Shelley outdid herself with a green bean casserole and old-fashioned creamed corn.

All three had collaborated on the turkey and a honey-glazed ham.

Maria even contributed the buttered mashed potatoes she had spent time gingerly peeling.

Everyone stood around the table and joined hands,

as Shelley asked Uncle Frank to deliver the Thanksgiving grace. He wasn't in much of a mood to thank God for anything, but he was cornered.

And so he began…

"Dear Heavenly Father, we thank you for all that you have blessed us with." *Blessed us with? What, like Shelley's health? Or how about Sarah's happiness? What kind of blessing will it be when Frankie no longer has a mother?*

He continued, "We don't always understand your ways."

Now there's an understatement, he thought.

"But we accept them and are grateful for the good things you provide in our lives, like our friends and our families."

He had to admit that Shelley and Frankie were pretty good things to have in his life.

"Father, bless this food you have provided, that it might nourish our bodies, as your Word nourishes our soul. Amen." *Good, that was over,* he thought.

He would have to have more conversations with this oh-so-benevolent God about a lot of other things he took issue with, but, right now, it was all about family. His anger could wait.

For the first time in many years, the usually empty antique dining table rang with the sounds of silverware on china, amid praises for the chefs of such a delightful spread.

Mothers admonished their sons to not take more than they could eat, and to eat everything they'd dished up.

After all, they said, there were starving children in Africa.

"Yeah, and if they're not careful, they'll put their eyes

out with something, too!" Tony chimed sarcastically, earning a not-so-stern rebuke from his father, who was trying not to laugh, himself.

"I can't believe you just said that!" his mother declared indignantly.

"I apologize for my son's insensitivity," she said to the rest of the diners.

"You're a hoot, Tony," Uncle Frank said, as he freely laughed out loud.

No one had eaten anything earlier that day, so as to have plenty of room for the feast. Slowly, steadily, the turkey became a bare-boned carcass, as did the ham, flanked by rapidly emptying bowls and platters. Conversation was sparse at first, muffled by mouths full of delicious food. Eventually, one by one, all the people seated there sat back in their chair, pushing leftover laden plates away.

"Anyone ready for dessert?" Shelley asked, knowing that everyone was stuffed to the gills. A chorus of contented moans of refusal greeted her.

"Maybe in a couple of hours," Uncle Frank answered.

"Yeah, that's the bad thing about Thanksgiving dinner," Tony postulated. "Ya eat it, and two days later, you're hungry again!"

"Where do you come up with this stuff, son?" Mike asked through his laughter, as everyone else joined in.

The dinner was a resounding success, men and boys alike belching their approval and being chastised by the women. As soon as one of the mothers made a move that looked liked cleaning up, every one of the guys fled for the front yard to toss football or sit on the porch steps chatting, while the women did the heavy cleanup work and prepared for dessert.

"My maw makes the best punkin' pie in the whole world!" Aubrey declared.

"Ohh…don't mention food!" an overstuffed Tony whined, wrapping his arms around his stomach.

Aubrey teased him, saying, "You mean you don't wanna talk about all that turkey, an' ham, an' green beans, an' sweet taters, an'…"

"Shut up!" Tony yelled at his tormentor. "Ohhh…I think I'm gonna die."

Frankie and Aubrey laughed and continued to tease him, running around and playing on the tire swing, while Tony lay on his back on the ground with a miserably full stomach, watching the grey clouds slowly meander by overhead, softly moaning his agony to the sky.

Uncle Frank had succeeded in his mission to have a blowout of a Thanksgiving Day celebration, satisfying his own sense of urgency to create memories of his sister, even though he hated the necessity of doing so. Pictures were taken to fill family photo albums, pictures that would be shared in the future with fond memories and sad lamentations.

Later in the evening, at Shelley's request, Ben was the last guest to leave.

"I know why you came, Ben, and I love you for it," she said, as they stood alone on the front porch. "It means more to me than you'll ever know."

"Aw, hell, now look what you've done," he said, choking back a sudden tear.

"Darlin' girl," he went on, struggling to regain his composure, "I'm only sorry I wasn't smart enough to take advantage of the free meal before. Ya sure you don't need help with them dishes? That's a pile of work you got there."

"Oh, don't worry about that," she replied. "I have plenty of help for that chore. Kathleen and Maria insisted on coming over in the morning. Well…Kathleen more than Maria. Between them and my two guys, we'll handle it. But thanks, anyway."

"That's good. For a second there, I was afraid you might accept my offer," Ben chuckled.

"Oh…you adorable old man!" she chided, playfully smacking him on his arm.

"Shelley…" he started, in a softer, more sincere tone, "you do this old man's heart a lot of good. I sure do love ya, girl."

He didn't have to say how much he was going to miss her. His eyes spoke that for him.

"I love you, too, Ben Ivey," she said, laying her head on his boney chest, as she hugged him closely. "I just wish Jack could have been here."

Though he couldn't see them, her watering eyes spoke of how much she would miss him.

"Yeah, that would have been just about perfect, now wouldn't it?" he said, his own eyes beginning to flood.

Winter silently made itself known one early December night, leaving a soft blanket of snow over everything to greet excited children in the morning.

A wonderfully deep, covering snow wasn't common in the South. No plows stood ready to clear the roads, so the schools were closed.

Not one word of protest was heard from a single child in town, but many parents groaned at the onslaught of snow-laden wet clothes and the inevitable colds that would accompany them.

Aubrey's farm had the perfect hill for sledding, and it was theirs exclusively. Buck let the boys play after they had helped him throw out blocks of hay for the cattle and stack firewood on the porch.

He knew he wasn't going to get much more out of them on the first day of a new-fallen snow.

Being from up North, Tony already had a Flexible Flyer sled. Frankie made a toboggan from a cardboard box, and Aubrey made do with an old tractor hood.

Each boy took turns on the other's sleds to see which one went faster, though that was never determined, because each run was more fun than the one before, regardless of which sled they used.

Tony's skill with his own sled allowed him to cut trails for the others to follow, weaving among trees and over ditches and using bumps on the hill as ski jumps.

Aubrey banged his nose on the front bar of Tony's sled during one jump, causing it to bleed freely and leaving a thin red line down the slope.

When the other two called it to his attention, he merely laughed, grabbed a handful of snow and covered his nose with it until it stopped bleeding. Far too much fun was being had to let a simple bloody nose interfere.

Aubrey tried hitching Rusty and Scooter up to Tony's sled, as he had read about in *Call of the Wild.* But the farm-bred dogs were not interested in pulling a sled, and had other plans of their own, each in a different direction.

Then he got the idea to hitch one of the mules to the sled. But his father said no, because his mules were trained to pull a plow slowly in a straight line, and pulling a silly, little sled all over the place at a run might put ideas in their heads.

This year, the snow hung around for more than just a few days. In fact, a little more snow fell every other day or so, much to the delight of the children and the chagrin of the parents.

The snow worked its magic on the town, as well, bringing a more festive holiday spirit than usual.

Merchants seemed more enthusiastic about setting out their Christmas decorations. Choruses of "Merry Christmas" rang out from every corner and on every street.

People in general seemed more cheerful and congenial.

The mood even infected Buck. Without waiting for the usual request from Sarah, he and Aubrey ventured out into the woods and cut down two nicely shaped cedars to use as Christmas trees. One was for his family, and one was for Shelley and Frankie, who were genuinely impressed by his act of kindness.

The next day he changed his mind and gave Aubrey permission to hitch the mules up to a sled.

The boys took full advantage of the occasion. It turned out that the old tractor hood made a better sleigh and could hold all three. The curved front of the hood kept them on top of the snow and would go sliding to the side whenever the mules changed directions.

Tony decided it was easier to guide the big beasts if he was on one of their backs. But Aubrey was sure it was just another excuse to ride.

He did his best to get the mules going fast enough to throw his buddies off of the makeshift sleigh, laughing hilariously when he succeeded.

Each time, Frankie and Aubrey pelted him with snowballs until he fell off the animal's back. Then they'd start all over again, and again, until Sarah finally called them in for hot chocolate, long after the sun had set.

Night sledding was always more fun when the snow reflected the light of the full moon.

Shelley really loved the snow, even though it made getting around more difficult. She relished the extra snow, knowing how unusual it was.

She and Frankie built a massive snowman in their front yard. It was so tall they needed a step ladder to put the eyes and nose in.

The Musketeers promptly filled it with BB holes after determining that it was alternately an abominable snowman, set on kidnapping innocent folks off to the high mountains, or an ice ogre intending to eat everyone.

It took weeks for the frosty apparition to melt after the rest of the snow had disappeared.

Christmas moved closer at an agonizingly slow pace, as it always does for boys of a certain age.

Pretending to be good for Santa was proving to be a grueling task, especially for Tony. Refraining from his usual pranks was proving to be very difficult.

Aubrey kept his perspective in check. The holiday was a holy day, celebrating the birth of his Savior. It was about Jesus, not Aubrey.

Past Christmases had taught him not to have the high expectations that other children had. Santa wasn't an anticipated visitor at the Denton home.

Buck still made his yearly sick comment about having fresh venison if he ever heard footsteps on his roof.

He even made sure to stoke the fire before going to bed. After all, ol' Saint Nick had never bothered to show up when he was a kid, so why should he show up now? His boys knew all about the fat, old fraud.

Frankie's anticipation was tinged slightly by his mother's illness hovering, ever-present, in the back of his mind.

Thankfully, she had not deteriorated as much as had been feared. A progressing weakness and a shortage of breath were only occasionally punctuated by spasms of pain, and she was usually able to conceal those from her son.

She couldn't conceal her weight loss, though. Clothes that once fit nicely now sagged on her diminishing frame. She began wearing loose-fitting clothing to minimize the impact.

She accepted every day as a gift and treated each accordingly, always looking for something positive in each day's events, but a withering reflection in the mirror each morning kept her mindful of the inevitable.

She and Frankie baked cookies and played board games frequently, and every evening, they would curl up together on the couch and watch television. She preferred comedies, her favorite being *I Love Lucy*, while Frankie preferred a wider variety, including Westerns and science fiction, like *Wanted – Dead or Alive* or *The Twilight Zone*.

At first, she imposed a bedtime, but more and more, she was content to let him fall asleep with his head in her lap. Then the television became nothing more than background noise, as she sat for long periods, cherishing her son's every feature, so many of which he had gotten from his father.

From his wavy black hair to his Romanesque nose, and when they were open, his crystal blue eyes. She inevitably ended up dabbing tears from her eyes, as she tenderly stroked his cheek. She didn't know if it was possible to miss someone after you died, but if it was, she would definitely miss her son.

HELL COMES HOME

On a cold grey evening, a couple weeks before Christmas, Buck stormed into the kitchen from the back porch, his mood particularly foul.

Aubrey and his mother were cleaning up after dinner, and the forcefulness of Buck's entry startled them, prompting an all-too-familiar fear in both.

"Goddamn dog!" he growled, casting a snarl at Aubrey. "The stupid bitch is pregnant again! I dun told you what I was gonna do."

What normally would have excited Aubrey now frightened him. He remembered how unhappy his father had been about the previous litter. He had become angry at the expense of feeding them, as well as at the effort it took to find homes for them. And the puppies were always underfoot.

Just then Sarah made a critical mistake. She reminded Buck that he had kept putting off getting Scooter spayed because it cost too much.

That ignited a furious tirade of abusive name-calling, culminating with him shouting, "I'll fix the bitch to where she'll never have another goddamned pup! You just watch."

He stomped out of the kitchen and into the hallway, where a large antique gun case held a respectable collection of shotguns and rifles, passed down through the generations. He yanked the glass-paned doors open and grabbed a 12-gauge automatic shotgun and loaded it. Raging angrily, as he stormed back through the kitchen, he threw the back door open. "I'll fix the bitch!"

"Scooter…" Aubrey whimpered and started after him, guessing what he had in mind, but his mother grabbed him out of fear for his safety.

Scooter lay halfway into her doghouse in the corner of the yard, idly chewing on an old bone by the light of an overhead string of bare bulbs illuminating the way to the outhouse.

Upon seeing Buck, she got up and walked trustingly toward him, wagging her tail and dipping her head in submission, her soft, brown eyes anticipating a possible treat of some sort, maybe some leftovers from the meal her sensitive nose had detected.

Standing on the porch landing, Buck raised the shotgun and took aim at the unsuspecting hound, as she carelessly ambled from one light circle to the next toward him, tail swinging side to side.

Through the kitchen window, Aubrey could see his dog walking toward her doom and screamed her name as loudly as he could.

Hearing her master's voice in such distress, she stopped and looked toward the house, her floppy ears perked.

Buck fired the shotgun, instantly killing his son's oldest, dearest friend. The sudden boom momentarily stunned mother and son.

Sarah struggled to hold Aubrey back, as he thrashed and screamed.

She had never seen Buck so full of rage. She feared that he might seriously injure Aubrey if he confronted his father.

Moments later, Buck stalked back into the kitchen.

"You bastard! I hate you!" Aubrey screamed at his father. The force of his anger caused Sarah to lose her grip on him. He flew across the room, ran headlong into Buck, and started pummeling him with all his might. The powerful blows made Buck flinch and further fueled his rage.

"Get off me, ya little shit!" Buck roared, as he pushed Aubrey off and then backhanded him across the face, sending him spilling across the floor in a daze and slamming into the refrigerator.

Sarah snapped.

Buck's heartless execution of the family dog was horrific enough, but seeing her son thrown so violently across the room was too much for her.

She could stand no more, and, without warning, she leapt at her husband, clawing and pounding his face as hard as she could....for the first time in her long-suffering life.

"You sonuvabitch, keep your filthy hands off my son!" she screamed, striking at him as hard as she could. The force of the blow broke her hand.

The dual assault on him fueled Buck's uncontrolled rage. A huge, calloused fist to her face knocked Sarah backwards and onto the floor. He kicked her in the side, as she tried to get up. He then straddled her, stooping to deliver more punishment.

"You fuckin' bitch!" he roared, as he vented all the

years of frustration onto her. *"I shoulda killed you a long time ago."*

Aubrey regained his senses and looked over to see his father slouched over his mother's body. He heard each sickening thud between curses, as each blow landed hard on his mother.

Hearing his father's threat and believing that he intended to beat his mother to death, the same way his grandfather had done to his grandmother, panic took hold.

"Stop...Stop!" he screamed.

He had to help his mother, but how? Then he saw the shotgun lying on the floor, where his father had dropped it.

As if he were watching someone else in slow motion, he saw himself crawl over to the gun and take it into one hand, as he used the other to help himself stand up. Still dazed from the blow his father had delivered, he stumbled toward the maniacal monster beating his helpless mother.

With every punch, memories of the beatings he had received over the years came back, harder and harder. He began trembling uncontrollably, as he raised the shotgun and pointed it at his father.

"Leave my mother alone!" he yelled.

"I said leave my mother alone!" he repeated angrily, when Buck failed to respond to his first warning.

Buck looked from the gruesome attack on his wife, over at Aubrey, who stood with the shotgun pointed at him. The demonic look on his father's face frightened Aubrey to his core.

Slowly standing up, Buck stepped over his badly battered, semiconscious wife toward the panicked boy, growling from behind gritted teeth, "I'll teach you, you little motherfu…"

The roar of the shotgun inside the house had a deafening effect on Aubrey, which only added to the surrealism of what was happening. Buck's body flew backwards, as a hundreds of tiny lead pellets found their mark, causing his chest to explode in a pink mist of blood and gore.

The shock of the recoil and the sound caused Aubrey to flinch and pull the trigger once again. The second shot went wide, obliterating the telephone hanging on the wall.

The world seemed to grind to a halt. Through the ringing in his ears, Aubrey could barely make out his mother's whimpers of pain.

Frozen in place by what he'd just done, he stood rooted for what seemed hours, rather than mere seconds.

"Aubrey…" he heard his mother gasp weakly through shredded lips.

"Aubrey, where are you?" she gasped again, desperation in her voice.

His mother's cries snapped him out of his paralysis. Panic flooded in again. He dropped the shotgun, as if it had suddenly become as hot as molten metal, staring in disbelief at it.

"*Maw…Maw!*" he cried, stumbling to her side, his father's lifeless body only inches away in a rapidly spreading pool of blood.

"I didn't mean to, Maw. Honest, I didn't," he blubbered, as he knelt down next to her. "He wouldn't stop, Maw. He…he wouldn't st…stop." His body was wracked with anguish. "He was gonna k-kill you!"

Sarah reached her broken hand up to brush tears from his eyes, but the pain caused her to withdraw it and use her other hand. Her vision blurred, as her eyes began to swell shut, and her speech became slurred.

"Aubrey, baby, Momma loves you," she said, as she began to lose consciousness.

"*Mama!* Wake up!" he cried desperately. "Please, Maw, wake up."

His panic grew worse by the second. He didn't know what to do. His thoughts scattered. Was she dying? What was going to happen to him?

His guts wrenched in agonizing confusion and uncertainty. His body shook with fear.

And then, as if a supernatural hand lifted the panic from him, he was suddenly able to think clearly.

He had just shot and killed his father, and now his mother lay bleeding and possibly dying, also. Oddly, he felt no concern for his father, but his mother, his precious mother, needed help, and he was the only one who could get it.

Waylon was at Irene's house for dinner and wouldn't be home for a while. He looked at the hole in the wall where the phone used to be. His options narrowed.

He realized what he had to do, so he leaned down and kissed his unconscious mother on her forehead, the only part of her face that hadn't been battered.

"I'm goin' ta get some help. Please don't die!"

He started to get up, but then took her injured hand and gently kissed it saying, "I love you, Maw."

As he stood up, he couldn't help but catch the sight of his father lying in his own blood. The urge to vomit rose in his stomach. Whether from the sight of the carnage or the revulsion for the man he now hated more than anything on Earth, he wasn't sure.

Thankfully, his clarity of mind held.

"Why?" he asked the dead man.

"Why didn't you love us?" he choked. "Why did you hate us so much?"

Breaking free of the sight, he raced out the front door without a coat, still wearing his house slippers. Slipping and sliding through shin-deep snow, he navigated his way to the gate at the end of the driveway, flung it open, and started at a dead run down the road toward Frankie's house, his slippers losing traction every so often, causing him to slip and stumble along at an awkward pace.

The thought of his mother lying on the kitchen floor, possibly dying, drove him onward through the slush and the cold. His mind began to reel again, as each step jolted a memory of abuse and pain at the hand of his father, alternating with the memories of the many acts of love from his mother showered on him.

The thought of Scooter lying dead in the snow only made things worse.

His rasping breath became a fervent and heartfelt, panting prayer, as he begged God for forgiveness and called for angels to watch over his mother while he ran for help.

Frankie lay prone on the living room floor watching *Zorro*, while his mother sat in her easy chair, working at her needlepoint. Suddenly, they heard the loud scrambling of heavy footsteps on their front porch. Then the pounding of desperate fists echoed through the house.

Frankie jumped up and ran to the door, feeling the urgency of the mumbled cries from the other side. He recognized the voice.

Throwing the door open, he saw Aubrey, completely distraught and gasping too wildly to speak. A river of tears flowed down his pale cheeks.

"What's the matter, Aub?" Frankie nearly shouted, seeing his best friend in such a state. "Did somethin' happen?"

Shelley followed her son to the door, the desperation in Aubrey's voice causing her alarm.

"I…I…I dun a bad thang!" he managed to say, between sobs. "I…dun …a terrible…bad thang! M… Maw's h…hurt real b…bad, too!"

"Come on in, sweetheart," Shelley said, as she urged him in out of the cold, putting her arms around his heaving shoulders. "What on earth has got you so worked up?"

He sniffled and heaved for a few long moments, and then sputtered, "I dun a terrible thang, Aunt Shelley, a terrible, bad thang!"

Shelley noticed his ice-caked house slippers and freshly battered face under the freezing tears. Whatever was wrong with him was bad enough to drive him out into the wintery weather and to run over a mile through snow and ice. She led him into the living room and wrapped him in a quilt she kept draped over the back of the couch.

"Aubrey, honey, you've got to calm down and tell me what's going on," she implored, with mounting concern.

Frankie had never seen Aubrey so upset. He couldn't imagine what could possibly bother his friend so much.

Still trembling from the cold and convulsing with sobs of grief, he finally managed to say "I…I shot 'im! I shot…my…paw! He's…he's dead an'…an' Maw's hurt bad!"

Shocked, Shelley yelped, *"What?"*

"I…sho…shot my paw," he repeated through heaving sobs.

Frankie felt as though he were in a bad dream. Did he just hear Aubrey say that he'd shot his father? He could only stand there with his mouth agape, too stunned to say anything.

His mother blinked back her disbelief and asked, "Wha…why?"

Aubrey made a great effort to collect his wits, and then he sniffed, "He…he shot Scooter." Then his chin wrinkled.

He sniffed some more and said, "An'…an' he was hittin' Maw real hard an' hurtin' her bad. She fell down, an' I begged him ta stop. He jus' k….kept on hittin' her, like he was tryin' ta kill her." He broke down into heaving sobs again.

"Oh dear God!" Shelley exclaimed, pulling the wailing boy close to her.

Frankie couldn't believe what he was hearing. Aubrey just told them that he had shot and killed his own father.

Why had Buck shot Scooter? Why did he beat Sarah?

Aubrey continued through gasps, "I pi…picked up the shotgun and told him ta st…stop."

His face contorted, as he said, "He…he jus' looked at me like he was gonna kill me, too. His eyes were cr… crazy, an' I was sc…scared. I don't remember, bu…but I musta pulled the trigger, 'cause I heard the shot an' saw him fall down."

Again, he broke down into spasms of grief. "I want my maw! I want my maw!" he whimpered desperately.

Shelley hugged him close, mumbling through her own shocked tears, "Oh, my God, you poor child."

They heard the crunching of tires on the gravel out front. Then a car door slammed, followed by footsteps crunching through the snow. As the sound of the footsteps started up the porch steps, Frankie yanked the door open again.

Waylon was just reaching for the screen door handle.

"Is Aubrey here?" he asked, his voice highly agitated.

Aubrey pulled away from Shelley. Seeing his little brother, Waylon rushed over and slid to a stop on his knees, embracing him tightly.

"You okay, Aub? He didn't hurt ya did he, lil' brother?" he asked desperately, tears of relief welling up.

He had gotten home mere minutes after Aubrey had gone for help, and he found his mother still lying unconscious next to his dead father. He managed to revive his mother and asked where Aubrey was.

Sarah had become alarmed at his question and sent him to search for him.

Not knowing what had happened, his mind flew into a panic. He desperately searched the house, and, finding nothing, he had a horrifying thought.

He ran to the barn and searched every stall and the loft. The relief at not finding his little brother's body tucked in a corner was tempered by the thought that it might be lying somewhere in the snow.

His own rage at his father grew wildly. Then he had a thought.

He's gone to Frankie's. After returning to the house and helping his mother to the couch, making her as comfortable as he could, he told her where he thought Aubrey had gone, and that he'd go get him.

"I'm sorry, Waylon. I didn't mean ta do it," Aubrey pleaded, his face buried in his brother's shoulder.

"He...he was hurtin' Maw real b...bad, an' he wouldn't stop!" he wailed.

Looking up into his older brother's face, he asked, "Is

M . . . Maw d…dead? Did he kill her, too?"

"No, li' brother, the bastard didn't kill Maw. Thanks to you, she'll be okay," he said, trying to reassure his distraught little brother.

"She told me what happened, or at least what she could remember. She said you saved her life, lil' brother." He was having difficulty holding his own emotions in check.

Waylon asked Shelley if he could use their phone to call the sheriff.

Aubrey's face paled, and his tear-wracked eyes widened.

"They're gonna lock me up, ain't they Waylon? I don't wanna go ta jail!" he cried, his voice even more desperate than before.

"Help me, Waylon. I'm scared!" he wailed.

"Calm down lil' brother; ain't nobody gonna haul ya off ta no jail," he said, as soothingly as his own agitation would let him. "You was just protectin' Maw, that's all. Sheriff Tanner's dun locked Paw up enough times ta know what kinda asshole he is…or was."

Waylon clearly did not feel as remorseful as his little brother was at losing their father.

Shelley saw resentment in the older brother's eyes where there should have been grief. His nostrils flared with anger, as he hugged his trembling younger brother close to him.

Holding Aubrey at arm's length, he looked intensely into his little brother's red, puffy eyes.

"Listen to me, Aubrey Denton!" (He only used his younger brother's full name when he was serious about what he was saying.)

"It isn't yer fault. Paw was wrong…flat out wrong ta

do what he dun," he reassured Aubrey. "He was a mean, spiteful man, lil' brother. All ate up with bitterness."

He paused and brushed Aubrey's unruly hair back with his hand.

"Lil' brother, I owe you an apology," he said, his own voice beginning to crack. "Hell, I knew what kinda mean sumbitch Paw was. He'd whooped up on me enough times fer me to know that he'd do the same thang ta you."

He choked momentarily, then said, "An' I didn't do nothin' ta help ya."

"Ya know, Aub, I never told you, but I been considerin' joinin' the marines, like Chet. Jus' ta git away from Paw. I been thinkin' that if I didn't, I was gonna kill him, myself."

A look of abandonment raced across Aubrey's face, stopping him in midsentence.

"Aw, hell, Aub," he grinned weakly, "I ain't gotta go nowhere now, an' I promise I ain't gonna leave you an' Maw all alone, neither.

"Yer my lil' brother," he choked out. "An'… Maw needs us both." He hugged Aubrey close to him and let his own silent tears flow.

Aubrey wasn't the only one he was trying to reassure, he realized. He needed it, too. He hadn't had time to process what had happened, and the reality was beginning to sink in.

"Lil' brother," he said after gathering his emotions, "you got more guts than me. You did what you had to do. I didn't." He finished speaking guiltily.

Shelley's tears where flowing freely, now. She knelt beside the two brothers and wrapped her arms around both.

She had never liked Buck; now she hated him, even

if he was dead. He hadn't been man enough to be a real father, just an ignorant bully who squandered the love of his family.

"You're a good brother, Waylon," she said, sensing the teenagers' need for comforting.

Frankie's head was spinning with fear and confusion. Fear of what might happen to Aubrey, confused that a son could hate his own father so much as to want him dead.

An impending loneliness began creeping into his heart. His mother would be gone all too soon. And now, his best friend may be taken away, as well. He was losing everything that brought joy into his life.

The moment passed, and then he felt guilty. His friend was in trouble, and this was no time to feel sorry for himself.

"Waylon, honey," Shelley said, gathering her wits, "let's go see about your mother. Aubrey…sweetheart, are you okay enough to go back home?"

"Y…yes ma'am, Aunt Shelley. I'm okay. Maw needs me," he bravely offered.

"I'll fetch 'im back home, Mrs. Albert," Waylon said. "I just need ta call Sheriff Tanner."

"No, hun," Shelley protested. "Let's all go together."

Turning toward the phone, she said, "You wait here with Aubrey. I'll call the sheriff."

Quickly, she dialed the sheriff's office and explained what had happened, as much as she could. Then she dialed a second number.

"Hello," Kathleen answered. "Oh, hello, sweetie. How are you?" A brief silence followed, and her face went pale.

"Oh dear God, you can't be serious. Oh sweet Jesus! Is he okay?" Another short silence, then, "Yes, of course.

We'll be right there."

She hung the phone up and turned to Mike, who had overheard the alarm in her voice and come to her side to see what was wrong.

"What is it?" he asked urgently.

She stood there for a few seconds, too stunned to speak.

"My God, Mike!" she finally managed. "I don't believe it. Aubrey shot and killed his father! Oh, Mother Mary, help us." She brought a hand to her mouth and began to tear up.

"He did what?" Mike was just as stunned as his wife.

With great effort, she told him what Shelley had told her, frequently having to stop and regain her composure.

"That sonuvabitch!" he growled, his contempt for Buck boiling over. "That lousy sonuvabitch!" His voice kept rising.

"I knew that sorry bastard was no damn good. He just couldn't stop pushing the boy, could he?" he ranted, as he walked to the hall closet to get coats for Kathleen and himself.

"Maria!" he called.

"What is it, now?" she grumbled to herself, annoyed at being called away from the TV program she was watching.

"Yes, Daddy!" she called back, in a condescending tone.

"Sweetheart, your mother and I have to go out. It's an emergency," he told her. "We need you to keep an eye on Tony for a while."

Hearing the urgency in his voice, her demeanor changed instantly. Her father was a rock. Nothing rattled him. Except now he was rattled….really rattled. More than she'd ever seen before.

"Okay, Daddy," she replied, much more respectfully. "What's happened?"

"I'll tell you when we get back. Just keep an eye on things, okay? We could be a while," he instructed, as he helped Kathleen on with her coat and grabbed his own.

"Aubrey killed his dad?" a disbelieving voice asked from behind him.

He turned to see his son standing there, eyes wide with fear and confusion. Kathleen hadn't seen Tony standing in the kitchen doorway when she broke the news to Mike.

"Oh my gawd!" Maria gasped, putting her hand over her mouth.

"Son," he said, dropping to one knee in front of Tony, "that's what we're going to find out. That was Frankie's mom on the phone just now." He was at a total loss as to what he should say next.

"I wanna go!" Tony begged.

Kathleen stooped down in front of him also and said, "No, baby. Not this time. You stay here with sissy, okay?"

"If it's true, and I don't know if it is," she fibbed, "but if it is, there will be things you shouldn't see or hear."

"We'll be back as soon as we can," she reassured him.

"And Tony," she said, drawing him into a motherly embrace, "Mommy loves you so much."

A range of emotions were dancing across the boy's face. Mike saw his son struggling. Taking his son by the shoulders, he said, "Buddy boy…. Aubrey is in some trouble, some real big trouble. He's going to need his pals like never before. You can be strong for him, can't you?"

Tony nodded, too stunned to speak.

"That's my man," Mike said, ruffling his son's hair.

"Maria," he implored, as he stood up. "Your brother needs you, okay?" He saw tears rising in his daughter's eyes.

"Yes, Daddy," she said in a quivering voice. She walked over to her brother and placed a protective arm around him. "We'll be okay."

No final instructions were given by the parents. What would they be, anyway? Get to bed on time? Don't watch too much TV? There was little chance that they'd do either.

Kathleen kissed each of her children on the forehead and then headed through the front door, as Mike was held it open for her.

Ten long minutes later, they pulled up in front of the Denton farm.

The wail of sirens broke the silence of the small-town night, as the sheriff's patrol car, then his deputy's car, and then a white Cadillac ambulance screamed by the Albert house just moments after Shelley's call.

Within minutes, Shelley was following Waylon home. Through the rear window of the old pickup truck, silhouetted by her headlights, she could see Aubrey's head leaning on his brother's shoulder.

They pulled up to the farm's gate. Even in the insanity of the night, the country-raised sheriff had thought to close it behind him. Shelley could see that Waylon was having a little difficulty convincing Aubrey to let him get out and open it. Aubrey was shaking his head, "No."

She couldn't blame him for not wanting to return to the house. She couldn't imagine the horrors running through his mind.

"Frankie, go open the gate," she ordered offhandedly.

Frankie jumped out and ran to the gatepost. Removing

the chain from its nail, he swung the gate open. Waylon drove through, followed by his mother, frozen gravel crunching beneath a thin veneer of snow as they passed.

Waylon continued up the winding and rutted driveway, as Frankie closed the gate, returned the chain to its nail, and hopped back into his mother's car.

Shelley pulled up in front of the farmhouse, next to the patrol cars and the ambulance. Waylon and Aubrey were climbing the front porch steps, the younger brother's arms wrapped tightly around the older one's waist.

Shelley and Frankie followed them into a scene neither of them would ever forget.

In the in the foyer stood a gurney with Buck's body on it, covered with a white, blood-soaked sheet.

Frankie was shocked and frightened by the sight. His head began to spin. All the detective shows and all the war movies could never have prepared him for this.

The blood was vivid red, not shades of grey, like on TV. Even the air smelled of blood. He felt his knees weakening, and the room seemed to close in. He heard a distant voice calling to him.

"Frankie…honey…are you all right?" The voice was familiar, but he couldn't remember why. The ringing in his ears turned into a buzzing, and then into a roar, and then all was quiet.

The next thing he knew, the familiar voice was calling frantically to him from beyond a wide gulf. Slowly he began to recognize the voice. It was his mother. She seemed desperate to get his attention.

But why? Where was he?

He felt as though he were lost in a dark forest, fear pawing at him from every direction. But slowly, as his mother's voice became stronger, the darkness began to fade, but not the fear. What was he afraid of? A light began to glow dimly overhead, growing brighter with every word his mother uttered.

Finally, bright light flooded in, as he opened his eyes. The light glowed behind a shadowed figure. Why was he lying on the floor?

"Frankie, baby?" the figure called to him, as he felt something cool swipe across his forehead.

As everything began to come back into focus, he recognized his mother. With crushing embarrassment, he realized he had fainted.

"Momma…what happened?' he asked in a raspy, hollow voice.

"I'm so sorry, baby. It was stupid of me to bring you here," his mother apologized. "This is too much for you. You passed out; are you okay? You scared me."

The gruesome sight had shaken her, as well. But her son fainting at her feet brought her back around. She smiled down at her blinking son and helped him stand up.

"I'm okay, Momma. I'm sorry. I didn't mean to scare you." Slowly, the events of the evening began coming back to him.

"Where's Aubrey?" he asked, concern for his friend suddenly flooding over him.

"He's okay, sugar," his mother assured him. "He's in the living room with his momma and Waylon."

"Is he okay?" the ambulance attendant inquired from nearby.

"Yes, he'll be fine," Shelley answered.

"I'm sorry, ma'am. I reckon we oughta get this thing outta here," he said, motioning to the body on the gurney.

Shelley noticed the insensitive referral to Buck as

a "thing." But then the attendant had probably seen so much of this sort of thing that he had built a wall against it.

"Hey Montie," he called to his partner, "give me a hand with this, will ya!"

Shelley quickly herded her son into the living room. Out of reflex, both she and Frankie glanced through the doorway leading into the kitchen, each one instantly regretting it.

A massive pool of blood covered the floor, except for a wide spot where the body must have been lying. Shelley jerked her eyes away, but Frankie's eyes locked onto the horrible sight and wouldn't move away from it. His mother looked down to see him grow pale again.

"Frankie!" she nudged gently. "Look at me."

He stood frozen in place, his eyes refusing to obey. Shelley swung herself between the gory sight and her son, kneeling down to face him in order to block his view.

"Frankie! Look at me," she repeated more firmly.

It took effort to force his eyes into complying. Finally, he focused on his mother, and the rushing sound in his ears began to fade.

Why was I so stupid? Shelley berated herself. *This is no place for an eleven-year-old boy.*

Her focus had been on Aubrey and Sarah, without regard to her own son. She regretted that she'd been so careless. But what was done, was done. Standing back up, she turned him away from the frightening sight and led him away.

Aubrey knelt down beside the couch where his mother lay. He was sobbing heavily again, his face buried in his battered mother's stomach.

"I'm sorry, Maw," he wept, "I'm sorry."

Sarah tried comforting him with her good hand.

The sight of her swollen face was painful to look at. Both eyes were turning an angry purple. One eye was completely swollen shut and the other a mere slit above a battered cheek. Her lips were swollen and cut in several places. Her movements were jerky and obviously painful, especially her left shoulder.

Buck had done his worst on the mother of his children. Shelley knew that if Aubrey hadn't done something, Sarah would most likely be dead.

Normally repulsed by violence, she found herself thinking that Buck had gotten what he deserved. It just broke her heart that it had been Aubrey who had given it to him.

Frankie saw Aubrey and his mother suffering. His mind was reeling. But, this time, fear was replaced by sympathy. He slowly walked over and knelt beside them, gently laying his head on her right shoulder and finally letting the dam holding his own tears burst wide open.

"I love you, Aunt Sarah," he croaked between sobs. He didn't know where that came from or why; he just felt he had to say it.

Even the stalwart old sheriff choked up.

"It's a goddamn shame, Jimmy, a goddamn shame," he declared to his wide-eyed and paling deputy.

"I shoulda shot the bastard when I had the chance," he said, referring to the time Buck had once again drunk too much at the roadhouse and had threatened him with the rifle he kept in the gun rack of his pickup truck.

"Son," he said to Aubrey, as he approached the grieving trio, "I hate to take you away from your momma, but I gotta ask you a few questions, okay? It'll only take a few minutes."

Aubrey lifted his head and looked at the lawman, panic flashing across his face.

"Don't worry, son," Sheriff Tanner reassured him. "You'll be all right. I just need some details for my report. Okay?"

"C'mon, Aub," Waylon offered.

"I'll stick with ya," he said, as he helped his trembling brother up.

The boys followed the sheriff back to the foyer, now empty of their father's body, to give their statements.

Kathleen and Mike pulled up to the farmhouse just as the attendants were loading the blood-soaked gurney into the ambulance.

"Oh, my God…oh, my God! It's true!" Kathleen gasped through her hands, as her husband opened the car door for her.

"Don't look, babe," Mike said, wrapping his arms around his wife. Even though he had seen much worse in the war, the sight still shook him, too.

This wasn't a battling warship, where you expected to see death. This was the town they lived in. This was far too close to home. This was where his son had played… often.

He shuffled his shocked wife through the creaking gate and up the porch steps. The door stood open in the glare of the pendulous bulb.

Mike saw the sheriff and the two boys sitting in the corner of the foyer, the sheriff pulling a notepad from his shirt pocket.

Aubrey looked up at them, and a shadow of guilt and embarrassment swept across his tortured face.

With the same-mindedness that comes with years of

marriage and parenting, Mike and Kathleen both hurried forward to comfort the frightened boy.

"I'm sorr..." Aubrey started, only to be hushed by Kathleen, who began planting gentle kisses on his troubled forehead, fresh tears welling up in her eyes.

"You don't have to apologize, Aubrey," Mike told him through a clenched jaw. "We'll get you through this."

Turning to the sheriff, he asked, "Does he need a lawyer? I've got a good one I can call."

"And you are…?" the sheriff inquired, standing up to shake Mike's offered hand.

"Oh, sorry; I'm Mike Carillo. My son and Aubrey are friends. I want to help."

"Glad to meet you, Mr. Carillo. I'm Earl Tanner, county sheriff," he explained unnecessarily.

"I wish it was under better circumstances. The name's familiar, though. You run the mattress factory out on 280, don't you?"

Mike nodded.

"We all want to help, Mr. Carillo. The little guy is gonna need all of it he can get."

"Please, call me Mike. Sheriff what…."

"Earl's fine," the sheriff interrupted.

"Earl," Mike nodded. Then he continued, "What happened here?"

"That's what I'm trying to find out, Mike. You might want to get hold of that lawyer you mentioned," he said.

Looking down at Aubrey and seeing the panic in his face, he added, "Just in case."

Mike squatted to get eye to eye with Aubrey. Taking a deep breath, he said, in as reassuring a voice as he could muster, "Aubrey….son, we….no, I promise you that I will do everything I can to help you and your mother. Don't be too hard on yourself, buddy. I know you, Aubrey. You were pushed into doing what you did, weren't you?"

Sheriff Tanner took an instant interest in what Mike was doing, but, instead of interrupting him, he simply stood back and listened.

Aubrey cast a furtive glance up at Waylon, who sat hovering protectively over his kid brother.

"Go ahead, Aub," Waylon urged, "tell 'em what happened."

Slowly and agonizingly Aubrey began recounting the horrifying events as well as he could. He grimaced, as he recalled the shotgun blast that killed his dog, and then withdrew into himself, as he sobbed out the description of how his father had pummeled his helpless mother while he lay on the floor not far away, unable to help.

His voice shrank to a whisper as he confessed to pulling the trigger that killed his father.

And then Aubrey fell silent.

Mike swallowed hard, unable to say anything. No one should have to go through the horror that Aubrey had gone through. He didn't doubt that he would have done what Aubrey had done, given the same circumstances, but Aubrey was just a kid.

Dead or not, Buck was a son of a bitch of the highest degree. He was unashamedly glad Buck was dead, but his heart ached for Aubrey. He knew the boy would be scarred for life, and the thought only made him angrier. "Bastard!" he mumbled.

His promise to the boy had not been an idle one, though. He was determined to get the best legal representation money could buy. He was not going to allow Aubrey to pay the price for his father's evil.

Sheriff Tanner couldn't recall when he'd gotten so

much information without having to interrogate any-one. He was grateful to Mike for making his job easier.

Even though he could never admit it while wearing a badge, he too, was glad to be rid of Buck, and all the trouble he'd caused.

One of the blessings of a small town is that you grew up knowing everybody else. One of the curses of a small town was that you grew up knowing everybody else.

Earl Tanner was no exception. He knew Buck from grade school, and like just about everyone else in town, he had been bullied by him at one time or another. Even after he'd been elected sheriff, Buck would taunt him to take the badge off and see how tough he was. There were several times he was tempted to do it.

Now Buck would become just an unpleasant mem-ory. Earl was glad for that.

His job was to make sure justice was served. In his heart, he felt it already had been served, with regard to Buck. But now Aubrey had to face it, and he wasn't sure how the boy would hold up. He would talk with the judge tonight, even if it meant getting him out of bed. He wasn't going to let Buck's legacy be the destruction of this frightened little boy.

Waylon wept silently, mumbling how he should have done something. Somewhere along Aubrey's recounting, Kathleen had placed her hand on Waylon's shoulder, to comfort him. Now she drew him close and wrapped motherly arms around the shaken teenager. Mascara streaked down her cheeks, but she didn't care. Nothing was pretty tonight.

"Mmm-hmm," the sheriff cleared the lump from his throat, as he stood up. "Aubrey, son…" he said, hesi-tantly, "I'm real sorry, but I'm afraid I'm going to have to ask you to come with me."

"Whoa….hold on Earl," Mike broke in as diplomatically as he could. "He's just a kid. The last place he needs to be is in your jail. What's he going to do? Run?"

"Mike," the sheriff replied, "there's a dead body involved. I have to take him into custody. I wish I didn't have to, but…"

Mike's mind was racing. Being locked up like a murderer would further devastate Aubrey.

"What if I posted bail and assumed custodial responsibility?" he interrupted, his businessman's mind kicking in.

Sheriff Tanner thought about it and then said, "Normally, I wouldn't do such a thing, but it sure sounds like it would be better for him. So….okay, we'll do that. I'll even let you come by in the morning to post the bail and take care of the paperwork, so you don't have to worry about it tonight, if you want."

"Earl, you're a good man," Mike told him, shaking his hand.

"Or a damn fool," the sheriff replied, wondering how badly the judge would chew him out for allowing it.

"When you say 'custody,' you mean you'll take him home with you and keep a close eye on him, right?"

"Absolutely I will," Mike assured him, his New York accent cementing the promise.

"I'll be right by his side all night long," Kathleen promised, still comforting Waylon. Even if Aubrey was able to get to sleep, she was sure he'd have nightmares, and she wanted to be there if he needed her. Mike's recliner sat next to the hide-a-bed couch, so that's where she would be.

Shelley had come into the foyer as Aubrey was reliving his horror, and she had heard what the Carillos where offering. Her affection for the couple grew tremendously. Not many people would so willingly insert themselves, their family, and their homes into such a gruesome situation.

Mike and Kathleen began to lead Aubrey out of the house. Shelley approached Waylon, as he stood to return to his mother's side.

"Waylon, honey..." she said to the largely ignored other son. "I would really like it if you and your mother came to our house tonight. She needs care, and you need to be away from all this."

"Thanks a lot, Mrs. Albert, really," he replied. "But I'll be all right, an' I can take care of my maw."

"Waylon," Mike said to him, in a concerned, but fatherly tone the teen had never heard from his own father.

"Be practical, son. Your mother needs medical attention, and you can't stay in a crime scene," he said, putting it bluntly.

"We're going to take care of your brother, so why don't you let Mrs. Albert help you take care of your mother, okay?"

Waylon thought for a moment, then said, "Yeah, I reckon yer right, Mr. Carillo; it's just that..." He trailed off.

"You've been a real man tonight, Waylon," Mike complimented earnestly. "Your mother and your brother need you to help them through this. Can you do that?"

"Yes sir, I can," he answered. Mike's man-to-man approach made him feel more like an adult than his father's insults and derision ever had.

Turning to Shelley, he said, "Mrs. Albert....me an'

Maw would be proud to stay with you tonight. Thank ya kindly."

"Come on, sweetie," she said, wrapping an arm around his shoulders. "Let's get your mother to a doctor."

Mike overheard the exchange, and, looking back over his shoulder, he said, "Shelley, make sure the hospital bills me for anything Sarah needs, okay? Call me if you need to."

"I love you so much," Kathleen said to her husband, as they walked to their car, Aubrey's trembling hand in hers.

"Thank you for everything."

"No need to thank me, babe. This little guy needs help," he said, stroking Aubrey's hair. "I'd be a first class asshole if I didn't do what I could."

"You could never be that," Kathleen replied. "Still, I appreciate what you're doing."

Aubrey rode in silence to the Carillo home, neither Kathleen nor Mike pressing him to talk. When they pulled up to the house, Mike said, "Give me a few minutes to go in and prep Tony. I know he'll want to ask questions, but I don't think Aubrey needs to be bothered, right now."

Kathleen sat in the front seat with her arm wrapped protectively around Aubrey, his head resting on her shoulder.

"Aubrey, darling," she started, "don't be too hard on yourself. You did what you had to do to protect your mother….and yourself. It's awful that you were put in that position, but you had no choice. Nobody is going to condemn you for it."

"And I promise that you, your mother, and Waylon are going to be taken care of, no matter what. We love you, and we won't let anything happen to you."

Inside the house, Tony bolted to the door as soon as he heard his father enter. Maria wasn't far behind.

"What happened, Pop? Is Aubrey okay? Did he really shoot his father?" he bombarded his father in a concerned voice.

"Slow down, son," Mike urged his distraught son.

"Have a seat, you two," he said, motioning to the living room couch. Both did as he told them.

"Yes, Aubrey is okay, son. In fact, he's going to be staying with us for a bit."

For once Tony sat still and didn't comment.

"And unfortunately, yes his father is dead."

Even though they were somewhat prepared for the news, it still came as a shock. Maria gasped and put her hand to her mouth, as tears began to well up in her eyes.

Tony's jaw dropped open in disbelief. Mike had been careful not to phrase the news in a manner that seemed to accuse Aubrey.

"It's a terrible tragedy for his family, and they're going to need all the support they can get. I convinced the sheriff to let your mother and me have custody of him for a while."

"Sheriff?" Tony asked. "You mean they were going to arrest Aubrey?"

"Well, I don't like putting it that way, but I suppose that's what you'd have to call it," Mike replied.

"But I'm not going to let that happen," he reassured his children. "He was just protecting his mother and himself."

Mike took a few quick minutes to explain to them what had happened, without going into unnecessary detail.

"Son," he said to Tony, "I know you're going to want to ask him a lot of questions, but for his sake...and as a favor to me...please don't do that. At least not right now. We'll all sit down with him together and give him a chance to tell his side, but only if and when he wants to. He's been through a terrible ordeal, and pushing him too hard will only hurt him more. Your mother and I know exactly what happened, so ask us, instead. Okay?"

"Okay, Pop," Tony agreed.

"And Pop...thanks for helping my friend," he whispered, on the edge of tears.

"I'm glad I can, son," he said, sitting down next to his son and hugging him close. "I'm glad I can."

"Poor Aubrey," Maria sniffed. "He's such a nice kid. What about his mom and Waylon?"

"They're staying with Frankie and his mom, for the time being," Mike answered. "She's in pretty bad shape, and Mrs. Albert is going to take care of her."

After he was sure his children were ready, he went to the door and waved to Kathleen to come in.

Aubrey stood in the foyer, his head hung in shame. Tony walked up to him and wrapped his arms around his big friend, saying tearfully, "It's okay, Aub. You're safe now. I won't let nothin' happen to ya."

Kathleen had to leave the room, as her own tears began to flow.

Mike stood there, choking back the lump growing in his own throat from the pride he felt for his son.

Maria joined her brother in embracing Aubrey.

Aubrey began to sob.

Shelley drove Sarah to the county hospital to have her injuries attended to. Waylon had refused to leave his mother's side, and she didn't want to leave Frankie at home alone. She took the time in the waiting room to talk to the two boys.

The shock of what had happened began to sink into Waylon. "It's all my fault," he said, trembling with guilt.

"I shoulda been home. I might coulda stopped that bastard from killin' Scooter."

The hateful reference to his father did not go unnoticed.

"Or I coulda been the one ta shoot 'im. Aubrey don't deserve this."

His rage began to mix with his feelings of guilt.

"Waylon…sweetie, you don't know that you could have stopped him," Shelley countered, sitting in the chair next to him.

"Your mother told me about the fight you had with him. He might have felt outnumbered and turned the gun on you, or your mother…or even Aubrey. It's terrible that it happened the way it did, but it could have been worse. Just be thankful that she and your brother are going to be okay."

"Honey, you're the man of the house now. They need you to be strong. Blaming yourself for something you had no control over won't help you. It'll only get in the way."

"Waylon…" Frankie croaked hoarsely, "Aubrey really loves you. He told me an' Tony so."

"He says you're the best brother in the world," he reassured him, not knowing how else to comfort the distraught teenager.

"Thank ya, Frankie," Waylon said. "Ya been a good friend ta him. I 'preciate that."

He forced a smile and turned to Shelley and said, "An' thank you, too, Mrs. Albert. I reckon yer right, but I jus' cain't help but think I coulda done somethin' if I'd been there."

"Your mother is a big believer in the Bible, isn't she?" Shelley asked him.

"Yes, ma'am; she is."

"Well, as I recall, the Bible says that God has a purpose for everything, right?"

He nodded his agreement, unsure of where she was going.

"Well…it seems to me that he intended Aubrey to be there to save her from being hurt worse…or maybe even killed. And maybe he kept you away to protect you from the same. Maybe?"

"I don't know, Mrs. Albert. He let me an' Aubrey get whooped up on all these years. That don't sound to merciful ta me. But I think I understand what yer sayin'. An' ya know, I think Maw mighta said the same thang. I'm jus' gonna hafta hold judgment on that thought fer a while. But I do 'preciate what you tryin' ta do."

"Well, we're practically family so…." she offered.

"Yeah, I reckon we are, at that, aren't we?" he said, offering a more relaxed smile.

"Ya think Aubrey's gonna be okay? I mean, I know the Carillos are some fine folks, an all; I'm jus' worried 'bout my lil' brother."

"He'll be fine," she reassured him. "It'll be a bit rough for him for a while, I'm sure, but he's got lots of love surrounding him."

"I reckon he does. I'm glad fer that. He's a good ki…"

The thought of what his brother must be going through broke down his defenses.

Shelley wrapped her arms around him, as he finally let loose a torrent of tears, her own heart breaking for him.

Frankie stepped over to Waylon and laid his hand on his shoulder.

"It's okay to cry…Aubrey told me so."

The following afternoon, Sheriff Tanner arrived at the Carillo residence with a sour expression on his face.

"Mike, I need to tell you something." he grumbled, as he entered the home, refusing the offer of coffee.

"What's that, Earl?"

"It seems my secretary, or rather my now-former secretary, couldn't keep her big mouth shut," he said, the muscles in his jaw tightening. "The ink on the report wasn't even dry before she was on the damned phone."

"She's supposed to keep things like this confidential. I'm considering pressing charges."

Mike stared down at his coffee cup, shaking his head. "That's only going to make things tougher on the Dentons."

"Well, I did leave out the part about you having custody, so you shouldn't catch too much grief," the sheriff offered.

"At least not right away, that is. But you know how little towns like this are."

"Yeah…I'm afraid I do," Mike said, huffing a frustrated breath.

"Jesus Christ, Earl. Haven't those boys and their mother been through enough?" he asked, exasperated at what he knew was coming.

"Yeah," Earl answered, "they damn sure have. Anyways, I just wanted to stop by and warn you. I'm on my way to see the DA. I'm gonna do some arm twisting to get the boy as easy a deal as I can. You may get a call from his office."

"No problem," Mike assured. "I took the day off and

I've already left a message for our legal staff in Atlanta. I'm sure someone there has the name of a good lawyer. We'll get Aubrey taken care of."

"Oh, and Earl...thanks. I appreciate what you're doing for Aubrey and his family. You're a damn descent fella." He shook the sheriff's hand.

"Back at ya, Mike. They're fortunate to have such good friends," Earl said, turning toward the door. "Wish me luck."

GENTLE PERSUASION

"Henry..." Aggie said coyly, as she twirled the graying hairs on Judge Henry Walton's chest, "I want to talk to you about Aubrey Denton."

"Aggie, you know I don't talk about cases pending before my bench," the Judge responded, propping himself up on one elbow to face her, as she lay next to him in bed. The morning light filtered through lace curtains and danced on her sleepy face.

"Henry, this isn't just 'a case'; you know that," she said, cutting off his protests as gently as she could.

"This is a little boy's life. This is going to affect him forever. At best, it's his second chance. At worst, it's his destruction. He's too good a kid to risk that. Henry, you know what an asshole his father was."

"Aggie, please," he implored, a little surprised at her unusually strong language. "I can't discuss the details of the...."

"And I don't want you to," she persisted softly. "I know nothing has been decided, yet. I'm not asking you to do anything unethical."

"I just wish you would consider what's going to

happen to him after all the courtroom debate and publicity is over," she pleaded, adding a gentle caress to the side of his face. The morning stubble tickled her fingertips.

"You can't simply send him off to Tullahoma to be thrown in with all those incorrigible juvenile delinquents. That would ruin him."

"I dare say, it might even kill him," she said, adding drama to her argument.

"There's a hospital in Memphis, just for children," she hurried on. "They have a psychiatric ward for troubled kids like him. Surely it's within your power to send him there. He needs help, not punishment. He's just a sweet little boy who was forced into an ugly situation beyond his control."

"Darlin', someone was killed," the judge reminded her. "I have a lot of things to consider; no plea has even been entered…."

"There's a real, live twelve-year-old boy involved, too," she cut in, an edge of irritation creeping into her voice.

"And not just any boy, either, Henry," Aggie defended. "I've taught thousands of children in my time, and I'm telling you, this boy has one of the most beautiful minds I've ever encountered. I've spent quite a lot of extra time with him, and he's such a delight to talk with and just be around. He's much more mature than his age would indicate…and we both know why. He has so much potential for good."

"Please, Henry….for me?"

"Trust me, Aggie…" Henry went on, "between you, Earl Tanner, Mike Carillo, and Reverend Greene I know the boy is something special."

"Hell, even my old law partner's daughter, Shelley,

came by to plead his case.....and yes, I do know all about his father, the sonuva…"

He caught the uncharacteristic show of emotion, and then went on, "The man has stood before me often enough to know what the boy was up against. I know his background and I do feel for him. Believe it or not, I do have his best interests at heart."

"But…okay, for you…and for him…I'll tell the DA to look into the hospital as an alternative," he conceded.

"You know…I really don't like having to send the boy anywhere," he said. "I don't enjoy that sort of thing, Aggie. I'm not as calloused as some folks seem to think. I'm not some damned hanging judge!" he defended, a slight hint of bruised feelings showing through.

"Of course, you're not calloused, sweetie pie," she agreed, playfully pinching his cheek.

"I wouldn't waste my Friday nights…or Saturday mornings, with a man who was," she grinned; then she kissed his cheek.

"So it's not just my dashing good looks and racehorse stamina that keep me at your back door, huh?" he teased scandalously.

The secrecy of their relationship was what made it so deliciously tawdry.

"Oh, heaven's no, stud muffin…I require that both heads work properly," she replied, with a beguiling grin.

"So now that they're both awake…" she said, snuggling closer to him, stroking his bare chest, a sultry smirk on her wizened face.

Judge Walton held Aubrey's arraignment in his chambers, not seeing the need for a public display. As he had promised, he and the district attorney agreed to remand custody of the fragile boy to the psychiatric ward of the

Children's Hospital in Memphis.

Aubrey spent a somber Christmas in his sterile hospital room. His mother and brother were there, as well as Frankie, Shelley, and the Carillo family.

But try as they might, it was a grey day for him. The hospital wouldn't allow the gifts his family and friends had for him, nor was there a decorated tree to lighten the mood. Even the cookies and candy his mother had brought for him sat untouched.

He'd been moody and deeply depressed since that awful night. He refrained from talking, and his usual peaceful attitude eluded him, along with his warm smile. He didn't think they would ever return, either.

Frankie sat on the bed next to Aubrey and placed his arm on his friend's shoulder, saying "Me an' Momma will keep our tree at home up until you come home, okay? Heck, I'm not even goin' to unwrap my own presents until you can, too."

He gave his mother a look, as if to ask if it was okay.

"That's a good idea," she said, admiring her son's attempt to console his friend.

"Well shoot….I already opened all mine, last night," Tony admitted, glancing guiltily at his mother, "but we still got all the ones we got for you."

"We can have an extra Christmas for him, can't we, Mom?" he asked.

"Of course we can," Kathleen answered cheerfully.

"Ya'll don't hafta do that," Aubrey protested glumly.

"I know we don't have to, Aub," Tony replied. "We just want to."

"I 'preciate that, ya'll, but I might be here fer a while."

"Oh…I don't know about that, Aubrey," Mike chimed in optimistically. "You're just here for an evaluation.

Your lawyer says it shouldn't be too long. I didn't tell you that, did I?"

The news seemed to brighten his mood, but only slightly. For the most part, he remained dour. He was still locked away from his family and friends. He still thought of himself as a murderer. He still felt as if he'd brought shame on his mother.

Though they showed no evidence of it, he was still afraid his friends would treat him differently when, or if, he ever got to go home.

Eventually, everyone left for the long drive back to Haleyville, leaving him with his self-flagellating guilt and self-loathing.

GRAMMA ANGEL

Just two weeks into the New Year, Aubrey sat on the edge of his bed, eyes fixed on the silhouette the homemade noose made on the wall of his room, as the afternoon sun shone through the thick, wire-meshed window panes.

His years of experience tying knots and wrangling mule harnesses made it easy for him to braid the deadly device from strips he tore from his bedsheets.

Each twist was ingrained with regrets of how sinful and how evil he had been and how he had let Jesus, his family, and his friends down. Each overlap reminded him of his shame in the eyes of others. He had even tested the makeshift tool of his self-execution to make sure it would support the weight of a murderer.

In his guilt-ridden mind, hanging himself seemed an appropriate punishment.

He had betrayed God, just as Judas had. He hadn't trusted Jesus.

Instead, he had taken matters into his own hands, just as Judas had.

He had murdered, just as Judas had.

No matter that his reasoning was flawed, impeded by

a false and overblown sense of guilt.

No matter how many times his family and friends had reassured him that he hadn't done anything so evil, remorse still strangled his heart, refusing to let him see any other alternative.

And now he was locked in a small room, so the doctors who knew about this sort of stuff could determine how bad he was and how bad he was going to be when he grew up.

Surely they would agree that he should be sent to a real prison to receive his real punishment…the electric chair.

He was convinced that the state was going to execute him, so again, hanging seemed appropriate. He would save his mother the shame of having her murdering son executed for the world to see.

Young children didn't kill themselves very often, so his room hadn't been made suicide-proof. He scooted the wooden chair into position under the noose that hung from an exposed pipe overhead. He stacked all the books he had in his room on the chair to add height to his final fall. The last book on the stack was the Bible his mother had given him for his birthday.

It would be wrong to use the Bible for this grim task, so he removed it from the stack. But his trembling hands fumbled slightly, causing him to drop the book to the floor.

As it landed, it fell open to the full-page color picture of Jesus gathering the children around him, as he preached to the multitude. The picture was one of his favorites, and it compelled him to pick the book up to examine the picture closely for the hundredth time…. for the last time.

Unheard by Aubrey, and unintentionally silent as a cat, the elderly woman cracked open the door to his room.

Why wasn't this door locked? Shouldn't there be a guard or a nurse sitting in the empty chair outside the door? she wondered to herself, as she quietly swung it partially open.

She saw the young boy on his knees. In his hands, she could see that he held a Bible. . . . She listened closely, and she heard his desperate prayer.

"I'm sorry, Jesus," he began, gazing watery-eyed at the image of his Savior. "I didn't mean ta shoot my own paw. I shoulda trusted you ta protect Maw. I was jus' scared and wudn't thinkin'."

His apology became a prayer, and his voice began to tremble with remorse.

"I…I know that killin' myself ain't right, neither," he apologized. "But, I jus' cain't look at myself in the mirror no more without thinkin' what kinda evil person I turned into.

"I know my paw wudn't a very nice person, an' he did whoop up on me an' Waylon a lot, but he didn't deserve ta be shot like that. 'Specially not by his own son. Maybe I coulda done somethin' dif'ernt, I don't know, but I didn't. I dun whut I dun.

"I know you said that no sin is too bad for you to forgive, so I hope that you'll forgive me fer this one, too. I don't reckon you'll ever want to talk with me, now, face ta face like I'd hoped ya would, but I'd sure like ta see yer holy face jus' once before I hafta go ta Hell fer my punishment. I hope you'll let me.

"I shoulda trusted ya, Jesus, an' I'm sorry I let ya down. I jus' don't know what I should do. If ya could help me now, I'd surely 'preciate it….even if I cain't get…. into

Heaven," he pleaded tearfully, choking on the last words.

The woman at his door felt her heart break for the confused little boy kneeling, and pleading for his very soul.

Then, her eyes were drawn to something dangling from the ceiling.

"Oh, dear God!" she gasped, announcing her presence.

Aubrey spun around to face her, startled at her presence. His surprised expression changed to confusion, then morphed into one of recognition.

Bewildered, he asked, "Are you an angel? Did Jesus send ya?"

It took a moment for the woman to take in what she'd just seen and heard.

On one side, the noose dangled, waiting for its victim and screaming silent accusations of hopelessness and misery.

On the other side, the horrible device's intended prey knelt, begging forgiveness and help from God.

"No, Aubrey," she started, choking back her shock. "I'm not an angel, but it seems that maybe I was sent by Jesus, just in time.

"Sweetheart, I'm your grandmother," she announced, a sympathetic smile gliding across her face, hiding the shock and horror of what she was seeing.

"My grandmother?" Aubrey replied, disbelievingly.

"But…I thought you were…dead," he said, as he slowly began to rise, his Bible still grasped tightly in one hand.

"I guess that would explain why you thought I was an angel," she smiled sweetly at her newly found grandson. "But, as you can see…I am neither dead, nor an angel."

"Did your mother tell you I was dead?" she asked. She

had treated Sarah dreadfully, and now she wondered if her daughter even wanted her around Aubrey.

"No, ma'am, she didn't," he said apprehensively. "But I reco'nize you from the pitchers Maw has on the wall. I jus' thought…I mean, Maw never talks much about you, so I jus' reckoned you was."

Without warning, he rushed forward and embraced her, weeping, "Gramma…please help me."

"Of course, I will, Aubrey; of course I will," she rasped through her own tears, returning the first hug her grandson had ever given her.

The desperation in his voice tore straight to her heart. The suppressed guilt of not having been there for her daughter and grandchildren broke down the final bricks of the wall she had so stubbornly built.

The heartbreak was rocking her to her soul, but even as guilt and remorse swarmed over her, she began to feel a warmth she had never felt before.

She kissed her grandson on the top of his head, as he clung tightly to his grandmother angel.

"Oh, Aubrey…child, you weren't going to hurt yourself, were you?" she asked gently, after she'd composed herself, even though the noose hung in open evidence to the contrary.

Feeling more ashamed of himself than he thought possible, he answered reluctantly, "Yes ma'am…I, uh…I was.

"Ya see…I shot my own paw and killed him," he confessed.

His head hung low to his chest, unable to meet her gaze.

"That's a terrible crime and a sin against God. I don't deserve ta live. It's what they do ta killers."

"Aubrey, may I sit down?" she asked, gesturing toward the bed and motioning for him to sit beside her.

"Yes ma'am," he said, stepping aside to let her pass between him and the noose.

"Child," she started, as she sat down, "I heard what you said to Our Lord. You really believe in him, don't you?"

"Yes ma'am, I do. Maw taught me an' Waylon all about him."

So you didn't abandon Christ, like I abandoned you, did you, Sarah? Good for you...good for you, she thought.

"That's very good. So you believe that God puts people where he wants them to be and makes things happen according to his plan, right?"

"Yes ma'am, I do," Aubrey answered, feeling his anxiety begin to melt, the way it always did when he talked about Jesus with others.

"Then you understand that you were in that kitchen for a reason and that God put you there for your mother's sake, don't you?" she asked, in a matter-of-fact tone.

She had read about the tragedy in her local newspaper and gotten further information from her secret friend in Haleyville.

"God put me there ta kill my paw?" he asked, doubting that it was true.

"No, sweetheart; God put you there to save your mother's life," she answered.

"But I killed my paw...an' killin's wrong," he protested.

"Your father was obeying his own master...Satan. Not everything is God's fault," his grandmother tried to explain.

"The Commandments say, 'Thou shalt not commit murder,' don't they?" she asked, getting a nod from him.

"They don't forbid you from defending yourself...or

to keep someone you love from being killed, do they?"

He shook his head.

"Did you think your father was going to kill her? And maybe even you?" she asked, getting another nod.

"So do I," she said with conviction.

"Sweetheart…what you did wasn't murder; it was self-defense," she offered.

"I think maybe God used you to stop Satan from having his way."

Then she went on, "Child, look at the Old Testament. Didn't God tell Moses and Abraham to destroy their enemies?"

"Yes ma'am," Aubrey said, seeing that his grandmother knew her Bible.

"But wudn't my…"

She held a finger up, stopping his protest. "I heard you apologize to Jesus for not trusting him, didn't I?"

"Yes ma'am. I shoulda…" he tried defending himself.

Stopping him again, his grandmother asked pointedly, "Are you trusting him now?"

Aubrey had to think about his answer for a second. "I…uh…I reckon maybe not."

"When you first saw me, you asked if I was an angel. Why did you think that?" she interrogated.

"'Cause I asked Jesus ta help me, an' I thought that maybe he'd sent. . . . " He trailed off, feeling it sounded silly.

"You thought maybe he'd sent someone to help?" she asked the obvious, her eyebrows arched in question.

"Does it have to be an angel? He sent you to help your mother. Are you an angel?"

His confused expression compelled her to go on.

"Aubrey," she continued, "a couple of weeks ago, I

was at the beauty shop. I picked up a newspaper that just happened to be opened to the page that had the story about what had happened to you. Do you think that was an accident?"

The look of surprised made her say, "Yes, the news did make it all the way to Georgia. Good news travels slowly, but bad news runs like a wildfire."

"Anyway, a voice told me that it was the time for me to set all my selfish pride aside and come see you….and hopefully even your mother. I believe that was God's voice answering your prayer, long before you prayed it, don't you?"

"Well….yes, ma'am, I reckon it could be," he answered, feeling the weight of his guilt slowly lifting.

"I s'pose that if I hadn't a been there, then Paw mighta murdered Maw, and then he'd a been sent to the 'lectric chair, huh?"

The thought of his mother being dead and his father on death row was far more disturbing to him than his own current dilemma.

Had God really put him in the kitchen that horrible night to save his mother's life? If that was the case, then maybe he wasn't a murderer.

"Gramma?" he asked, relishing the good feeling the word gave him.

"Yes, sweetheart?" she replied, also cherishing the title.

"If God uses someone ta do somethin' that's normally a bad thang…like whut I dun….ya think he forgives them for it?"

"I'm sure he does," she answered, knowing her grandson had turned a corner in his feelings about himself and what he'd been through.

"That's good," he said, nodding thoughtfully to himself. "Then I reckon maybe he even forgave Judas, since he was only fulfilling what God had planned, huh?"

Beatrice Pickard had never heard such a postulation before.

"I suppose it's possible, maybe even probable," she conceded. Her grandson's insight amazed her.

"But I know that you are wrong about one thing."

"Whut's that, Gramma?"

"Jesus will never turn his face away from anyone who seeks it," she reassured him.

"I can tell you with all confidence that he waits for the day when he can talk to you…face to face. He would never keep you out of Heaven for this. He loves you too much to do that."

Aubrey's heart soared at her reassurances.

Of course, Jesus wouldn't turn his back on me. He promised that he wouldn't. How could I be so stupid? he admonished himself.

He reached his arms out to her, and she immediately drew him into hers. The feeling of hugging his own real-life grandmother felt like a soothing flow of warm water over his entire body.

The sensation of holding her grandson rang bells of joy in her heart. If only….

"Gramma?"

"Yes, darling boy."

"Where have you been?"

The simple question speared her heart as nothing had since her husband had died.

"It's not 'where' I've been, Aubrey; it's 'what' I've been," she corrected.

"I have been selfishly stubborn and unbelievably stupid. When I read about you, the word 'forgiveness' kept flashing in my mind.

"It hit me like a Mack truck. I call myself a Christian, but I forgot that forgiveness goes both ways. My idiotic pride kept me from forgiving your mother, yet I expected Christ to forgive me."

"What did Maw do that needed forgivin'?" he asked.

She realized that Sarah had never told him about her teenage mistake. Now wasn't the time to lay more worries on the troubled boy.

"Honey, your mother didn't do anything but seek out the love she wasn't getting at home. That's my fault, not hers," she confessed.

"If I had been a better mother, then…"

"Mommy?" a surprised and haunted voice whispered from the still-open doorway.

She raised her watering eyes to see Sarah staring in disbelief at her, as if she, too, were seeing a ghost…or an angel.

"Mommy…is that r…is that really you?" Sarah asked, in a cracking voice.

Not knowing how her daughter would react, Beatrice answered cautiously, as she rose from the bedside, "Yes… it's…really me. Is it okay that I…"

Sarah dropped the package she had from her good arm and rushed forward to embrace her long-lost mother. The sling and cast on her other arm made it cumbersome; it was something she had ached to do for too many years.

It was something her mother had ached for, as well.

"Oh…Mommy…Mommy…" Sarah sobbed. "I've missed you so much."

She broke down, as tears of joy began to flow freely.

"Where have yo….no, no, it's okay. You're here, now; that's all I care about."

"I sure haven't been where I should have been, my darling girl; I'm so sorry," Beatrice pleaded, her backlog of heartbreak breaking through, as she stroked her daughter's hair and examined the healing wounds on her face.

Sarah lovingly laid her head on her mother's shoulder, as she whimpered, "Mommy…Mommy."

The two women embraced for several long minutes, swaying and rocking in each other's arms.

Finally, Beatrice pulled away just enough to cup Sarah's face in her hands and to start kissing her wet cheeks, carefully avoiding the stitches near her mouth.

"Oh, my baby, I've done you so wrong," she sniffed. "Can you ever forgive this foolish old woman?"

"I never blamed you, Mommy. It was my fault. I was the one who…" Sarah tried to confess.

"Hush…hush, baby girl. Don't ever apologize again. It was never your fault," Beatrice corrected.

"It was always me. I was horrible to you. I pushed you too hard. And may God forgive…I blamed you for your father's weak heart. It was never your, baby, never your…" Sobs of regret choked off her words of contrition.

Hearing his mother call her mother "Mommy," as a little girl would, made Aubrey realize just how human his mother was. It made her more real, more approachable. It made all the things she had done for him over the years seem as much as acts of friendship as the acts of a loving mother.

Seeing this and realizing how close he'd come to being completely wrong about God's will and capacity for forgiveness, he decided that his first assessment of his grandmother had been more correct than even she realized.

"I reckon you really are an angel after all, Gramma," he said, distracting them from each other.

Remembering that she hadn't yet acknowledged him, Sarah started to introduce her son to her mother...for the first time.

"Mommy, this is my pride and joy. I named him after my big brother."

"I've already met this wonderful young man. I think your brother would have been so proud of his namesake," Beatrice replied. "Your father would have been so proud."

"I may have been a stubborn old bitch," Beatrice confessed. "But I wasn't completely heartless and stupid. I couldn't help myself. I just had to keep track of you and your family."

"You did?" Sarah asked, genuinely surprised. "I thought you had forgotten us."

"Oh, Sweetheart...I could never do that," Beatrice replied, feeling the stab of guilt plunge deeper. "But, yes, I certainly did keep up."

"I had a little help, though. You remember Mrs. Emory and her daughter, Natalie?"

Sarah nodded, recognizing the two gossip icons from her church.

"Well, I swore them to secrecy on the Bible and stayed in touch with them over the years through letters and sometimes a call. They even managed to sneak a Kodak or two of you and your boys at church picnics and such. Aubrey made a wonderful Joseph in the Christmas play." Then, she smiled down at him.

"It must have been absolute torture for Millie to keep it to herself," she laughed. "That woman just loves to gossip. But you seem surprised, so I guess the old girl can keep a secret, after all. She'll be relieved to hear that she doesn't have to anymore. I can just see her now…patting herself on the back for all the old bitties to see.

"But, as I told Aubrey, I think it was really God who brought me here today," she confessed, gesturing toward the now-innocuous suicide device hanging from the ceiling.

Sarah turned to look, and her eyes widened, as she screamed, "*Aubrey!* Oh, my God! Oh, son…"

Suddenly panicked, she scooped him from the bed-side nearly as angry at him as she was fearful for him.

"Why would you….?" she asked. Her fear overtook her, as he began to sob again, as she nearly crushed him with her embrace.

"I'm sorry, Maw," he strained to apologize through her vice-like hug.

"It was really stupid, I know. Gramma made me see that. But Jesus sent Gramma jus' in time, so…" he added, hoping it would help, not realizing the gut-wrenching fear and pain a parent would feel at the thought of their child committing suicide.

"He has your faith, Sarah," her mother complimented. "You've obviously done a great job. Better than me. I am so proud of you."

Sarah released him, and, without wasting a second, she quickly moved the books from the chair and climbed onto it to take the hateful noose down from the pipe it was attached to.

"Thank God no one else saw this," she said, cram-ming the homemade rope into her purse.

"They'd have thrown a fit and locked you up in much different room than this," she gently scolded Aubrey, not allowing the thought of him actually succeeding to enter her mind.

After she stepped down from the chair, Aubrey pointed to the wall and called their attention to the shadow of the Cross that the sun's rays through the window pane made, replacing the tragic silhouette the noose had previously made.

Thank you, Jesus, he thought to himself. *I shoulda known you'd be there for me.*

His mother's attention returned to the package she had dropped. She picked it up and handed it to Aubrey.

"Honey, here's some fresh clothes for you. We have to go talk to the doctors and then to Judge Walton," she instructed.

"He's driving all the way up here to talk to you and see what the doctors say. Go get cleaned up while Momma talks with Gramma, okay?"

Aubrey loved hearing "Gramma" as much as Sarah and her mother did. It filled a hole in all their lives that had lain open far too long.

Aubrey went into the bathroom and showered, while his mother and grandmother caught each other up on the past decade and a half of their lives.

He was attempting to comb his unruly hair and, he was thinking that maybe the Judge would let him go back home to his friends and….

Uh-oh, he thought.

"Maw," he called out, as he returned to the room.

"Yes, darlin' boy?" she answered.

"Um…I think I dun something else stupid."

As was his usual routine, Frankie retrieved the mail for his mother. On this particular Saturday, as he thumbed through the envelopes, he spotted a familiar scribble on an envelope with his name on it.

"Awright," he said out loud and pulled the letter from the bunch. "Cool."

Aubrey had written him from the hospital. He carefully tore the end of the envelope to extract the letter, as he walked into the house. He began reading it with a broad smile, happy to hear from his best friend.

But then his smile melted into a frown….

"*Momma…Momma!*" he shrieked, stamping his feet in terror. "Nooooo!"

Shelley heard his panicked cries and came rushing into the foyer from the kitchen.

"What is it?" she asked urgently.

"Aubrey…" was all he could manage, his face screwed into an agonized expression.

"What?" she said, taking the letter from his shaking hands….

Dear Frankie,

What I done was a terrible thing. And if I'd been a grown-up, they would have put me in the electric chair for it. But since I'm just a kid, I suppose they will just keep me locked up until they can. Plus, what I did was a sin against God.

So since the guvermint won't execute kids, I figure I better do it myself. It's what I deserve.

You been the best friend I could of ever had. I thank you from my heart for all that you done for me. We had lots of fun. I'm sure sorry for all the stuff that's happened lately. I hope you don't think too badly of me.

Tell Tony that he was a good friend, too, and to keep on not letting anybody push him around.

Tell him I'm proud of him.

Tell Uncle Frank thank you for me. He's really cool, and you're right, he's the best uncle in the whole world. Don't ever listen to anybody saying bad stuff about him.

Give your mom a hug for me. She sure is a supernice lady. I'm real sorry she's so sick.

Take good care of Rusty, too. His momma was a dang-good dog and a good friend, too.

Please remember me in your prayers. It might sound funny, but I love you guys, and I'm going to miss all of you.

One last thing: please hug my maw for me, and tell her how much I love her. And Waylon, too.

> *Your friend forever,*
> *Aubrey*

"Oh, Jesus...no!" she gasped, not knowing what else to say.

Frankie stood with his fists balled against his eyes, as his body convulsed with sobs.

This is not possible, she thought, pulling Frankie close to her, as much to comfort herself as to comfort him. *I've got to call Sarah. No, wait...she's on her way to Memphis.* Her thoughts were racing around in her head. *I'll call the hospital. What was the name? Oh, yes, Kathleen would know.*

"Momma...Aubrey wants to kill himself," Frankie squeaked in disbelief, trying to regain his composure.

"Why, Momma, why?" he pleaded. "It wudn't his fault."

"I know, baby, I know," she said, trying to comfort him.

She took the envelope from her son's hand to examine the postmark. *Two days,* she thought. *Maybe he hasn't done anything, yet. Poor Sarah, she'll be devastated if anything happens to him.*

"Momma's got to make some calls, honey," she said, releasing him and moving toward the phone in the kitchen, with Frankie only steps behind her.

Just as she reached for the phone…it rang, startling her.

"Hello," she answered nervously. "Oh, thank God it's you, Sarah."

"Frankie just got a le…" she started in a panic, then stopped in midsentence and listened intently for a couple minutes.

Frankie watched the panic drain from her face, only to be replaced by a curious welling of tears, as she bit her lower lip and fanned her face with her free hand.

"Oh…praise God…praise God," she whispered hoarsely.

"What is it, Momma?" Frankie asked impatiently.

"Hold on a second, hun," she said into the receiver.

Kneeling to face him, she said, still in a whisper, "He's okay, sweetie. This is his mom. She's there with him. And…" she couldn't hold back her tears, "so is his grandmother."

"Grandmother?" Frankie responded. "I thought he didn't have a grandmother."

The new piece of information succeeded in distracting him from his own panic. "But he's okay? Can I talk to him?"

"Yes, baby, he's just fine," she answered. "But, right now, he's with the doctors." Holding a finger up, she stood back up and returned to the telephone conversation.

"Okay, hun. Thank you so much for calling. I read his letter and almost fainted. Frankie was beside himself."

She listened for a few seconds.

"I sure will, and you be sure to tell that little shit that he scared the living daylights out of us...then hug him real tight for me...for us. Oh, and, Sarah...I'm so happy for you. I can't wait to meet her. Okay, hun. Bye-bye."

After hanging the phone up, she grabbed Frankie in a deliriously happy hug. He hugged her back, just as enthusiastically.

"How 'bout some milk and cookies?" she offered. "Momma has something wonderful to tell you."

She recounted everything Sarah had told her, choking up at key points, but pushing on to deliver the good news.

"Do you remember Judge Walton?"

Frankie nodded, his mouth too full to answer.

"Well...it seems that Aubrey's grandmother showing up really impressed him. His mother said that it showed him that there were sufficient adult relatives in Aubrey's life for him to be released into his mother's custody, and that..." she choked up again, "and that the State isn't going to press charges against him."

She cupped his face.

"He's free, Frankie," she declared joyously. "Nothing is going to happen to him."

Frankie nearly choked on the cookie in his mouth, as he started to cheer, spraying crumbs across the table like a lawn sprinkler.

They both laughed heartily at the sight.

"The doctors want him to stay for a few days more, but after that..." she giggled, "he's coming home!"

Frankie was now as giddy as he had been panicked just minutes before.

CHET'S SURPRISE

A week later, Sarah heard a knock on the front door of the farmhouse.

"What now?" she mumbled, a little annoyed at being distracted from her task at hand. She saw a familiar figure through the chiffon curtain that covered the door window.

"Oh, my Lord…*Chet!*" Sarah yipped, throwing the door open and nearly knocking him off his feet, as she embraced him in a joyous hug.

"I can't believe it's you," she wept happily, as she rocked him in her arms.

"Thank God you're safe. When did you get in? I'll bet your folks are just delirious to have you home safe," she said, looping her arm in his and guiding him into the living room.

"Two days ago," Chet answered, "I got emergency leave so I could come see about you and Aubrey… and yes, Mom and Dad smothered me with hugs the first day. They barely let me out of their sight, but they thought it was a good idea for me to come on down as soon as I could."

His eyes scanned her fading bruises and stitches, then the living room full of half-packed boxes, each one holding Denton family heirlooms and memories. He turned a quizzical look toward his aunt.

"I'm selling the place," she answered his unasked question.

"Why?" he asked incredulously.

"Darlin', there's just too much bad history here," she answered sullenly. "Too much pain haunts these walls."

"Are you sure you really want to?" he asked. "I mean… it's been the family farm forever."

"Yes, I'm sure. In fact, I have to," she replied.

"Aubrey practically begged me not to make him come back here. I can't remember the last time Waylon slept here. The boys just don't want to live here anymore… and, quite frankly, neither do I."

"This place may have held happier memories for others before us, but we just don't have that many. I haven't told your mother yet, but I don't think she'll object too much. She had her issues with this place, too," she finished, remembering the horror stories Betty had told her of brutality and abuse at the hands of her father.

"I'm actually staying with Shelley Albert; Waylon is, too," she informed him. "It helps me to be away from all this, and she needs someone to help her, so…."

"I understand," he said. "I don't suppose I can blame you. You and the boys had it pretty rough with Uncle Buck."

He really did understand. He knew Buck, but he couldn't help feeling a little remorse over the thought of the family farm being sold. This is the house his mother grew up in, and he'd spent many summers here.

But it was also the house his grandfather he'd beaten

his grandmother to death in, and his uncle had nearly done the same to his aunt. He knew about the abuse his mother had suffered, too. It was a shame that his grandfather and his uncle had done so much damage to the family, but what was done could not be undone.

He had to admit…he agreed that it was better to move on, for everyone's sake. Memories would survive, and perhaps even become a little sweeter, or at least more tolerable, with time.

"Mom told me about how she was the only one at Uncle Buck's funeral," he said. "That's a pretty sad thing."

Sarah didn't reply. She had been in the hospital. Aubrey and Waylon had refused to attend.

In fact, Waylon had gotten hold of some moonshine, and in a drunken rage, he had gone to the cemetery and urinated on his father's grave.

Changing the subject, Sarah said, "Mike Carillo, Tony's father, has managed to find a buyer for me. It's a gravel company that wants to quarry the place for all that limestone out front. Only a businessman would have thought of that, and he's a good one.

"You know what's ironic?" she asked. "That's the part of this place I'll miss the most.

"Those big ol' rocks were a playground for my boys… and you, too, as I recall," she said, smiling at him and patting his hand.

"It was someplace they could escape to," she said. "Someplace they could get away from the never-ending chores and criticism…and abuse."

"I used to love to watch my babies play there when they didn't know I was looking," she reminisced. "They seemed so happy then.

"Sometimes, when they were at school, I used to

venture down just to walk among the little forts they built….and to retrieve the knives, pans, and all the other things they'd sneak out of my kitchen to play with." Then she laughed.

"I'm sorry things turned out so bad for you, Auntie," he offered, wrapping his long, muscular arms around her. "I wish I could've done something."

"Done something?" she replied, pulling herself back to look him in the eye. "Chet…darlin' boy, I can't begin to tell you how much you've done for my boys over the years. Baby, you made summertime tolerable for them. You gave them something to look forward to, especially Aubrey. You know how much he adores you. You're like a guardian angel to him. You should see how he brags about you."

"Thanks, Auntie," he blushed. "But I just can't help but feel that maybe if I'd been able to reach Uncle Buck, then…"

"Stop," she said firmly. "Don't you dare take on guilt that doesn't belong to you. Your uncle was…well…" She found it difficult to finish what she was going to say.

"I know, Auntie. No need to say anymore," he said, feeling her pain.

"Well, what can I do to help you out here?" he continued, hoping to lighten the mood.

"You can sit your handsome self down in the kitchen and let your old aunt make you some lunch," she insisted.

They sat in the kitchen for several hours, among scattered boxes, harbingers of the impending abandonment of the century-old family home.

Sarah avoided the unpleasant subject that hovered in the room like a seething ghost. She sat with her back to the place on the worn linoleum floor, where her life nearly came to an end.

Instead, she asked about Vietnam, about the war, his friends, and the country itself.

But, eventually, Chet wanted to know what had happened. His eyes kept straying to the plywood patch on the wall, where the telephone used to be. Now he knew why he wasn't able to call ahead.

With a great deal of difficulty and self-control, Sarah managed to retell the terrible story.

"That's just not right," the combat-hardened marine said, with watering eyes, after she finished. "Poor Aubrey must have been devastated."

"Yes, he was," she said. "But Gramma Pickard has been spending a lot of time with him."

"Gramma Pickard?" he asked, taken by surprise.

"Oh…that's right," she said. "I didn't tell you, did I?"

She proceeded to tell him about the reunion, including the noose Aubrey had fashioned, drawing an audible gasp from him. She told him that her mother had rented a hotel room close to the hospital so she could visit her grandson.

"She's with him every day. The doctors say she's a godsend. He has really come around since they've been spending so much time together. They've grown so close. It's just wonderful."

She hesitated for a second and added with a constricted voice, "I got my mommy back, too."

"I'm real happy for you, Auntie," he said, reaching over to touch her hand. "I can tell it's been good for you." The smile on her face was evidence of that.

"Speaking of things from the past," he started, "I'd like to meet Frankie Albert…and his mother, if that'd be okay."

"I have something for them," he said cryptically.

"Of course you can. They live just down the road. I'll introduce you," she offered him.

"Actually, Auntie, I'd rather go alone…if you don't mind," he said. "I'd be more comfortable if was just the three of us. I hope you understand."

"Oh?" she replied, slightly put off by his request. But, seeing the seriousness in his eyes, she didn't protest further. "Well, I suppose that'd be okay. Will it take long?"

"I don't think so, but…" he responded.

"I'll tell you what," she said. "I'll just whip something up for my dinner here, and then you can come get me when you're done. How's that sound?"

"Are you sure?"

"I'll be fine, hon. Just don't be too awfully late. She needs her rest, and, quite frankly, so do I."

"Okay, I promise."

A little later, just as twilight began overtaking the day, Frankie was in the front yard, teaching Rusty to fetch his new Frisbee. He watched a familiar old truck pull up in front of his house.

But instead of Aunt Sarah, a man in a U.S. Marine Corps uniform got out and strode toward the gate, smiling and waving at him.

"Howdy," he greeted.

"That's a fine lookin' dog ya got there," he said, nodding at Rusty. "You must be Frankie."

Frankie was mesmerized by the uniform. He had never seen a marine in dress greens before.

"Yes sir, I am," he answered clumsily. Then it struck him.

"Are you Aubrey's cousin Chet?" he asked.

"Lance Corporal Chet Gordon at your service," he

grinned, offering his hand to the awestruck boy.

"Wow!" Frankie sighed, shaking his hand.

"You're just the man I wanted to see," Chet continued. "Is your mom home?"

"Um…yeah, she sure is. Come on in," Frankie offered eagerly, dashing for the porch steps, Rusty hot on his heels.

"He looks just like his mother," Chet said, gesturing toward the dog.

"She was a good ol' hound," he added; a touch of sadness in his voice.

"Aubrey told us about you fightin' Commonist in Veet-nam," Frankie said, mimicking Aubrey's mispronunciation of both words and earning a chuckle from Chet.

"Uh, yep that's right," he replied. He decided not to correct his cousin's best friend. The boy would learn soon enough, especially if the war dragged on, as it had been dragging on for too many years.

"Momma…hey, Momma!" Frankie called out, holding the door for Chet. "You'll never guess who's here."

"Who is it, baby." Shelley called back, as she walked into the foyer.

Seeing a tall, dark-haired, handsome man in dress uniform standing before her caught her off guard. A brief image of Jack flashed before her, eliciting a slight gasp.

Chet saw one of the prettiest women he'd seen in a long time emerge from the living room and come to a sudden, surprised stop. The fleeting look of recognition that swept across her face made him wish it was for him. But he knew it wasn't.

"Howdy, ma'am, I'm Chet Gordon…Sarah Denton's nephew," he announced, offering his hand.

"Oh, yes, of course," she said, gathering her thoughts, as she shook his strong hand.

"Sarah has told me so much about you," she said. "I'm so pleased to meet you."

"Please…come in and have a seat," she offered him. "Would you like something to drink? I think there's still a cold beer in the fridge."

"No thanks on the beer, ma'am, but if ya got a soda pop, that'd be great."

"Of course, but we only have grape Nehi; is that okay?" she asked.

A marine preferring a soda pop to a beer struck her as almost comical, but she figured his preference had been made more out of polite respect than a real desire for a soda pop. "It's Frankie's favorite."

"My favorite, too, ma'am," he answered.

"Frankie, go fetch a soda for Chet, okay hun?" she asked, motioning Chet into the living room.

"Sure thing," he said, dashing off to the kitchen.

Blushing, Shelley found herself straightening her blouse, as she followed him and wishing she had her hair in something other than her usual ponytail…and hoping her illness wasn't too obvious.

"So…" she started, "are you home for good?"

"Actually, I'm home on emergency leave. On account of what happened to Aunt Sarah and Aubrey," he answered. "But I had only another month left in country, so I don't believe they'll be sendin' me back."

"Good. I'll bet your folks are happy about that," she said. "I know your aunt must be. She fretted so much over you, ya know."

"Yes ma'am, she is. I'm pretty happy about it, too. It ain't much fun over there."

Shelley noticed that Chet had referred to himself as Sarah's nephew, not mentioning his uncle, even though Buck was the blood relative.

"Ma'am, I really appreciate all you've done for Aunt Sarah. She told me all about you and Frankie…and the Carillos, too. I'd like to meet them while I'm here. Aubrey wrote that Tony is quite a character. I'm really grateful that there were folks like ya'll around for them."

"There's no need to thank us. Your aunt and cousins are like family to us. They've done as much for us, if not more. And, yes, Tony is a hoot."

Then she added, "But I absolutely adore Aubrey. He's so…serene. And Waylon is such a wonderful young man. Your aunt and I have grown quite close, too. I just love her to pieces."

"Yeah…she's a special lady," he said.

An awkward silence fell, neither one knowing how to continue.

"So…" Shelley started, "what brings you to our humble home?"

"Well, actually I have a real special reason for being here, ma'am," he replied.

"Oh? What might that be?" she asked, just as Frankie returned with three bottles of Nehi.

"I thought you might want one, too," he said, as he handed his mother one, getting a cocked eyebrow from her.

"Thank you, Frankie," she said in that motherly tone that told him she could see right through his scheme to get one for himself.

"Thanks, buddy," Chet said, tipping the bottle back and taking a long, satisfying drink.

"Ahhh!" he gasped. "It's been ages since I've had one

of these."

Realizing that she was staring, Shelley looked away and coughed lightly.

"Well…" Chet began, looking at Frankie to cover his own awkwardness, "Aubrey wrote me a bunch of times, and he told me all about you, Frankie. And you, too, ma'am."

"Please…call me Shelley. 'Ma'am' sounds so old," she insisted.

"Well, you sure ain't that," he let slip.

"Um…" he started, his embarrassment showing in his bright pink face. "I'm sorry. That was outta line."

Shelley's own blush revealed her own embarrassment.

"Oh, that's all right. No need to apologize. I don't get many compliments, these days."

Why on Earth not? Chet wondered to himself. *You're beautiful.*

Her condition had caused her to lose a lot of weight, but she had not yet assumed the gaunt, frail appearance she feared would come, as the disease consumed her.

"Um, where was I?" he asked out loud, trying to get back on subject.

"You said Aub wrote you all about us," Frankie said helpfully. *Why are you guys turning red?* he wondered.

"Oh yeah," Chet said, continuing, "He says you've been a really great pal. I appreciate that. He told me all about your mom, too."

"I'm terribly sorry to hear about it, Ma…I mean, Shelley," he said.

Seeing the shadow slip across her face, he felt like kicking himself. Such a pretty face shouldn't be painted with pain.

"He even told me about your Uncle Frank," he hurried

on. "He sounds like a heck of a guy. He's a fireman, huh? I'd like to meet him, someday."

"Yeah, he's a pretty far out guy," Frankie gushed.

Donning a more serious tone, Chet said, "He also told me about your dad and what happened to him."

Frankie's grin disappeared.

Chet moved on.

"He told me that he was a soldier and that he died in Vietnam."

Shelley's own demeanor changed, as well.

"What could Aubrey tell you about that?" she asked, looking at Frankie accusingly.

"Well, he didn't tell me how it happened," he explained. "Just that it did."

Frankie recalled how Aubrey seemed to interrogate him about his father, asking things like where and when. At the time, Frankie thought he was just being an interested friend, but now his real motives were revealed.

"I told him," Frankie confessed.

"It was okay, wasn't it?" he asked, feeling that maybe he'd revealed something his mother had not wanted him to.

"Of course it was, honey. That's what friends are for," she said, assuaging his apprehension. "In fact, I'm glad you did."

"I'm sorry, Chet," she said. "Please continue."

"Well, bein' marines, we play a lot of poker in our downtime. One of our company supply clerks lost a wad of cash to me and was scramblin' to find a way to pay me off. I wasn't all that worried about the money, but it was the principle of the matter. A debt is a debt, and he owed me. Then I hit on an idea.

"I gave him all the information that Aubrey had sent

me and told him that if he found something out for me, we'd be even. The scrawny little fella jumped at the chance. I think I scared him a little." He grinned.

Chet had inherited the imposing build of the Denton men.

"Our captain found out what he was doin', and we both nearly got our asses handed…sorry, I mean…we both nearly got into a mess of trouble. But after I explained to him what I was tryin' to do, he actually wanted to help. And that's a good thing. His bars cut through a bunch of red tape.

"Anyways, I finally got a copy of what is called an 'After Action Report.' It tells what happened the day your daddy was, um…. killed," he said, looking Frankie in the eye. "Do you want to hear about it? You don't have to, if you don't want to."

Frankie nodded, not really sure he did want know. What if his father wasn't the hero everybody thinks he was?

"Is it okay?" Chet asked Shelley. "I mean, I'm not trying to intrude or stir up painful memories, or anything like that. I just thought he might want to know about his father…the way I would want to know if it was mine."

She thought for a moment, then asked Frankie, "Are you sure you want to hear this?"

Again, he nodded, "Yes, Momma, I do. He was my dad. I wanna know all about him."

"Okay, then," she said to Chet, fighting back her own apprehensions.

"Not too graphic, though," she gently warned.

"Oh, no ma'am, I wouldn't do that," Chet assured her.

Looking at Frankie, he said, as if reading his thoughts, "Don't worry, buddy. He really was a hero."

"I'll skip all the military jargon and just give the important details," he started.

"As you know," he said to Shelley, "he was with some of the first combat troops to be sent over there. His job was to help scout out potential bases of operation and such, and also to try to gain the confidence and the trust of the people.

"To do that, one of the things they did whenever they went into a hamlet . . . that's what they call the villages over there . . . anyway, one of the things they did was to give medical treatment to anyone who was sick or hurt and to vaccinate the kids against some of the diseases they have over there.

"Well, when Charlie…that's what we call the Viet Cong fighters…when Charlie would get wind of it, they would go into those same villages and do horrible things to the people, even kill 'em. Sometimes, they'd even cut off the arms of the kids that got vaccinated."

Frankie's eyes shot wide open in shock. *What kind of people would cut a kid's arm off just for getting a shot from a doctor?*

"I'm sorry," Chet apologized. "I guess I got a little carried away."

"That's okay," Frankie allowed meekly. "It's the truth, right?"

"I hate to say it, but…yes, that's just one of the terrible truths of this war," Chet said, shaking his head in dismay.

"They do a lot worse," he said, remembering the booby traps and the other horrendous things he encountered during his walking nightmare in the jungle.

"Well…according to the report, one of the boys from the hamlet your dad's platoon visited earlier that morning caught up with them later that afternoon.

"He told them that the Viet Cong were heading toward their village and that the people were scared that they'd be tortured or killed.

"Your dad was the platoon leader, so he ordered them back to the village as fast as possible to protect the people, until they could get some choppers in and evacuate them to safety. They managed to get back there just before Charlie did.

"Your dad took half the platoon and set up a defensive perimeter between the village and the V.C., while the other half rounded up the villagers and withdrew to a safe L.Z. (that's a landing zone)...to wait for the helicopters.

"But about a half a dozen women and children had been hiding in one of the hooches...er...huts. They had been overlooked and left behind. Your dad ordered the rest of the platoon to fall back and escort the stray villagers to safety with the rest of the group, while he stayed to cover them with the S.A.W.; that's the M-60 Squad Automatic Weapon."

"It's a machine gun that uses belt ammunition," he explained, seeing Frankie's quizzical expression.

He cast a glance at Shelley, only to see her wringing her hands, with an expression of deep anxiety on her face.

Shit! he thought, shifting uncomfortably. *Maybe this wasn't such a good idea.*

"Go ahead," she said, reading his thoughts. "We're okay."

Chet cleared his throat and continued.

"The report says that, about that time, an enemy force of about thirty men engaged your dad and his men in a firefight. Three soldiers stayed behind with him, so the others could get away.

"I won't go into the details…like I promised, so I'll just say that your dad and those three men gave their lives so the people of that village could escape.

"After the choppers hauled the villagers off, the rest of the platoon went back to the village to help your dad. They were too late to save him and the other men, but they destroyed what was left of the enemy. According to the report, there weren't too many V.C. left to destroy.

"It seems your dad and the other three soldiers had kil…um, eliminated over half of the attacking force…all by themselves."

"Frankie," Chet said, leaning close to him to look him in the eye, "there were over fifty people in that village, mostly old men, women, and children. Your dad was directly responsible for saving their lives. You have every reason to be proud of him. He was a hero in the truest sense of the word.

"He brought honor to his uniform, and whether they like it or not," he said, recalling the hateful welcome he received from the long-haired war protesters when he got off the plane, "he brought honor to his country. I only hope I can be as good a marine as he was a soldier.

"I saw the medals he got. A Silver Star with a "V" for valor is a pretty high honor, ya know."

Frankie returned his gaze with watering eyes.

"Thanks, Chet," he managed to squeak out.

Chet reached his hand out and patted Frankie on the shoulder. "Are you okay with all this?" he asked.

"Mmm-hmm," Frankie managed.

The scenario of his father desperately fighting to save people he didn't even know was overwhelming. He realized how much he missed the father he never really knew. Finally getting the real story of how his father died was bittersweet.

His father really was a hero…but he was still gone, nonetheless.

"You've been a good friend to Aubrey. He wrote me and told me how you wondered about your dad a lot. I thought this might help you understand what kind of man he was. I hope I wasn't wrong."

"I understand," Frankie said softly. "It helps. He's my dad."

Chet heard a light sniffing sound.

Shelley was attempting to dab her tears with her hand.

Chet quickly reached into his jacket pocket, pulled out a handkerchief, and handed it to her.

"I'm sorry," he apologized. "I hope I didn't upset you too bad."

"No…" she sniffed, "you didn't. It's just that this is the first time I've heard what happened."

"Really?" Chet asked, genuinely puzzled. "I'd have thought the army would have told you all about it back when it happened."

"They wanted to," she replied. "I just didn't want to hear it then. I was pretty angry about losing my husband. Details would have only made things worse."

"This was a good thing you did, Chet," she said, dabbing at her eyes. "I needed to hear it, too. I'm past the anger, and Frankie needs to know about his father. Jack's memory deserves the truth. Thank you."

"I'm okay, now," she said, half-lying and handing his handkerchief back to him.

Damn it, Jack…your son needs you…I need you!

He tucked it back into his jacket, feeling the widow's moist tears.

"Would you like to stay for dinner?" she offered, attempting to change the mood and surprised to find herself hoping he would.

"I'd love to," he accepted, gazing briefly into her watery eyes. *Life is so damned unfair.*

She returned his gaze with a warm smile. He reminded her so much of Jack.

Dinner was a pleasant, even cheerful event. Frankie bombarded Chet with questions about Vietnam and the U.S Marine Corps, while Shelley's interests were about the Denton family's history.

Chet made a point to ask Frankie about his hobbies and interests, prompting Frankie to scramble upstairs to fetch some of the models he and Aubrey had built.

He asked about Uncle Frank, as well. His aunt had told him of the fireman's own hardships in Haleyville.

He struggled not to show what he began to feel was inappropriate interest in Shelley. It was a task he found increasingly difficult, as the evening wore on. A growing urge to hold her in his arms and to comfort her threatened to overtake him.

Not one mention was made about her illness by anyone.

Chet glanced at his watch and realized that he'd gone on too long.

"Oh Geez! I forgot. I have to go get Aunt Sarah. She's gonna take that wooden spoon after me for being so late," he joked.

"Don't worry," Shelley assured him. "I'll tell her it was my fault."

Out on the porch, he gave Frankie a manly handshake and held Shelley's soft hand in a lingering, gentle grip, relishing her touch.

"I'll be back with Auntie in a little bit. I hope I haven't kept ya'll up too late."

"Not at all," Shelley replied. "I couldn't go to sleep right now, anyway."

"Me, neither," Frankie chimed in, getting a raised eyebrow from his mother, he added, "But I s'pose I'd better try, huh?"

"Good idea," she agreed.

The short drive to his aunt's farm was filled with conflicting, unexpected feelings. A year and a half of the mayhem of combat had numbed some of his emotions and sharpened others.

He had not had time to decompress from a war environment, nor had he had time to process his family's tragedy.

He wasn't sure if the reason for his attraction to Shelley was that she was the first "round eye" woman he'd encountered in over a year whom he wasn't related to.

Or perhaps it really was just a normal attraction to such a pretty woman, no matter how much older she was than him.

This was a different kind of minefield he was treading in, but he knew that he'd have to be equally careful, lest further damage be done to an already-wounded heart.

"Someone's watch must have run down," Sarah admonished with a grin, as Chet hurried into the living room.

"I'm sorry, Auntie. I just got carried away," he apologized.

"Oh, I'm just messin' with you," she chuckled at his discomfort. "I had plenty to keep me busy."

A little later, as he was telling his aunt about the evening, describing a simple roast-beef-and-potato dinner as though it were a royal affair, Sarah said, "Honey, be real careful. I know she's a pretty woman, and I sure can't blame you for seeing that, but you know about her condition…and her loss. I would hate for anyone to get hurt."

Chet blushed, embarrassed by his transparency. But then, his aunt had always been able to see right through him. Even when he was a child, she could read his thoughts. Usually, it didn't bother him, because she was always discrete about it, but sometimes, like now, it was a little unnerving.

"Auntie," he protested politely, "I know what you're saying, but don't worry; I'll deal with it. I know it would just complicate things. But if she is going to, um…die," he said, forcing the word out, "don't you think having another friend would be a good thing?"

"A friend would be wonderful, Chet," she said, in a motherly tone, "but sometimes friendship can be mistaken for something else. Especially by someone who has been alone for such a long time, and in her case, someone who knows they don't have a lot of time left. She's been hurt a lot in so many ways."

"Geezus, Auntie," he flustered, "I've been around a lot of death. I've seen women and little children gunned down or blown to pieces. I've had buddies die in front of me, even holding my hand," he choked, with unexpected emotion, "so why does her death fuck me…"

"I'm sorry, Auntie," he apologized. "I'm not used to being around civilized folks yet."

She smiled her acceptance of his apology.

"But why does her dying mess me up like this?" he admitted, straining to understand his sudden rush of emotion.

"I don't know, honey. I suppose you expect to see death on a battlefield, but not in your own hometown. Or...maybe, if I suspect right, you feel something for her that you never felt for the strangers, or even your buddies.

"A young man's heart is a volatile and vulnerable thing, hard to control.

"I can't tell you who to fall for...I couldn't even tell myself that," she lamented. "All I can do is caution you to be very careful."

"But you know your old Auntie's here, if you need me," she said, reaching across the table to pat his hand.

"I know, and I really love you for it, too," he said, squeezing her hand in return.

"So..." he started, changing the subject, "when can we go see Aubrey?"

"We can go tomorrow, if you want. He'll be so surprised to see you. It'll be such good medicine for him. He's fretted something awful over you. He misses you so much."

"Yeah, I miss the little guy, too."

Shelly watched the old truck rattle away, lingering for a long moment, as she gazed into the darkness past the last streetlight.

"Chet's a really nice guy, huh, Momma?"

Her son's question distracted her from her thoughts.

"Yes, baby, he is," she smiled.

"How 'bout helping Momma with the dishes before you head off to bed?" she said, turning back into the house.

This is just plain crazy! she thought. *He's so young. I'm old enough to be his mother.* Though not strictly true (Chet was born when she was only thirteen), it may as well have been. *It must be the uniform.*

It couldn't be his warm, brown eyes, or the hint of curly, brown hair above his high and tight marine haircut. Nor could it be his gentle, Southern voice or the strength in his hands, as he tenderly held hers.

No…it had to be the uniform. It made her long for Jack. For the first time ever, the vision of Jack that she carried so deeply in her heart seemed ever-so-slightly fuzzy.

"You okay, Momma?"

Frankie's voice snapped her back to the sink full of dishes. She looked to see Jack's blue eyes looking up at her, filled with concern.

"I'm okay, baby. I was just thinking about your daddy," she said, pulling another dish from the sudsy water.

"Yeah, me, too," he said, resuming his chore of drying the dishes his mother had washed.

"It was really nice of Chet to tell me about my daddy. He's a really cool guy."

"Yes, it was. But you know who else deserves a thank-you?"

"Who's that?"

"It was Aubrey who told Chet about your daddy, in the first place, wasn't it?"

"Yeah, I guess it was. He's a good friend, isn't he?"

"He's wonderful. You're very lucky. Most people never get to have such a thoughtful friend."

"When's he comin' home? I can't wait to see his face when he opens his Christmas presents!"

Though Christmas was long past, Tony and Frankie had agreed not to open the gifts Aubrey had delivered to them just days before the tragic event. Shelley had agreed to leave a tree up until Aubrey came home, but she opted to replace the dying cedar that Aubrey and his father had cut for them with their old, familiar, silver artificial tree.

Sarah still had the gifts she and Waylon had gotten for Aubrey, as did the Carillos. Uncle Frank promised to be there, as well.

And now, even his grandmother was going to share her first Christmas with him.

Jesus' birthday had always been Aubrey's favorite day, and everyone had joined in to plan a special one, just for him, regardless of when that day might be.

"Well, Aunt Sarah said it might be soon," Shelley told him. "In fact, she's supposed to go to Memphis tomorrow. I'm sure that Chet will be going with her."

"Wow, Aub's gonna flip out! He's always talkin' about him."

"Well, I can see why," Shelley commented.

"I think Aub loves him the same way I love Uncle Frank."

"I think so, too, baby."

A short time later, after Frankie had gone to bed, Sarah and Chet arrived back at the Albert home.

"I hope you don't mind, hon, but I brought a stray along," Sarah joked, nodding at Chet. "He offered to stay at the farm, but I…"

"Now that would have been an insult," Shelley protested, feigning indignation. "Besides, Waylon called to say that he'd be staying at Mark's house, tonight. So Chet can use his bed."

"He's not going to be happy about missing you," Sarah said to Chet, getting a modest smile from him.

The three sat around the kitchen table, laughing and even crying from time to time, until long after midnight.

As Shelley began to rise from the table to go to bed, her face paled, and she dropped heavily back into her chair.

Sarah immediately jumped up to rush to her side.

"Are you okay, sugar?" she asked, getting a brief nod from Shelley. "Come on. I'll help you to bed, okay?"

Shelley smiled her thanks, but then she looked over at Chet, and her pale face went crimson red with embarrassment, mortified that the handsome young man had seen her in such a state.

"I'm sorry," she apologized. "I…uh…"

"Please don't apologize," Chet smiled as warmly as he could through his own alarm.

"I understand. Auntie told me all about it. Is there anything I can do?"

"No, thank you; I'll be all right after a good night's sleep. I'm just a little weak, that's all," she continued to apologize.

"Oh, there is one thing you can do, if you will," she remembered.

"You name it," he said, as cheerfully as he could.

"Rusty needs to be let out. He's taken to staying up with me until I go to bed, but he's not entirely housebroken, yet."

"You bet," Chet replied, grateful to be of some help, however small.

Frankie lay awake gazing out his window, the dim light from a full moon silhouetting the model cars and tanks lined up along the sill; he was thinking about all he had learned about his father.

The anger he had held onto for so long began to diminish, as he replayed his father's heroism in his head. Now he knew that people weren't just trying to make him feel better when they said his father was a hero…a real hero.

It somehow made him feel more confident in himself. Surely, he would be just as heroic, if he ever needed to be.

At least, he hoped he would be...if he ever needed to be.

Shelley gazed out at the moon from her bed, tears rolling from her cheeks to the pillow. Thoughts of Jack persisted, as she stroked the pillow next to her, where his head should be resting, denying her any sleep. But as twilight dreams began to finally creep upon her, brown eyes replaced his crystal-blue ones, and curly, brown hair replaced his wavy, black locks.

Chet fell asleep, holding the handkerchief stained with widow's tears, as he listened to the soft, nearly inaudible tones of his aunt's payers from the next room. He was home...he was safe...but he was confused.

"Sweet Heavenly Father," Sarah prayed softly. "Thank you for bringing Chet home safely to us, and please watch over those he left behind in that terrible place.

"Thank you for all you have done for me, for the crucible you have brought me through, and the point you have delivered me to. But, most of all, Lord, thank you for saving my Aubrey and returning my mommy to me."

IT'S GOOD TO BE HOME

"Dang, boy…you sure have grown!" a familiar and cherished voice echoed into Aubrey's room.

"Huh?" he started.

"Chet…Yahoo!" he yelled, springing from his bed, where he'd been passing the time reading *White Fang*.

Forgetting his own size, he nearly bowled Chet over, as he ran to embrace his cousin in an iron hug.

"You're here! You're okay!" he yelped gratefully. "I cain't believe it."

"Well…you'd better believe it, little buddy," Chet reassured him. "But you ain't so little anymore, are you?"

"When didja git home? Have ya seen Maw an' Waylon? Wait'll ya meet Frankie…and Tony. How long are ya home…fer good, I hope? You don't hafta go back, do ya? Guess what? I got a Gramma!"

"Whoa…slow down, hot rod," Chet laughed, responding to the barrage of questions. "Now, let me see. One…I just got back a few days ago, but I'll be here for a while.

"Two…your mom is here with me; she'll be here in a moment. She's talking with the doctors, but I haven't seen Waylon yet.

"Three…I already met Frankie, but not Tony.

"Four…yes, I'm home for good, and, no, I don't have to go back.

"And five…I heard about your grandma, too. That's fantastic. I can't wait to meet her. Did I miss anything?"

"I sure missed ya, Chet. I reckon ya heard about what happened, huh?" he asked, less enthusiastically after releasing Chet and sitting on his bed.

"I heard," Chet answered, taking a seat next to him.

"Ya know, cuz, I'm sure a bunch of folks, a lot smarter than me, have already talked with you about the right and wrong of it," he said. "And I think you know all that already…right here." He patted Aubrey on his chest.

"So I'm just gonna talk to ya as a man who has had to, um….well, do drastic things to stay alive," he counseled.

"Focus on the necessity of having to do what you had to do. Don't let extra bags of guilt weigh you down. You can't turn back the clock and undo it. You can only move forward and make sure you're ready when the next bad thing comes your way. That way, you survive. Otherwise, ya kill yourself slowly from the inside out.

"But I came here to give you some good news, not a lecture that you don't need."

"What's that?" Aubrey asked, happy not to dredge up sickening details, just so some doctor or other adult could analyze every little nuance.

"Well, right now, your mom is downstairs, signing papers so we can take you home."

"Wha…?" Aubrey half-whispered.

"You mean I can…? *Far out!*" he shouted, jumping up and dancing a silly jig.

"That's right, G.I. The orders are being cut, so let's get your duffle packed," Chet said, standing up and straightening his dress greens.

"Now get moving; this ain't no time to dallyfu . . . I mean dilly-dally . . . around," he barked like a drill sergeant, catching himself before his bunker language slipped out.

"Aye-aye, Lance Corporal, sir," Aubrey snapped to attention and gave his best imitation of a regulation salute, getting a perfect one in return.

By the time Sarah got to his room, he had gathered his meager collection of books and clothing together and was pacing back and forth in anticipation.

"Maw, Chet told me," he said gleefully, wrapping his arms around her waist. "I'm goin' home! No more doctors and no more of the yucky stuff they call food here."

"That's right, baby. You're comin' home with Momma. Gramma's on her way up. She's going to ride home with us. And no, you don't have to torture your stomach anymore, but…" she said, "you'll have to come back here every couple of weeks for a while, so the doctors can make sure your getting better."

"Oh, Maw, do I really have to?"

"Yes, son, you do. But it's just a couple of hours at a time," she said, adding, "I'm pretty sure we can find things to do when we're here. I hear there's a nice zoo in Overton Park."

"A zoo? Really?" he replied, his disappointment vanishing.

"That sounds outstanding, lil' troop. Heck, I might have to join ya for that one," Chet injected enthusiastically, giving Sarah a wink.

"Yeah, an' maybe Frankie an' Tony can…"

"Let's not get too far ahead of ourselves," his mother broke in. "One thing at a time. Let's get you home first."

As excited as Aubrey was to get back to his brother and friends, the long drive eventually became monotonous.

While his mother and grandmother seemed to have an unlimited number of things to talk about, he and Chet had fallen silent in the spacious back seat of Kathleen's New Yorker, each wrapped up in his own thoughts about the dramatic changes in their lives.

Glancing over at his cousin, Aubrey noticed an intense look on Chet's face, as he seemed to be staring out the window at something a thousand miles away.

"Whatcha thinkin' 'bout?" he asked, bringing Chet back into the present.

"Aw, nothing," Chet answered, in a hollow voice, adding, "And everything."

"Veet-nam?"

"Yeah, buddy…Veet-nam," he replied, managing a grin.

"I still got buddies back there. I'm sure they'll be okay, but still…

"I went through a lot with those maniacs. I hope you never get to understand, Aub. The movies make war look a whole lot . . . well, softer . . . than it really is."

"What's it really like?"

"I don't really know how to explain it. I mean…well, for one thing, there ain't no Audie Murphy over there, takin' on whole companies all by himself.

"It's not a regular war, with front lines and all. You don't know for sure who the enemy is. Most of 'em wear those goofy, ol', black, pajama-lookin' outfits instead of a uniform." His gaze returned to the sparse clouds dotting a blue sky.

"The guy smiling and waving at you from the rice

paddies is the same guy shooting at you at night. You know the people hate you. Hell, they even have little kids carrying AKs or hand grenades.

"Everything is booby-trapped, too. A guy from another company was killed when some gook bitch handed him a baby with a live grenade in the blanket." He spat bitterly.

He continued rambling, unaware that the conversation in the front seat had stopped.

"Even nature hates you, over there," he went on. "Poisonous snakes hiding in the trees, and spiders the size of a dinner plate everywhere."

"One time, we found a pit with a dead tiger in it, surrounded by human bones," he described. "The A.R.V.N. lieutenant that was with us said that betting on how long a prisoner would last against a starving tiger was one of Charlie's favorite sports.

"And then you come home to hippies that spit on you and call you a baby burner," he grumbled sourly.

"I don't think my country is very proud of me, but that don't matter. I'm proud of myself, and I'm especially proud of those crazy bastards I left back in the jungle.

"Fuck those smelly hippies!"

"Oh....dammit!" he growled at himself, turning to see a mortified Aubrey staring at him, mouth agape, then noticing that everyone was quiet. Gramma Pickard had turned sideways in her seat.

"I am so sorry," he said to everyone in the car.

"I just got caught up and...." His head sank to his chest in embarrassment, contrition stifling his apology.

"I lost my son over Germany," Beatrice said, as though it were the most natural thing to say. "I still have all his letters. He tried to hide it, but I could tell he was scared.

I just can't imagine the hell you've been through. But I will tell you that I am grateful to you, and to all the boys like you. And I am so very grateful that you came back to us whole and healthy. Oh, and I agree with you about the hippies."

"I'm real proud of ya, Chet," Aubrey offered, still shocked at what his cousin had revealed.

"Why do them hippies wanna spit on ya? Are they on the enemy's side?"

Collecting his wits, Chet answered, "Ya know, Aub, I think that maybe they are. Back in Nam, we got stories about them waving the flag of the enemy and burning ours. We heard about movie stars calling us murderers and saying that we should be put on trial for war crimes. Even the news reporters act like we are the bad guys, claiming that the war is lost and that we should cut and run, even though we've never lost a battle. I don't know, Aub. This country just doesn't feel the same as it used to."

"Spiders as big as plates? That's just creepy. Yuck!" Sarah interjected lightly, as she drove, getting a laugh from everyone.

The road leading into Haleyville happened to be the same road the Denton farm was on. Aubrey was relieved when his mother didn't slow down at the gate. He couldn't help looking at the place, as they passed by.

"Maw, who's takin' care of Kitt an' Aida?" he asked, concerned for the animals he had worked and cared for and had so recently played with.

"Honey, Mr. Gooch bought them a couple of weeks ago."

Old man Gooch was a relic of a bygone era. He barely had electric lights and no indoor plumbing at all. He stubbornly insisted that a good mule team was worth more than any newfangled tractor. It was a point he made repeatedly, when he came to their farm to buy hay and a steer or two every year, asking Buck if he'd managed to get the old Farmall running yet, knowing that he hadn't.

"I'm glad," Aubrey said. "Mr. Gooch knows how to treat 'em right. I think they'll be happy there." He knew that he would miss the cantankerous beasts and wondered if he would be able to visit them.

"Well, he sure got a good team," Chet added.

A few minutes later, Aubrey was dumbstruck, as they pulled up outside Frankie's house. A huge banner made from sheets hastily sewn together read, "Welcome Home Aubrey" in big, black, painted letters.

Frankie and Tony had taken lookout posts at the side of the road and had dashed inside to announce their arrival, as soon as they saw the big, gold luxury car.

Just as Sarah came to a stop, the front door flew open, and all the people he knew and loved started flooding out of the house, led by his two buddies.

All the hugs and pats on the back made him feel like a returning hero, which at first was a little uncomfortable, but soon the celebratory mood infected him, too.

As promised, there was a belated Christmas celebration, in which Aubrey was inundated with gifts. He nearly made himself hoarse thanking everyone repeatedly. But soon, the welcoming home became the focus.

He was particularly proud to introduce his grandmother to his friends, shifting some of the attention to her.

Frank had to keep his thoughts in check when he met Beatrice, knowing how much pain she had caused Sarah by abandoning her so long ago. But a whisper from

Sarah made the task easier.

Shelley shared some of her brother's feelings, though not as intensely. But seeing the glow on Sarah's face as she introduced her mother helped those feelings dissipate. After all, water does flow under the bridge.

In a fleeting moment, when neither Frankie nor Tony was hanging on him, Aubrey approached Mike.

"Mr. Carillo, Maw told me all that ya dun for me, an' for her," he said. "I don't know how I can thank ya properly, but I do want you ta know that I think yer a great man….an' a good dad for Tony." He offered his hand.

"No thanks are needed, Aubrey, but what you just said is more than enough," Mike replied, taking Aubrey's hand and getting a surprisingly firm handshake.

"You know," he continued, "there is one thing that you could do, if you've a mind to."

"Anythang you want, Mr. Carillo, anythang at all," Aubrey offered, happy to show his gratitude.

"It would be a tremendous honor if you would call me 'uncle.' You know, like you do Uncle Frank," Mike requested. "And I'm pretty sure Mrs. Carillo would be just as pleased to be called 'aunt.'"

"I believe the honor would be all mine, sir. An' I'd be right proud to," Aubrey gushed, feeling like the luckiest kid in the world.

He was back with his friends and family, and his family had just grown some more. Now he had two uncles, two aunts, and a grandmother.

Hiding in the back of his mind, and silently cheering, was the promise of no more brutal beatings, either.

The party went on into the evening, as the spread of snacks and finger foods that Shelley and Kathleen, and even Maria, had prepared began to disappear.

Aubrey and his buddies fell seamlessly back into their Three Musketeer mode, running like maniacs around the house, until their mothers joined together and ran them outside.

Chet and Mike chatted for a while, as only fellow military men could. Frank joined them, and the conversation shifted to cars and sports and other "guy" things.

Maria flirted with Waylon, and Waylon flirted back, each one earning piercing looks from their mothers, when they were caught in their hawklike sights.

As the celebration came to a close, it occurred to everyone that the Albert home was in need of a "No Vacancy" sign.

Mike and Kathleen insisted that Beatrice come home with them, since they had an empty guest room, adding that their hide-a-bed was also available.

Maria suggested that someone, like maybe…Waylon, could sleep there, getting a stern *"Are you out of your mind, girl?"* glare from her mother. Mike cast an intimidating look at Waylon, causing him to shrink behind Shelley and his mother.

Instead, Chet was invited, which didn't really disappoint Maria.

After the guests were gone and the boys were up in their rooms Shelley had started to climb the stairs, when a wave of weakness overcame her.

Fortunately, Sarah had taken to helping her make the nightly climb and was close behind to catch her.

"Are you all right?" she asked urgently.

But Shelley didn't respond as quickly as she normally did. Her weakness and pain seemed more pronounced.

Taking her by the elbow, Sarah guided her up to her room and helped her to bed. As she began to lie back,

Shelley's grip tightened on Sarah's arm.

"It hurts," she gasped, almost inaudibly.

Sarah felt helpless. All she could do was comfort her and give her medication.

After she had left the room, Shelley decided that just one more painkiller would help.

It did.

That night, she had some of the most vivid dreams of Jack that she had ever had.

Getting Aubrey back in school proved to be problematic. Principle Pike was resisting, saying that some of the parents had expressed deep concerns about having a "killer" sitting in the same class with their little darlings, however innocent he may be.

Sarah knew that her son would be ostracized and made to feel like an untouchable outcast among his peers.

Miss Shockley had suggested a retired friend of hers as a private tutor, and Mike had insisted on paying for it, so Aubrey attended school at Shelley's dining room table.

Not surprisingly, his grades actually improved drastically, and since his tutor was a former English teacher, so did his vocabulary and diction, albeit slowly.

Frankie and Tony weren't sure that having a teacher in their home every day was something they would enjoy very much, though.

At school, both fiercely defended their friend, whenever somebody was foolish enough to make snide remark about him, earning them newfound respect from the other kids, even the bullies.

Miss Shockley began stopping by to visit Aubrey at least once a week, often helping Mrs. Bastion with his lessons, but usually just to sit and talk with the boy who had come to be her all-time favorite student.

Back at school, she had grown tired of all the gossip and speculation surrounding Aubrey's tribulations, sometimes even by other teachers. She badgered Principal Pike until he agreed to let her give a "civics" lesson for the whole school in the form of a mock trial, with players and circumstances very similar to those of Aubrey's case.

Judge Walton even agreed to sit as judge in the trial, undoubtedly influenced by her persuasive ways. When the defendant was found to be not guilty, the result was a slight shift in sympathy in favor of Aubrey.

His life had begun to change for the better. He now had a grandmother, and his mother's injuries had fully healed. He was living in the same house as his best friend's, and his beloved cousin was safely out of the war.

Most significantly, he no longer had to fear brutal beatings for just being a kid. Even though he had lost his oldest friend when Scooter was killed, Rusty was around to help fill that void.

KATY

In the following weeks, Shelley became weaker and more dependent upon Sarah for the day-to-day running of the now-full house. Most of her time was spent reclining on the couch, watching soap operas and game shows.

Some days, she never left her bed.

Even though Aubrey was now his permanent roommate, Frankie struggled to keep his spirits up for his mother.

The specter of the inevitable was beginning to hover in the background for everyone.

Chet had opted to stay in Haleyville and to take over the chore of selling off the farm equipment and tools and of shutting the Denton homestead down. Many of the family heirlooms and treasures were being stored in Shelley's garage, to be sorted through at some later date. The rest was either sold at auction or donated to charity.

One early spring day, after Sarah had served lunch to Aubrey and Mrs. Bastion, the phone rang.

"I'll get it!" she called out, as if anyone else would. Half the calls were for her, anyway.

"Hello, Albert residence."

"Sarah? This is Betty."

"Hi, darlin'. How are things going up there? Keith and Cheryl doing all right?"

"Oh, Lord, yes," Betty exclaimed. "You know Keith and his gadgets. We just got a shipment of those new miniature cassette recorders from Japan. He's been playing with them all day, even recording his belches, the goofball. You know, those things will fit inside a clutch purse. Amazing what those crafty Japanese can come up with."

"As for the little princess, Heaven forbid her friends should see her with her square old mom and dad," she huffed.

"When they become teenagers, you end up wishing you had raised chickens instead. At least then you could kill 'em and eat 'em," she cracked sardonically.

"Well if it makes you feel any better, I haven't seen Waylon for more than ten minutes in a day for weeks, now. That Irene has got him snookered," Sarah countered.

Then she continued, "So to what do I owe the pleasure of your call?"

"You know me too well," Betty admitted embarrassingly. "Truth is, hon, I didn't call to talk about my quirky hubby or my snooty daughter. I need your advice on something."

"How can I help, sug?" Sarah asked.

"Yesterday, Katy, our office girl, came in with a black eye," she explained. "She tried to cover it with makeup, but that only made it look worse."

"It seems that worm she's married to thinks it's okay to smack her around," she spat.

"I was absolutely mortified. My heart broke for the poor girl. Keith was beside himself, cussin' up a storm, he was so mad. I've never seen him that worked up before. She's been with us since she got out of high school. She's almost like a second daughter to us.

"He insisted that she stay at our place last night. She was too upset to argue. In fact, I think she was relieved not to have to go back. Poor baby was so traumatized."

"I let her use Chet's room," she rambled. "I'm sure he won't mind."

At her end of the line, Sarah drew a slow, deep breath. It was a subject that was far too familiar to her. She understood why Betty had called.

"The little darlin' hasn't even been married for a full year," Betty continued. "And she's such a pretty thing."

"She kept asking what she had done wrong, and I kept telling her that she hadn't done anything wrong, except marry the wrong man. What can I do to help her, Sarah? I just don't know. Should I…"

"What's her name again?" Sarah interrupted. If she was going to do what was on her mind, she should at least know the girl's name, and Betty was beginning to ramble, as she always did under stress.

"Hmm? Oh! Uh…Katy. Katy Williams. Her married name is Moore, but I'm pretty sure it won't be for long. As soon as she feels safe enough, Keith and I are going to…"

"Betty," Sarah interrupted again. "Sweetie, listen to me before I change my mind. Put her on a Greyhound first thing in the morning. Send her on down to me."

"What? Oh, honey, no," Betty protested. "You don't need another burden. What with a sick woman and two boys to care for, on top of what all happened. I didn't call to pawn my problems off on you; I just wanted some advice…you know, from someone who…"

"Someone who's been through that particular brand of Hell?" she finished for her.

"Oh no, darlin', that's not it….well, I guess maybe….." she stammered. "Sometimes my big mouth just won't give it a rest. But really, hun, Keith and I…."

"Betty…Betty…you can't handle this," Sarah declared. "No offense, sweetie, but you have no clue what she's going through. God love you for wanting to, though.

"You have a husband who adores you and, to my knowledge, has never even raised his voice at you, so how can you possibly relate to what she's going through? This girl needs to know right now that it's not okay to be a punching bag. She needs to know that she deserves better. I don't want her, or any woman, for that matter, to make the same mistake I did and saddle herself to a life of misery and regret.

"So just send her on down, okay?" she concluded. She thought she heard a whimper at the other end of the line.

"To tell you the truth, Shelley's been getting weaker lately, and I could use an extra set of hands sorting things out from the farm and keeping up with the boys.

"Sarah…sweet, sweet Sarah, I love you so much," Betty sniffed. "Surely the Lord has a special pair of golden wings waitin' just for you.

"Okay. I'll send her to you, first thing tomorrow. I'll have Keith go with her tonight so she can get some of her stuff. I'll make sure he takes a couple of our biggest dock workers with him, too, just in case that cowardly weasel is there.

"But, according to her, he spends most of his time… and money…at some honky-tonk called Slim's.

"I'll tell her what's up. I do believe she'll be relieved. She already knows about how Buck treated you, and I think that just scares her more. She's been petrified that Steve might find her here and cause trouble for us. Keith keeps reassuring her that she's safe here, even though I think he's a little concerned for me and Cheryl. He checked the gun cabinet, and he's asked when Chet was coming home a couple of times. He's no coward, though, God bless him. Sarah, honey are you sure you want to do this?"

"No, not really, but it's something I feel I have to do it anyway," Sarah said. "I wish somebody had done it for me. At least there aren't any kids."

Sarah sighed, then added, "She's not pregnant is she?"

"No...no, that's one blessing," Betty assured her.

Sarah fought back a flood of emotions, "Call me and let me know when she's supposed to get here. Chet and I will pick her up."

"Speakin' of Chet, how's he doin'?" Betty asked, hoping to change the mood. "He doesn't call his momma as much he should. Is he eatin' you out of house and home yet?"

"Oh, he's been just wonderful," Sarah gushed. "I couldn't have gotten anything done without him. He's such a blessing. Thank you for letting him stick around a while longer."

"How is Shelley doin'?" Betty chanted on. "You said she's getting' weaker. That doesn't sound good."

"It's not good. I talk with her doctor regularly. He says he's not sure exactly how much longer she has, but is sure that it's not much.

"Ever since she had to quit working, she spends her time crocheting or watching TV. Sometimes, when she has the energy, we go for short walks, but that's getting less frequent lately.

"Frank comes down as often as he can and takes her for rides out in the country. Last week, he took her down to Stone Mountain to watch them carve it. Frankie wanted to go, too, but I explained to him that his mother needed some time alone with her brother. He's been so brave through all this, but Aubrey tells me that sometimes he cries himself to sleep, the poor baby."

"How's Aubrey handlin' everything?" Betty asked. "That boy has been through so much. Is he still in therapy?"

"Uh-huh. Momma and I take him to Memphis every other week. She fawns over him the whole time, and he eats it up like candy. He's so tickled to have a grandmother. He calls her Ma'amaw. I swear I don't know where he gets that country twang of his, but that's Aubrey. The therapist says he's doing remarkably well. He seems to think that gaining a grandmother and all the love and attention she gives him, so soon after experiencing such brutality from his father, has been a saving grace."

"I'm so happy for you," Betty commented. "It must be wonderful to have your mother again. I'll bet the boys are just ecstatic."

"That is an understatement, my dear," Sarah countered. "Aubrey is absolutely head-over-heels for her. Waylon is a little more reserved, but I can tell he's really happy about it. It's so nice that they have someone in their lives who praises them and builds them up, instead of constantly tearing them down the way their father…" she stopped.

"I'm sorry, I shouldn't talk about your brother like that," she apologized.

"Don't you dare apologize, Sarah; you're absolutely right," Betty said, her voice cracking slightly. "My brother was a brute. Just like his bastard father. I'm just thankful that your boys didn't inherit that foul gene."

"How about you, Sarah?" she asked. "You're carrying the weight of the world on your shoulders, but how are you holding up, hun?"

"Betty, I don't have time to feel sorry for myself; there's just too much to do. Shelley has been magnificent. She can read me like a book. When things pile up, she's always there for me. The tears the two of us have shed could fill a lake.

"But my strength is in the Lord and knowing that I am needed. I have my boys and Momma. It helps that we aren't living in constant fear. We'll make it through. I am so grateful to have so much love around me."

"I know what you mean," Betty replied. "I count myself as one of the luckiest women in the world."

"I'm thankful that you have someone like Keith," Sarah said. "He's such a wonderful man. Men like him give the women of the world hope." Sarah was diverting the subject from her own burdens.

"Yes, he is a wonderful man," Betty said.

Sensing Sarah's desire to change the subject, she added, "Well, darlin', I gotta let you go. I think my ever-lovin' man just pulled up.

"Ya know, for some reason, I just got the urge to show him just how special I think he is. That little baby-doll nightie he got me for our anniversary oughta do the trick." She felt suddenly happy.

"I'll call you tomorrow as soon as I know somethin'. And Sarah…I really do love you, and I'm so glad you and Aubrey are okay."

"I love you, too, sweetie. Tell Keith I said hello and give Cheryl a big hug from me, okay?"

"I sure will, bye-bye."

Sarah hung the phone up and poured herself a cup of coffee. She had a lot to think about, but first, she had to explain to Shelly that she had just invited yet another wounded heart into her home.

To her relief, but not at all surprisingly, Shelly not only understood, but she also seemed elated that Sarah had insisted on helping the young woman and that she could be part of that help.

The big house was filling up with people who loved and cared for each other, and that is just what she needed.

She confided in Sarah that lately, she had been having dreams of Jack more frequently. She didn't mention the extra painkiller she took every night to help bring those dreams. Each time seemed more real than before, and waking was becoming less desirable.

More often than not, she woke in tears, his name on her lips. She wondered if it meant that she was getting closer to being with him.

Then, the warmth of that thought would run cold with the guilt of leaving Frankie behind. She had long since stopped praying for a miracle and now only prayed for her son to be happy.

Early the next morning, Betty called to tell her when Katy would be arriving. Chet moved his things into the room Frankie and Aubrey shared and set up a pallet on the floor, over the protests from both boys that he take one of their beds.

"Boys, I've had to sleep in wet foxholes in the jungle during the monsoon season. This is just fine," he assured them.

As soon as he left, they stripped the blankets from their beds and made pallets of their own.

"Hey, Frankie, ya think our moms will let us camp out in the backyard next time it rains?" Aubrey asked eagerly. "We could use that pup tent Uncle Frank gave you. That way, we can pretend it's a foxhole in Nam an' we're guardin' the perimeter, jus' like Chet did."

"That would be cool, but probably not. You know how moms are. If they ain't warnin' ya about puttin' your eye out, they worry about ya catchin' your death of pneumonia, whatever that is."

"Yeah, yer right. My maw would probably throw a fit, too."

Naturally, just the mention of playing war triggered a firefight with a force of imaginary "commonists" trying to overrun their firebase in the jungle, their beds serving as bunkers.

After they had fought off the attack, Frankie asked, "So…who's this lady your mom and Chet went to pick up?"

"I dunno. Aunt Betty called Maw, and Maw told her to send her down."

He paused for a moment, then added sullenly, "I heard Maw tellin' Aunt Shelly that her husband beat her up."

Then he fell silent.

Frankie could see the turmoil in his face, as he slumped his shoulders and continued, "I cain't understand it, Frankie. Why would ya want ta beat up someone you say you love? It don't make any sense. Did your paw ever hit your maw?"

"Nope, I don't think so. My dad was a hero, an' heroes don't beat up girls…or women, especially their wives."

Then he noticed a wrinkle in Aubrey's chin, and said, "Aw, man…I didn't mean that your…"

"Naw, man…my paw was a asshole," Aubrey choked a very rare profanity.

"He didn't deserve Maw, an' she sure didn't deserve him."

They both fell silent, but, just then, the familiar tinkling music of the ice cream truck lilted into the room through the open window.

"Hey…I got fifty cents," Frankie declared. "I'll race ya!"

The boys thundered down the stairs and burst through the door amid Shelley's calls from the living room for them to slow down.

Sarah and Chet arrived at the bus station early to make sure Katy wasn't left standing alone.

"What does she look like?' Chet asked.

"No idea," Sarah replied. "Your mother just said she had long, black hair and would be wearing jeans and a pink tank top.

"Honey, she's been through a lot and might be a little shy, especially around men. I want to have a couple minutes with her first when she gets here, so why don't you wait by the doors, and I'll bring her over. Okay?"

"Sure thing, Auntie; I understand," he answered. "Ya know, I'll never understand men that hit women. What fucking cowards!"

"Oh, shi...I mean…I'm sorry, Auntie, I'm trying."

Sarah turned an amused face to her nephew, "I understand, hun. Just remember that a real lady doesn't find that kind of language attractive and a real gentleman doesn't use it….and a truly smart man doesn't need it."

"Consider me duly reprimanded, ma'am," Chet said,

snapping to attention and eliciting a lighthearted laugh from his aunt.

To their surprise, the bus pulled into the station on time. Sarah went to the gate, as Chet retreated to the lobby entry, unconsciously assuming a military parade rest stance, as though he were guarding a post.

One after another of the passengers exited the bus, until a young woman in blue jeans and a pink tank top could be seen backing out of the bus, as she assisted an old black woman who was hobbling down the steep steps with a cane.

"Bless ya, child. May the Lawd Jesus watch over you," the gracious elderly lady said, as Sarah walked up.

That's a good sign, Sarah thought, as she approached the couple.

"Katy?" she called out.

"I'm Sarah. How was your trip?" she asked, introducing herself and offering her hand.

"Actually, it was wonderful, thanks to Hattie here," Katy answered, turning back to the older woman. "She's been such a delight to talk to…and so helpful."

"Oh, it ain't no thang, honey child," Hattie shrugged.

"I just couldn't stand seein' them hard ol' tears in such pretty eyes. Jus' remember, baby: one rotten man don't mean they is all bad. Hopefully, the Lawd'll put a man in yo life like my Herbert, God rest his lovin' soul."

"This is Sarah Denton," Katy introduced. "She's my friend's sister-in-law, and she's taking me in for a while." She smiled a hopeful, but uncertain, smile at Sarah.

Hattie turned to Sarah, saying, "It's a precious thang y'all are doin' fo her. She dun told me what all she knows about you an' what you yo'self has been thoo.

"I think maybe Jesus dun brought her to the right

place," she said. "God bless the both of ya." She smiled a toothless grin.

"Bye-bye, Sugah," she winked at Katy.

"Bye-bye, Hattie. Maybe I'll see you around town. I'd love to meet those grandkids of yours."

"Ya nevah do know, now do ya?" Hattie replied, patting the young woman's hand and getting a warm hug in return.

"Well, there's my son. Ain't he a handsome one?" she said, pointing to a portly middle-aged man in bib overalls, a broad, toothy grin welcoming his mother home.

"What a nice lady," Sarah said, turning toward the gateway door, just as another bus belched sooty smoke, announcing its departure.

Inside, Chet's sharp eyes watched for his aunt and the new addition to their household. When they fell on Katy, his heart skipped a beat. He froze at the sight of the most beautiful creature he'd ever gazed upon.

Then, to his chagrin, Sarah stopped and faced the goddess in blue jeans, delaying his meeting her that much longer.

"Katy, hun, that's Chet over there, Betty's boy."

"Oh, I'd know him anywhere," she responded. "Mama Betty has his picture everywhere and reads his letters to all of us in the office."

"He's cute," she giggled.

Hmmm, Sarah thought.

"Well, be that as it may, as you know, he just got back from Vietnam, and he's still getting used to 'the world,' as he calls it, so please excuse any slips, okay? He's really a sweetheart, and I love him to death. I don't know what I'd do without him."

"I know. Mama Betty told me all about it. I feel so bad bringing my little problems onto you."

"Little? Honey, don't ever think your experience was just a little problem. That's how I felt at first and look how it ended for me." Sarah corrected.

"No, Katy, your problem was every bit as big as mine. We're just going to nip it in the bud. Okay?" She took Katy's hand into hers.

"Thank you, Mrs. Denton. I don't know how to..."

Sarah held up her free hand, stopping her and saying, "First off, call me Sarah. Secondly, no thanks are necessary. I wish someone had helped me early on, so it's my pleasure and my blessing to be here for you.

"Now, let's get going; Chet is looking a little impatient," she said, smiling and nodding toward him.

Chet saw his aunt gesturing and suddenly felt embarrassment flush over him. As the two women approached, he felt his knees trembling and his pulse increasing.

Take it easy, Marine! She's just a girl.

When his aunt introduced him to the dark-haired angel, he squeaked a pubescent "Hi," then croaked a more masculine, "I mean ...hello. I'm Chet," eliciting a snicker from his aunt and a grin from Katy.

"Hi Chet," the violet-eyed vision spoke, causing the rest of the world to fade in the light of her beauty.

"I'm Katy," she said, extending a hand of ivory perfection, highlighted with pink fingernails that matched her own blush.

A jolt of elation shot through him, as he took her hand in his.

"Ahem," his aunt cleared her throat, after what seemed both forever and far too short a time. He reluctantly released the pleasantness of her warm hand.

"Oh…yeah, um, sorry, I…uh…well, where are your bags?" he stammered, looking for a distraction.

"Well, Chet, they usually set them on the ground next to the bus," his aunt intoned sarcastically, barely able to contain her amusement.

"I only have one, it's the blue Samsonite. Thank you so much," Katy answered, coming to his rescue.

The drive to Shelley's house was an annoying distraction for Chet. Sarah sat up front, while Chet drove the borrowed Rambler. Katy sat in the backseat.

After Chet nearly ran off the road for the third time, Sarah couldn't resist teasing him, "Chet dear, please keep your eyes on the road. We'd like to get home in one piece."

Chet's eyes snapped away from the rearview mirror. Katy's petite beauty had captivated him, but as he took in each exquisite detail, he began to notice the bruise that showed through her makeup.

An all-too-familiar feeling began to creep up on him. He recognized the rage he felt toward the enemy when a comrade was wounded, or, worse, when a buddy was killed. The urge to tear apart and destroy whoever had done it was overwhelming. He felt his core trembling. No one had the right to cause such harm. The rage had served him well in the war zone. It had helped keep him alive, but now his stomach wrenched with angry efforts to control it.

Only after he felt his aunt's hand gently squeezing his forearm, while she said, "Chet, darlin' we're here," did he realize the white-knuckled grip he had on the steering wheel.

"Are you okay, baby?" she whispered.

"Huh? Oh, yeah. Sorry, Auntie," he said. "I was just lost in thought. You know…the jungle and all." He was

trying to excuse his distraction, flushed with embarrassment that Katy should see him lapse so.

"I understand," she comforted him.

A soft hand rested on his shoulder, as Katy looked
into the rearview mirror and into his eyes.

"Thank you, Chet, really. You're very sweet," she said,
tenderly squeezing his shoulder and maintaining a sweet
gaze that peered into his soul.

"Thanks," was all he could manage, without breaking
down.

He opened the car door, loath to pull away from the
comfort of her touch but equally loath to let the rage
inside find its way out.

He had left the war, but the war had not yet left him.

Retrieving Katy's suitcase, he slammed the trunk of
the car harder than he'd intended. Seeing both women
eyeing him with concern, he simply said, "Sorry," then
strode past without a word, embarrassed yet again.

"Poor baby," Sarah said. "That war must have been a
real hell for him."

But she knew that the war was only part of it. She felt
the rage, herself. Katy seemed so delicate, so fragile.

"I'm sorry," Katy apologized, unconsciously bringing
her hand up to her bruised cheek.

She also felt that Vietnam wasn't what brought Chet's
anger on. She felt an instant connection with the dash-
ingly handsome man. It was a feeling that both thrilled
and frightened her.

"I'm sorry, too, Sweetie. I'm sorry that you had to go
through your hell, Chet through his, and me through
mine," Sarah said, sadness echoing in her voice.

"But at least we have a life to look forward to. You're
about to meet one of the sweetest people God ever cre-

ated. She's going to die soon, leaving an absolutely adorable little boy without a mother. If we must be sorry, let's be sorry for her."

Then she added, "Let's not show it, though. She needs to be uplifted, not pitied."

Katy wondered how Sarah did it. Betty had told her every brutal detail, breaking down in tears when she told how her own brother had savaged his family. How did she endure it? How had she kept her wits when her son had killed his father? How could she bear to watch her friend die such a slow death?

How could she take on yet another burden?

"I hope I can be as much a woman as you are, Sarah," she said, looking up at a real-life Wonder Woman.

Sarah stopped in her tracks and looked back at the diminutive, young woman. A rush of compassion overwhelmed her. She reached out and embraced Katy in a warm, motherly hug.

Katy returned the embrace, feeling the love that exuded from Sarah.

I'm safe.

A tear trickled down her cheek.

"What do you think you're doing, girl?" Sarah scolded Shelley, as she struggled to get to her feet and to greet Katy.

"I am welcoming a guest into my home, like my momma taught me. What does it look like I'm doing?" Shelley fired back, sticking her tongue out playfully.

"Hi. I'm Shelley, and you must be Katy."

"Yes ma'am, I am," Katy replied politely.

"Welcome to my home...to our home," Shelley said, offering a frail hand.

"But please, sweetie, drop the 'ma'am' part. I'm not as

old as I might look."

"Oh, you don't look old at all. It's just habit," Katy said.

"And a good one, too," Shelley offered. "But since you're going to be staying with us, Shelley will do just fine. Please come in and sit with me. Would you like some iced tea?"

"That would be wonderful," Katy replied.

Shelley started for the kitchen doorway, but Sarah cut her off, saying firmly, "Greeting someone is one thing; fetching tea is quite another. You know what the doctor said. Stay off your feet, and let me handle things."

"Yes, ma'am, Captain Ma'am," Shelley said, giving Sarah an unimpressive salute.

"Okay, now it's your turn to drop the 'ma'am.' You know I'm right, so just skedaddle on back to your Lazy Boy . . . Chet?"

"Yes, ma'am," Chet said and snapped to attention, giving a perfect U.S. Marine Corps salute, then winking at Shelley.

"Now, I can smack you if I need to, young fella; your momma gave me permission. Not that I need it," Sarah threatened, half-raising her hand.

Chet scrambled out of reach and gently took Shelley's arm. "Let's get out of here, before she gets the razor strap."

"Katy, would you give me a hand, darlin'?" Sarah asked. The two women strode into the kitchen.

"I wanted to speak with you for a minute about what all is going on here," she said.

"As you know, Shelley has breast cancer. It's inoperable, and before you ask, she won't do that new chemotherapy, because there's no guarantee, and she doesn't want to prolong the trauma for Frankie." So she explained to Katy briefly.

"That's her little boy. You'll meet him when he gets home from school, in a little while. Anyway, she stood by me during my troubles, and the Lord has blessed me with the opportunity to take care of her.

"Now, I don't expect you to do anything you don't want to do. It's difficult to watch someone dying right before your eyes, especially someone as sweet as her. So don't feel obligated. You just focus on healing your own self. You have enough on your plate, as it is.

"We're just happy to have you here. In fact, when I mentioned it to her, she was insistent that you come down here, where you can feel safe."

"If it's all the same to you," Katy smiled, "I would really like to help out as much as possible. My mother was a registered nurse at Baptist Hospital in Louisville. She used to take me to work with her, when Daddy had to work double shifts. I'm actually thinking of becoming a nurse myself, so it would be a pleasure to help, if that's okay."

Sarah cupped Katy's delicate face in her wizened hands, saying, "I think that nice lady . . . Hattie was it? . . . well, she was so right when she said Jesus brought you here to us. Okay, we'll talk to Shelley and let her know.

"To tell you the truth, darlin', I could use the extra hands. Chet helps out with the boys and all, but there's only so much a man can do. That's why God made women."

"Now, sweet tea or plain?" she concluded, turning to the task at hand.

"Sweet," Katy answered.

"So Chet is staying here, too?" she asked, then blushed, realizing what the question had revealed.

"Only for a little while, sugar," Sarah answered, not

bothering to conceal a broad grin.

"He has to report to Camp Lejeune for a spell, while they process his discharge; then he'll probably head back to Kentucky."

Noting a faint look of disappointment on the young woman's face, she added, "Or maybe not. He seems to like it here. We'll see what the good Lord intends."

Oh, I hope so, he is just gorgeous!

Her thoughts brought a blush to her face. She was amazed that she could even think about another man so soon after being so badly treated.

But there was something about Chet that grabbed her by the heartstrings and that forced all thoughts of her soon-to-be ex-husband from her mind.

She knew and loved his mother and father, and Cheryl had always treated her like a big sister, so it was only natural that Chet should be just as wonderful as they were.

And his aunt! Wow! What a woman!

After all that she'd been through, nobody could blame her if she had chosen to be bitter and resentful, but Katy saw none of that. Instead, she saw strength and peace, as well as a desire, maybe even a need, to serve according to her faith.

She had barely been in town an hour, and already she felt at home.

"Do you think it would be okay if I called my mother?" she asked, "I can pay for the long distance."

"You'll do no such thing…pay, that is. Of course, you can call your folks. I'm sure they're worried to death about you."

"Well, Daddy passed away a couple years ago, but Momma's a worrier, so…"

"You go right ahead. There's an extension in the upstairs hallway, if you want some privacy."

"Thanks. I'll be as brief as I can."

"Take your time, sugar," she said. "Family is important. But, first, I want you to meet the light of my life. He's in the dining room with his tutor."

Sarah introduced Katy to Aubrey and Mrs. Bastion, amused at the way Aubrey blushed and stuttered, trying not to gawk.

Excusing herself, Katy skipped up the stairs, happier than she'd been in a long time and excited to tell her mother the good news.

Lost in her thoughts, she spun around the large round banister post at the top of the stairs and ran right into Chet, as he was returning from putting her suitcase in her new room.

Out of instinct, they grabbed each other in a steadying embrace, each as surprised as the other.

"Uh…excuse me," Chet stammered first, "I…uh…was just putting your….um…things in…um…your…room." His face flushed red, as his tongue was failing him rapidly.

"Thank you. I was just…coming up to…make a call," she stammered, equally as flushed and tongue-tied.

Neither seemed in a hurry to break contact or to look from each other's eyes until Katy shook herself back to reality and looked for the phone.

"Oh, yeah…yeah, it's right over there," Chet said, reluctantly looking away and dropping his hands from her waist to point the way.

"Thanks," she whispered demurely, sidestepping the befuddled man. Reaching for the phone, she noticed she was trembling. She could still feel where his strong hands had caught hold of her. She steadied herself for a second before starting to dial.

Chet stood transfixed, his heart thumping wildly in his chest. Unconsciously, he raised his hand to touch his arm where she had caught hold of him. When he finally moved, he was so distracted that he nearly stumbled down the stairs.

"Are you okay?" Sarah asked, seeing the bewildered look on his face.

"Huh? Oh, yeah, I'm fine," he answered unconvincingly. "Hey, I…uh, I think I'll go pick Frankie up from school, if that's all right."

"I'm sure he'll love it. Besides, the air will do you some good," she answered, nearly laughing out loud. She knew that look. She'd had had it once, in a lifetime ago.

Still, she would have a talk with her nephew about the delicacies of a healing heart.

A short time later, he returned, with Frankie close behind. The boy was eager to meet the woman Chet had described so glowingly.

Aubrey met him at the door, saying, "I think I know what angels look like, now."

When Katy rose to greet them, Frankie blurted out breathlessly, "Wow! You're right, Chet; she is beautiful."

Sarah nearly choked on her iced tea, and Shelley burst out laughing.

Chet turned beet red and stood frozen, like a deer in the headlights of an oncoming truck, too mortified to say anything.

Katy flushed bright pink, but she kept her composure.

"You must be Frankie," she declared, grinning modestly.

"I recognize you from your school pictures in the

hallway," she said, offering her hand to him. "I'm Katy, and I'm real pleased to meet you. Your mother has told me so much about you."

Frankie was mesmerized. "Uh-huh," was all he could manage to say.

"Okay," Sarah said. "Close your mouths before the flies get in. It's not polite to stare." Sarah tried hard not to laugh.

"Frankie, darlin', would you fetch the mail?" Shelley asked, breaking the spell Katy had cast on them.

"Huh? Oh…sure thing, Momma. Come on, Aub," he said, punching Aubrey in the arm. Recovering their wits, the boys raced out the front door.

"I…ah…" Chet stammered, then abruptly turned and headed for the kitchen, still red in the face and mumbling something about "killing those two."

As soon as he was out of the room, all three women burst out laughing.

Outside, Frankie and Aubrey were walking back from the mailbox, mail in hand.

"Katy sure is pretty, isn't she?" Frankie asked.

"She sure is. I think Chet likes her," Aubrey answered. "I seen Waylon act the same way when he first met Irene, all goofy an' stuff. She sure is pretty, too."

"Yeah, she is. You don't think we're gonna act that way when we get girlfriends, do ya?"

"Heck no, I ain't gonna," Aubrey insisted.

"Me, neither," Frankie said, just as adamantly.

Later that evening, Chet walked out onto the front porch, intending to go for his nightly run. As he began stretching, he noticed his aunt sitting in the porch swing.

"Oh, hi Auntie, I didn't know you were out here."

"Hi, sugar," she said. "Come on over here. Your old

Auntie wants a word with you." She patted the swing beside her.

Uh-oh, Chet thought, as he sat next to her. "What's up?" he asked, as innocently as he could.

"I think you know, don't you?" she said, her eyebrow cocked.

"Katy, right?"

"Yes, Katy."

"Auntie, I . . . ," he started, feeling another talk about affairs of the heart coming.

"Hush and listen," she gently ordered. "The girl has been through hell. A hell I know all too well. I had your mother send her down because I thought I might be able to help her get over it. But, in reality, I think helping her just might help me. Do you understand what I'm trying to say?"

"Actually, I do," he answered sullenly.

"The first time I saw one of my brother marines get killed, I was a mess. But another guy who'd been through it before took me under his wing and helped me keep my sanity and channel my anger. The next time it happened, it didn't feel any better. I was just able to cope with it. Next thing I knew, I was helping the new guys out the same way.

"It's a God-awful thing to see someone you know, someone you just had chow with or just played poker with, get blown to pieces. I still have bad dreams," he explained, more then he'd intended. "I'm sorry, Auntie. I'm sure you didn't need to hear that."

"It's okay, baby. I understand more than you know." The bloody scene she awoke to after regaining consciousness that terrible night was etched into her mind forever.

"It's a crying shame that people are capable of doing

such things to each other. And it's a crying shame how they tend to blame God for it, absolving Satan of any responsibility. But I digress.

"Anyway, we were talking about Katy…and you," she said. "Give her time, baby, and give yourself some time, too."

"What do you mean?" he asked, knowing full well what she meant.

"You know good and well what I mean. You couldn't be more obvious if you had a neon sign hanging over your head. You're falling for her. You couldn't take your eyes off of her all through dinner. To tell you the truth, it was almost comical watching you two avoiding each other's stares. Shelley said she thought you two would end up with whiplash." Then, she chuckled.

"She saw it, too?" he asked guiltily.

"Of course, she did. She's no fool. But don't worry. She thought it was cute. She actually hopes you two get together."

"Really? You mean she's not…you know."

"Jealous? Lord, no," she replied. "Don't flatter yourself, sweetie. That woman is still way too in love with Jack to ever consider anyone else."

Then, noticing a slight deflation in his expression, she took his hand into hers and continued, "She talked to me about the first encounter you two had."

Chet blinked at that.

"She said you are an adorable man, and she admitted to being momentarily distracted…but just a little."

That revelation made him feel slightly better.

"But she also said that it made her feel as though she were somehow cheating on Jack and that it made her miss him that much more."

"I understand. It makes me feel better in a weird sort of way. I kinda felt guilty about how I felt at first. I didn't want to get my hopes up, or hers, you know, all things considered."

"We keep drifting away from Katy, don't we?" she commented.

"Auntie, she's the most beautiful thing I've ever seen in my life," he capitulated. "At first, I thought it was just because I haven't been around women who weren't either hookers or refugees for such a long time, but that's not it. Shelley's a beautiful woman, too, but Katy is just so…."

Just then, the screen door creaked open, and Katy walked out into the soft glow of the overhead porch light. The shadows it cast upon her gave her an exotic appearance that shot through Chet like high-voltage electricity.

"Oh, there ya'll are. Isn't a beautiful night? So peaceful," she sighed.

"Just look at the fireflies. I haven't seen them in ages. We don't get them in the city," she said, stepping to the edge of the porch and looking up.

"And the stars…I can actually see the Milky Way," she exclaimed. "I never realized how much the city lights blotted them out. Y'all feel like taking a stroll?"

Sarah could feel Chet flinch

Oh well, so much for giving it time, she thought, smiling to herself.

"No thank you, darlin'; I have to get the boys into the tub and to get Shelley tucked in.

"But, I'm sure Chet wouldn't mind. Would you Chet?" she asked, winking at him.

"Uh…well, I…uh…of course, not, I'd…I'd love to," he stuttered, trying not to sound too enthusiastic.

"Are you sure?" Katy teased. "I don't want to impose."

"Oh, he's sure, all right," Sarah joined in. "And what better escort than a big strappin' marine to keep the boogeyman away?"

Resigned to the inevitable, she figured she might as well have some fun with it.

Wait until Betty hears about this. She'll flip.

She and Chet rose from the swing and walked toward Katy. Sarah reached up and playfully pinched Chet's cheek, saying, "Now you remember what we talked about."

Then she turned and went into the house.

"What where ya'll talking about?" Katy inquired.

"Oh…nothin'. Just stuff," he said, slightly peeved at his aunt.

"Shall we?" he said, stepping off the porch and gesturing toward the walkway.

"It's so nice here," Katy said, as they passed through the gate.

"Your aunt says you like it here. Do you plan on staying after you get out of the marines?" she asked, hopefully.

"Yeah, it is nice here," he answered, dodging her inquiry. "I used to come down every summer for a few weeks to help on the farm. Mostly to help, that is, but Auntie's cooking is to die for. Mom always said she thought Auntie was trying to fatten me up."

"I just love your mom and dad. They've been so wonderful to me. Your dad is quite a character."

"Yeah, he's a quirky little guy. But a fella couldn't ask for a better dad," Chet answered affectionately.

"I remember when we first got our Touchtone Princess phone. We'd only had those clunky old black, dial types before.

"He sat there for an hour. trying to play tunes on it. Mom just about hit the ceiling when we got the phone bill, though. It seems he had made several long-distance calls without realizing it. She grounded him from using it for a week. It was hilarious!" He laughed.

"Yep, that sounds like Poppa Keith, all right," she chuckled, then said, "You don't mind me calling him that, do you? I miss my own daddy so much, and your father was always such a comfort."

"I don't mind at all," he conceded. "You're not the first one of my friends to call him that. He's got a generous heart. So does Mom. They've helped more than a few folks past hard times."

"So...am I your friend?" she asked, looking up at him, the full moon's light dancing in her eyes.

Chet stopped walking and turned to face her. He felt exposed.

"Well...yes, of course, you are. I mean. . . . " He hesitated. "I want to be your friend. I want to be..."

He stopped himself from blurting out his true feelings. He wanted to say that he'd fallen head first from the second he laid eyes on her. He wanted to say that he wished for nothing more at that moment than to scoop her up in his arms and to taste the sweetness of her kiss. He wanted to say that he would never let anyone or anything ever hurt her again.

"I want that, too," she whispered; then she reached out and slipped her hand into his.

She had stopped loving Steve long ago, after finding out about his unfaithfulness, resulting in the first beating. Getting over a broken heart wasn't an issue for her. Feeling safe and wanted was.

Chet's reaction to her bruised face had touched her

deeply. His gentle manners and boyish clumsiness around her made her feel desirable again. That he was so drop-dead handsome helped, too.

He felt as though she'd peered straight into his heart. The feel of her soft, delicate hand in his made him light-headed. He tenderly squeezed her hand and nearly gave into the urge to kiss her. But remembering his aunt's words, he resumed walking, albeit on shaking legs.

Katy responded to his gentle gesture by leaning her head against his muscular shoulder, as they walked silently down the moonlit road.

She was sure he was going to kiss her, something she wanted as well, but she understood his hesitation.

In fact, it endeared him to her even more. Most guys she had ever known would have wanted to take advantage of having her alone this way. It was a good sign.

After a short time, they picked up their conversation from where they had left it. They laughed about his dad's misadventures with modern gadgets and took a more somber tone when they talked about what Sarah, Aubrey, and Waylon had been through.

She comforted him when he told her of the horrors of the jungle, doing him a huge amount of good, since he hadn't yet really spoken about them to anyone else.

Not until they had reached the bridge that crossed Mill Creek, about halfway between Shelley's house and the Denton farm, did he realize how far they'd walked.

"You know, Aubrey and I used to fish off this bridge," he reminisced. "But we should probably head back, before Aunt Sarah comes looking for us."

"He's such a sweet boy," she said. "And Frankie, too. I'm glad they have each other. Everybody needs some-one to help them over the bumps."

"Yes, we do," he replied. "God knows we've all hit a few, haven't we?"

"We certainly have," she said, adding, "but it's like Momma Betty says: "'We are the sum total of our experiences.'"

THE PHOENIX

Over the next couple of months, Katy grew closer to Shelley, as she fawned over her, serving her every need and cheerfully helping Sarah around the house.

Aubrey and Frankie stumbled over each other, trying to please her, melting under her violet eyes whenever she asked them to do something.

Sarah milked the advantage for everything it was worth, often having Katy ask them do various chores around the house.

All Katy had to do was preface her request with, "Would you fellas please…." and whatever she requested was eagerly granted, the boys often competing to do it faster or better than the other.

Sarah and Shelley were wildly entertained by their drooling efforts to be perfect gentlemen for the raven-haired beauty.

She accompanied Shelley to her doctor appointments, getting advice from him and learning about all Shelley's symptoms and treatments.

Several times, she tried to get Shelley to give chemotherapy or radiology a chance, only to be gently, but gratefully, rebuked by Shelley, who had resigned herself to her fate.

Still, Katy continued to research what scarce materials she could find, hoping to discover some sliver of hope.

To her dismay, the town's library was almost completely devoid of anything useful concerning cancer of any type. The doctor had provided some addresses she could write to and ask for literature, but even the American Cancer Society had little to offer, except suggestions on how to make a patient as comfortable as possible in their last days.

Medical research into breast cancer lagged far behind that of other types, such as lung cancer. Katy assumed that the reason was that more famous men were dying from that particular type. Breast cancer was a woman's cancer and wasn't openly discussed in polite society, nor did it have an easy villain to blame, like cigarettes.

One small regret Katy had was that eventually Chet had to report to Camp Lejeune. But he had promised her that he would come back to Haleyville, much to his parent's disappointment.

However, after Sarah explained things to them, their disappointment changed to hopeful anticipation.

Though neither Chet nor Sarah had implied even so much as an engagement, Keith immediately hired the best divorce attorney he could find on Katy's behalf, giddy at the prospect of having her for a daughter-in-law.

Katy counted the days until Chet's return, her heart harboring hopes of her own. Sarah found herself counting them as well, secretly becoming just as eager as his parents.

In the meantime, she became Shelley's personal nurse, her own troubles long forgotten. She established a daily medication and exercise routine for Shelley, though the walks were becoming shorter and the medications more frequent.

With help from Kathleen, she put together a special diet, using the list Kathleen's cousin had sent her. But Shelley's appetite continued shrink, as the weeks passed, as did her strength, though not her spirit.

Sarah was impressed by her determination.

If hope could cure Shelley, then Katy was a magic bullet.

But she knew better, and so did Katy. It became increasingly difficult for them to conceal their growing sadness. But they knew that it was of paramount importance not only to Shelley, but to the boys, as well, that they do so.

Frankie struggled more than anyone to hide his slowly crumbling heart. Several times, Katy had found him off in some corner of the house or out in the yard, quietly crying.

Usually, she left him alone, not wanting to embarrass him or interrupt his dealing with the inevitable. Other times, she couldn't restrain herself from tenderly wrapping her arms around him and sharing his grief.

For his part, Aubrey sought the comfort of his mother's arms when his own sadness became too much. More so than the others, he sought solace in prayer.

Shelley was deeply touched by the efforts of those around her.

At night, feelings of gratitude mixed with those of guilt often made it difficult to fall asleep.

Katy had begun to notice that her pain medication was disappearing faster than it should and had questioned her about it. Shelley convinced her that the pain was getting worse than it really was and that she was taking the pain pills more frequently than she really was. Katy, in turn, had convinced the doctor to increase the prescription.

Eventually, climbing the stairs became too strenuous for Shelley, and she decided to live what was left of her life in her bedroom.

The large bedchamber had been her parents' and was situated on the morning side of the house, with a wide bay window overlooking the back yard and the woods beyond. She recalled with fondness the many times she had found her mother sitting in her grandmother's old rocking chair, softly humming and crocheting one of the many doilies or afghans that still decorated the house.

Upon hearing of her retreat, Keith sent down a new compact color TV for her to watch her soap operas and game shows on. Very often, others in the house would join her, eating their meals off TV trays, as they kept her company.

But, increasingly, she chose to simply rock to and fro and to gaze out the window, contemplating her life and the effects her death would have on those she loved so dearly.

Uncle Frank visited as often as possible, cheerfully regaling the Musketeers with tales of the brave firemen he worked with.

But his focus was always on his beloved sister. He, too, could often be found on the back porch in tearful anticipation.

More often than not, Sarah sat at his side, his head on her shoulder, as they comforted each other.

Early one spring evening, Shelley heard a soft knock on her door.

"Come in," she beckoned, wondering who it was.

"Oh, hi, Aggie," she cheerfully greeted her old teacher and new friend.

"It's so nice to see you. Please, have a seat," she said, motioning to the overstuffed chair Frank and the boys had wrestled upstairs for her visitors.

"You look wonderful, dear," Aggie complimented, leaning down to hug her.

"It's nice of you to say that, but…"

"Humor an old woman, child," Aggie insisted. "Accept the compliment."

"Okay, thank you. You look great, yourself."

"I said humor…not bullshit, but thank you," she countered, continuing, "How are you doing?"

"As well as can be expected, I suppose," Shelley answered, trying to be as upbeat as she could.

"Well, I suppose that was a rather inane question, wasn't it?" Subtlety was never a strong point for the aging woman.

"Oh, that's okay. Actually, I'm glad you stopped by. I've been wondering how Frankie has been doing, you know, with the other kids and all."

"He's doing fine," she said. "He's such a brave little trooper. I speak with Mrs. Delgado about him frequently. She's a wonderful woman and a great teacher. All her students love her. They say she's very entertaining."

"Unlike a certain 'Dragon Lady' we know," she said, unapologetically.

"Oh, now, you weren't that bad," Shelley defended.

"Oh, yes I was," Aggie grinned, "And I still am.

"Anyway, she says that Frankie is doing fine. I can assure you that nobody bothers him, especially with his friend Tony hovering over him like a mother hen. That little guy is a real fireball when it comes to protecting him. It's rather comical, like watching a Chihuahua guarding sheep," she chuckled.

"It's not just Frankie he defends, either. Just the other day, Mr. Pauley had to pull him off a boy who had made a disparaging remark about Aubrey. He's quite a loyal friend."

"Yes, he is. His parents have been great, too. Did you know that Mike insisted on covering all of Aubrey's and Sarah's legal and medical expenses?"

"Yes, I know. They're extraordinary people," Aggie agreed. "The attorney they hired was very good."

"So…how is the judge?" Shelley asked, with a sly grin.

"Now how would I . . . ?" She started to protest, but, seeing Shelley's accusing smile, she capitulated, "He's doing fine, dear." A faint pink rose in her cheeks.

"Don't worry; your secret is safe with me. In fact, I think it's scandalously delicious." Shelley winked.

"Well, sweetie, if you've guessed, then I'm sure others have, too," she said.

"But let the tongues wag as they may. I'm too old to worry about that sort of thing," the elderly matron said defiantly, getting a well-needed laugh from Shelley.

The two women chatted for a while longer, until Aggie excused herself. On the way out, she visited briefly with Aubrey and Frankie.

Later that evening, Frankie was in his mother's room, watching Gunsmoke with her, when she winced in pain that seemed more pronounced than he'd seen before.

"You okay, Momma?" he said, rushing to her side in alarm.

"Not really, honey," she gasped honestly. "Could you help Momma to bed?"

She leaned heavily on her son, as he helped her the

short distance between her chair and the bed.

Up until now, he had managed to hide his fear and pain, but as she lay back on her pillow, he couldn't hold back any longer.

"Momma," he sobbed, laying his head on her shoulder, "I don't want you to...go."

He couldn't bring himself to use the word "die."

After a short time, he whispered hoarsely, "I wish I was a Phoenix bird."

"A what?" she asked, forcing the pain back.

"A Phoenix bird," he explained, through tear-flooded eyes.

"Mrs. Delgado read us a story about it from somethin' called mythology," he explained.

"A Phoenix bird lives for a thousand years, and then it builds a nest that catches on fire and burns it up. But after it burns up, a whole new bird rises up from the ashes and lives for another thousand years."

Feeling a little perplexed, Shelley asked, "Well, honey, why would you want to do that?"

"No, that's not it, Momma," he sniffed.

"I don't wanna burn up or anything like that, but some people used to believe that when a Phoenix bird cries, it's tears can heal wounds or cure any disease, and even stop someone from...from dyin'," he managed to say.

"I wish I were a Phoenix bird; I really do," he sobbed, wiping the tears from his eyes with his finger and looking at them remorsefully and then at his mother.

"So do I, baby; so do I," she choked, as her own tears streamed down her cheeks.

GOING HOME....FINALLY

"Auntie?" Katy asked, as she placed Shelley's dinner plate on the tray she had prepared.

"Yes, darlin'?" Sarah replied, from her post in front of the suds-filled kitchen sink.

That Katy had started calling her "auntie" further stoked her hopes for the young couple.

"I'm getting worried about Shelley, I mean, more than usual. She just seems so distant lately," she explained. "Sometimes when I'm talking to her, I can tell that she's not really listening. It's like she wants to be somewhere else."

"She does, sweetheart. She wants to be with Jack," Sarah elaborated. "But she doesn't want to leave Frankie or her brother, either. It's a hard place to be for her to be in.

"To tell you the truth, I think she's drifting away from us and doesn't even realize it. There's no doubt she loves us, but maybe subconsciously, she realizes that her time here with us is growing short, and so she allows herself to drift more towards Jack."

"So you believe there is a life after you die?" Katy asked.

"Of course I do," Sarah answered, in a matter-of-fact

tone. It's what Christ promised. Don't you?"

"Well….I never really thought too much about it," Katy replied, feeling far less certain.

"Sorry, sweetie; I shouldn't have put like that. It's only natural that you wouldn't, being as young as you are. Young thoughts are on the life that is in front of you, as it should be."

"That's okay," Katy allowed. "I've thought about it some, but mostly it's been that I hope to see people like…well, my daddy and memaw when I die, but it's not like I know I will. How do you get there?"

"It's called 'faith,' sugar. It can be a hard thing to acquire. Some folks never do."

"Have a seat," Sarah said, and she motioned toward the kitchen table, drying her hands with a dish towel.

Taking a seat herself, she began, "You see, darlin', faith can be simply believing in things we take for granted, like, say, . . . gravity. It has always been there and always will be. We can't see it, taste it or touch it, but we feel the effects of it constantly, and so we don't doubt it or question it. That's an easy kind of faith to have. Even animals have that kind of faith.

"But faith in God is much more difficult. It takes a willingness to believe that there are things out there that we can't, and never will, completely understand or be able to explain. Not even with science. The truth is that science can't fully explain gravity, either. But because the effects are ever present and provable, it's accepted on faith as a fact.

"Much more difficult to explain and impossible to prove scientifically are the very real effects that faith has in and on the everyday lives of those capable of having it."

Seeing the quizzical expression on Katy's face, she explained, "The Bible tells us that not all people will have the ability to believe in something they can't touch or see…in fact, most people don't.

"Even some Christians can only believe up to a point, and then the world scares them into trying to justify or prove that which they are not capable of proving.

"That doesn't mean that skeptics are bad or stupid. It simply means that they have an unrecognized limitation within themselves. It's a limitation that only allows them to believe that, someday, maybe science will answer all their questions and prove all their points.

"But that, in itself, is still a kind of faith in something they have no real control of.

"Sadly, many of them take great delight in ridiculing the faithful. They assume an intellectual superiority and make themselves feel better by calling us mindless sheep, or worse. But we forgive them for it and pity their emptiness, however vehemently they may deny it.

"A vital aspect of religious faith is that those of us who have it don't need proof of God's existence. His Word and his promise is enough for us. I think that's the part that really bugs the skeptics and the cynics the most, since they require proof of everything, including their own existence. But I've digressed, haven't I?"

"Not really," Katy replied. "I think I understand…sort of."

"Darlin'," Sarah continued, "put it this way. If I didn't have faith, then I would have to believe that everything in the world, everything in my life, and all the beautiful achievements of mankind were merely the result of random accidents. I would have to believe that even truth doesn't really exist, since human thought would be just an accident, too. Now, that might be okay for some folks, but it just wouldn't work for me.

"I went through years of unmitigated hell, with only my faith to carry me through. Chances are that, without my faith, I wouldn't be alive today.

"There's a story in the Bible that teaches how a piece of metal is plunged into a blazing furnace and then hammered on. This happens repeatedly, until, eventually, the beleaguered metal becomes a mighty sword.

"Life with Buck was my furnace and my anvil. Through his brutality and anger, by the grace of God, I was forged into the woman I am today, though I would never recommend it to another woman.

"But because of it, I had the strength to pull myself and my boys through the horrific events we've been through, lately.

"And so, here I am today, believing in God more than ever before, because he has delivered me from the infernal ordeal. I have the strength to be here for Shelley and Frankie…and for you.

"And it's not just my own faith. The Lord gave me Aubrey. Can you see my darlin' boy without the faith he relies so heavily upon? Can you believe that a heart like his was the result of a chain of random accidents?"

"No, Auntie, I really can't. He's an amazing little boy," Katy agreed. "But he has you to guide him."

"Yes, but only to guide him and to nurture what God alone had created in him. No science known to man could do that. I can only imagine how powerful a force for good he will be when he grows up.

"Did you know he's thinking about becoming a minister?" Sarah bragged.

"That doesn't surprise me," Katy said. "He'll be a

good one."

"He certainly will," Sarah agreed.

"So do you see how my faith allows me to believe what Christ has promised? It allows me to believe that I will go to Heaven and that I will see my big brother and my father when I get there.

"Maybe she doesn't realize it, but Shelley's faith makes her believe that she will be with Jack when she leaves this mortal world behind. Her faith is born out of a deep and abiding love for him. That is her gift from God, and it will carry her into his light. Jack's purity of heart and love for humanity means that he will be there waiting for her."

"So if I learn to believe like you and Shelley, I will get to see my daddy?" Katy asked.

"Well, sweetie, belief isn't something you learn. It's more like something you give into, something that makes itself apparent to you. You learn to remove the obstacles from your heart and your mind. You learn that your faith is not dependent upon the approval of others. Then you can begin to receive the gifts of peace and strength that faith brings you."

"This is all pretty heavy stuff, Auntie. I'm going to have to think about it," Katy said, rising from the table. "And read about it, too. Do you have an extra Bible I can borrow?"

"You can have mine, sweetheart," Sarah offered. "And if you have any questions, which I am sure you will, just ask me or Aubrey. He knows his stuff."

"Oh, I don't doubt that. Well, I'd better get this up there before it gets cold," Katy said, lifting the tray of food she had prepared for Shelley.

"Here ya go, Shell," Katy said, as she set the tray on

the nightstand and started helping Shelley into a sitting position.

"Auntie and I just had a really intriguing conversation."

"Oh…about what?" Shelley responded, her voice weak with fatigue.

Auntie? A good omen.

"It was about faith and believing what God has promised," Katy answered, as she placed the bed tray across Shelley's lap.

"Well, you couldn't have found a better person to have that conversation with. She sure has helped me… tremendously."

"Actually, we…ah…we talked about seeing our loved ones when we…um…" Katy stammered, realizing that it might be too sensitive a subject for the dying woman.

"When we die?" Shelley finished for her.

Seeing Katy's discomfort, Shelley continued, "Don't worry, honey. It's a subject rather dear to my heart, right now."

"In fact, I find myself thinking quite a lot about it, lately," she concluded, somewhat morosely.

"Oh, Shelley," Katy whispered, her eyes beginning to water.

"Katy, darlin' girl, you're going to have to accept that I'll be leaving soon."

Patting the bed beside her, she said kindly, "Here, sit by me for a moment."

Katy sat on the bed, and Shelley took her hand.

"Honey, I've accepted it. To a degree, I even welcome it. I hate that I'll be leaving my precious boy, my brother, you, Sarah, and all the rest. But it is what it is. What could have been done…wasn't done, and that's nobody's fault but mine. Maybe if I hadn't been so ignorant or so deep in denial...well, who knows? But I was, and so... here I am.

"But I've had a good life. And that's because of all the people I've shared it with. Sure, at first, I was angry; who wouldn't be? But, now, the thought of being with Jack again, and knowing Frankie will be taken good care of, I can accept it."

"Auntie said you knew you would be seeing Jack again," Katy sniffed, bravely holding her composure. "She said your faith comes from your love for him. It must be a wonderful kind of love."

"It is. It really is. But love doesn't always feel good. My love nearly destroyed me when I lost him. But my love for Frankie saved me. Having him pulled me through the darkest times. Missing Jack made me terribly lonely, to the point of physical pain, but my love for him also kept me warm through all the cold nights. And now . . . " She trailed off.

I'm coming home, Jack...soon.

"Something tells me that you just might find a love like that, yourself," she finished, causing Katy to blush. "Or maybe you already have?"

"You think so?" Katy asked, a girlish twinkle replacing the sadness in her eyes.

"Honey...I saw it the first day you got here. Cupid pegged that boy right through his big ol' heart. And I think he struck a bull's-eye on yours, too," she chuckled.

Turning her attention to the tray in front of her, she asked, "Now, what delightful treat did you prepare for me tonight?"

Katy smiled gratefully. "It's a new recipe. Lentils and rice soup, with chicken breast."

"Oooo...yummy!" Shelley declared enthusiastically.

Though her appetite was down to nothing, she still enjoyed what little she could bring herself to eat, and she knew that Katy had put her heart into making it for her.

Later that night, as the light of the full moon played across her face and the rest of the house was asleep, the pain deep in her chest was not allowing her to fall asleep, even though she had taken the extra pill.

Without clicking the nightstand lamp on, Shelley poured what she thought was just another pill into her hand. In her grogginess, she didn't realize that she had, in fact, poured three additional pills out.

As she had hoped, she began to drift into the familiar haze, where Jack always waited for her. But, tonight, his presence seemed just a little more real than it had before.

"Jack?" she called out, in her dream.

"I'm right here, babe," he answered, his voice just a little stronger than usual, "waiting just for you."

Her heart soared. There he stood, just out of reach. She glided forward, and her hand touched his. She was surprised at such a real feeling of his hand in hers.

"Oh, Jack," she crooned, not wanting the feeling to end.

Suddenly, a blinding flash of light came from out of nowhere, and Jack was gone. Her eyes flew open, as a spasm of pain rampaged through her body.

"No...no!" she whimpered. "Jack, please come back."

The cold moonlight highlighted a stream of tears flowing down both sides of her face and onto the pillow.

He was there. It was real, so real. She had to go back. Sobbing quietly and desperately, she reached for the yellow plastic bottle that promised his return. In a delirium of panic and overmedication, she poured several more pills into her hand and washed them down with the glass

510

of water on the nightstand.

The pain still raced in her chest. She wasn't sure if it was the cancer or her heart breaking.

Slowly, through her tears, she felt the pain relinquish, giving way to a wonderful feeling of lightness. The usual haze was gone.

She heard the melodic symphony of falling water and turned to see Sweetheart Falls, glittering under as glorious a spring day as she had ever seen.

"Hi, babe."

Spinning around, she saw him leaning casually against Proposal Rock.

"Been waitin' for ya," he said, straightening up and walking toward her, his crystal-blue eyes sparkling and his disarming smile flashing his love for her.

"What…why…?" She couldn't speak; her feet felt frozen in place. This dream was so very different from all the others she had been having.

"I'm here, babe, and I'm never going away again… never," he declared, in a voice she had missed for so long, a voice so clear, it had to be real.

Opening his arms to her, he asked, "Well, are you gonna make me walk all the way?"

Suddenly, she found herself running to him and falling hard into his arms. She felt the embrace she had missed and had craved so many thousands of times. It was more real than reality itself. She felt as though she were a part of him, more than ever before.

"It's okay now, babe. You're where you belong.

"I've missed you, my love, more than you can possibly imagine," he assured her. "But I've never been far away from you."

"Oh, Jack, I know…I know," she sobbed through

tears of absolute joy. "Are you really here? Please say that you are."

"Yes, babe, I'm really here, forever. And so are you," he replied, the joy in his voice ringing through. "I'm sorry for leaving you the way I did. I hope you forgive me."

She basked in his loving embrace for what seemed an eternity, unwilling to let him go, for fear it might be yet another dream.

Then she felt his strong hand gently tilt her face to his.

The man she loved with every fiber of her being, the man she knew she had always loved and would love through all time leaned down and kissed the kiss she had so desperately missed for so very long. A kiss that lasted forever, yet was far too short.

All the pain she had ever felt, in her heart and in her body, evaporated into a rapidly fading memory.

When at last they broke the kiss, he smiled the most beautiful smile she had ever seen in all of creation and whispered, "There's a couple folks who've been waitin' to see you."

Turning aside, with one arm still wrapped around her waist, he motioned toward the ancient oak tree that stood in front of her house. Standing next to the old tire swing was a middle-aged couple beckoning her with open arms and broad smiles.

"Mommy…Daddy?" she whimpered, taking slow, unbelieving steps toward them.

"Yes, baby, Mommy's here," Emma McKinney called out, moving briskly toward her daughter, embracing her as only a mother can, gently stroking her daughter's hair.

"We've missed you so much, my darling girl," she said, as her father joined the embrace.

"I'm really sorry that your mother and I had to leave that way," he said, echoing Jack's apology. "I know it was hard on you and your brother, but we were never far from you, either."

"Oh, Daddy," Shelley cried.

She was home. A delirious rapture washed over her. She felt her heart would explode with happiness. She knew that she would never be alone or never suffer again.

"How's that grandbaby of mine?" her father asked.

Shelley felt an instant panic, "Oh no, Frankie. What about Frankie? Oh, my poor baby."

"Now, Robert," her mother chided. "You know good and well how he is."

Turning back to Shelley, she brushed her cheek reassuringly, "Don't you fret, sweetheart. Frankie will be just fine. He's in good hands…the best he could possibly be in."

"Now that is a fact," her father said. "Your brother… my son, is a good man. Make that a great man. That's something I didn't tell him when I could have…when I should have. It's my greatest regret, the stone I must carry. But I'm told that I'll get the chance to fix that…at some point."

"Babe," Jack broke in from the seat of his '32 Deuce coupe, now idling noisily next to her.

"I have it on the highest authority," he said, nodding upward, "that his little friend is held in high regard around here; so is his mother. Plus, with you and me watching over him, our boy will be just fine."

"How 'bout a cruise?" he offered, reaching over to open the door for her.

"Wake up sleepyhead; time for my almost-famous waffles," Katy called out, as cheerful as the spring morning that shone through the drawn curtains.

Setting the tray on the nightstand, she gently shook Shelley. Getting no response, she shook her again, saying, "Come on, now, it's nearly nine. Do you plan on sleeping the whole day away?"

Still getting no response, worry began creeping up on her.

"Shelley?" she said more urgently. "Shelley, wake up."

Grabbing Shelley's limp hand, she felt the coldness of it and immediately placed her fingers on the dead woman's jugular vein, getting no pulse.

"Oh, my God!" she gasped.

"Sarah…Sarah!" she yelled, running out of the room.

Sarah came rushing out of her room. "What is it?" her voice reflecting the urgency in Katy's.

Too panicked and distraught, Katy could only point to Shelley's room, her hand covering her mouth.

Sarah stopped, as she entered the room. Intuitively, she knew that her friend was gone. Crossing her arms as though holding herself in an embrace, she choked back a guttural sob and dropped heavily on the bed next to Shelley's lifeless body.

Katy stood riveted in place for a few endless seconds and then slowly made her way back to the doorway.

Sarah sat clasping Shelley's hand in hers, pressing it to her tear-stained cheek. "Tell Jack hello for me," she said softly.

Then clasping the hand to her breast, she began rocking gently and humming softly to her friend, tears flowing freely down her sorrow-wizened cheeks.

Katy broke out into convulsing sobs and sank to her knees, burying her face in her hands.

Footsteps echoed up the staircase, as Aubrey and

Mrs. Bastion ascended to find out what the commotion was about.

"Aunt Shelley?" his young voice squeaked, as he shuffled unsurely into the room.

"Maw?" he whimpered, slowly kneeling beside the bed. Seeing his mother lost in her grief, he laid his head on Shelley's shoulder and began to cry.

"Oh, my Lord," Mrs. Bastion gasped, cupping her hand to her mouth and turning away from the unexpected sight, knowing full well what had come to pass.

After what felt like forever, Sarah reached down and stroked Aubrey's hair, his face still buried in grief.

"Come on, son. She's gone to the arms of our Lord. We have things to do," she beckoned, as she rose from the bed.

Katy was still on her knees, her head leaning against the door frame, makeup streaking her face. In shock, she looked up with a lost expression when Sarah stroked her head.

"She's with Jack now," Sarah whispered.

Katy merely nodded and rose to her feet.

Then, without warning, she collapsed into Sarah's arms and began sobbing again.

"It's my fault," she croaked between sobs.

"No, it's not," Sarah admonished gently. "Why would you say that?"

"Look at the pill bottle," Katy wailed, pointing to the overturned container.

Sarah hadn't noticed that detail, but she refused to let the young woman blame herself.

"You didn't do that. You had no way of knowing."

"Yes, I did," Katy protested, sobbing. "I convinced… her doctor to…increase her…dosage."

She took Katy by her shoulders and shook her lightly.

"Stop it, young lady," she said sternly, distracted from her own grief. "The doctor knew what he was doing. He wouldn't let anyone convince him of anything he didn't believe was necessary."

"Oh, Katy," she said, drawing her into her arms. "She wanted to be with Jack. Nothing you said or did had any effect on that. Don't torture yourself, sweetheart. Be grateful for the time you had with her. She loved you. She told me so…and I love you."

"I love you, too," Aubrey offered, wrapping his arms around both women.

"Hey, yo, Frank," the fireman called out across the empty engine bay. "You got a call!"

"Can't you take a message? I'm kinda on the busy side," Frank grated.

Dammit, Charlie. Can't it wait till I get home?

"Who is it?"

"Somebody named Sarah."

Instantly, he dropped the firehose he was inspecting and rushed over to the phone.

"Sarah, what is it? How's Shelley?" he begged urgently.

He felt as though a bolt of lightning had raced through him. From the depths of a cavern he heard, "Frank? Frank, are you still there?"

He responded mechanically, "Yeah….Sarah. I'm…. when?"

A few agonizing moments later, he said unsteadily, "I'll be there tonight. Thank you, Sarah…for everything."

"Geez, boss! What happened?" the other fireman asked, as Frank placed the receiver back on its cradle, "You look like you seen a ghost."

"My sister…she, ah…she…died last…night," he

replied, not believing the words himself.

Then in a brief moment of lucidity, he said, "Eddie, tell the chief that I have to take some time off, okay?"

"Sure thing, boss," Eddie answered. "Is there anything else I can do?"

"Thanks, but...I gotta go," Frank answered, rushing off, before his fellow hero saw him cry.

He had to force himself to pay attention to traffic, as he slowly rumbled home.

"My God, Frank, what happened?" Charlie Hunter asked, seeing Frank's face, as he came through the door of their suburban home, surprised to see him home so early.

"Shelley," was all Frank could manage to say, his gazed fixed on some distant point in the universe.

"Oh, no," Charlie moaned, knowing instinctively what had happened. He wrapped his arms around Frank, allowing him to finally break down.

A short time later, still in a daze, Frank tossed his overnight bag into the passenger's seat, reluctantly coaxed the powerful engine awake and waved goodbye to Charlie, who stood red-eyed at the front door.

Though it was little more than a three hour drive, he knew it would be the longest drive of his life.

"Are you happy, God?" he spat bitterly, as he merged onto the interstate and began his sad journey.

A short while later, he looked up into his rearview mirror and saw lights of the tan-and-black state trooper sedan flashing.

"Great," he growled to himself. "Just what I need."

But after seeing the fireman's identification sticker on his windshield and hearing of his loss, the trooper let Frank go with his condolences and a plea for him to drive safely.

As he drove, his anger subsided, to be replaced by fond memories of his baby sister.

Her giggling laugh whenever he made funny faces for her, the way she pouted when he made her mad. He could still feel the proud hug she gave him after he had beaten Tommy Babbins up for calling her a boogerhead.

He recalled the protectiveness he felt, when other boys stared at her blossoming beauty, and the indescribable pride he felt, as she walked down the aisle to marry his best friend.

The cheers, "It's a boy!" were as clear today as they were on that wonderful day.

He relived the insurmountable grief she had suffered when she lost the love of her life.

And now…he had lost her. The fractures that had torn his heart asunder grew with every memory.

After what seemed an eternity, he slowed the car to a crunching stop in the gravel outside his childhood home.

For a moment, he entertained the ludicrous hope that Sarah had played some cruel joke to get him to come for a visit. But he knew better. Sarah could never be so insensitive, especially when all she had to do was say, "We miss you; come see us."

He wasn't sure how long he sat there, avoiding the inevitable reality. At some point, he noticed the front door open and a familiar form emerge into the porch light that chased back the fading twilight.

Sarah walked slowly to the gate, and as she opened it, he marshaled the courage to get out of his car and trudge numbly into her sympathetic arms.

"Is she…?" he started to ask, glancing toward the house.

"No, Frank," she answered instinctively. "The funeral home has already taken her. Come on in; there's a little boy who needs his uncle."

As usual, Sarah knew just what to say. Her words tugged at him.

Frankie needs you. Quit feeling so sorry for yourself. Yeah, she was your sister, but she was his mother. You knew this was coming. It's your time now!

He passed through the gate, just as he had done a thousand times before, yet the sense of foreboding made it feel strange to him.

Only then did he notice the Carillos' gold Chrysler and Aggie's coffee-brown-and-black Edsel parked nearby. Though he appreciated the support of friends, he dreaded what waited beyond the screen door ahead.

He stopped for a moment and took a sweeping look at the yard he and his sister had played hide-and-seek in, the tree fort he had forbidden her, a mere girl, from playing in, and the tire swing he spun her and pushed her high in.

For a fleeting instant, he thought he saw his mother and father standing next to it, arms open and beckoning him.

Earlier, Sarah had asked Mrs. Bastion to call Aggie at the school and relay the news to her, asking her to personally bring Frankie home without telling him. None of them wanted Mr. Pike involved, and Aggie had no qualms about telling the prying lout to mind his own business, when he asked why she was leaving early, with a student in tow.

Though it broke her heart, she honored Sarah's request

not to tell Frankie what had happened. She understood and appreciated Sarah's sense of duty to her friend, plus she knew that Aubrey would be there to comfort his friend.

What she hadn't been prepared for was the soul-wrenching wail that emitted from the broken-hearted child. Though normally stalwart and controlled, she found herself retreating to a private corner to surrender to her own overwhelming flood of grief.

"Momma…Momma! Please come back! I'm scared!" Frankie begged, as the appropriately respectful mortuary attendants wheeled his mother's body out of her house for the last time.

"Momma, don't leave me. Please don't leave me," he pleaded, as he fell to his knees.

"She'll be okay," Aubrey comforted, kneeling down beside him. "She's with Jesus now."

"No!" Frankie screamed. "I hate Jesus! I don't want her to be with him. I want her to be with me. I don't want her to be an angel. I want her to be my momma. I want her…to…be…my…"

He fell over into a fetal position and sobbed uncontrollably.

Aubrey looked helplessly up at his mother, his own eyes flooding. Sarah reached down and helped her son up, leading him out of the room.

"He don't mean it, Maw; he don't mean it," he choked.

"Of course not, baby. He's just hurting real bad. Jesus understands," she said soothingly.

Katy quietly knelt beside Frankie's convulsing figure, gently stroking his ruffled hair, her own well of tears long since emptied, though her heart continued to break.

Eventually, Frankie fell into a quiet malaise, silently

sitting in his mother's favorite spot on the couch, clutching her afghan and staring at a blank television. Katy sat close by, but not so close as to crowd him.

The Carillo family arrived shortly afterwards, Kathleen uncharacteristically without makeup and visibly upset. Mike offered his condolences, as Maria shuffled over to where Frankie and Katy sat.

Tony couldn't bring himself to get out of the car, so Aubrey went to him and saw him in the backseat, crying. He quietly joined him, sitting silently on the seat beside him, until Tony had decided he could confront the grief with a brave face for Frankie. Ironically, when he went into the house, the sight of Miss Shockley comforted him, somewhat.

Aggie went to the two boys, stooped down, and drew them into a sympathetic hug.

When Frank finally walked through the door, with Sarah close behind and holding his hand, a pall of silence fell upon the room. All eyes turned sympathetically toward him, all except for Frankie's. Focusing entirely on his nephew and oblivious to everyone else, he hesitated briefly, then walked slowly over to him.

Your father was an orphan, and now you have become one. The tragedy of the thought seared through him.

"Frankie…Bambino?"

As if his uncle's voice was an alarm bell, Frankie jolted upright and turned to Frank. Without a word, he flew into his uncle's waiting arms.

"She's gone, Uncle Frank," his cracking voice barely audible.

"She's an angel now, isn't she? Just like you said," he whispered, burying his face into his uncle's neck.

"She always has been, Bambino; she always has been."

That night, Frankie insisted on sleeping in his mother's bed. He wanted to be close to her one last time, to smell the fragrance of her perfume once more and maybe even dream about her. Before getting into the bed, he offered up a short prayer to her.

"Momma…I miss you," he managed over his tears. "I know you're an angel now and that you're probably with my daddy."

Swallowing hard, he proceeded, "Please tell him hello for me, and Gramma and Grampa, too."

Remembering what he'd said earlier, he added, "And please tell Jesus that I didn't mean it when I said I hated him. I promise to take care of Uncle Frank, just like you asked me to…but it's gonna be hard without you."

As more tears flowed silently down his cheeks, he continued, "Momma, I'm not gonna say good-bye, 'cause you promised me that you would always be with me, right here," he said, patting his heart.

"Aubrey says that I'll see you when I go to Heaven. I hope you recognize me, 'cause I'll be all grown up then. I'm glad you're not hurting anymore. I love you, Momma," he finished.

He reverently pulled the bedcovers over him and laid his head onto the pillow, where his mother's spirit had departed this world. As he reached to turn the lamp off, he spotted the place where his tears had fallen on the sheet.

"I wish I were a Phoenix bird," he whispered; then, he closed his eyes, in hopes of seeing his mother just once more, if only in a dream.

A FINAL FAREWELL

It was a pleasant late spring day when Shelley was laid to rest between her parents and Jack in the family plot, forever surrounded by those she had loved in life. Her father had purchased the private plot, cordoned by a waist-high, intricately latticed wrought-iron fence, when she was just a baby.

Hers was only the most recent among the many markers and monuments in the aged cemetery, dating back to antebellum times, silently reciting the history of the town.

Sarah stood with her arm entwined in Frank's. Aubrey, Waylon, and her mother stood next to her.

Frankie held his uncle's hand, too numb to cry. Ben stood next to Frankie, a grizzled hand on the boy's shoulder.

Kathleen, Mike, Tony, and Maria stood on the opposite side of the casket.

Chet was in full-dress uniform at the foot of the open grave, with Katy on his arm, his parents and his sister next to him.

Aggie, Judge Walton, and Reverend Greene completed

the group within the private plot, while a dozen or so who had known her stood outside the fence, forming a solemn circle.

Reverend Greene delivered a heartfelt eulogy, recounting Shelley's gentle nature, his all-too-brief friendship with her, and the courage she had showed through her trials, stopping at times to force back his own emotions.

Afterwards, Frank waited with his nephew, as the last rose was placed on her bronze casket, shaking the hands of the mourners and nodding their gratitude, but not daring to speak, lest they break down once again.

As they started to walk away, Frank noticed that Ben had remained behind. To Frank, he looked as old as the many weathered statues that surrounded them…except that statues didn't shed tears and Ben's were freely tracing the wrinkles in his sorrow-wracked face.

Frankie walked up to the old man and wrapped his arms around his waist. Frank noticed that Ben was wavering slightly and rushed over to support him.

"She really is gone, isn't she? My Shelley girl is really gone," Ben whispered hoarsely, then collapsed into Frank's arms.

"You still have us," Frank assured. "And you always will."

"Will I?" Ben asked. "I mean…you and my boy here will be gone to Nashville, soon. I know you mean well, son, but he won't be showin' up at the shop on Fridays anymore.

"It's bad enough that my life will never be brightened up by my Shelley girl's smile again. Pretty soon, I won't even have him around to give me a reason to keep on goin'. I might just as well close up shop and rust away," he sniffed, in a rare moment of self-pity.

"I'm sorry, son. It's not your fault. I shouldn't be layin' this on you. I just don't know what I'm . . . " His words froze in his throat, as he fought to hold his composure.

"Ben," Frank started, "why don't you come to Nashville with us. I've got plenty of room, and we'd love to have you. You could still teach Frankie…."

"I appreciate that, Frank, I really do," Ben smiled sadly. "But that's not likely to happen. What would an old, small-town bastard like me do in the big city? You're gonna have enough on your hands, tryin' to raise a boy, as it is, without havin' an old man around to clog things up."

A thought began to form in Frank's mind.

"Ben, I do volunteer work with the fire crew down at the Fairgrounds Speedway on race nights. One of the tech inspectors just retired. I know some people in the front office, and when they hear about your racing background, I'm sure I could get you on there," he offered.

"Whoa son, slow down. I appreciate what you're tryin' to do, but I'm too old for that kind of stuff. Hell, I'm too old to be doin' what I'm doin', as it is," he protested.

"Thank you, son, but…no, I can't do that. Don't worry about me, Frank. Just do me the kindness of callin' from time to time and maybe even payin' a visit when you can."

"I'll call you, Uncle Ben…every Friday," Frankie vowed, his sad eyes turned up to the lonely man.

"I promise I will. And we'll come visit you to, a bunch of times, won't we, Uncle Frank?"

"I'm holdin' you to that, squirt," Ben smiled down at him, as he forced his bad knee to bend so he could kneel and face his surrogate grandson. "You're gonna have to;

I still got a half a box of Baby Ruth bars at the shop…and I hate peanuts.

"Dammit, boy, I'm sure gonna miss you!" His voice cracked, as he hugged Frankie.

"I promise, too," Frank added. "You know, Ben, Shelley and Frankie aren't the only ones who love you."

"Now godammit, why did you have to go and say somethin' like that?" Ben ranted, as he struggled back to his feet and yanked Frank into a surprisingly tight hug.

"I might not have said it, but I hope you know that I have always loved you," he whispered hoarsely. "If I'd ever had a son of my own, I hope he'd have turned out like you.

"Now you two get on outta here, so I can have a word with my Shelley girl," he ordered, nudging them toward the gateway.

"See you at the wake?" Frank asked.

"No, son, I wouldn't do too good there; too much heartbreak floatin' around," he replied. "I got a bottle of Jack and a heart full of memories. I'll have my own wake."

"Fair enough," Frank yielded. "I'll stop by before I leave town."

"Knock softly," he winked. "Now git."

He waved them off, turning back to Shelley's coffin.

Laying a lone, white rose atop all the red ones, he placed his hand on her casket.

"I miss you already, girl. This hole in the ground ain't nothin' compared to the hole in my heart.

"Shelley, I just wanted to thank you for, um…for lettin' me into your life and for sharin' Frankie with me."

"Now don't you worry about him; that brother of yours is a mighty fine man, and we both know how much he loves that boy. The boy calls me 'uncle,' but I sure wish it had been 'grandpa,' because you're the daughter I never had, but always wanted....but 'uncle' is good, too.

"Tell Jack, 'Howdy,' for me. Tell him his boy is learning his engines real well and that he knows which end of the screwdriver to use. Oh...and tell him that I fixed that bad valve on the number-four cylinder, so Frankie's gonna get a hot little buggy...when he gets old enough."

"I hope you like your cof . . . " He choked back an audible sob, hesitated, then continued, "I hope you like your coffin, darlin'. It's the nicest one I could find. Nothin's too good for my Shel . . . " He fought back a wave of emotion.

"Frank fussed at me for spending so much, but, hell, it's only money. Speakin' of which, I haven't told Frank yet, but I've been puttin' money back for a while, so Frankie can have a good college education, so don't worry about that, either.

"Well...I reckon I should be going now and leave you to the arms of the angels. I'll be visiting you from time to time. I sure hope God is as forgiving as your friend Sarah says he is, because I want nothin' more than see you and Jack again.

"She sure is one fine lady, that Sarah. You know, I think she carries a torch for Frank, and I might be a daft, old curmudgeon, but I honestly believe he's got special feelings for her, too. But who knows?

"Anyway...good-bye for now, Shelley. I love you, darlin'. Always have and always will...like the Good Book says, 'Even until the end of time.'"

Slowly, Ben left the fenced-in plot, reverently closing the rusting gate behind him.

"God...you'd better let me through those Pearly

Gates of yours; I ain't takin' no guff offa St. Pete, neither, because the pure hell of takin' Shelley and Jack away from me is payment enough for a lifetime of sins. No offense intended, Lord. I'm just lettin' you know what I'll be expectin'," he challenged, in a whispering growl.

Frankie and his uncle caught up with Sarah and the others at the limousine.

"Is Ben coming to the wake?" she asked.

"No, he's got other plans," Frank replied, as he opened the door for her and the boys.

"I asked him to move to Nashville with us, but he refused. I guess he's too rooted here. I don't know what he sees in this shabby, little town."

"He sees his life and all his memories here, Frank," Sarah answered gently.

"When he built that car with you and Jack, he was building a reason to be," she said. "This is where Shelley brought love to him in the form of her home-cooked meals, and it's where he treated Frankie like his own grandson. This is where he felt loved and needed. Just seeing the same sidewalks you walked on brings you back to him. You can't ask him to give all that up." Then, she squeezed his hand.

"This might be a shabby, little town, and he may grumble about it, but it's his shabby, little town."

"How do you know all that?" he asked, puzzled at her familiarity with Ben, since she had only recently met him.

"Shelley told me all about him. She really loved him," she answered.

"He seems like a nice man, if a bit crusty. I may visit him, myself. She said he likes spaghetti."

Her words penetrated him deeper than she knew.

"Sarah, if I asked you to…" he started.

"Shhh," she motioned, lightly pressing a finger to his lips. "Let's talk about this later, okay hun?"

"Sure thing, Dumplin'," he submitted.

He had planned to ask her to move away, as well, confident that she'd be eager to do so, leaving Haleyville and all its bad memories behind. But after hearing what she just said, he wasn't so sure she wanted to be rescued from what he had been so certain was her prison.

At first, Frank was uncomfortable having the wake at his house, feeling that it would only lend bad memories to his family home, but Sarah reminded him that death was a natural part of family life.

Unlike the fear, anger, and pain that had permeated her home, forever casting it as a place of misery fit only to be demolished, the McKinney/Albert home had been filled with love and caring.

Enshrining Shelley's memory there would give it intangible and immeasurable value to Frankie.

As usual, Frank couldn't argue with her logic.

Kathleen had insisted on managing the wake, along with several women from Shelley's church. Feeling that enough tears had been shed, she was determined that it would not be a morose and depressing affair.

She had spent enough time with Shelley to know her tastes in music and had assigned Maria as disk jockey. Finger foods, iced tea, and lemonade were laid out in the dining room and on the back porch.

Of course, she had a pitcher of her special "mother's punch" tucked away in the refrigerator.

A small gallery of pictures had been carefully arranged in the living room for all to celebrate, ranging from Shelley as a baby all the way to her as a beautiful bride.

Upon seeing the love that she had put into her efforts, Frank was glad that his sister would be remembered this way, in her own home.

"Uh, you do know that punch is loaded, don't you, Reverend?" Frank asked Neal Greene, in a secretive tone.

"I'm counting on it," the preacher replied, surprising Frank.

"This is a nice wake. Kathleen did well. I guess it's good that a Catholic planned it. I don't think Motown would be playing if a Baptist had."

"Yeah, she did a good job; bless her heart," Frank agreed.

"Good folks, the Carillos," Reverend Greene commented.

"Frank, I need to speak with you, and this is as good a time as any," he said unexpectedly.

Oh, no, here we go!

"With all due respect, Reverend, I'm not really in the mood for a . . . " Frank started.

"Frank," Neal interrupted, "give me a chance. I'm not going to preach, and it's not about that, anyway. That's a subject for some other time. Okay?"

Frank drew a deep breath, realizing that it would be monumentally rude to not let the man who had just delivered such a decidedly beautiful eulogy for his sister to at least have a few words.

"Sure, Reverend. I apologize for being so crass."

"Ah, forget it," Neal waved. "But please call me Neal. That's really my first name. 'Reverend' is just a title I get to hide behind while I scare the hell out of people over their immortal souls."

"It can be fun, ya know," he chuckled, getting a genuine laugh from Frank.

"Anyway, what I wanted to talk to you about was a conversation I had with your sister, not long ago. Actually, I have something to give you, too. It's out in my car.

"Come on," he nodded toward the back porch. "Let's sneak out the back."

"Whatever you say, Rev...er, Neal," Frank said. He was intrigued by the minister's casual attitude.

The men were able to slip out the back door without being noticed.

"This is a beautiful yard," Neal complimented. "The lawn is perfect."

"Yeah, it was my dad's pride and joy. Of course, I had to mow the damn thing every week, once I could reach the mower handles. But thanks."

Exiting the yard through the driveway gate to avoid the cluster of guests near the front walkway, Neal led him to a dark blue Mustang and opened the trunk lid.

"Mustang, huh...are you a Blue Oval Boy?" Frank asked.

"Well, not strictly speaking. I kinda like some the stuff Mopar has put out lately, but I really like my little pony.

"Are you a Bowtie Bubba?" Neal parried, nodding toward Frank's Corvette.

"Nah, not really, just a speed demon. Actually, Shelley's husband and I built a '32 Deuce coupe back in high school. Ben Ivey has it in his garage. I'll show it to you sometime."

"I'd like that. Shelley told me about it."

"She did? Hmm...so what else did she tell you?" Frank asked guardedly.

"That's why we're out here," Neal replied, retrieving a

large manila envelope from his trunk.

"Ya see, Frank, Shelley was more interested in her big brother's life than I think you realize. Shortly after you were promoted to assistant fire chief, she called your boss, a Chief Harrigan, I think," he said, getting a confused nod from Frank.

"Well, apparently, you've been keeping secrets," he taunted, but, seeing Frank's demeanor stiffen, he quickly added, "No, not that. Like I said, that's a discussion for a different day of your choosing."

"I'm talking about these," he said, pulling several newspaper clippings from the envelope.

"She wanted something special to show Frankie, so she asked your boss if there had been any announcements about your promotion in the papers.

"He told her that it wasn't just the promotion that had been reported on but that several of your commendations had made the press, as well.

"It seems that a lot of people owe a debt of gratitude, if not their very lives, to you personally for risking yours.

"The chief put her in touch with the Banner and the Tennessean, and they sent her these," he explained, handing the clippings to him.

"I'm proud to stand in the presence of a real, full-fledged hero. I try to save souls once a week, but you save lives on a daily basis." he exaggerated, offering his hand to Frank.

Shaking his hand, Frank blushed, as he scanned the clippings in his hand.

"It's, uh….it's my job, Neal. Any one of the other guys would have done the same thing. In fact they have," he protested.

"And, no doubt, they have clippings of their own, too.

Ya think they hide them?" Neal countered.

"Come on, Frank; don't be so modest. It's okay to feel good about something like this. Too much modesty is a sin...or at least it should be.

"Your sister wanted her son to be proud of you, just like she wanted him to be proud of his father. It was important to her. She asked me to show these to him when she was gone, because she knew you'd be too modest to. But I thought you should know first.

"I'm not interested in embarrassing you, Frank, but I agree with her. He's lost a lot, and so he needs a lot. I know it's probably going to be a bit uncomfortable for you, but putting you on a pedestal will mean the world to him."

"But..." Frank stammered.

"Frank...about that other thing," Neal said pointedly, "this will go a long way in helping him deal with that. Being a certified hero gives him something to counter the negative things he's going to hear about...well, the other thing. Your sister thought so, too."

In his heart, Frank knew Neal was right, and so was Shelley. But he was still not comfortable with what he felt was undue adulation for just doing his job.

Reading his thoughts, Neal added, "Consider the people whose lives you saved. It was pretty significant to them. Do you think it's fair to them to call it just another day at the office?

"So what do you think? Does Frankie have the right to adore his uncle even more than he already does? Or should he regard you as just another guy...with issues?" Neal lobbed at Frank.

"Now that's dirty pool," Frank growled defensively.

"Call it what you want, but your sister was thinking

about her son…your nephew…and you. I happen to agree," Neal replied, taking the clippings from Frank and slipping them back into the envelope.

"How 'bout you? Are you up to being the center of that boy's universe? You may not have asked for it, but there it is. This is something you can't move to another city to get away from, Frank."

"Aren't you supposed to comfort people through hard times?" Frank asked accusingly.

"Well, that is the myth, but I think my duty lies more in telling the truth. Or would you rather I blow smoke up your skirt just to make you feel all warm and fuzzy?"

"No, I suppose not," Frank capitulated. "So when do you plan on building this pedestal?"

"Well, Sarah seems to think that sooner is better than later," Neal answered cryptically.

"So Sarah knows, too, huh?"

"Well, of course she does, Frank. She was Shelley's best friend and confidante. But I will say that she was not the least bit surprised; in fact, she acted as though it was to be expected from you. She, ah…well, let's just say that she thinks very highly of you, very highly."

"What do you suppose they're talking about?" Kathleen asked, nodding toward the two men, as she joined Sarah, Beatrice, and Aggie in the front porch.

"Well, if I know the good reverend, he's probably throwing a bit of cold water in Frank's face, God love him," Sarah replied.

"I hope he's not too rough on him," Aggie added. "Frank never was good at being put on the spot, as I recall."

"Oh, I wouldn't worry too much. The reverend's hammer is covered in velvet," Sarah assured. "He knows what he's doing."

Meanwhile, Frankie had retreated to the tree fort, along with Aubrey and Tony. Too many people were expressing their sorrow for his loss, not realizing that every well-intended time they did so, it only served to remind him of the devastation he felt to his very core. His ability to shed tears had temporarily faded, but his ability to feel the pain had not.

The three boys sat in silence, Aubrey and Tony instinctively understanding his need for their presence but not for their words.

Finally, after a seemingly interminable silence, Frankie said, "She was always afraid we'd fall out and break our necks."

"Or at least put an eye out," Tony added, getting a welcome burst of laughter from the other two.

With that, each one began to recount happy stories about his mother and lavish praises for the wonderful things she did for them, or baked for them, especially Aubrey.

"Ya know, I think maybe 'Saint Shelley' fits better than 'Aunt Shelley,'" Tony offered.

"Yeah, Tony. I think maybe your right," Aubrey agreed. "She sure was an angel in real life."

"I sure was lucky, wasn't I?" Frankie postulated.

"Yeah, ya were. We all were," Aubrey offered.

Again, silence fell upon the tree fort, but it was a happier silence than before, as the three boys remembered her in their own way.

"That's a damn fine boy you raised, babe," Jack said to Shelley, as they sat next to each other on the broad branch across from the rickety tree fort, watching the boys.

"I wish I could have been there," he lamented.

"You were, Jack, every day," she acknowledged, her head on his shoulder. "You were."

Things moved rapidly over the next few days. Chet returned to Camp Lejeune to finalize his discharge, and Katy returned to Kentucky with Betty and Keith to finalize her divorce.

Leaving Sarah and the boys was difficult for her, but she vowed to return as soon as he could.

Frankie and Aubrey were heartbroken at her departure and didn't wash the lipstick she left on their cheeks for days afterwards.

"Thank you for takin' care of my momma," Frankie told her.

"Thank you for letting me, sweetheart," she replied. "She was a really nice, wonderful lady, and I know that she loved you so much."

"Auntie," she said, taking Sarah's hands in hers, "I don't have the words to tell you how grateful I am for you and all the love you've shown me. I love you; I really do. And I mean it when I say that I'll be seeing you again, soon, I hope."

"I don't doubt that, darlin' girl. In fact, if I know that nephew of mine, I'm sure we'll be seeing each other quite a bit. He's a good boy. He has his daddy's heart, you know."

"God, I hope so. Papa Keith is such a doll."

"Yes, he is. Betty sure got lucky with that one."

"She sure did," Katy agreed, wholeheartedly.

"But then, so did you," Sarah added.

"Maybe someday, Auntie, God will bring a good man into your life."

"That's okay, sweetie. I already have two good men in my life. I'm getting a little long in the tooth to hope for anything more."

"Don't say that, Auntie. You're not old."

"No…just worn out and damaged," she lamented with a grin.

"Truth is, I kinda like being free from the demands of a man."

And the beatings…and the derision…and the neglect.

"I still have faith that someone good will come your way," Katy insisted.

"Faith? So you were listening after all, huh? " Sarah teased. "You take care of yourself, baby. And keep that big lug in line for me, okay?"

"Oh, I will," Katy promised.

Frank signed the necessary paperwork concerning custody of Frankie, and Sarah began organizing things for their pending move to Nashville, something she dreaded deeply.

He asked her to take care of Frankie, while he returned home to prepare a room for him and made arrangements with his soon-to-be new school. She gladly accepted, loath to let Frankie go at all, especially to a big city where he had no friends to comfort him and soften the blow.

She also dreaded the effect it would surely have on Aubrey.

Frank had asked her to move to Nashville with them, but, like Ben, she declined for reasons she had already intimated to him in the limousine, adding that her mother was moving back to Haleyville, as well.

He offered to sign the house over to her, claiming that he had neither use for it nor desire to live in it. But she refused that, as well, saying that even if he didn't want it, Frankie might, someday.

He was bewildered that she and Ben would choose to stay in a town that had only mistreated them. She had explained to him that pain, like anger, resides in the heart, not on a map. Even though the reminders were still there, it was up to one's spirit to triumph over them and denude them of their power to hurt. Running away only gave them life.

The last part had cut him deeply, and he wasn't sure whether she had intended to do so or not. But he was sure that, whatever her intents, they were not malicious. The woman didn't have a mean bone in her body.

The drive home was a blur of introspection. Had he run away with his tail tucked between his legs? Had he handed a victory to the few poisoned minds that had condemned him? Had he made it easier for them to cast their hateful aspersions on his family? By the time he got home, he felt ashamed of himself for being such a coward.

Dammit, Sarah. Why do you always have to be so right?

CHARLIE'S REVELATION

"Good morning, sunshine," Frank said to Charlie, as he walked into the dinette. "It's a beautiful day out there."

"Morning," Charlie replied in a measured tone. "Yes, it is nice."

"What's the matter?" Frank asked, noticing his mood. "Is something wrong?"

"I need to talk with you," Charlie said, placing the plate of bacon and eggs in front of Frank.

"Uh-oh, that doesn't sound good. What's up?"

Charlie could be moody at times, but this felt different.

"You know I love you, Frank, but I've been doing some soul searching lately, and I think it's best if we go our separate ways." He made his announcement unexpectedly, and did so quickly, lest he not be able to make it at all.

"What?" Frank responded, stunned at the announcement. "Why do..."

Charlie interrupted, holding his hand up, "The truth is...I don't think you're committed to this relationship, or even this lifestyle, for that matter."

"What the hell, Charlie?" Frank protested, pushing

his breakfast aside.

"Please Frank…this is hard for me to say, so just hear me out," he implored, pausing to gather his emotions.

"The time I've spent with you has been wonderful. You've been good to me, but these last few months have given me pause to reflect on our relationship, and it hurts me to say this, but I don't think your heart is really in it.

"Our relationship has been rather one-sided. Even going back to when we met. I came onto you, and when you didn't reject me, I was ecstatic. You're a gorgeous man and a fireman, to boot…a gay man's dream.

"And ever since, I've tried to draw you out of your self-imposed closet. But I know now that you were never in the closet I thought you were in.

"Mind you, I wasn't trying to complete your conversion. Being gay isn't something you can convert to or from; it's just something you either are or are not.

"I thought I was helping you to fully accept what can be terribly hard to deal with. But it has finally sunk in.

"You live in a different closet."

"What do you mean, Charlie? You're really confusing me."

"Confused is a good description, because you are confused, Frank. But you're confused about being straight, not gay. I mean, nothing about you says 'gay.' Not your wardrobe, not your taste in music, not your hobbies or other interests."

"Aren't you stereotyping, Charlie?" he asked, feeling a bit perturbed.

"Yes, I am. But stereotypes exist for a reason, Frank. There's always some element of truth in them.

"At first, I thought it was interesting, even quaint, that you were so nonobvious. But, after a while, it began to get old. Drag queens annoy you, and you hate going to the clubs. Whenever we have friends over, you just can't relax.

"You want another stereotype? When I first moved in, there were no paintings on the walls. Your furniture was mismatched and minimal, at best. Car magazines were all you had on that tacky, old coffee table, and your dirty uniforms were scattered all over the place. Just look around you, I have done all of this," he said, sweeping his arm toward the tastefully decorated living room, "and I don't think you even appreciate it."

"That's not true. I do appreciate it. It's really nice," Frank countered.

"'Really nice'? Do you hear yourself? That's how a straight man would talk," Charlie railed.

"You are the straightest gay man I've ever known. You're more comfortable with your straight self than you've ever been with your supposedly gay self. You've never once shown that you even have a feminine side."

"Oh? What should I do? Wear a dress?" Frank spat sarcastically.

"Don't be glib with me, Frank McKinney," Charlie warned. "You know what I mean."

Raising his hand again to ward off another protest, he continued, "I've seen a change in you, especially since you've reconnected with your friend, Sarah."

Frank sat defensively up in his chair.

"Don't get me wrong; I'm sure she's a wonderful person, and I've seen how much she has helped you get through these hard times. And that's the point.

"You've been leaning on her far more than you ever leaned on me, and yes, I am jealous; I don't like being replaced. But I am also able to see what you don't seem to be able to."

"What's that?" Frank asked curtly.

"That you're in love with her."

"What? Come on, Charlie, that's ridiculous."

"Is it? When you talk to her on the phone you call her "Dumplin'". You don't have a pet name for me though, do you?"

"Charlie, that's something that I…" he started to explain, but, seeing Charlie's expression, he stopped.

"No matter how hard I have tried, I have never been able to reach you the way she can so easily, and it hurts me, Frank.

"You didn't even ask me to go to the funeral with you. I can understand why, and I would have declined if you had, for your sake, but you didn't give me the chance. You know I love you, but I don't know that you love me."

"Aw, come on, Charlie. That's not fair."

"See what I mean? Even now you can't say it. Frank, I'm going to ask you a question I probably should have asked a long time ago…have you ever even been with a woman. Did you and Sarah ever…you know, have sex?" he asked uncomfortably, not sure he really wanted to hear the answer.

"That's none of your business," Frank protested sternly, an embarrassing anger emerging.

"I take that as a 'no' on both counts," he retorted, almost relieved.

Frank sat in silence. Charlie had struck a nerve.

"Frank, how do you know for sure that you're really gay? Or you can put it this way: how do you know you're not straight if you've never even been with a woman?

"I have been and I didn't like it. It was awkward and uncomfortable. That's how I can be positive that I prefer men. But you can't be.

"I never knew about your friend Robby until I over-heard you talking to her about it. I had to ask you to tell me about it, and when you did, it got me to thinking. And what I think is that you have been fooling yourself all these years out of a sense of guilt over what happened to him. I think you confused missing him with loving him. I'm sure he was a sweet boy who really was in love with you but who just couldn't take the rejection or the humiliation, and I think you've been trying to make it up to him ever since. In fifteen years, you've had what… three boyfriends, including me?

"I think that losing a male friend that you were so close to, so comfortable with, somehow convinced you that you could only feel that way with other males.

"You told me that you and Sarah dated soon after he died, 'comfort dates,' you called them. But I think it was too soon after his death, and all the emotions you couldn't let out made you afraid that if you got close to her, something might happen to her, as well. So you never gave her a chance to help you get your head on straight."

"Gee, Charlie, I thought you were an accountant, not a psychiatrist. You seem to have me all figured out," Frank said sourly.

"No, Frank, I don't have you figured out. It's just what I think," Charlie fired back angrily. "But maybe you do need therapy."

Frank bristled at the comment, but chose not to say something that he might regret. Besides, some of what Charlie was saying was beginning to make sense.

Reaching over to the kitchen counter, Charlie retrieved the manila envelope that contained the newspaper clippings Neal had given Frank and tossed it onto the table in front of Frank.

"You know what else I think?" he asked. "I think you have a death wish, too. You could have been killed in any one of these cases, and you nearly were killed in at least three of them.

"Frank, you can't bring Robby back by killing yourself, and you can't punish yourself for someone else's choices. That is just plain stupid….and goddamn selfish, too.

"Think about this…what if you had been killed? Where would your nephew be, now?"

"Now that's hitting below the belt, Charlie."

"No, Frank, it's hitting the bull's-eye. As much as it hurts me to say this, I just can't waste anymore of my heart trying to save you from yourself. It seems that Sarah is far better equip…" a sudden jolt of emotion caused him to choke, "…far better equipped for that rescue mission than me.

"So do yourself a favor, Frank. Do me a favor. Go to her and let her help you figure yourself out, and if by some miracle I'm wrong about this….well, I'll always love you. But for now, I have to say good-bye." Charlie finished speaking and turned away, walking quickly down the hallway to the bedroom.

Frank sat in stunned silence. Charlie had not merely hit a few nerves…he had pounded them into ground meat. A cynical inner voice began berating and heckling him.

You know he's right, don't you? You are some kind of idiot, Frank. Did you really think that pretending would help you with your phony martyrdom? Robby was honest; you're a fake. You dishonor and mock his memory. Just how many lives do you have to mess with before you pull your head out of your ass and face what you really are?

Hey, buddy. I have an idea that's right up your alley. Why don't you run away from this, too? You can always pawn Frankie off on someone else...like Sarah. I'm sure she'd just love another shot to the heart from you. What a cowardly prick you've been.

How many people have carried your selfish little lie to their graves? Your parents? Jack? Your trusting sister?

Say...why don't you bring Frankie into this mess you call a life. Maybe he'll pretend to be something he's not, just like you, and mess his own life up, too.

You disgust me.

Frank laid his head back and stared at the ceiling, as tears began to roll down the sides of his face.

I hate me.

The voice mocked, *You should!*

After a while, he heard Charlie walking by. Looking up, he saw the suitcase that proved his now ex-lover was serious.

He got up from his chair and walked toward him. Intending to tell him good-bye, he opened his arms.

But Charlie waved him off and instead offered his hand, as though he were simply completing a business transaction, saying, "I'd rather not have a good-bye to remember, so let's just shake on it and part like men... straight men...so you'll be more comfortable with it," he jabbed. "I'll make arrangements to get the rest of my stuff later."

Frank took his hand, saying "Charlie, can't we...."

"No, Frank, we can't," he said, with heartbreaking finality.

After Charlie had gone, Frank lay on the couch... Charlie's couch...thinking about what had just happened.

He felt miserable. Instinctively, he knew that Charlie was probably right. As he lay there, he began to feel the urge to call Sarah.

I'll bet Sarah has the answer...maybe she is the answer. I should call her.

No, I need to see her and talk to her in person.

Then it dawned on him. The thought of seeing her, touching her, and hearing her voice made him feel better. He stood up, shook off his malaise, and went to his room to pack an overnight bag.

I need you, Sarah, now more than ever. I think maybe I do love you. I've got to know for sure.

Thirty minutes later he was driving down the highway, carefully keeping his speed under control. He didn't need another encounter with the state troopers to distract him from his mission, a mission to save his sanity, his heart, and maybe even his life.

By the time he had left the interstate for the rambling country roads that led to Haleyville, he had mulled through his feelings and replayed Charlie's blistering admonitions several times over.

Was it possible that he had squandered so much time and emotion and had hurt those closest to him for no good reason?

Had he shamed his parents and embarrassed his friends over his own misguided guilt?

Had he hidden out in a world he really didn't belong in, just to avoid his own flaws?

Had his selfishness condemned Sarah to all those years of brutality and neglect?

Thunderstruck by the thought, he suddenly wondered if seeing her was such a good idea. Would he have the courage to face her? Did he have the right to? Would his long overdue apology hurt her or anger her? His stomach knotted up at the thought that maybe, once again, he was only seeking to make himself feel better.

The elation he had first felt at seeing her and telling her everything he wanted to tell her suddenly became a fear that she would reject him and his unforgivably late apology.

Would he lose his dearest friend?

Only Sarah held the answers to his questions. As always, it was going to have to be her strength that would get him past the crashing waves that threatened to smash his soul against the jagged rocks of emotion he had blundered upon.

For better or for worse, he really needed her now.

For better or for worse? How ironic!

SARAH'S REDEMPTION

Sarah was surprised to hear the familiar rumble of Frank's Corvette through the screen door, as he pulled up. He hadn't called as he normally did, causing her some concern. She hoped that nothing was amiss, as she cleared the lunchtime dishes from the kitchen table.

Aubrey and Frankie had gone to Lake Owen with Tony and his father, and they would be gone for several hours, leaving her alone in the house with a rare period of peace and quiet. Having Frank show up unexpectedly was a pleasant surprise. Time alone with her best friend was rare, and she was glad for it.

"Hi, Dumplin'," he called from the front walkway. "How's my favorite girl?"

Frank had always made her feel special, and now that she was free to bask in the feeling, she relished every moment of it.

"I'm doing wonderful...now," she returned. "What brings you back home so soon?"

He had returned to Nashville only four days ago, after helping her get various household affairs in order for the pending move.

Her reference to "home" was not lost on him.

"I, ah…I just had to see you, Sarah," he answered, with an unexpected urgency in his voice, not using his pet name for her.

"What's wrong, sweetie?" she asked, sensing that something was indeed amiss.

"Is there any of Kathleen's special punch left over? I could really use a stiff drink, right about now," he replied, raising her concern even higher.

"No, hon, but I do have some lemonade, and that bottle of Jack Daniels is still collecting dust in the cupboard."

"Good enough," he said, as he reached to embrace her.

As soon as he touched her, an intense tingle he had not previously noticed swept over him, causing him to flinch ever so slightly.

Sarah noticed his reaction and said, "Something's up Frank. You're behaving mighty strangely. Please tell me what's wrong; you're worrying me."

"Oh, trust me, Dumplin'; that is exactly what I had in mind, but first…that bottle?"

After he had poured himself a potent Jack and lemonade, they settled onto the couch, facing each other.

"Okay, Frank, the suspense is killing me," she pleaded.

"Well, I guess the best thing to do is dive right in, so here goes," he started.

"Charlie and I are no more. He broke up with me this morning."

"Oh, Frank. I'm so sorry," she sympathized, though a secret part of her felt guiltily pleased.

"Don't be, Dumplin'; I think maybe it's for the best."

"But why?" she asked. "I thought you two were happy together."

"I thought so, too, but apparently not," he said, rising

to his feet and wandering to the lace-curtained window that overlooked the side yard.

"He, ah... he seems to think that I'm not, uh...not committed to the relationship...not really...gay."

Somehow, saying it out loud suddenly made it feel more like the truth.

"What?" she asked. "Now that just doesn't make sense. Why would he say something so crazy?" She joined him at the window.

"Well, he admitted to being jealous of, um...of you, as a matter of fact," he said, taking a long sip from his drink.

"Me? Why in the world would he be jealous of me?"

The secret part of her felt a sense of satisfaction.

"Well...it's like this..."

He proceeded to recount what Charlie had said, in nearly every detail, except the part about him being in love with her. He wasn't yet sure that he should reveal what he had begun to believe.

She shifted uncomfortably, when he mentioned the part about never having been with a woman. He tactfully left out Charlie's question about the two of them, not wanting to embarrass her...or himself.

"I'm so sorry Frank. I didn't mean to come between you two," she apologized, cupping his cheek in her hand. "I didn't know."

"Of course, you didn't, Dumplin," he said, and placed his hand over hers and brought it around to kiss her palm.

"How could you have known?"

Then, to his own surprise, he drew her into an embrace that felt more loving and intimate than ever before, pressing his body against hers and feeling the tingling grow to a crescendo, fueling a sudden overwhelming desire for her.

She freely fell into his arms and laid her head on his chest, as though it were the most natural thing in the world for her to do. She wrapped her arms around him and passionately returned his embrace. A warmth and a need that she had never felt before began to grow like a wildfire.

In a voice that felt strangely foreign, yet desperately familiar, and with a sincere tenderness he could not remember having ever experienced, he said, "I love you Sarah."

"I love you, too, Frank," she replied, after a stunned moment, wonderfully confused and not knowing what else to say.

"No," he said pulling back slightly, her face inches from his. "I don't think you understand, I mean…I love you…Sarah. As in, I am in love with you."

"Frank…you don't…I mean, you're not…"

Her words were cut short, as his lips met hers, surprising her and sending an electric excitement through her entire body. For a split second, she felt she should pull away, but the heat of his lips against hers felt so right, overwhelming her with a desire she had kept buried since high school.

She returned his kiss as passionately as any woman had ever kissed any man.

Feeling her response ignited a desire that had never revealed itself in all his adult life. Holding her and kissing her felt as though it was the only thing in life worth living for. All the years of doubt and self-loathing fell away like a grey mist before a brilliant sun.

Time lost all meaning, as they reveled in the final realization of a passion they both had needlessly buried all those long, torturous years ago.

When at last they parted their kiss, her first thoughts were to say, *"We shouldn't be doing this"* or, *"This is a mistake."* But those were words her heart would not let her say.

Instead, she stood gazing into the warm, green eyes that had stolen her heart long ago and now held her captive.

In a quivering voice, she softly cooed, "I love you, Frank. I always have."

"Charlie said he thought I was in love with you," he whispered. "I thought it might be possible, but, until this very minute, I didn't realize just how true it is."

"My God, Sarah. Why was I such a selfish fool? All this time I could have had you for my own. I could have spared you..."

"Shh...be still, my love. We both have suffered our choices, but that only makes this moment that much sweeter," she assured him tenderly.

"You said he asked how you could be sure. Let me help you to answer that question," she offered. Gently pushing away from him, she took his hand in hers and began to lead him toward the stairs.

"Sarah, I, ah...don't know how...."

Pressing a soft finger to his lips, she said, "And I don't know how it feels to make love to a man who truly loves me and cares for me. I think we are both long overdue. Don't you?"

Frank found himself deliriously ascending the stairs in the hands of his own special angel.

Sarah felt as though a wonderfully sweet force was guiding her, as she closed the bedroom door behind them.

Later that evening, Frankie noticed a strange, giddy

behavior in his uncle, and Aubrey saw a lightness of being in his mother that made him wonder what miracle had taken place.

He had never heard her hum to herself, as she prepared dinner, and the smile that fixed itself on her face, especially in her eyes, seemed to have chased years from her face, revealing a beauty he had never noticed before.

The boys cast confused glances at each other over dinner.

"What the heck is goin' on?" Aubrey wondered out loud, as they sat on the front porch steps, eating peach cobbler.

"You saw it too, huh? Uncle Frank is acting really weird."

"Uncle Frank? I was talkin' about Maw. She ain't never been that happy. I ain't never heard her hum like that before," he mused. "I don't know what it is, but, to tell ya the truth, I hope it stays."

"Yeah, me, too. Did you see how they kept smilin' at each other? It's almost like they..." A sudden thought occurred to him, "Aw, man! You don't suppose they like each other, do ya?"

"Well, of course, they like each other. They've been friends since high school," Aubrey answered, without a clue.

"No, you big dummy," Frankie chided. "I mean 'like' each other, you know, like boyfriend and girlfriend."

"Aw come on, man. That's just goofy. Uncle Frank's a gay guy, and Maw's a married..." A light switch flipped on in his head, as he went on, "No, she ain't a married woman no more, is she?"

"Nope. And you've seen the way they talk to each other whenever Uncle Frank is here," Frankie surmised.

"Ya think maybe a guy can get un-gay?"

"I dunno. Maybe."

"I think maybe he can," a voice behind them said, startling them both.

Snapping their heads around, they looked up to see Uncle Frank standing behind the screen door.

"Or maybe a guy can realize that he wasn't really a gay guy to begin with," Uncle Frank speculated.

He had intended to come and share the firefly show with them, but, hearing their conversation, he decided that it was a good opportunity to be honest and open with them. There had already been enough secrets in his life.

"You're right Bambino. We do 'like' each other," he said, as he opened the door. "In fact, I hope it's all right with you Aub…I'm in love with your mother, and I know now that I always have been."

Aubrey's brow furrowed in thought; then, in the same manner a father might asked his daughter's suitor, he asked, "Does she love you back?"

"Yes, baby boy, I do," Sarah's voice answered from behind Uncle Frank.

She stepped through the door and wrapped her arms around Frank, resting her head against his shoulder.

"Is that okay, baby? It's really important to me that you approve."

Aubrey glanced down for a moment, causing Sarah a flash of consternation.

Then he cocked his head up at her and said, "Yeah, Maw, it's okay."

Rising to his feet, he moved to her and said, "In fact, I'm real glad about it. I ain't never seen you so happy, so yeah, it's okay with me. An' I'll bet Waylon will be just as happy about it, too."

"How about you Frankie?" Uncle Frank asked.

"So you're not really gay? And you really do love Aunt Sarah?" he queried, following Aubrey and rising to his feet.

"Yes, I do love her, and no, I'm not gay…anymore. Apparently, I never really was. Trust me, buddy. It's as surprising to me as it is to you, but that's what my heart tells me. I'm just sorry it didn't tell that me a long time ago."

"Momma would like this," Frankie said, wrapping his arms around his uncle's waist. "Are ya'll gonna get married?"

"Well, we haven't got that far yet, but…" Frank trailed off, leaving the distinct possibility open.

"I hope so," Aubrey added, joining in on the hug.

RIGHT BACK WHERE
I STARTED FROM

"I'll be back as soon as I can, Dumplin'," Frank promised, as he held her close in the open gateway, reluctant to let her go. The previous day had been such a delightful epiphany that he hated to leave her for even a minute, much less a week.

"It might be a few days, though," he said. "I hope Chief Harrigan doesn't get too mad. This is short notice. He really went to bat for me with the promotion and all. But he's a great guy, so…" He tossed his duffle into the passenger's seat.

"I'm sure he'll understand," Sarah reassured him. "Are you sure you want to do this?"

"Sarah, it's taken me half a lifetime to wake up to how much I love you and need you. I don't care if I have to work in Mike's mattress plant. I'm not going to be away from you anymore. So, yes, I am absolutely positive about this. Are you sure?"

"Oh, get out of here," she replied, slapping him playfully on the shoulder. "Am I sure? Hmph! You just drive carefully, and come back soon."

"Believe me…nothing can keep me away, Dumplin'. Call me if you need to…or if you just want to," he smiled.

A week later, Frank knocked on the door of the Haleyville Volunteer Fire Brigade Chief's office.

"Enter," Chief Shelby Stoner boomed out.

Frank opened the creaking door and stepped into a veritable museum of firefighting. Antique brass hose nozzles served as paper weights, bookends, and a desk lamp. Tattered leather helmets with polished brass badges and scorched overcoats hung on pegs scattered around the room.

Models of horse-drawn engines and early antique gas-powered engines graced the shelves that made up two of the walls. On a third wall, pictures of firemen dating from recently all the way back to the Reconstruction covered every available space.

In the middle of the dusty room, a huge, ornate oak desk was covered with various personal mementos and pictures, guarded by a life-sized, hand-painted ceramic Dalmatian sitting beside it.

Behind the imposing desk sat a weathered, but equally imposing, man.

"I've been expecting you," he said, as he leaned back in his worn leather throne.

"You have?" Frank asked, completely taken by surprise.

"You are Frank McKinney, aren't you?" the chief asked.

"Uh, yes, I am. How did you know?"

"Have a seat, son," Shelby offered, motioning to a comfortable-looking armchair placed at an angle to the desk.

"Coffee?"

"No thanks," Frank declined.

"Oh, bullshit," the chief chuckled back.

"I've never met a fireman in my life that didn't drink the stuff like it was going out of style. Besides, it's my own secret brew. I got it from a hard-assed, old bosun's mate, back when I was a fightin' fires on carriers in the Pacific," he bragged, pointing to a picture of a group of sailors posing beside a dive bomber, some with hoses draped over their shoulders.

"A little chicory mixed in with a dash of salt," he said, as he poured a cup for Frank, not bothering to ask if he wanted cream or sugar, because real men don't use that sissy stuff.

Frank accepted the cup and took a sip of the bitter brew, feigning his approval.

"So you're wondering how I know who you are, eh?" Shelby started. "Well, son, it seems you have a bit of a fan club."

"A fan club?" Frank replied, thoroughly perplexed.

"Yep, a fan club," the chief parried.

"Starting with that cranky old bastard, Ben Ivey."

"He does all our mechanical maintenance. The other day he came by and started ridin' my ass to get a 'real' fireman for a change and not just these 'half-assed glory monkeys,' as he so quaintly refers to my volunteers."

Frank smiled. *That would be Ben, all right.*

"He followed that with, 'Someone like Frank McKinney.'

"And then there's Reverend Greene," Shelby said. "A real nice man. Not your usual stuffed-shirt preacher. He was a helluva lot more civilized about singing your praises. He showed me these." Shelby opened the drawer and pulled out what was rapidly becoming the ubiquitous newspaper clippings Frank had seen in so many unexpected places.

"You got a pair of brass balls hangin', son. At least that's what Chief Harrigan thinks."

"Chief Harrigan?"

"Yes, Chief Harrigan. You know, your old boss," Shelby taunted.

"He called yesterday. A polite fella...a real professional...at least until he found out that I was a fellow swabby. Then he got real about it and called me a sonuvabitch for stealin' his best man. I like him."

"That is what you're here for isn't it...to sign on with us?"

"Well...I did come to ask if you had any openings," Frank answered, overwhelmed by what he was hearing.

"No, I don't have any 'openings.' I have a 'need,'" the chief countered gruffly, leaning forward ominously. "I want to retire, and I need someone whose ass is worthy of this chair. Are you that man?"

"I...don't know. I hadn't anticipated..." Frank stammered.

"Quit stuttering, boy," Shelby barked brusquely. "And you had better learn to anticipate. That's part of the job. I run a crew of well-trained, qualified volunteers, with a few rookies mixed in.

"But no professionals...and not one with anywhere near your training and experience. It's a bit different than the fun you had in the big city," the chief understated, "and you'll have to get the hang of rural firefighting.

"A barn fire is a mean sonuvabitch, and panicked animals can be downright dangerous. And then there's the public relations part. We ride in several parades a year. You gotta answer the same stupid questions a hundred times and pose for pictures with bratty kids who think your engine is a playground. Think you can handle it?"

Frank was taken aback by the coarseness of the chief and the unexpected offer he was being given. He was still trying to figure out how it all had come together.

"Well?" the chief demanded.

"Chief, I, uh . . . . " He hesitated.

Then Sarah came to mind. Her courage and strength and her unhesitating willingness to face life's challenges inspired him.

"Yes, Chief, I can. When do I start?"

"That's what I wanted to hear, son," Shelby said with satisfaction, leaning back in his chair again.

"How's next Monday sound? Here, take this down to McCarthy's Tailor Shop and get outfitted," he said, handing Frank a handwritten purchased order for his uniforms.

"Welcome aboard, Lil' Chief," he said, rising to his feet and offering his hand to Frank.

"Me and the boys have a monthly meeting down at Gerty's Diner every first Saturday. Seven p.m. sharp. Damn good fried chicken and plenty of beer. It's all free. The town's way of saying thanks. See ya there.

"Oh…one more thing before you go," Shelby hesitated; then he asked, "Those rumors I've heard about you being gay. Are they true?"

Surprisingly, Frank wasn't thrown by the question.

"The truth is…if you'd asked me two weeks ago, I would have answered 'yes.' But thanks to the love of a good woman, I've discovered that I have been fooling myself; so, no, I'm not gay. Not anymore."

Chief Stoner looked hard at Frank for a few long seconds, then said, "Must be one helluva woman. I'm sure there's a good story behind that, maybe someday we'll talk about it over a bottle or two, but that's a damned honest answer, and that's all I wanted. I really don't give a shit one way or the other. It's your business. I just don't like secrets....or liars. That's good enough for me. Consider the matter closed."

"I just had the weirdest interview I've ever had," Frank said, as he entered the living room where Sarah sat watching *The Edge of Night*.

"Oh? What do mean?" she said, rising from the couch to meet him.

"I just met with Chief Stoner. What a salty old dog! He knew who I was before I even got there. It seems ol' Ben and Reverend Greene paid him a visit, campaigning on my behalf. Even Chief Harrigan called to sing my praises."

"Oh...well . . . ," Sarah began sheepishly. "I have to plead guilty on two of those counts."

"Really? Why is that?" he asked, an accusing brow cocked at her.

"Well, I told Reverend Greene that you were moving back here and jokingly mentioned what you said about the mattress factory," she explained, as she moved in baby steps toward him, like a contrite school girl, batting her eyes for him.

"He said it would be a ridiculous waste of talent and resources for you to do that. I guess he felt like he owed it to you to speak to the chief."

"And Ben?" Frank inquired, doing his best not to give into her demure cuteness.

"Oh, now, Frankie had a hand in that," she betrayed.

"When he heard that you were going to move down here instead of taking him to Nashville, he begged me to take him to see Ben.

"That old man is nuts about you, ya know. He got so choked up, when Frankie told him, that all he could was dance a little jig and keep thanking Jesus. He hugged me so tight I thought he was going to crack my ribs. He really is a sweetheart of a man. I can see why you love him so much. I had nothing to do with Chief Harrigan, though. Maybe he has a higher opinion of you than you know."

"What am I gonna do with you, girl?" Frank asked, pulling her into his arms.

"Well, you could start with a kiss; then we can see what that leads to," she teased, her school-girl demeanor suddenly becoming deliciously seductive.

"A very worthy suggestion, my love," Frank replied, gladly taking her up on it.

EPILOGUE

Chet drove his parent's station wagon past the corner bar in the industrial part of town. The flickering neon sign over the doorway proclaimed it as "Slim's Tavern."

This was the place. Parked across the street from the dingy bar was the bright orange Camaro with the black Playboy Bunny emblazoned on the sail panel behind the door window, just as Katy had described it.

So Stevie boy thinks he's a lady's man, eh? What a maggot!

Parking the wagon half a block away, he exited the car and marched purposely toward the bar, steeling himself for one final combat mission.

It was nearly closing time, and the street shimmered with water from an earlier summer shower. Aside from his car and the Camaro, only three or four other cars sat scattered up and down the block.

Good. No witnesses.

Glancing through the half-curtained window, he saw four people inside, the bartender and three young men laughing and drinking at a corner table.

One marine, three drunks, no problem.

He urged the heavy door open, immediately drawing the attention of the burly man behind the bar. The heavily muscled forearms told him that the man could be a problem. The three loud patrons in the corner seemed inconsequential, by comparison.

But the genuine smile that crossed the man's face when he saw Chet's green-and-tan uniform gave some comfort.

"Step up, Marine. The first one's on the house. What'll ya have?" the man offered cheerfully.

Relaxing only slightly, he noticed that the chatter from the men in the corner had stopped.

"A Jack, neat...no, make that a double shot of tequila," Chet replied, his voice as even as he could make it.

"Tequila, huh? Whatever you say, son," the bartender said, flicking a quick glance at the now-silent drunks and giving Chet another once over.

"On leave?" he asked Chet.

"Yeah, you could say that. Just back from Nam."

"Semper Fi, brother," the big man said, placing a second shot glass beside Chet's and filling both.

"Master Gunnery Sergeant Larry Brewer, retired...at your service. My friends call me Slim, believe it or not," he said, looking down at his paunch.

A wave of relief washed over Chet. The 'Gunny' may not help him, but at least he wouldn't hurt him.

"Gunny, huh? Shoulda figured.

High and tight," Chet quipped, motioning at the man's graying, but regulation, burr haircut, "'Nam?"

"Naw, son, dubya-dubya two...Tarawa and Iwo...and Korea," he answered, eliciting a look of genuine awe from Chet.

"To our beloved Corps," he said, raising his glass and knocking back his drink. Chet followed suit.

"Oo-rah!" the retired marine exclaimed proudly.

"Oo-rah!" Chet replied, just as proudly.

"You got somethin' on your mind?" he asked, nodding toward the three men who were now eyeing Chet's uniform.

"Sorry, Gunny; personal business."

"That dog don't hunt, son. This is my place. I'm the only ass kicker allowed."

"What makes you think I'm lookin' to kick some ass?"

"Well, for one thing, back in my day, tequila was fightin' water," he said, staring straight into Chet's eyes.

"Plus you're missin' your cover, your collar hardware, and your chest candy," he said, pointing to several tiny holes in Chet's blouse, just above his left pocket.

"I'm guessin' you left all that in your car, because you don't want some civilian lowlife goin' home with a souvenir. Right?" he finished, looking once again at the three men, who were now rising from their chairs and walking toward the bar.

"Ooo-wee! Ain't he perty?" the tallest of the three taunted, as they approached Chet. "Looks like a bellboy, don't he?"

Wham!

In the blink of an eye, Slim had pulled out a baseball bat and slammed it on the bar, getting the full attention of everyone.

"You maggots come into my bar and mock my Corps? Get the fuck out before I knock what little brains you dickheads just might accidentally have outta your dumb-fuck skulls," Gunny Slim threatened, his eyes narrowing dangerously, as he started out from behind the bar.

The man looked so fearsome that even Chet took a half step back.

565

"Now settle down, Slim. Pigmeat didn't mean any-thing by it, didja, Piggy?" the one with the Clark Gable mustache and dark, slicked-back hair said, raising both hands defensively.

"Naw, huh-uh," the one called Pigmeat answered. "It's jus' that these fellers with their fancy uniforms come in an' think that they can git all the women."

"You see any women here, ya stupid jackass?" Chet challenged, squaring himself for combat.

"Stand down, Marine!" Gunny Slim barked, with a familiar authority that caused Chet to freeze.

"I said there'd be no ass kickin' here unless I was doin' the kickin'. Is that clear?" he roared.

"Aye-aye, Gunny," Chet responded, out of habit, nearly snapping to attention.

The third man snickered.

"Shut up, ya piss ant, before I knock what remainin' teeth you have out that smelly pie hole you call a mouth," Slim growled.

The grin vanished instantly from the man's face.

"You chickenshits have come in here and harassed our boys in uniform before. I shoulda kicked your sorry asses out then." Slim then glowered at the men.

"Well, I ain't repeatin' that mistake. Get the fuck out and don't ever come back, or so help me gawd, I'll beat you to a bloody pulp."

"*Now get out, I said!*" he shouted.

All three men scrambled for the door.

"Hey!" Slim yelled, stopping them in their tracks. "You deadbeats owe me nine bucks for the beer."

Moustache tossed a ten-dollar bill on the floor and sneered, "Keep the change."

"I could have taken 'em," Chet said, after Slim was

back behind the bar.

"With one hand tied behind your back, no doubt, son," Slim agreed.

"But those three, and others like 'em, go around pickin' fights with GIs, and the cops 'round here treat you service boys as badly as those smelly-assed hippies do. No respect.

"Besides, son, haven't you done enough fightin' for a while? You mighta killed one of 'em outta pure instinct. Then where would you be?"

Chet drew a deep breath. "I suppose you're right, Gunny. Thanks," he said, offering his hand. "Lance Corporal Chester Gordon. My friends call me Chet, soon to be civilian Chet Gordon."

"Damn glad to meet ya, Chet," Slim replied, taking his hand in an iron grip.

"Now tell me…all three or just one?"

"Just one. A nutless rat named Steve Moore."

"That'd be the pretty boy with the moustache," Slim offered. "A real douche bag."

"Yeah. Fits the description his ex gave me," Chet confirmed.

"Why? If I may ask."

"He beat her up pretty badly."

"Is that right?" Gunny Slim intoned, his voice becoming menacingly low, as he straightened up.

"She your girl, now?"

"Soon to be my wife," Chet answered.

"All the more reason for you to let this go," Gunnery counseled. "You don't want to start a marriage with her visiting you in the pen, do ya?"

"No, but I just can't…."

Slim held his hand up, silencing Chet.

"Son, let someone with experience in the matter handle it."

"You?"

"Yeah, me. My baby sister's ex used to whoop up on her regularly. I didn't find out until he'd put her in the hospital. Then me an' five of my little buddies" he said, holding a gnarled fist up, "had a discussion with the worm.

"After he got out of the hospital, he couldn't sign the divorce papers and get to the Greyhound station fast enough. He told the cops he'd fallen down a long flight of stairs.

"Baby sis is doin' just fine, now. Remarried to a flyboy captain, but I'll overlook that," he grinned.

"Hey now, don't dog the flyboys, Gunny. They saved our asses a hundred times during Tet at Da Nang."

"Chosin Reservoir, too, son," Slim said, refilling the shot glasses.

"To our winged guardians, God bless 'em," he said, raising his glass.

"God bless 'em," Chet followed.

Iwo, Tarawa, and *Chosin? Wow!*

"Now seriously son," Slim said, the grin disappearing from his face. "Let me handle it for you. It'd do this old recon grunt good. I got friends. I'll put the word out. After I'm through with him, that creep won't be able to walk into a bar anywhere in this town, without gettin' his ass whipped. It'll be fun. You can get on with your new life in peace. Good enough?"

Chet thought for a few seconds. The old Gunny was right. He'd had enough of fighting. He wanted peace. He knew the ex-marine would keep his word to a fellow jarhead. Knowing that the scum-sucking maggot would be getting back what he'd dished out made him feel better.

Still, it would have felt good to break a couple of the coward's bones himself.

"Aye-aye, Gunny. I'll stand down, if I got your word."

"Don't doubt it for a minute, brother."

The two warriors shook hands.

Chet insisted on helping Slim clean up and close the bar, since the latter refused to take payment for the drinks. When the doors were locked, Slim grabbed a half-empty bottle of Johnny Walker, and each reminisced about wartime experiences, as only warriors could.

They shed tears for lost comrades and laughed about tales of outrageous behavior only they could appreciate. Finally, though loath to end their tribute to the Corps, Chet said good-bye, promising an invitation to his wedding.

Slim waved, promising to show up.

This is how it should be, he thought, as he drove through the deserted streets of early morning. He felt a welcome peace settle over him.

His mother no longer cried herself to sleep, worrying about him, and Katy's beautiful smile bespoke of her love for him.

What more could he ask for?

Yeah...this is good.

His aunt had told him that angels come in many surprising forms.

Apparently, one of his angels was the grizzled, old Master Gunnery Sergeant Larry Brewer.

His other, more significant angel was, beyond any shadow of a doubt, Katy.

It was time to get back to his angel.